THE REAPER

The Reaper, Book One of the Chimera Chronicles

Cover and Interior Layout Design by Inspire Books

ISBN: 978-1-950685-02-8
E-book ISBN: 978-1-950685-03-5

Library of Congress: 2019903863

Printed in the United States

THE REAPER

Book One of the Chimera Chronicles

ROB JUNG

HAWK HILL
LITERARY
AN IMPRINT OF INGRAM

ALSO BY ROB JUNG

Praise for Cloud Warriors

"Wow, I loved this book! Such a unique read … With a hint of the paranormal this story took me out of myself. An adventurous trip, with a good cast of characters. Highly recommend!"

– Hannelor Cheney, NetGalley

"From the extravagant trappings of upper echelon 'Bay Area' environs to the steamy, teeming Peruvian jungle, Rob Jung's multilayered novel contrasts the incivility of the highest forms of civilization to the honor and civility of the "uncivilized" people of the wilderness. Get *Cloud Warriors*, you will love it!"

—Paul Whillock, Goodreads

"A story that includes encounters with the spirits, a powerful magical potion that could change the world, and a clash between ancient and modern civilizations that places Professor Castro at the heart of one of the biggest discoveries (and potentially the most dangerous changes) humanity will ever face. Readers of thrillers that incorporate scientific discovery, deadly special interests and manipulation processes, and confrontations between ethical and moral purposes will relish *Cloud Warriors* for its fast-paced action and satisfying blend of adventure with a touch of extraordinary powers and intrigue. Especially recommended for readers who look for the kind of high-octane action, complex plots and powerful characterization mastered by such big names as Michael Crichton, H. Rider Haggard and Philip Kerr."

—Diane Donovan, Midwest Book Reviews, Senior Reviewer

"An amazingly literate, engaging novel with a unique premise and characters with whom you immediately empathize. Highly recommended, and definitely not the last book by Mr. Jung that I'll be reading."

—Cindy McBridge, NetGalley

"A beautifully written, fast-moving novel with such an original, well researched plot that it has you hooked from page one and doesn't let you off until the final page has been turned...A hugely enjoyable book that I wouldn't hesitate to recommend to anyone."

—Veryan Williams-Wynn, Author of *The Spirit Trap*

DEDICATION

To Kathy: for her love and patience, for her support and for her contribution to *The Reaper.*

Come, grow old with me.
The best is yet to be.

ACKNOWLEDGMENTS

Storytelling is an individual endeavor, but publishing a book is a group effort. There are so many to thank for their unselfish effort in making *The Reaper* a reality.

So, thanks, to Kelly Langdon, Jessica Shannon Mueller, Marc Thompson and Michael McBride for their invaluable critiques of my work. You make me a better writer. Thanks to the two Nans, Strauss and DeMars, to Shelley Kubitz Mahannah, my wife, Kathy Stoller-Junghans, and to Denny Maas, my beta reading team, whose insights and feedback helped polish the story. Thanks to my old newspaper buddy, Gary Evans, for his mentorship. Thanks to Lynn Hanson for her excellent proofreading, and to Terry Heller for her equally excellent editing. Thanks to my publicist, Tiffany Harelik. And, finally, thanks to all of you whose brains I picked and ears I bent as we shared the seven-year journey of writing *The Reaper*.

AUTHOR'S NOTE

Each of my novels is based upon an actual historical fact or event. In *The Reaper,* that event is the disappearance of Joan Miro's mural, *El Segador, Catalan peasant in revolt,* which he had been commissioned to paint by the Spanish government for display at the 1937 Paris Exposition. The mural became popularly known as *The Reaper,* and it is around that still-lost work of art that this story revolves. The details about the painting, the Paris Exposition, the architecture and art work of the Spanish pavilion, and the Spanish civil war are historically accurate. The story, however, is entirely fictional as are the characters except in the case of historical characters who appear in fictional settings.

Rob Jung

PROLOGUE

The artist backed away from the wall, careful not to trip over the crumpled drop cloth and detritus cluttering the floor. He looked up at the painting that had absorbed all his creative energy for the past two months. He beheld the enormous, angry head, wearing the traditional farmer's cap, balanced on a stalk of a neck. A raised fist at the end of a scrawny arm held a scythe, poised to strike a blow. The painting rose eighteen feet to the ceiling of the second level of the pavilion, as much a symbol of a struggle for independence as a work of art.

He had intended it to be so.

He had named it *El Segador*, a tribute to the Catalonian farmers who had fought for independence three hundred years earlier in what became known as The Reapers War. Like so many others before and after, they had fought valiantly but lost, and his beloved Catalonia was still part of Spain. Even as he stood there, another civil war was wracking Spain, and Catalonia was the epicenter. His family farm outside Barcelona had been overrun, and he had been exiled in Paris for a year.

A rotating gaggle of spectators watched as the painting evolved. Most assumed it was the reason that the Spanish exhibition hall, unlike the other pavilions at the 1937 Paris World Exposition, had not opened its doors. Oblivious to their stares, or that two months had passed since other countries had opened their exhibits, the artist stood motionless, contemplating. The brush in his right hand, lush with paint, seemed anxious to return to its task, but instead he turned and placed the verdant brush in a half-filled can of turpentine. He picked up a smaller brush, carefully trimmed a stray bristle, dabbed it in a splotch of black paint on a well-used pallet and returned to the painting. He kneeled and deftly stroked his signature on the bottom of the painting:

Miro.

1937

MONDAY, NOVEMBER 22, 1937

PARIS

Through the glass front of the austere pavilion, Francois Picard watched as twilight descended upon Paris. December's rains had come early, and a gray sky spit out a steady cold spray. Gusting winds whipped passers-by on the Jardins du Trocadero, turning rain drops into stinging missiles and rendering umbrellas inverted.

The stark interior of the pavilion, with its sharp corners and hard surfaces, invited the chill inside. Picard shivered involuntarily. His thin security guard uniform, two sizes too big for his skinny frame, was insufficient to ward off the psychological frigidity caused by the tempest outside and barren architecture within.

He squeezed the ash off his smoke with nicotine-stained thumb and finger, inserting the stub into a crushed pack of Gitanes. The main level of the building was empty except for the three large pieces of art commissioned by the Spanish government specifically for the 1937 Paris Exposition. Two were huge surrealistic paintings, one by Joan Miro called *The Reaper,* the other a bizarre black and white twenty-five-foot-long mural titled *Guernica,* by Pablo Picasso.

Their harsh style and lack of color added to the vapid feel of the building, and Picard disliked both.

Contrarily, the mercury fountain in the center of the hall mesmerized Picard. Alexander Calder, an American, had fashioned his fountain-cum-mobile out of aluminum, and had chosen mercury rather than water as the liquid medium. Picard would often stand and watch the mercury ooze through the labyrinth and dribble against the last teardrop-shaped fob. That dribbling element, with its silky silver flow, kept the fountain in constant motion, leaving him to marvel at the mind that had created this perpetual movement. Calder's fountain reinforced Picard's admiration of all things American and, by contrast, his disdain for all things Spanish.

It should be a quiet night, he thought, running his stained fingers through his thin, sandy-colored hair.

For that he was thankful. There had not been many in the five months since the pavilion opened. The civil war was going badly for the Spanish government and funds intended to sustain the pavilion, Spain's presence at Expo '37, were diverted to the war effort. As a result, Picard had become the lone security guard. His work schedule, twelve hours a day, seven days a week was not difficult, mostly giving spectators directions and finding parents of lost children, but it was constant and exhausting. Tonight, perhaps, he would sneak in a nap.

The sound of umbrellas being retracted and shaken drew Picard's attention. Two men, one short and bulky with a shuffling gait, looking disheveled in his three-piece suit as though he had been traveling all day, and the other, taller, smartly dressed in a blue topcoat with silk handkerchief in his lapel pocket, fedora and walking stick, had entered the pavilion. Though dressed fastidiously, the focus of the taller man was an outrageous mustache, curled upward into needled points.

They walked directly to *The Reaper.*

"His best work." "Incredible." "Historical significance." "Priceless." The short man was clearly American, while the mustache spoke in Spanish-tinged broken English.

Picard could hear the words clearly, amplified by the flat, unadorned surfaces of the empty pavilion.

A young couple, and then a group of six or seven, came into the pavilion; a few tenacious fair-goers, undaunted by the weather, trying to squeeze in as many exhibits as possible before the 9 p.m. closing time. The couple strolled to Calder's fountain and stood transfixed as the mercury slithered and dribbled its way through the maze. The group made its way toward the stairs to the second level, tittering and pointing toward the two men standing at the foot of *The Reaper.*

As more people entered, Picard's hope for a nap faded. He picked up a newspaper from his desk and scanned the front page of *La Republique.*

A story below the fold reported that the ongoing civil war in Spain continued to favor the military forces of General Franco. A related story about negotiations between the two sides mentioned the secession of Catalonia as a proposed way to end the war and save the Republican government from what appeared to be certain defeat at the hands of the pro-monarchy military. According to the article, Catalonian secessionists who had been supporters of the elected government in the early fighting were attempting to use the civil war as leverage to gain long-sought independence. Joan Miro was mentioned in the article as an important figure in the movement because of his paintings, including *The Reaper,* that championed Catalonian nationalism.

Picard finished the article and checked his watch. Fifteen minutes to closing. The two men and the young couple who had been admiring *The Reaper* were now on the second level. The larger group had made quick work of the exhibit and left without Picard noticing.

"Fifteen minutes to closing," he announced from the top of the stairs, then turning, he returned to his desk on the main level. Minutes later the young couple walked past and uttered "*Gracies*" in his direction. He acknowledged the Catalan salutation with a nod. At 8:59 the two men descended the steps and walked directly to Picard's desk.

"*Parlez vou Anglais?*" the American inquired.

"I…speak little…English," stammered Picard, his chinless lower jaw quivering in embarrassment at his inability to converse understandably in the language of the country that he so admired.

"Who is the owner of that painting?" The man spoke slowly as he pointed toward *The Reaper.* Picard shook his head, trying to indicate that he didn't understand the question, but leaving the impression that he didn't know the identity of the owner.

"What is going to happen to that painting at the end of the Exposition?" was the American's next question. Picard shrugged, shaking his head, his face a bright red.

"Tell the Spanish authorities that I'd like to buy that painting," he said, a little louder, color starting to rise in the American's cheeks.

Picard did what most people do when they don't understand. He nodded.

The man with the mustache stepped forward.

"Excuse me, *monsieur,*" he said in perfect French, clipped with a Catalan accent, "Would you please give this note to the person in charge of this pavilion."

He handed a hand-written note to Picard, who nodded and put the note in his breast pocket.

"Oui," he said, relieved that he had understood at least that part of the conversation.

WEDNESDAY, NOVEMBER 24, 1937

Picard knocked on the director's door and entered in response to a grunt that he interpreted as an invitation.

"Director Puig, I was asked to give you this." He handed the folded note he had been given two nights before to the director. He had forgotten it until looking in the vest pocket of his uniform jacket for a match to light a cigarette.

Puig opened the note, read it, and exhaled a derisive snort. He tossed the note on his desk.

Picard did not move.

"Is there anything else?" the director asked, his tone reflecting his displeasure with the note's message, or with Picard, or with life in general, one could never tell with Director Puig. He had been appointed to the position not for his people skills but because he had been instrumental in raising funds to pay for construction of the pavilion.

"There, ah, have been rumors of, ah, a demonstration," Picard stammered, color rising in his cheeks.

"Such rumors have been frequent. I am fully aware of them," Puig said, dismissing the diffident security guard with a flip of his hand.

"But I thought, with only four days before the Exposition closes, perhaps we could have extra security," Picard said, standing his ground.

"If I thought it was necessary, I would have arranged it."

Picard backed out of the director's office, his head down.

For the first time in days the sun seeped through the overcast. By noon the skies were clear and the early morning trickle of visitors had become a torrent, swelling total attendance at the eight-month-long exposition to well over thirty million.

At approximately 2 o'clock a swarthy young man standing just outside the pavilion entrance, dressed in typical student garb, began to shout through a bullhorn: "We are fighting for the freedom of Spain. For the freedom of all who will not be under the thumb of the throne and the tyrant Franco!"

Heads swiveled. Most fair-goers on the Trocadero quickly moved on, but a few stopped. Two men appeared, carrying a stepladder. They unfolded it and taped a poster above the pavilion entryway. Then they moved the ladder to the middle of the esplanade, where the orator and his bullhorn climbed up several steps to gain leverage on the crowd. "We will never give up! We are Spaniards! We are not afraid of the Nazis or their puppet Franco!" he shouted, gesturing toward the poster. It quoted Spanish President Manuel Azana: "More than half a million Spaniards are standing ready with their bayonets in the trenches. They will not be walked over."

A few more passersby stopped to listen.

Picard rushed through the entrance, out onto the esplanade, read the poster, and shouted at the man with the bullhorn: "Take this banner down immediately." The two ladder-men stepped between Picard and the speaker. The security guard retreated back into the pavilion and ran to Director Puig's office.

"Monsieur Director, there is a demonstration on the esplanade!" Picard shouted in a high-pitched voice as he burst through the office door. "They have taped a banner above the main entrance."

Puig glared at Picard, rose slowly from behind his desk and, without losing eye contact, walked punctiliously out of his office.

The crowd had grown significantly in the minute Picard had been in Puig's office, now numbering close to a hundred. The director stood for a moment, considering the situation. "Lock all the doors," he ordered Picard. "I will call the gendarmes."

Picard locked the front entry doors and stationed Monique, his favorite tour guide, by the locked door to redirect visitors wanting to leave. He quickly made his way toward the back where he enlisted the help of the second guide. He armed the lock of the self-locking back door and instructed the guide to let people out, but not to let anyone else into the pavilion.

When he returned to the front, the crowd had swelled. A second speaker had replaced the first on the ladder, shouting more words of Spanish nationalism and gesturing in the direction of the Eiffel Tower across the Seine River to the southeast. But it wasn't Mr. Eiffel's tower that was the target of his ire. It was the hulking German pavilion where a line of *Wehrmacht* was now forming as a human barrier against the demonstration.

Several demonstrators moved to the outer edge of the crowd, shouting expletives at the German soldiers, shaking their fists. Sirens in the distance signaled oncoming gendarmes, fueling the thickening tension.

Picard turned his head to find Director Puig standing beside him, watching the developing frenzy outside.

Pop! Pop! Pop!

Picard looked back just in time to see the man with the bullhorn pitch forward off the ladder, a red splotch spreading on the front of his shirt. Screams of terror preceded by only seconds the collapse of the glass front of the pavilion as the crowd crushed in panic to flee the gunfire.

Picard threw up his arms to protect himself as the thick glass shattered and collapsed upon him.

THURSDAY, NOVEMBER 25, 1937

They kept Picard overnight at Hospital Ste. Perine for observation.

"He could have been killed," was the whispered exclamation he overheard on multiple occasions in nursing staff conversations. He learned that Director Puig had not been so fortunate. He had been cut badly by the shattered glass and had lost a lot of blood.

"What about Monique?" Picard asked, and was informed that no one named Monique had been admitted to the hospital.

He was discharged with bruises, a gash on the side of his head with eight stitches, a thundering headache, and a bottle of laudanum with instructions to take it when needed. His request to see Puig was refused. The director was still unconscious and his condition was critical. Picard went home and slept.

FRIDAY, NOVEMBER 26, 1937

He arrived at the pavilion at 8 a.m., an hour before opening, sporting dried blood on his jacket, gauze wrapped around his head, and a laudanum high. The glass front of the building had been replaced with wallboard, and there were still workmen scurrying about. The front entry doors were intact but, when they closed behind Picard as he entered, the adjacent walls swayed unsteadily. Or, perhaps, it was the laudanum. He couldn't be certain.

With the glass front now a solid wall, the inside of the pavilion was dark, but Picard still squinted as he tried to focus. Nothing seemed to have been harmed by the collapse. He shuffled to the switch that activated Calder's fountain, but the movement of the mercury and aluminum fobs created instant nausea, and he frantically grabbed for the switch and turned it off. Holding his breath to keep from vomiting, he turned to go sit at his desk and realized it was gone. It had been in the path of the falling glass wall and had been no match for the heavy glass. He paused, bewildered.

"Are you all right, Monsieur Picard?" Monique was suddenly beside him. He had not heard her come in. He touched the bandage on his head, and she caught him just as he wobbled unsteadily. "Let me help you to the director's office."

A zombie in a bloody, baggy uniform, Picard was relieved to let the petite tour guide take control. With one arm draped over her shoulder, he rested most of his weight on her as she steered him into the director's office and lowered him onto a chair. "I'll get you some water," she said.

He lifted his head just off the desk when she returned. She was the most beautiful vision he had ever seen. She set down the water.

"Can I get you anything else?"

"How did you…uh…did you get…um…hurt?" he stammered.

"No. I'm fine. Can I get you anything?" she repeated.

Picard shook his head; a mistake.

"No," he said softly and laid his head back on the desk.

"Three shots were reported. One of the demonstrators was hit twice. He's still alive. Shots were from a .38," Detective Claude Ormonde said as he concentrated on the thin stream of coffee he was pouring into a small white cup in front of Pierre Gaudin, weekend crime reporter for the *Paris-Soir.*

".38? Walther PPK?" the reporter inquired, raising an eyebrow.

"Don't know yet, but it would seem to fit. The Walther is the Wehrmacht's standard issue. They wouldn't let us question any of the guards or look at their sidearms, of course. They claimed diplomatic immunity," Ormonde said. "We're seeking a warrant."

"That's ridiculous! The Expo is not an embassy. Their pavilion is under French jurisdiction!" Gaudin's decibel level was elevated enough to draw attention from the other gendarmes in the precinct station.

"I know," sighed Ormonde, "but they wouldn't cooperate so we have to go to the courts. Even then I'm still not sure they'll comply."

"What about the person who was shot?"

"He was shot in the chest and in the shoulder. He's in bad shape. Probably won't survive," the detective responded.

"Was the demonstration about the civil war?"

"Of course, and they didn't have a permit." Ormonde sighed again, reflecting his growing frustration with trying to keep order in the escalating tension that gripped Paris. Civil war to the west, military buildups to the north and south, strikes throughout the country—France was in peril on every front and those, like Ormonde, charged with keeping peace and order were facing a deteriorating situation. It was compounded by Expo '37 where the Nazis and the Communists were in a stare-down, upbraiding each other on a daily basis as the two competing ideologies fought for the hearts and minds of the millions of Europeans attending the Expo.

"He was one of the speakers," Ormonde said, continuing to answer Gaudin's questions. "Andres Duron, or at least we think that's his name. There were a couple hundred at the demonstration, but the demonstrators we talked to weren't much help in identifying anyone. Apparently, the speaker was blaming the Germans for the mess in Spain. Then the shooting broke out. One witness said there were rocks thrown at the Germans but we didn't find any on the esplanade, and it's not like the Germans to clean up after themselves. We have a couple of the rally organizers in lockup, but we can't charge them with anything more than loitering or demonstrating without a license. We've questioned them, but so far we haven't gotten anything that would shed light on the shooting. They're full of opinions but short on facts."

"Anything else I should know?" Gaudin asked, scribbling notes as he finished the last of his coffee.

"When the gunfire started, the crowd panicked and rushed the front of the pavilion. It was mostly made of glass and part of it collapsed," Ormonde replied. "A lot of people got cut and several were trampled. Four or five were taken to the hospital and twice that many were treated at the scene. None of the injuries were serious except for the director of the pavilion. He got his throat slit by flying glass and is in poor condition. Lost a lot of blood."

"Name?" asked Gaudin.

"Puig. Jose Vergas Puig."

Pierre thanked the detective for the coffee and the information and made his way out of the precinct station. Later, he would convince Ormonde to let him talk to the two organizers in custody.

It took nearly an hour for Gaudin to get to the entry gate to Jardins du Trocadero. No parking spaces presented themselves so he pulled two wheels of his old Renault onto the sidewalk, next to a hydrant. He placed his "Press" card on the dashboard and went in search of the Spanish pavilion.

Gaudin was bumped several times as he made his way through the crowd on the esplanade. *Unusually large for a Monday,* he observed, *probably because it's the last week.* He checked his pockets to make sure they had not been picked in the jostling throng. His belongings were intact, but a feeling of unease crept over him as he passed between the monoliths that were the German and Russian pavilions. The eagle perched on a swastika sitting astride the taller German pavilion and the bulky bronze workers brandishing hammer and sickle atop the squat Russian exhibition hall were poised for combat, a perfect reflection of the creeds they represented, magnified by heavily-armed soldiers flanking the doors and creating a gauntlet through which spectators were forced to walk.

The foreboding feeling disappeared as Gaudin passed the German building. Two gendarmes were watching a covey of workmen busy rehanging doors and finishing the last work on the boarded-up front of the Spanish pavilion.

Gaudin nodded a greeting to the gendarmes who stood and watched him climb the two long flights of steps that led to the second level entrance to the pavilion. He tried the door. It was locked. He trudged back to ground level and to the gendarmes, whose backs were now turned. He detected a smirk as he showed them his press credentials.

Once inside, he asked to see the person in charge of the pavilion and was led to an office with an open door, a light shining from within.

Gaudin knocked lightly.

"Oui. Entrez."

Gaudin stepped through the doorway and introduced himself. "Can you tell me about the riot and what happened here on Saturday?"

Picard sat at the desk, a vacant stare on his face. The gauze bandage wrapped around his head, which had slipped over one ear, cut diagonally across his forehead.

"I tried to warn him, but he wouldn't listen," Picard said in a monotone.

"Warn who? About what?

"Director Puig. I told him we needed more security, but…" Picard trailed off.

"What's your name?" asked Gaudin.

"Francois Picard. Security guard for the Spanish pavilion," he said, refocusing, a tot of pride creeping into his voice.

"Can you tell me what happened here on Wednesday?" Gaudin repeated.

"There was a riot. Shooting. The glass wall collapsed on me. I don't remember anything after that until I woke up in the hospital," Francois said. "I don't know what happened."

Gaudin quickly realized that no useful information would come from Picard. "Are you alright? Can I get something for you, or take you some place?" he asked as he prepared to leave.

"I need to secure this place," Francois replied in a leaden voice.

Gaudin mentioned it to the gendarmes on his way out. "He may have a concussion, or perhaps he's in shock. Check on him once in a while." They nodded in agreement, but Gaudin doubted that they would.

Picard sat at the director's desk, his head thumping in pain with each heartbeat. He was vaguely aware of ringing in his ears. He wanted to sleep. He lay one cheek on a pile of papers on the desk. A familiar folded note caught his attention just as he was about to close his eyes:

> *"I have a buyer for El Segador. The government needs money. My buyer is willing to pay a good price in U.S. dollars. S. Dali."*

Details eluded Picard's damaged brain, but a vague recollection of two men slowly formed, followed by the hazy outline of a plan. He touched the stitches and winced. *They owe me for this.* He reached for the telephone and dialed the number under Dali's name.

"Mr. Dali? I can arrange for the sale of *El Segador* to your buyer."

FRIDAY, LATE AFTERNOON, NOVEMBER 26, 1937

The young man stood for several minutes beside the hospital bed, his face a mask of concern. Finally, he turned and walked out of the room and out of Hospital Ste. Perine. Three blocks down Rue Chardon he entered a patisserie and took a seat between two older men huddled over coffee and pastries. Except for a man behind the counter, they were the only people in the place.

Without looking up, the one wearing a fedora spoke: "And?"

"He is still in critical condition. I would not have been able to see him if he wasn't my brother," Renaldo Puig answered.

"I am sorry," the other man said. "It is unfortunate that Jose was hurt. No one expected the crowd to react in that manner. Were you able to speak to him?"

"No. He's still in a coma," Renaldo went on, "and his vocal cords have been damaged, so even if he wakes up it is unlikely he will be able to speak."

"So, we do not know if he has made arrangements for delivery of the painting," the Hat said, looking up from his plate.

"No."

The three sat silently.

Eventually the Hat continued. "We must make sure *El Segador* is delivered, Renaldo. You must find out whether Jose arranged it. Tell them you are his brother and that you are just making sure that the art work in the pavilion is properly taken care of. Tell them that it was Jose's greatest concern, and now that he is injured you are doing your brotherly duty to make sure his wishes are followed and his good name maintained."

Renaldo pondered the assignment. "Whom should I ask for?"

"There must be an assistant director. Talk to him. He should know."

"And what if Jose did not make arrangements? What then?" the third man asked.

"We will figure out a way," the Hat responded. "It has to be delivered to the warehouse in Sitges. Franco's people will take possession of it there. Our job is to make sure it gets there."

"Why don't we just keep it in a warehouse here and let the secessionists come and get it?" asked Renaldo. "They are the ones who want the painting. Franco is going to give it to them anyway, and the French don't care."

"You do not understand the art of politics, my young friend," said the Hat, draping his arm over Renaldo's shoulders. "It is in the giving that the meaning lies. Franco is agreeable to Catalonia seceding from Spain to end the war quickly, but he wants to be sure that we will be an ally and trading partner for his new government. By giving this painting as a gift he shows his good will and support for Catalan independence, and we show our gratitude by entering into a trade agreement with him. It will be a big step in accomplishing both his goals and ours without any more bloodshed."

If you hadn't shot Duron we wouldn't have to do this, and my brother wouldn't be in the hospital, Renaldo fumed, seething under the weight of the man's arm. *If you were worried about bloodshed you shouldn't have pulled the trigger.*

The Hat's excuse for shooting Duron—that he was a supporter of the monarchy who was trying to create an incident with the Germans that would derail Catalonia's secessionist plans—didn't ring true with Renaldo. If that were true, why did he need to shoot him three times? He suspected that there was bad blood between the two and the Hat had used the opportunity to settle an old score.

The civil war was the best opportunity in centuries for Catalonia to gain independence from Spain. Jose Puig had been the chief architect of the treaty between the secessionists and the Franco junta. Renaldo agreed that the Barcelona-based federal government had to be sacrificed for independence and, now that his brother was no longer able to orchestrate the delivery of *The Reaper*, Renaldo was bound by familial loyalty and political zeal to carry on his brother's work.

FRIDAY EVENING, NOVEMBER 26, 1937

Puffs of burnt rubber spurted from all four tires as a ponderous Junkers G-38 touched down at Orly Airport. As the behemoth slowed from its 100-m.p.h. landing speed a string of four armored cars, sandwiching three Mercedes limousines, emerged from behind a hangar and sped across the runway. In perfect German precision the cordon stopped just as the plane's massive fuselage spewed out stairs that slowly descended to the tarmac. Uniformed soldiers, gripping nineteen-millimeter MP28s in quick-response mode, materialized from the armored cars and flanked the limousines. Their collective gaze swept the airport with scrupulous intensity.

The first two men down the steps, one in uniform, the second in a business suit, disappeared into the lead limousine. They were followed by a dozen more passengers who crammed themselves into the two trailing limos. The carefully choreographed maneuver, from touchdown to exit, was over in five minutes. The vehicle caravan, swastikas fluttering from the fenders, surged out of the airport, turning north on Avenue de Fontainebleau toward downtown Paris.

"Tomorrow is a proud day for you, Albert," said the man in the uniform, seated facing the other passenger in the lead limo.

"*Ja, mein Fuhrer*, and for the Reich."

Adolph Hitler and Albert Speer watched the twinkling lights of suburban Paris glide past, a fitting entry into the city called *La Ville-Lumiere*, the City of Light. The sweet scent of pomade from Hitler's hair, mixed with the redolence of the leather seats, was a not-unpleasant addition to the ambience in the limousine.

"I love this city," Hitler said, breaking the silence as the caravan entered Paris proper, crossing Boulevard Massena and passing an open space that would, in later years, become known as *Jardin Joan Miro*. "We must be careful not to destroy it."

"*Ja, mein Fuhrer*. There is much beauty here that could never be replaced, too much art and architecture, too much history."

"The architecture and the history we will leave, but the art will go to Berlin," Hitler responded. "You will make Berlin the most beautiful city in the world, and I will make it the greatest cultural center in history—the city of the new enlightenment."

Albert Speer nodded. He had designed the colossal stadium in Nuremberg where the Nazi party held its rallies, and where his friend, Adolph Hitler, had risen to power five years earlier. Speer's architectural design of Nuremberg Deutsches Stadion had won him a *Grand Prix* from the World Exposition's architectural jury, much to his surprise and the surprise of the Nazi hierarchy. Speer envisioned the Exposition's closing ceremony tomorrow when he would be awarded the prestigious prize, along with a gold medal for his design of the Exposition's German pavilion.

Hitler and much of the Nazi party brass, who had opposed taking part in the Exposition until Speer convinced them of the propaganda value, had decided at the last moment to come and share in the glory of Speer's celebrity status.

"I wish to see this painting by Picasso." Hitler interrupted Speer's thoughts. "The one he calls *Guernica*. I want to see if it justly glorifies our Luftwaffe." Hitler's lips curled under his mustache in the pretext of a smile, but his grey eyes remained stone cold.

"That painting is at the Spanish pavilion where there was a riot and a shooting," Speer warned. "It is not safe."

"I am the Fuhrer. I will not hide because of a demonstration by some rabble!" Hitler seemed to increase in size as his tone became bellicose. "The world will know true German courage!"

"*Ja, mein Fuhrer.*" Speer sank back in his seat. *His ego is too big. It makes the Fuhrer take foolish risks,* he thought.

A perfect full moon was climbing out of the Paris skyline as Picard waited on the park bench. Cars traveling west down the Rue de L'Universite toward the Eiffel Tower slowed as they approached the signature structure of the 1898 World's Fair. No one took notice of the lone seated figure.

Lights from the opposite bank sparkled off the surface of the Seine

River as he dreamed what America would be like, and how it would be more wonderful with Monique. Another car approached and he tried to clear his mind of his fantasies that involved her. He knew it was important to concentrate on his plan, but details kept getting intermingled with his flights of fancy that only temporarily assuaged the headache that continued to hammer him.

After twenty minutes Francois began to doubt if the American would come, but one recurring thought kept him glued to the hard bench: *This is my chance to go to the United States. There is opportunity there, and I will not have to fight in the war.*

A large black car slowed as it passed him, then accelerated and turned left on Avenue de La Bourdonnais. Minutes later the same car came slowly down Quai Branly and came to a stop in front of him.

Picard, standing up too quickly, had to grab the back of the bench until the dizziness passed. Unsteadily he made his way to the car. The back door swung open and he ducked inside. Sitting next to him was the American.

"*Monsieur* Picard. You have been injured." The American said. A man in the front passenger's seat interpreted his concern into French.

"It is nothing," Picard said. "Excuse me for my appearance. We had an incident at the pavilion yesterday. That is why I am here."

"I don't understand."

Picard related what had happened, including Puig's injuries. He purposely exaggerated the danger in which the riot had placed *The Reaper* and his role in keeping it unharmed.

"As you know, the government of Spain is desperately in need of funds to support the war effort." Picard barely recognized the sound of his own voice. Someone else seemed to be in control of the rehearsed words he was speaking. "Because of the need for haste relative to the risk to the works of art at the pavilion, there was no one else available to meet with you," he continued. "Even though I am French, I am a sympathizer of the Spanish government and a loyal friend, so they have entrusted me with the task of delivering the painting to you."

"You do not even know who I am." The American's tone challenged Picard's authority, although his expression was passive.

"You come recommended by Monsieur Dali, and that is enough." Picard had anticipated such a question. "And payment must be in United States dollars. Cash. So, who you are is not so important to the government as is your money."

"And how much U.S. money does the Spanish government wish to be paid for this painting?"

"One thousand U.S. dollars," was Francois's immediate response.

"That is a very large amount of money." The American would have paid ten times that amount, but his demeanor showed no sign of surprise at his good fortune. "How would I receive delivery if I were to agree to pay that astonishing sum?"

This was the risky part for Francois; the part that his head hadn't been able to organize, so he improvised. "You send a truck to the Spanish pavilion Sunday at 2 p.m. I suggest you contact Lipp Moving. They are handling the removal of all art work from the pavilion. I will leave word at the gate that your truck will be coming. Make sure that you send an extra workman with your truck. I will be there to let them in. They can take down the painting and load it into the truck. When the painting is loaded, they can give me the payment." Picard surprised himself. His impromptu plan sounded like it might work.

Francois had picked 2 p.m. because it was in the middle of the closing ceremonies. People would be distracted. No one would question him because of the events of today. In his plan, Francois would be gone just as quickly, heading for the United States with Monique and money in his pocket.

"And you will give me a receipt showing payment and a bill of sale transferring the title of the painting to me, of course."

It was detail Picard had not considered. "Of course," he said.

"And how will I be sure that the one thousand U.S. dollars actually gets to the Spanish government?"

Picard hesitated. "Because I will deliver it to them," he said, sounding offended. "Please call at exactly 9 a.m. to confirm. I will be in my office." He gave the American the phone number for the pavilion

The American, nodding, reached across Picard and opened the car door.

"Good evening *Monsieur* Picard," he said, happy to be rid of the larcenous, undersized security guard.

Despite several hours of digging, Gaudin had learned little about the shooting or the demonstration. The security guard at the Spanish pavilion remembered nothing, and the tour guides' recollections were of popping noises, people running, and walls collapsing, but few specifics.

He had been stonewalled by a Wehrmacht officer at the massive German monument to Nazi rapaciousness. The officer had refused to give his name, nor acknowledge that there had been a demonstration, nor even that a shooting had taken place.

At Hospital Ste. Perine the medicos had refused him access to either the shooting victim or the Spanish exhibit director, both of whom were in critical condition. All others injured at the demonstration had been treated and sent home. Gaudin got their names. Only one had a local address.

In a final deadline-beating effort to breathe life into his story, Gaudin returned to the dingy precinct station, hoping to get access to the two demonstrators being held in custody.

The desk sergeant, sitting behind a beat-up metal desk beneath a single yellowing lightbulb, gave him a nod and a directional thumb, and Gaudin walked through the door of the squad room into a cacophony more frantic than usual.

"What's going on?" he shouted in the direction of Ormonde whose shiny, bald head bobbed above the milling crowd of uniformed gendarmes, criminals, suspects, friends, families, and hangers-on that always inhabited the squad room.

"Hitler and the whole fucking German government landed at Orly an hour ago!" Ormonde bellowed above the melee.

Gaudin's first reaction was *invasion*, then, instantly: *Nazi party officials wouldn't personally be leading an invasion.* He grabbed the nearest phone and dialed the newsroom. They already knew about the German "invasion" and had reporters working on it.

"How's your story coming?" the editor wanted to know.

"I'm just about to talk to the demonstrators that are in custody," Gaudin responded, hoping his statement was true. "Then I'll file my story." The editor gave his okay and Gaudin hung up. He knew his piece, if he could get confirmation of German culpability for the shooting, would run as a sidebar to the new, big story of the day.

Hitler will probably love it, he thought.

Ormonde, immersed in organizing security for the unexpected arrival of the German government, was too occupied to be concerned with the two demonstrators in custody. His permission to allow Gaudin to question them was given without hesitation.

Forty-five minutes later Gaudin left the interrogation room with a new twist. The first detainee, sporting bruises on his face, claimed that he saw someone in the crowd shoot Duron. The shot, according to him, had not come from the Germans, although his beating had. The second prisoner said that he was in the crowd that had gathered in front of the Spanish pavilion to support the Spanish government in the civil war when a group of thugs advocating independence for Catalonia infiltrated the rally. There had been shouting and shoving between the two groups before the shooting, although the second detainee couldn't corroborate where the shots came from or why he had been arrested.

On his way out Gaudin confirmed with the desk sergeant that neither of the detainees were suspects in the shooting, then borrowed his phone to call the hospital. Duron or Puig were still unavailable for an interview. He drove back to the newspaper and pecked out the story on his ancient Hermes typewriter.

The headline in the *Paris-Soir* on Saturday morning read: *Hitler Arrives in Paris for Exposition Finale.* Below the fold a single column headline over Gaudin's byline read: *Germans Not Responsible for Expo Shootings Says Eye Witness.*

SATURDAY, NOVEMBER 27, 1937

Monique pulled her hooded cloak tightly around her shoulders against the early-morning wind whistling down the Seine. She walked across the Pont d'lena bridge thinking about the proposition she had received the previous evening from Picard.

In slightly slurred words he had told her he was going to America as soon as the Exposition closed. "There's going to be a war with Germany," he had said. "I will buy you a ticket. You can come with me. We'll be safe in America."

Had he been serious?

Although she had worked with Picard for the past five months, she and the skinny security guard had seldom spoken beyond pleasantries or work-related matters. She certainly wasn't attracted to him, nor did she think she had given him any reason to believe so. She had always considered him timid and a bit wimpy. But with the Expo closing tomorrow, and no employment prospects, she pondered his offer.

She shuddered at the prospect of traveling with Picard, but it would get her to America. She could dump him as soon as they got to New York.

Bang! Bang! Bang! Her thoughts were interrupted by the noise.

A German soldier was pounding on the main door of the Spanish pavilion. A second soldier, in an officer's grey uniform, turned as she hurried toward them.

"It is two hours before the pavilion opens, Messieurs," she shouted above the banging.

"The high command of the German Reich...," the officer paused in mid-sentence as Monique arrived, shrugged off her hood and shook out luxuriant chestnut tresses.

"...wishes to tour your pavilion, Fraulein," he continued, the tone of his heavily accented French mellowing. He extended his hand, which had been resting on his sidearm, as a peace offering.

"We thought it may be less burdensome if we came before you opened to the public, perhaps in one half hour," he said

"I think that would be fine," she said, flashing her radiant tour guide smile.

The officer bowed smartly, pivoted and left. Monique watched as he walked away, his broad shoulders filling out the uniform, the heels of his polished black boots clicking on the esplanade. She was only vaguely aware of the other soldier walking beside him.

Monique found Picard slumped over in the director's chair, his head on the desk.

"Monsieur Picard, are you, all right?" she asked, gently shaking his shoulder. He stared at her, uncomprehending, looking like a bandaged cadaver.

"Are you all right?" she repeated.

Picard shook his head, a mistake. His headache ratcheted to a new level.

"The German high command will be here in a half hour to tour the pavilion," she said in a whisper, trying to save Picard any further pain. "I can guide them. You should lie down."

He looked at Monique with a crinkly smile and laid his head back on the desk. Monique quietly closed the office door, concluding that the previous night's offer had been delivered in a state of delirium caused by the laudanum.

At precisely 8:30, in response to a polite knock, Monique unlocked and opened the pavilion door. The handsome German officer looked down at her, his ice-blue eyes smiling. She stepped aside.

"Please come in."

Two heavily armed soldiers stepped around the officer, their eyes and the barrels of their MP28s sweeping the interior of the pavilion. A nod gave the all clear signal. The young officer did a crisp about-face and ushered the German high command into the pavilion.

Monique recognized Hitler, an average-sized man in a baggy brown suit with piercing, unhappy eyes. He looked small in comparison to the uniformed hulk, dripping in medals, immediately behind him: three hundred plus pounds of General Hermann Goering. Others followed, some in uniform, most in civilian clothes, with two more armed soldiers providing security at the rear.

Picard, roused by the commotion, wobbled out of the director's office and hesitated at the sight of the German uniforms. Gathering his courage, he walked unsteadily toward them.

"This is Monique Fontenot," he said without introducing himself. "She will be your tour guide." With that he turned and, in a hurried shuffle, returned to the director's office, closing the door behind him.

Monique broke the silence caused by Picard's awkward behavior.

"I must apologize for Monsieur Picard. He was injured when the wall collapsed." She nodded toward the boarded-up front wall of the pavilion.

"Shall we start our tour? My German is not so good, but I will do my best, unless you would prefer French."

"French will be fine, Monique," the young officer said, pleased that he now knew her name. "I will interpret. We are primarily interested in looking at the works of art. Mein Fuhrer and General Goering are both quite famous artists, you know."

She led them toward Calder's fountain in the middle of the main floor. The mercury that oozed its way through the fountain-cum-mobile transfixed all but three of the German contingent: the young officer openly ogling the pretty tour guide, and Hitler and Goering staring across the auditorium at the black and white mural on the far wall.

"Is that the Picasso painting?" Hitler's voice cut off the young officer's translation in mid-sentence. All eyes turned in the direction he was pointing.

Monique understood the words "Picasso" and "painting" and nodded, triggering an en masse movement of the Germans across the terrazzo floor to the security rope in front of the twenty-five-foot-long mural. Goering, in the lead, stopped to take in the scope of the painting as Hitler swept past him and unsnapped the security rope, dropping it to the floor.

"Wait, Mons..." was all Monique could get out before Hitler stepped past the barrier, stopping inches from the painting. She looked in protest to the young officer, but he only shrugged in resignation, holding up his hand apologetically to stop her from saying anything further.

Hitler peered at the painting, moving up and down its length; occasionally stepping back to get a wider perspective. His sallow complexion turned pink. The room held its collective breath.

"It's a travesty!" he shouted. "A disgrace!"

Color drained from several faces and heads began to nod.

"It's a mockery," Hitler roared, his face now a full-blown scarlet and his volume escalating. "Who can tell what it is? It does not even show our Luftwaffe. The painter should be shot! THIS PAINTING MUST BE DESTROYED!"

With that he turned and stormed from the pavilion, followed in rag-tag formation by half of the entourage. The door viciously banged shut behind them, causing the temporary board wall to shudder and sway, before settling back in place

Monique stared in shock, her mouth open. She had not understood all of his words but she knew that the Supreme Commander of Germany was supremely angry. Her legs turned to jelly and she reached for the closest thing to steady herself, the arm of the young German officer. He seemed not to notice, standing with eyes wide, unsure of whether to follow Hitler or stay.

"Mein Fuhrer is a bit off his feed this morning." Goering broke the awkward silence. "I think he is angry because our Wehrmacht didn't shoot the demonstrator yesterday."

He chuckled at his own joke. No one joined him.

"I rather like the painting, but if the Fuhrer says it is to be destroyed, well, then, it must be," he continued, then turned to Monique with a syrupy smile and said, "Let us continue our tour, shall we?" The young German officer only interpreted the last sentence.

The remainder of the tour was leaden. Monique had lost her verve, and the young officer's amorous intentions deflated in the fury of Hitler's tirade. As the remaining Germans filed out, Goering held back, beckoning the young officer to him.

"I think you should stay, Heinrich, and get better acquainted with the young Fraulein," he said in a conspiratorial tone. "Find out what you can about their plans for *Guernica* when this building is torn down next week. Whatever else you can accomplish is up to you." The

General's eyes twinkled. Heinrich nodded, thankful once again that he was aide-de-camp to Goering and not Hitler.

Returning to a conversational tone, Goering switched subjects. "What do you think of that painting, Heinrich?" pointing toward the upper landing and *The Reaper*, nearly as tall as *Guernica* was wide. "Do not the Spanish have a strange view of the world?"

Heinrich nodded.

Goering smiled. *We can destroy a painting for the Fuhrer. It just may not be the one he thinks it is.*

Antoine Lipp was a simple man.

He owned two trucks. With the help of his son-in-law, whom he paid only enough to support Antoine's oldest daughter, he moved furniture and freight around the city of Paris. He owned a warehouse where he employed two dockworkers, at minimal wages, to handle the freight that moved in and out. He belonged to social clubs and fraternal organizations. He went to mass every Sunday. He provided for his wife of thirty-five years in what he considered a generous manner, but it was meager by comparison when measured against the lavish lifestyle he led with his mistress.

He had built a reputation as a good businessman: his prices were fair and he was careful with his customers' goods. It did not make him rich, but it did provide a steady stream of business—business that included moving and storage of delicate and valuable items such as antiques and works of art, for which he charged premium fees.

Ordinarily that was a good thing, but now it was presenting Antoine Lipp with a dilemma.

A month earlier, thanks to a referral by his niece, Monique Fontenot, Lipp had agreed to move several pieces of art for the Spanish government. The man with whom he negotiated the contract, a Monsieur Puig, was the director of the Spanish exhibit at Expo '37. The contract required removal of the art from the Spanish pavilion on Jardin du Trocadero between November 29 and December 4. He was to store the art at his warehouse for up to 10 days during which time Puig was to notify him of where to make final delivery.

Because of the civil war in Spain, Lipp insisted on being paid for his services in advance, with an additional "risk" premium. His fee also included a substantial sum so he could purchase an insurance policy in case any of the art was damaged or lost. Lipp, of course, already had such a policy.

Three days ago, a man had visited Lipp's office. He had identified himself as Sergio Mendez, curator of an art museum in Madrid. Senor Mendez also hired Lipp to remove a painting from the Spanish pavilion and hold it at his warehouse. The painting, identified by Senor Mendez as *Guernica* by Pablo Picasso, was to go on display at his museum after Expo '37 was over. Another freight carrier would pick it up at Lipp's warehouse and take it to Madrid.

As before, Lipp used the Spanish civil war to his advantage, insisting on payment in advance, and once again his fee included a charge for an insurance policy, and for a separate pickup even though he would pick up *Guernica* at the same time as the other Spanish art work.

Lipp thought it odd that Puig had not arranged for the removal of this painting in the earlier contract, but then the Spanish were unpredictable, and the earlier contract didn't identify specific art pieces by name.

All had seemed right until Lipp received a telephone call yesterday from a third person asking him to remove a piece of art from the Spanish pavilion.

The caller was an American who also wanted a large painting removed, but this one was to be delivered to Marseille. He had said it would take two people to remove the painting, and that he would pay twice the usual charge because of the short notice. The painting had to be picked up at the pavilion on Sunday at 2 p.m. and had be delivered to a freight forwarder at Bassin d'Arenc in Marseille by six the following morning.

Antoine agreed to take the job provided payment was delivered before noon. The American assured him that it would be, and also assured him that the gate guards at the Exposition would be expecting him. He told Lipp to ask for Monsieur Picard, the pavilion security guard, when he arrived. Picard would direct him to the painting.

Now Lipp sat drumming his fingers on his desk, pondering what to do. From the American's description of the size of the painting he was certain it was the same painting that Senor Mendez had hired him to remove. And could it also be one of the paintings that Director Puig had asked him to move?

Lipp went to a file cabinet and located the Puig contract. It listed numerous paintings, two of which were extremely large. None of the art was identified by name or artist.

Perhaps there are many large paintings, he thought. *Maybe the American and the Spanish museum curator were getting two other large paintings. But if that were true, surely Masseur Puig would have mentioned it to prevent me from taking the wrong paintings. Could it be that all three, Puig, Mendez and the American, wanted him to remove the same piece of art? If that is so, then two of them are thieves.*

Lipp saw an opportunity.

The thieves couldn't claim he had taken their money without admitting that they hired him to deliver a stolen painting. He would be able to keep all three fees. On the other hand, if he did accidentally deliver it to one of the thieves, and one of the others proved he was the rightful owner, Antoine would claim he was duped, or that it had been stolen from his warehouse. He would, in that case, dutifully refund his fee to the rightful owner and collect on the insurance. Either way he was getting paid three times for the same job.

Another shewed business deal. Now he only had to figure out which of the two were thieves.

The phone in the director's office rang. Ring. Ring! RING! RIINNGG!!

Jolted out of his stupor, Picard finally answered. "Spanish pavilion. Security."

"Officer Picard, I am confirming that there will be a truck at the gate at two o'clock, but I have some bad news." Francois immediately recognized the American's voice.

"What?"

That is the only kind of news there is, Picard thought.

"One thousand dollars was more than I had expected to pay for the painting, and now the shipping costs are far higher than I expected because of the size of the painting. I can only afford to pay you eight hundred dollars."

Picard thought for a moment. Eight hundred would buy him and Monique passage to the United States and still leave him with more than five hundred dollars. He could accept the American's new offer, but it irritated him.

"I, too, have some bad news," he said.

The American was silent.

"The Miro painting is painted on the tiles of the wall," Picard continued. "You cannot pick up the painting at two. You will have to wait until the Exposition is over. Then you can send someone to dismantle the wall so you can take your painting."

"Officer Picard, that is not possible," the American said. "I am leaving Paris this evening and will not be available to supervise the removal of the painting tomorrow. There must be some way for us to remove the painting today."

"I don't see how," Picard answered.

"Allow me to send my workmen at two and see if it can be done. If it cannot, then we are out nothing except the time it takes to try."

Picard thought for a moment. "All right," he agreed.

"Please make sure you have the bill of sale ready today in the event we can move it," the American said before he hung up.

"The man is an idiot," the American said to himself after he hung up. "He is not only a thief, he is a complete fool."

When he had first discussed *The Reaper* with Dali, he was informed that the painting had been done on Celotex, the same wall board from which the walls of the pavilion were constructed. Miro had chosen Celotex for two reasons: it would make the painting look like it was part of the building, and it was free. The sheets Miro used were left over from the construction.

And, although the finished work was 18 feet tall and 12 feet wide, when disassembled it broke down into six sections, and, most importantly, each section was attached to the actual wall of the pavilion by a simple set of brackets which could be easily removed.

Already paying only one-tenth of the painting's value, the American realized that Picard's ignorance presented an opportunity to depress the price even further.

Picard informed the gate guards that Lipp Moving Company would be sending a truck at two o'clock to pick up the remaining debris from the collapse the day before, "and probably some other items as we start to close down the pavilion." They assured him they would send the truck through.

He stopped at a food wagon on his way back to the pavilion and ate a croissant. The bread seemed to soak up some of his jitters. He looked at his watch. Nearly ten thirty. Pedestrian traffic was starting to pick up on the esplanade. Work crews were busily preparing the Trocadero for the closing ceremonies. He watched as bunting was attached to the grandstand railing and stage where the speeches would be made and awards presented.

Fresh air seemed to ease his headache. Warm sunshine felt good on his weary body.

With a big sigh, Picard ambled back to the pavilion. He went up the steps to enter through the second floor, prolonging his time in the sun. Once inside, he scanned the room. There was a reasonable crowd, all seemed in order.

"There is a man here to see you," a tour guide informed him. "He is waiting for you in the director's office."

Annoyed that the American may have sent his workmen early, Picard hurried to the director's office. To his amazement, he found a young man flipping through the papers on Puig's desk.

"What are you doing?!" he challenged the visitor.

The young man looked up. "I am Renaldo Puig," he introduced himself. "I am the brother of Director Jose Puig. Are you the assistant director?"

"I am the security guard," Picard shot back, piqued by the audacity of this visitor. "May I see some identification?"

Renaldo showed him his national identification card that confirmed his name, Spanish citizenship and residence in Barcelona. Satisfied, Francois eyed the young man and thought he saw a resemblance to the director.

"I am sorry about your brother. Have you seen him?" he asked Renaldo.

"He was still unconscious when I left him little more than an hour ago."

"That is too bad. What can I do for you?"

Renaldo started the speech he had been rehearsing: "My brother was greatly concerned with the safety and protection of the art work of this pavilion. He spoke of it to me often. Now that he is injured, I am here to carry out his wishes. I do not want something to happen that would tarnish his good name. Do you know if he has made arrangements to have the art work safely removed?"

Picard found such an expression of brotherly concern out of place when directed at someone as condescending and arrogant as Director Puig, but he saw no benefit in offending the young man.

"Yes. Yes. Director Puig arranged for everything. He was very diligent in that manner." Picard said it although he had no idea whether the director had, in fact, arranged for removal of the artwork.

"Do you have the name of the mover?" Renaldo asked. "I would like to contact them to make sure everything is in order."

Picard caught himself before blurting out the name of the freight company that would be removing *The Reaper* in a few hours. "I'll have to find it for you," he parried. "Perhaps I could call you with that information."

"I'm sure it's here in Jose's office," Renaldo said. "I know you're busy. As long as I'm here I'll go through his things and find it."

Picard felt trapped. He could order the young man out of the pavilion, but he seemed very determined. That might cause a confrontation, or he might come back later with more people. He didn't want him here at two o'clock!

"All right, but the pavilion will be closing at one for the closing ceremonies. You'll have to leave by then," Picard lied, and left.

Renaldo rummaged through his brother's desk, looking for some indication of who was going to remove the pavilion's art works. As he turned to start his search in the filing cabinets, the phone on the desk rang. Renaldo hesitated, then gingerly picked up the handset.

"Hello," he said.

"Monsieur Picard?"

"No, this is Renaldo Puig."

There was a hesitation on the other end of the line. "Director Puig?"

"No, I am his brother."

"Is Monsieur Picard there?"

"No. Can I take a message?"

"Please tell him that Antoine Lipp of Lipp's Moving Company called, and that one of my trucks will be at the pavilion to pick up the painting at one thirty rather than two o'clock."

"Which painting are you picking up?" Renaldo asked.

"I don't know. Monsieur Picard is to identify it for us when we arrive," Lipp answered. "I just want to make sure he'll be there at one thirty."

"I'll tell him," Renaldo responded, then added, "Do you know who is picking up the other paintings from the pavilion?"

"I am."

"When will you be doing that?"

"Sometime next week."

"Did my brother talk to you about a painting named *El Segador*?"

"No," Lipp answered, "but I am to pick up all of the art work so I'm sure that painting is included if it is at the pavilion."

"Where are you to deliver the art?" Renaldo continued to probe.

"Director Puig will tell me. For now, it will be stored in my warehouse."

"My brother has been injured in an accident and is in the hospital," Renaldo said. "I will find out from him where the art is to be delivered and get the information to you."

The younger Puig took down the address and phone number of Lipp's company and accepted Antoine's condolences.

"How many large paintings are there?" Lipp asked at the last moment. "Your brother forgot to write down the number, but I know there are at least two that are about twenty feet long. Are there any more large ones that you know of?"

"I'm not sure," Renaldo said, "but I believe there are just two."

Andres Duron died of his bullet wounds, his protest brought to a violent end. Ormonde's case instantly became a homicide.

He stood outside the examining room window at the Paris morgue, watching the chief coroner doing the routine autopsy that was required for all murder victims. Finished, the coroner washed off the blood, took off his gloves and apron, and left the examining room.

"Anything out of the ordinary?" Ormonde asked.

"Nothing we didn't already know. He died of a gunshot wound. The one in the back killed him. Punctured a lung and severed an artery. Bullets were .38 caliber."

"Any way of telling which directions the shots came from?"

"I'd have to know how he was lying after being shot to tell you that," the coroner said.

Ormonde left the morgue and went in search of the ambulance drivers who brought Duron to the hospital. He would also question the emergency room personnel who had treated the others injured at the demonstration, and then check with the station to see if the third bullet, the one that had not hit Duron, had been found.

He was hoping that Gaudin's story was right, that the bullets hadn't come from the German security guards. Then he'd have a chance to solve this murder.

The ambulance driver drew a diagram for Ormonde, showing him the position in which they had found Duron's body. He didn't know if Duron had been moved between the time he was shot, and the time he picked up the body.

In the emergency room, Ormonde leafed through the admission reports from the previous day. From the time of admittance, and the nature of the injuries, it was relatively clear which of the patients had come from the demonstration. He copied names, addresses and phone numbers. He would have one of his investigators at the station follow up. He went upstairs to the post-operative critical recovery area and asked the head nurse if Duron had had any visitors. Her check of the log indicated that there were none. His inquiry about Puig was met with bad news. He had not regained consciousness and the surgeons were pessimistic, both about his recovery and about his ability to talk if he did recover. She said that Puig's brother, Renaldo, had come to visit him. He had been there about an hour ago and stayed only a few minutes. Ormonde copied down his name and address from the visitor's log.

"May I speak to the person in charge here?" Ormonde asked, showing Monique his credentials.

She pointed to Picard, across the pavilion's main floor: "That is Monsieur Picard. He's in charge."

"A gendarme to see you," she said as they approached Picard. Inner muscles constricted, and color drained from his already-pale face.

Ormonde identified himself, again flashing his badge. "I'm here investigating the shooting," he said.

Picard's stomach muscles relaxed and in staccato fashion, he gave Ormonde his best recollection of what had happened. He also mentioned that Director Puig's brother was in the director's office.

So that's how a French security guard came to be in charge of the Spanish pavilion? the detective mused. *Nervous little fellow.*

Ormonde asked a few more questions and indicated that he would also want to talk to any pavilion staff that was on duty that afternoon.

First, however, he made his way to the director's office and stopped outside the slightly open door, listening to one side of the end of a telephone conversation. The speaker was speaking French with a decidedly Catalan accent. When the call ended, Ormonde stepped inside.

"Renaldo Puig?" he asked, showing his badge. Puig visibly jerked in reaction to the badge. He nodded.

"I'm here investigating the shooting that led to the injury to your brother," Ormonde continued, introducing himself. "Were you here yesterday when it happened?"

After a pause, Renaldo answered. "Yes. I was in the crowd. How did you know my name?"

"Tell me what you heard and saw," continued Ormonde, ignoring the question.

"I heard gunshots and everyone started running."

"Did you see the man get shot?"

"No. I was talking to the person next to me when the first shot was fired," Renaldo answered. "Then it was just running."

"Were you one of the people who ran toward the front of the pavilion?" Ormonde motioned in the direction of the boarded up, formerly glass wall.

"No. I ran down the promenade," he said, pointing in the opposite direction of the German pavilion.

"Did you see the German security guards?"

"Yes."

"Did the shots come from the direction of the German security guards?"

"I don't know." Renaldo hesitated. "Maybe. Probably, since I ran in the opposite direction. I don't really remember. I just ran."

"Did you know the man who got shot?" Ormonde continued.

"I knew of him. I didn't know him personally."

"He's dead." Ormonde said it bluntly, trying to elicit a reaction from Puig. A tic in his cheek gave away that he knew more than he was saying.

"How was it that you were in the crowd yesterday?"

"I come here often to see my brother," Renaldo said, doing his best to recover from the news of Duron's death. "I just went out to see what was going on."

"Was there anyone in the crowd that was heckling the speaker or showing any hostility toward him?"

There was a long pause. Finally Renaldo answered: "No. I didn't see anybody, but I heard some in the crowd were not in favor of the rally."

"Heard from who? Can you give me names?"

"Nobody specific, but I can ask around."

"Why were they not in favor of the rally?

"I don't know. Maybe they were Franco supporters."

Ormonde asked where Renaldo was staying while in Paris, then handed him a card with his phone number on it. "Call me if you remember anything more, or learn the names of anyone who was opposed to the rally," he said.

On his way to interview Monique and other staff members, Ormonde passed the security guard. "Did you see Director Puig's brother here yesterday?"

"I've never seen him before today," Picard answered.

He watched Ormonde climb the steps toward the second level. Something the detective had said made Picard consider, for the first time, how odd it was that the Spanish government had not been in contact with anyone at the pavilion since the demonstration four days earlier. There was no assistant director, Director Puig made sure of that, preferring to keep everything under his personal control. He didn't delegate authority, and he was the only one who had contact with anyone from the government. Picard didn't even know to whom Puig reported. There was no one who knew how to inform the Spanish authorities when the director was injured. It was the one loophole in Puig's management style that he had not counted on. Unless they read the morning newspaper, the Spanish government would not even know their appointed director was on the verge of death.

A stroke of luck for me, Picard thought, still clinging to the thin hope that *The Reaper* might be his ticket to the United States. *Now if I can just get this gendarme and Puig's brother to leave.*

He walked down the stairs to *his* office. Renaldo Puig was still there, sitting in *his* chair and looking pale.

"Did you find what you were looking for?" Picard asked brusquely, showing no concern for the young man's apparent distress.

"What? Oh, yes. He called and they're coming at one thirty," Puig said, absent-mindedly.

"Who called, and who's coming at one thirty?" Picard asked, annoyed.

Puig pushed his handwritten note across the table at the security guard. "The company that my brother hired to move the art work."

Francois read the note. *Merde!*

"Very well," he said. "You are done then? You have found out what you want?"

"Yes," Renaldo responded, getting up from the chair. "Monsieur Lipp said he was picking up a painting today. Which painting is he picking up?"

"I'm not sure," he said, the response taking too long. "I may have him take as many as he can."

Renaldo nodded, knowing a lie when he heard one.

Ormonde sat on a rickety folding chair across the table from the second of the demonstrators. The austere interrogation room smelled of old smoke with a metallic tinge. He offered a cigarette to the prisoner and lit it, then lit his own, clamped between his thick lips.

He had questioned the first prisoner without learning anything new. Ormonde knew that he would have to release them both, but for now it was good to have them easily available.

He took a long drag off his cigarette and asked, "Do you know Renaldo Puig?"

The man slowly nodded his head, looking pensive, as if trying to conjure a memory to attach to the name. "The Puigs are from Barcelona. Influential. I think Renaldo is the youngest."

"Why would he be in Paris?" asked Ormonde.

"His brother is here. He directs the pavilion where we had our rally," was the response. "Maybe he came to see his brother."

"Did you see him at the rally?"

"I don't know that I'd recognize him if I did see him."

Ormonde was accustomed to chasing dead ends. He questioned the man again about the events of the prior day, but his story was consistent and nothing new was learned. He informed him of Duron's passing. The man was clearly distraught.

As he considered if there was anything he hadn't covered, Ormonde tossed out a "throw-away" question to buy time to think: "Are the Puigs active in Spanish politics?"

"More in Catalonian politics," the prisoner said. "I've heard that the pavilion director is big into the Catalonian independence movement. I don't know about the younger one."

"Are you Catalan?"

"No. I'm from Madrid," the prisoner responded.

"Aren't the government and the Catalonians fighting on the same side in your civil war?" The detective continued to probe this new vein, hoping for gold.

"We're doing the fighting," the prisoner responded with an edge in his voice. "They haven't done much of anything, but at least they didn't fight against us, until recently."

"What do you mean?"

"Word is that the Catalonians are trying to cut a deal with Franco. If he'll give Catalonia independence, they will withdraw their support of the government."

"Would that end the war?" Ormonde asked.

"Much of the territory that we control would be given up," sighed the demonstrator. "The government would collapse, I think."

Ormonde thought for a moment, then asked: "How did a Catalonian secessionist become the director of a pavilion paid for by the Spanish government?"

The prisoner shook his head. "I have no idea."

Ormonde ordered the release of the two demonstrators. He wasn't going to charge them with something as trivial as demonstrating without a permit—not with a murder to solve and the courts already overflowing.

Besides, Renaldo Puig had just become a "person of interest" in the murder of Andres Duron.

First, we will get The Reaper *to Barcelona. Then we shall take care of that murderous bastard, Edgardo The Hat.* Anticipation of revenge for his brother was ample motivation for Renaldo.

He caught a taxi outside Pallais de Chaillot to the hotel where he was staying. Edgardo the Hat and Antonio were waiting for him in the lobby.

"I have the name and address of the company that is picking up the art work," Renaldo told them after they had left the lobby and gathered in his room. He lay a crumpled piece of paper on the bed and did his best to smooth out the wrinkles.

"This Senor Lipp," he said, pointing at the name of the moving company written on the paper, "told me that he is to pick up the art work next week and will hold it at his warehouse until further orders from my brother. I told him that I would get the orders from my brother and pass them on to him."

"Did he accept that?" asked Edgardo.

"He said he would take direction from me," Renaldo said, stretching the truth.

"You have done well," said Edgardo, draping his arm over the young man's shoulders.

"What should I tell him?" the young Puig asked, pulling away from the older man's embrace and cigarette-tainted breath. "I could tell him to take it to Barcelona."

"Then this little deception could be traced directly back to you. You might find yourself in a French prison," Edgardo chuckled. "I think it better that we find another moving company to pick up from Senor Lipp's warehouse and deliver to Franco's men. I will contact them to see if they have a suggestion on who to use. Then, if there are problems, it will be Lipp's problem, not ours."

"I saw the painting when I was in the pavilion. It's very large," said Antonio, speaking for the first time. "Make sure that Franco's men know that. And the mover must be someone experienced in handling paintings. We don't want it damaged by some clumsy dock worker."

"It is three or four times the height of man," Renaldo confirmed. "At least five or six meters high and half as wide. We will need a big truck to move it."

The Hat thought for a moment.

"I will call a mover from Sitges that I know," he said, changing plans. "If he doesn't have the expertise and equipment, he will know someone that does. It is better if we don't use a local moving company. It will be more difficult for the French gendarmes to question a mover from Catalonia."

The men sat for a moment, Renaldo thinking about the phone call from Lipp which he had luckily intercepted.

"There may be a small problem," he said.

The heads of both men jerked up.

"In my conversation with Lipp I learned that he is picking up a painting at the pavilion today at one thirty. When I asked the security guard which painting, he lied. He said he didn't know, and that he might have Lipp pick up many paintings, but I could tell he was lying."

Both men simultaneously looked at their watches. They had only two hours before Lipp was to arrive at the pavilion.

"Why would they be picking up one painting today, while the Exposition is still going?" asked Edgardo.

"Exactly," Renaldo replied. "There is something going on here that isn't right."

"You must return to the pavilion and see which painting is being moved this afternoon," Edgardo ordered.

"The security guard was not happy to find me in my brother's office, and seemed to want to get rid of me," Renaldo responded. "Perhaps it would be better if Antonio went. He would look like any other spectator and could watch what is going on without being identified."

Edgardo thought for a moment.

"You and I will wait outside the Exposition," he said, pointing toward Renaldo, "and, if they are moving *The Reaper,* we will follow. If it goes to Lipp's warehouse, fine. If it goes somewhere else, we will hijack the moving truck."

All three men nodded.

If that is the case, Renaldo thought, *there will be more bloodshed. Edgardo will see to that.*

"Antonio, go to the Exposition. Now." Edgardo ordered. "Find out where a freight truck would enter the grounds. There will be some special gate for that. We may need a place to hide the truck. I will check with Franco's men and with my friend in Sitges to see if there is a friendly warehouse here to park the truck for a few hours, if needed. Call me back when you locate the entry gate. Renaldo and I will be parked outside the gate by one forty-five. If they are taking *The Reaper* it will take some time for them to remove a painting that large. Come find us as soon as you know if *The Reaper* is being moved."

Antonio left the hotel room. Renaldo seethed at the prospect of spending the next hour, alone, with the murderer, Edgardo.

Lipp hung up the phone.

So, Director Puig is in the hospital, he mused. *And there are only two large paintings. There is great opportunity here, but which of my customers are thieves? Which painting are they trying to steal?*

He had decided to go to the pavilion earlier than scheduled to determine if the picture he was to remove today for the American was the same as the one that the Spanish museum curator wanted. He also wanted to see how difficult it was going to be to detach the large paintings from their wall-mountings.

The phone call to inform the security guard that he was coming early turned out far better than Lipp could have imagined. The Director was the only person with whom he had dealt, and with him out of the picture, no one would know exactly what Lipp was hired to do. Puig's brother was only a minor obstacle. He did not seem sure of himself on the phone, and if Lipp took charge of the situation, he doubted that the brother would challenge him. The whole situation was ripe for harvesting, and he, Antoine Lipp, would be the reaper.

Puig was the first to ask for my services, so I must presume he is the honest one, he reasoned.

On the other hand, the instructions Puig had given Lipp were vague, at best, giving him ample room to arrange for other ultimate destinations for the paintings, perhaps for his own personal benefit.

He is employed by the Spanish government, Lipp thought. *They are losing a war and there is little future there. He will surely be arrested, or executed, when the government falls, if he returns to Spain. Perhaps Puig sees this as his escape plan.*

Lipp's thoughts turned to the American. He had insisted that the painting be removed at two o'clock today and delivered in Marseille no later than six tomorrow morning. The money had been delivered in an envelope in francs. No receipt had been requested. The note accompanying the delivery confirmed that he should ask the security guard which painting he was to remove, and also indicated that someone representing the American would meet him at the pavilion at two.

If this was, in fact, a theft, and Lipp was reasonably certain that it was, having the security guard involved reduced Lipp's risk significantly. If something went wrong, he would maintain his innocence. He was just a poor freight hauler hired to do a job taking direction from the security guard. Even if something went wrong he would have earned his fee, or so he would try and convince anyone who challenged him.

The curator, on the other hand, seemed to Lipp to be legitimate. He was the only one without a possible ulterior motive, or at least none that Lipp could conjure. He had paid with a draft drawn on a governmental account in Valencia. He was the only one who identified the painting. He had given specific instructions about how the painting was to be moved. *But why did he contact me only three days before the end of the Expo? Is he really a curator of a museum?*

To which of them should he deliver the painting? That was Lipp's real dilemma. That, and how could he keep the fees paid by all three?

Those were the questions Lipp pondered as the clock ticked into the afternoon.

Picard looked at his watch: 12:30 p.m. He had emerged from the director's office to find sunshine streaming through the parts of the pavilion that weren't boarded up. It had brought out a huge crowd for the final weekend of Expo '37. The pavilion was packed, and movement was made difficult by the out-of-order main entrance. The vibration and general instability made evident when Hitler slammed the door on his way out that morning had convinced Monique and the other guides on duty to lock the entrance. The crowd could only enter or exit through the second level, meaning that the staircase was constantly jammed with traffic going up, going down, or standing still to look at *The Reaper.*

"Monsieur."

Picard turned to face three suits.

"Monsieur, I am Luis Araquistain, Spanish ambassador to France. This is Dr. Enrique Goma who is here to take over directorship of this exhibit, and this is Sergio Mendez, curator of El Prado Museum in Madrid who is here to help Dr. Goma transfer the artwork following the close of the Exposition tomorrow."

Picard's jaw dropped.

"We learned yesterday of the riot and of Director Puig's unfortunate injury," Araquistain continued. "We would like to thank you for handling the situation under very difficult circumstances. Please be assured that the Spanish government appreciates it very much."

"I…ah…I…thank you," Francois stammered, trying to collect himself. The headache that had receded below the surface exploded like Bastille Day fireworks and a wave of nausea swept over him.

"Are you all right Monsieur?" the ambassador asked, seeing the bandaged security guard suddenly grow pale.

"Oui" was the weak reply.

"Perhaps we should go to Director Puig's…ah…Dr. Goma's office?" Araquistain suggested politely. The party of four joined the throng on the staircase and pushed their way to the main level and the director's office.

There were only three chairs, and barely room for those. Picard stood, uncertain.

"Please. Sit down," the ambassador said, gesturing toward a chair. "What is your name?"

"Merci. Francois Picard." He sat and felt his nausea slowly subside.

"If you would be so kind as to answer a few questions for Dr. Goma and Senor Mendez perhaps you could leave for the rest of the day."

"I can't!" Picard recoiled. "Uh…there is an ongoing investigation of the demonstration, and I have to be here when the gendarmes arrive."

"And," he added, after a pause, "the man who Director Puig hired to remove the art work is coming this afternoon."

Mendez interrupted: "Lipp is coming this afternoon? Why?"

Merde! He knows Lipp.

"Uh…to see how difficult it…ah…will be to remove the sculptures and the large paintings," Picard lied, still trying to gain traction on the slippery slope his outburst had created.

"I can meet with Lipp," Mendez declared curtly. "There is no need for you to be here."

"I am fine," Picard said, his voice stronger now. "I have worked here since the beginning and I have duties to perform. I will not abandon them because of a bump on the head.

"Besides, I must be here in case the gendarmes come back," he added, repeating the earlier lie, hoping it sounded more convincing this time.

"Very well." Araquistain acquiesced, despite a scowl from the curator.

After several minutes of questions, the ambassador excused himself, satisfied that everything was under control, and indicated that he would return to the embassy.

Nothing is under control, thought Picard ruefully. *It is all out of control.* He had no idea how prescient he was.

Less than ten minutes after the ambassador made his exit, there was angry pounding on the locked main door. Picard unlocked it, opened it a sliver and announced through the crack to the people standing there: "This door is closed, please…"

Before he could finish, a man expensively dressed in wool britches and a madras shirt, interrupted: "It is now open. I am here to get my art work." He was not physically intimidating, but his demeanor left no room for discussion. Four men in uniforms befitting janitors or service technicians stood behind him.

"Are you Monsieur Lipp?" Picard asked.

"I am Pablo Picasso and I have come to take my art work."

Picard, reduced to a state of shock for the second time in the last twenty minutes, stood in the now-fully opened doorway, staring at the famous artist.

Picasso gave a curt "Merci," and attempted to push past the dumbstruck security guard. Picard's arm shot out to block his entry.

"Just a moment!" he blurted. "Stay here." Picard turned and hastened to the pavilion office to present the newly-appointed director with his first crisis.

"Pablo Picasso is at the main entrance," he informed Dr. Goma. "He has come to take his painting."

"What?" Goma and Mendez bellowed in unison.

Mendez bolted for the office door and Picard stepped aside to avoid being trampled. The curator, followed by Dr. Goma, charged across the pavilion floor abandoning all decorum.

Picasso and his workmen had not heeded the "stay" order. They were already working at the edges of *Guernica.*

"What are you doing?" bellowed Mendez.

Picasso turned and faced the curator, like a bulldog protecting his territory.

"Senor Picasso, what are you doing?" Mendez repeated, his bellicose tone turning servile.

"I am taking my painting," Picasso responded in a monotone.

"But it is the property of the Spanish government," declared Mendez.

"I have not been paid!" Picasso's voice elevated only slightly. "Until I am paid, it belongs to me. I have come to take both *Guernica* and my sculpture. Clearly, they are not safe here. You are very lucky that they were not damaged in the riot.

Mendez stood, his mouth open with nothing coming out.

"If you could just leave them until we close the pavilion tomorrow, I'm sure I can arrange payment through the embassy," Dr. Goma interceded, the authority of his new position an ill-fitting garment.

"Who are you?" enquired Picasso.

"I am Dr. Enrique Goma, director of this exhibit."

Undeterred, Picasso pressed forward. "Dr. Jose Vergas Puig, the original director of this exhibit, and I agreed that I would be paid for these works. I'm sure you are a fine man and will honor the commitment of your predecessor . . . particularly since it is in writing."

Picasso paused for theatrical effect, and then removed a folded piece of paper from his pocket. Handing it to Dr. Goma, he continued: "I have requested payment several times. I am not a beggar nor a charity! I am taking them now unless you pay me immediately."

Mendez found his voice and turned to the security guard. "Stop him!" he shrieked.

Picard sized up the workmen, turned and retreated to the office, followed by Mendez spewing accusations that alternatively questioned Picard's courage and Picasso's mendacity.

Picard dialed the local precinct station. "This is Francois Picard, security guard at the Spanish pavilion at Expo '37. There is an altercation here and I need help. Please send someone immediately." He listened to the confirmation from the other end, hung up the phone and left the office, ignoring the raving curator.

People had gathered at the upper level railing to watch the altercation as main level spectators closed around the combatants. One inadvertently bumped the new director, who staggered backward into the crowd. A punch was thrown, and with it random hostility ignited like dry tinder.

Picard blew his whistle as hard as he could, the shrill blast causing his head to explode in pain but accomplishing its intended task. Clenched fists, fingers wrapped around lapels, even shouts and curses froze in mid-air, caught in tableau.

"I have called the gendarmes!" Francois said softly, in deference to the pounding in his skull. "They will be here in a few minutes. No one will be removing anything from this pavilion until they get here."

The near-whisper from the bandage-swathed security guard, in the midst of the escalating crisis, was as surreal as *Guernica* itself—but it had the surprising effect of quieting the crowd.

Picasso returned to his controlled, in-charge demeanor. "We shall wait for the gendarmes and see who is entitled to my art," he said confidently.

When he thought no one was looking, Dr. Goma gingerly touched the back of his head where he had been struck. He nervously pulled at the cuffs of his suit jacket to straighten wrinkles that weren't there. This appointment was supposed to be a small reward for years of service. The role as caretaker for a few days while the pavilion was disassembled would allow him to add "World's Fair Pavilion Director" to his resume. But in less than an hour he had been punched, bruised, insulted, and forced to confront a national hero, Pablo Picasso. And now the gendarmes were coming. He wanted nothing more than to leave, returning to the peace of academia.

The two sides each staked out a piece of the pavilion floor. Approaching sirens could be heard in the distance.

Goering had been obsessing over *Guernica* since he left the Spanish pavilion, pondering which wall of which of his villas it would grace. He had decided to have it hung behind a series of tapestries that he had recently "purchased" from a Jewish merchant. The tapestries could be rolled up when he wanted to show off *Guernica*. He would, of course, have to make sure that Hitler would never see it, but that would not be difficult. He and the Fuhrer were not exactly social friends. *The Fuhrer's appreciation of art is so limited, so mundane,* he thought. *No wonder he was a failure as an artist.*

Of course, Goering could not utter those sentiments aloud. He had told Hitler that he would make sure that the Picasso painting would be "taken care of." He had chosen his words carefully so that he could disavow having lied to his Fuhrer if something went wrong. Even as such, he knew that subtle nuances of language would not save him if Hitler discovered the ruse. *I'll give the painting another name, so that even if he hears something from another who sees it he will not make the connection.*

For the moment, however, his concern about such things was secondary. He was fastidiously reviewing himself in a full-length mirror in preparation for the closing ceremony. A knock on his dressing room door was followed by Heinrich's entry.

"That was quick," Goering said, still looking in the mirror, but now with one eyebrow raised.

"I am having lunch with her at one o'clock," Heinrich reported.

"Good," the General replied, "You will need to be on the dais at 2:00 p.m. tomorrow. Until then, you and the Fraulein should get well acquainted."

Goering continued his primping.

Heinrich saluted, thrilled at the prospect of spending the next twenty-four hours with Mademoiselle Monique.

A movement near the now-unlocked main level door caught Picard's eye. Monique was waving to get his attention. "I'm leaving now," she mouthed the words.

Antonio, standing at the second-floor railing watching the dispute over *Guernica* unfold below him, saw the interchange between the security guard and the young woman, and drew logical, but erroneous, conclusions. He watched as Picasso and his workmen formed a defensive line in front of the painting.

So it is "Guernica" and not "El Segador" that they are trying to move, he thought. Antonio looked at his watch: 1:05 p.m. *They must have come early.*

He wandered away from the railing and gradually made his way down the steps to the main level. There he stood for several minutes, oblivious of the crowd milling around him, trying to interpret everything that Miro had put into the painting. He was in awe of Miro's vision, of his tribute to Antonio's forefathers. Catalan pride swelled in his breast.

Gendarmes spilled through the lower level entrance, drawing Antonio's gaze away from *The Reaper.* He watched the gendarmes approach the security guard, then fan out around *Guernica* and the knot of people who surrounded it.

It was one fifteen. He faded into the crowd and out of the pavilion. As he descended the steps he saw the police cars parked on the esplanade. He failed to notice a second moving truck parked at the pavilion entrance.

Lipp and his son-in-law, Georges, had arrived at the pavilion minutes earlier, Lipp's anxiousness to see the paintings firsthand escalating the pace of his usual leisurely lunch. What he learned at the pavilion, Lipp reasoned, would show him which of his customers were thieves, which, in turn, would help him decide to whom he would deliver the painting. It would also help him, he thought, to devise a plan that would allow him to keep all three payments.

He was in a hurry to get to the task at hand but an unmarked freight truck parked at the pavilion entrance, similar to his own, was not what Lipp had expected. Following his usual cautious instincts, he climbed the stairs and entered the pavilion on the second level to scope out the situation before identifying himself to the security guard.

Georges followed in his wake like an abused puppy.

As they entered the pavilion they were swept to the upper level railing by curious fair-goers rushing to see the ruckus below. The melee was brought to an immediate halt by the piercing screech of a whistle.

The man, wearing a rumpled, dirty uniform, with his head wrapped in bandages, seemed a strange choice to be in charge, thought Lipp, but a quick scan of the pavilion revealed no one else who might be a security guard.

Monsieur bandage-head must be my contact.

Then he recognized Senor Mendez.

This is most curious! I am glad I did not just blunder into this.

Lipp continued to watch the scene play out below. He was in no hurry. The American's agent wasn't due for at least forty-five minutes, giving him plenty of time to find out which painting he was to remove. He ordered his son-in-law to stay at the railing and then extracted himself from the throng and took a quick tour to count the number of large paintings. He was relieved to learn that the director's brother had been correct. There were only two.

Lipp was halfway down the stairway between floors when six gendarmes poured into the pavilion. After the events of the prior day, French law enforcement was not about to leave itself vulnerable to a charge of untimely or inadequate response.

The officer in charge directed two of his squad to the left and two to the right while he and the sixth gendarme approached the crowd and *Guernica* head-on. He spotted Picard and altered his course.

"What happened here?" he asked, indicating Picard's bandaged head.

"That is from Wednesday's riot," Picard said.

"Did you make a call for help?"

"*Oui*," Francois responded. "We have a disagreement here. This man," he turned, pointing first toward Picasso, and then to *Guernica*, "claims that painting is his and he has come to take it. That is *Monsieur* Pablo Picasso."

"That," Picard continued in a still-soft voice, "is *Monsieur* Mendez. He is the curator of a museum in Madrid and claims that the painting belongs to him and his museum.

"And this," Picard continued his introductions, "is Dr. Enrique Goma who has just been appointed the director of this pavilion. He represents the Spanish government."

The lieutenant, enthralled to be introduced to the great Pablo Picasso, barely heard the rest of the introductions, until Picard mentioned "director of the pavilion." The gendarme turned to Dr. Goma.

Lipp, from his perch on the stairway, could see a lot of nodding and gesturing as the gendarme questioned the newly-minted director. He kept one eye on the security guard, hoping that he would separate himself from the pack so that he could approach him, but Picard did not move.

The conversation became a great deal more animated, and louder, when the lieutenant began questioning Mendez. The curator was punctuating the conversation with arm-waving and shouting almost entirely in the direction of Picasso and the painting. Lipp used the distraction to complete his descent to the main floor and work his way through the crowd toward Picard.

The lieutenant could be heard repeatedly assuring Mendez that there would be no "stealing" of paintings under his watch while, at the same time, trying to separate himself from the impassioned curator. Twice he stopped Mendez from following him as he attempted to approach Picasso. After the second time, the sixth gendarme stepped in and herded Mendez back to a spot beside Director Goma.

Picasso and the gendarme began a quiet discussion. Again there was a great deal of head-nodding, this time mostly by the lieutenant.

From the few short yards away it appeared that the famous painter was convincing the gendarme of the merit of his claim. It was more than Mendez could stand. He dodged around the sixth gendarme and charged the painting, Picasso, and the lieutenant, shouting Spanish epithets. Before anyone could reach him he was in Picasso's face, his eyes bulging, his face florid. The melee threatened to explode once again as the workmen dashed to their employer's defense, and the gendarmes rushed in to restore order.

Another piercing whistle blast caused momentary paralysis among the combatants, just enough to allow one of the gendarmes to wrap his arms around the angry Spaniard. He pulled Mendez away from the equally incensed, but less combative, artist, and order was quickly restored.

Lipp's ears were ringing. He had been standing just behind the security guard when Picard enlisted his whistle for the second time. As the bedlam subsided, he stepped beside the security guard and, through the corner of his mouth, introduced himself.

At first, Francois didn't comprehend what the person standing next to him was saying. He was trying his best to maintain control of "his" pavilion, and he didn't need further distractions, but as the man stood there, looking at him expectantly, the words sunk in.

"This is not a good time, Monsieur Lipp," he whispered.

"I understand," the mover answered in an equally surreptitious tone, "but I need to know if that is the painting I am to move today." He pointed at *Guernica*.

"No. It is that one," Francois responded, jerking his head in the direction of *The Reaper*.

"Merci."

Lipp thought for a moment, watching the tense situation, and then did something contrary to his normally cautious nature. He stepped forward and shouted, "Excuse me!"

Heads turned toward the big man as combatants swiveled to face this new challenge.

"Excuse me," Lipp repeated, with slightly less volume now that he had everyone's attention. Addressing himself primarily to the gendarme lieutenant, he continued: "I am Antoine Lipp. My company has been hired to remove the artwork from this pavilion, and to store it in my warehouse. I may be of help in this disagreement."

Mendez, seeing Lipp as an ally, immediately rushed to the mover's side, greeting him like a long-lost brother. Lipp nodded in acknowledgment, wishing the gendarmes had kept a better grip on the annoying, incendiary Spaniard.

"It is apparent that there is a dispute over who is to take this painting," he continued, gesturing toward *Guernica* as he walked toward the lieutenant. "Since I have already been hired to remove this painting, as well as all of the other art, I would be happy to remove it and store it in my warehouse until the dispute can be resolved and it can be delivered to its rightful owner."

Mendez tagged along behind Lipp, his head bobbing in agreement. Picasso moved closer to listen, being careful to stay out of reach of the museum curator.

"This pavilion is to be demolished in the next few weeks." Lipp continued addressing the lieutenant. "This painting can't be left here during demolition. My warehouse is a safe place, it is not far from here and it is insured."

"This man was hired by that madman!" Picasso injected, referring to both Lipp and Mendez who were now standing side-by-side. "He will not touch my painting!"

"You are correct, Monsieur Picasso, that I was hired by this man," Lipp responded in a conciliatory voice, "but I have met him only once before today for less than a half hour. He paid me to move your painting to my warehouse. I owe him no allegiance beyond that, and he has already paid for my work so you will not be charged for the removal of the painting or the storage in my warehouse. If it is determined that the painting is, indeed, yours, I will deliver it to your studio at no additional charge."

"Well?" asked the gendarme, looking back and forth between the painter and the curator.

Mendez was incensed that Lipp had shown no loyalty to him, and, in fact, had been deferential to Picasso, but having *Guernica* in Lipp's warehouse, rather than Picasso's studio, was preferable. Suppressing his emotions, he nodded. He was certain that the Republican government would not deny him the money to pay Picasso.

Picasso was not so quickly convinced, but further conversation with the gendarme made it clear that he was not going to be allowed to remove the painting. Finally he agreed to have Lipp take the painting to his warehouse provided that he, Picasso, would supervise the removal and storage of the painting

The suddenly affable mover, and the Spanish painter, exchanged phone numbers and agreed to coordinate the time for removal of the artwork.

Picasso and his crew left, followed a few minutes later by the squadron of gendarmes, less one. The officer in charge had commended Picard for keeping the situation from getting out of hand. He indicated that he would leave one of his men to help assure that calm was maintained.

Goma and Mendez repaired to the director's office to report to the ambassador about the events of the past hour.

Picard sidled up to Lipp.

"Someone is going to be here at two o'clock to see if *The Reaper* can be moved without tearing down the pavilion wall," he said.

"Your buyer has told me to meet the man," Lipp whispered. "We are of the same understanding, but I have not seen anyone yet. I shall wait for him by the painting."

The crowd had thinned by 2:00 p.m., as most fairgoers took time off for lunch. Picard descended the steps to the main level and saw Lipp standing in front of *The Reaper,* in conversation with the American and a third person. Picard glanced toward the director's office, and then around the pavilion, making sure that neither Dr. Goma or Mendez were out-and-about. Relieved that he saw neither, he approached the three.

"We shall remove it after six o'clock. I can still get it to Marseille in time," Lipp was saying, through the third person, an interpreter.

"How late can you remove it and still get it to Marseille?" the American asked.

"Nine p.m."

"You can actually remove it?" Francois asked in a low, incredulous voice.

"It will be difficult," the American said, "but it can be done without taking down the wall."

Lipp raised an eyebrow. *Why would anyone think you would have to take down the wall to remove the painting?*

"Can I have a word with you in private?" Picard said to the American.

"I will inventory the other art work," Lipp offered. This whole scenario was playing out much better than he could have expected, *but someone here doesn't know what he's doing*, he thought.

Out of Lipp's hearing, Picard inquired: "Do you have something for me?"

"I do," the American responded, "I will give it to you when the painting is out of the pavilion and in Monsieur Lipp's truck. I will have to give some of it to him because of the added difficulty of removing the painting."

"I understand," said Picard, relieved that he was at least going to get something for his effort. "Do you know how much?"

"We have agreed on 1,000 francs."

Picard could hardly contain himself. He would still receive over seven hundred fifty U.S. dollars. He was on his way to America! With Monique.

"I can meet you here at eight and let you in."

"I will not be here this evening," the American said, "but I can give your payment to Lipp with instructions to give it to you once the painting is loaded into his truck."

Antonio slid into the back seat of the Citroen parked two blocks from the Exposition's freight entrance.

"I have seen *The Reaper.*" His voice was choked with emotion. "It will rally all true Catalonians to the cause of liberty."

Renaldo, who had also seen *The Reaper*, was surprised by its effect on the older man. He did not understand how this painting instilled such passion. His brother Jose, twenty years his senior, had tried to explain the capacity of Miro's painting to instill nationalist pride, but to Renaldo's generation it was just another strange painting. Perhaps it was understandable only to those who saw themselves as lifelong victims of a corrupt and oppressive government—those who had so often tried and failed to break free from Spain.

The nationalistic fervor was lost on Edgardo. In fact, to him the painting had the opposite effect: it made people emotional and emotional people did stupid things. As a soldier, completing his assignment was all that mattered and there was no room for stupid things, only for cold, calculated actions that accomplished his mission.

"Are they moving it today?" he asked.

"No," Antonio responded. "The argument was all about Picasso's painting, *Guernica.* The famous man, himself, even showed up to take the painting. A bunch of other people claim the painting belongs to Spain. It almost turned into a riot, but the gendarmes were called. When they came, I left, but all the argument was about *Guernica. The Reaper* was never mentioned."

"Good." Edgardo said. "You saw nothing that suggested that *The Reaper* would be removed today or taken anywhere other than the mover's warehouse?"

"Nothing."

"Did you see the movers?" Edgardo continued. Antonio's expression changed to confusion.

"What movers?"

"A Lipp Moving Company truck entered the Exposition not fifteen minutes ago. Didn't you see it?"

After a pause, a meek "no."

"Merde!!" exclaimed Edgardo. "So the mover is here and we don't know what he is going to do!"

Antonio sat silently in the passenger seat, looking at the floor

"*Idiota,*" Edgardo insulted him. "Go back to the pavilion and find out what is going to happen with *El Segador*!"

Antonio got out of the car and slunk away, relieved to be away from the angry soldier. Edgardo seethed in silence. Renaldo was also silent, his plans for Edgardo The Hat occupying his thoughts.

Five minutes later an unmarked moving truck left the Exposition and drove past the parked Citroen. Three police cars followed minutes later. More minutes passed and Antonio returned on foot.

"Did you see the movers?" Edgardo pressed him before he had fully entered the car.

"There were several men standing in front of *El Segador,* including a security guard. They were talking but I couldn't get close enough to hear what they were saying."

There was silence in the car. Renaldo and Antonio cowered in anticipation of a violent outburst from Edgardo but, instead, in a forced, calm voice, he said, "We shall wait."

A half block away two men watched the Citroen. They had heard the report on their radio that the incident at the Spanish pavilion had been resolved. They had watched as the police cars left the Exposition, and as Antonio returned to the car.

"What do you suppose they're up to?" one of the plain-clothed occupants asked.

"I'm not sure, but Ormonde says we need to keep a tail on this Renaldo Puig. As long as he's in that car, we wait," said the second.

Several miles away on Rue de Beaux-Arts, the American sat in the rear seat of a black limousine, looking at the front of Pierre Loeb's art gallery.

It had been surprisingly simple to arrange a meeting with Joan Miro.

A call to the North American Newspaper Alliance office in Valencia, Spain, had gotten him in touch with his childhood friend, Ernest Hemingway, a longtime admirer of Miro. Hemingway's purchase of a Miro painting named *The Farm* in the 1920s had become something of a legend. Typical of Hemingway, he had won the right to buy *The Farm* in a dice game with another would-be purchaser, then didn't have the money to pay for it. Miro, always the gracious gentleman but perhaps not the best businessman, had agreed to accept payment in installments allowing Hemingway time to raise the money.

Now Hemingway was covering the Spanish civil war for several Canadian and American newspapers. He had come to Paris on Friday when rumors started to circulate about the German high command attending the closing ceremony of the World Exposition. Hemingway, whose pro-Republican government leanings were well documented, sought a firsthand opportunity to confront the German brass about its support of the Spanish army. A story linking the German military directly to the Franco-led insurgency might help rally American and Canadian support for the shaky government.

But even with the potential of a significant story at stake, he was not too busy to help out an old friend.

"Al! How the hell are you?" Hemingway growled into the phone when he had returned the American's call. "And what are you doing in Paris?"

Ernest Hemingway and Algur Dreyfus had both grown up in suburban Chicago, the offspring of comfortably wealthy families. They had met as boys in Charlevoix, Michigan, where both families spent their summers. Dreyfus was the older of the two by a year, but Hemingway was the ringleader—the alpha dog of a group of preteen boys who spent their summers creating one adventure after another, skipping into and out of the minor trouble that boys of ten or twelve are prone to get into.

The friendships held through the early teens. But as the members of the group grew older, discovered girls, and stopped summering in Charlevoix, friendships waned. Only Dreyfus and Hemingway had stayed in touch. Dreyfus ascended through the ranks of the industrial world, developing a reputation as a smart dealmaker with a keen understanding of the value of a dollar and the knack for accumulating lots of them. Hemingway, meanwhile, found fame, if not fortune, in writing. His mad-dog approach to life, which he exercised unabashedly in the middle of some of the great historical events of the time, gave him a larger-than-life persona and made him a frequent media darling. During the thirty years since Charlevoix, they had corresponded regularly and met occasionally. The meetings usually resulted in great stories and major hangovers.

"Hem, I'd like to meet your friend, Joan Miro." Dreyfus had said, after the pleasantries had been dispensed. "I saw one of his paintings in the Spanish pavilion at Expo '37 and decided I wanted to add some of his work to my collection. Could you arrange a meeting?"

Hemingway was only too happy to do so. “In fact,” he exclaimed. “I’ll go with you. I haven’t seen Joan in a couple of years.”

And so it had happened. The chauffeur opened the curbside door and offered his hand. Dreyfus took it for leverage and pulled himself out of the back seat. He entered the gallery and was immediately engulfed in a bear hug from the large, mustachioed man who was his friend, “Hem.”

“Al! Damn! It’s good to see you,” Hemingway boomed, a large hand on each of Dreyfus’s shoulders, holding him at arms length. “You haven’t changed a bit.”

“It’s only been a couple years,” Dreyfus said, accustomed to the ebullient greetings of his friend.

“Really? Feels like I’ve lived ten years since we last saw each other.”

“You have,” Dreyfus chided. “I’ve only lived two.”

Hemingway roared with laughter.

“C’mon,” he said. “I’ll introduce you to Joan.”

Miro was a handsome man, not large of stature, with his hair slicked back and shirt unbuttoned enough to expose a mat of chest hair. He gave the impression of being fastidious, perhaps obsessively so.

The men chatted about numerous matters: Hem and Miro reliving a few old times, Miro telling how he and his family had come to Paris on holiday and had been stranded because of the civil war. He told of how his friend and benefactor, Pierre Loeb, had agreed to let him use part of his gallery as a studio so that he could work and earn a living. There was much talk of politics, the civil war and the brooding presence of Germany that hung over it all.

Finally the talk turned to the reason for the meeting.

“I have seen *The Reaper* at the pavilion, and admire it very much,” Dreyfus said.

“That work means a great deal to me,” Miro responded. “Are you familiar with the Reaper’s War?”

Dreyfus apologized that he was not, and that set off a lengthy monologue on Catalonia’s unending battle for independence from Spain and of the Reaper’s War, another of the uprisings that had failed, but in its bloody failure had become a coalescing memory in the hearts and minds of the Catalonian nationalists.

"Because we, Catalonia and Spain, are all fighting for our very survival against a hideous enemy, I painted *The Reaper* to give inspiration and courage. I donated it to the cause of freedom," volunteered Miro.

"Al wants to see some of your paintings," Hemingway interjected, cutting directly to the point of the visit. "Have you got anything like *The Reaper* you could show him?"

"Most of my work is still in Catalonia," complained Miro, "but I have several that I've done since I've been here in Paris."

The threesome, who had been sitting on comfortable sofas in the gallery's viewing room, rose and went to a back corner of the building that was currently serving as Miro's studio. Along the way the artist pointed out several of his works hanging on the gallery walls. None of them were what Dreyfus had in mind.

In his small, neat studio Miro explained each of the works that were on the walls and two that were sitting on easels. He showed particular pride in the multiple textures he had been introducing into this new works. As he listened, Dreyfus scanned the room.

"What's this?" he asked, pointing to a painting sitting on the floor, leaning against a wall behind one of the easels.

Miro picked it up and laid it on the top of a table, carefully rearranging several bottles and brushes to make room. "This is actually painted on the same material as *The Reaper*," the Catalan painter explained. "I had to cut the bottom off some of the panels on which *The Reaper* is painted to fit them into the space I was given at the pavilion. This painting is on one of those pieces I cut off."

"Does it have a name?"

"I just call it 'Composition,'" Miro replied. I have many paintings that I call composition until I find a name. Sometimes I never do."

"I like this one. Would you sell it?" Dreyfus asked.

"Of course," the artist responded. "I have also painted others on the same material."

He showed them to Dreyfus, but the American liked the one he had first spied leaning against the wall.

The bargain was struck quickly: $1,800.00 U.S. Dollars. Miro seemed pleased at the price.

"Times sure have changed," boomed Hemingway, recounting how he had paid 5,000 francs for a Miro painting named *The Farm* in 1924. "Sixty seven dollars back then. What would you pay for it today?"

Dreyfus shook head. "More than I can afford," he said.

Miro nodded, a wan, melancholy smile crossing his face.

Dreyfus was back in his limousine, staring at a receipt: "Sold to Algur Dreyfus, Chicago, Illinois, United States of America. One composition, oil on Celotex fiber board. One thousand eight hundred U.S. Dollars," it said. The signature on the receipt, "*Miro*," was clear and unmistakable.

Composition was in the car's trunk, carefully wrapped and cushioned. The receipt he would use to convince customs officials that *The Reaper* was legally his.

Monique's thrill of having her arm folded into the arm of the handsome German soldier as they walked the esplanade, continued through lunch.

"May I take you to dinner this evening?" he had asked as they parted company back at the Spanish pavilion, and she had gladly accepted.

Upon his return to the German pavilion he was informed that Goering had left instructions with the head of security to provide Heinrich with whatever assistance he requested. In a brief, sworn-to-secrecy conversation with the German security director, Heinrich divulged his assignment: to carry out the Fuhrer's demand that the painting in the Spanish pavilion be destroyed. Heinrich did not have to emphasize the gravity of the required task. Hitler's rage had done that.

His meeting complete, Heinrich changed into civilian clothes, donned a cap and sunglasses, and went back to the Spanish exhibit, his budding relationship with the vivacious Monique giving him perfect cover for spending time there.

He noted two men dressed in the fashion of workmen moving from place-to-place on the second level, making notes about each poster, painting and exhibit. From the railing he saw Monique working on the main level. He also saw a man in a business suit inspecting *The Reaper,* paying particular attention to the clips that held the painting in place. A short while later four men, including one of the workmen and the pavilion security guard, met in front of the painting held a brief conversation. The man in the suit and the security guard continued their conversation after the others had left.

Heinrich descended the stairway to get another look at *Guernica.* He was aware of his commander's love of art, but this particular painting was completely different from anything Goering had *collected.* To Heinrich it looked like a bad dream, but a critique of the painting was not the purpose of his inspection. *How would he move a painting this large?* That was the puzzle he was trying to solve as he stood looking at the mural.

"Can I help you Monsieur?"

He turned to the brilliant smile of Monique. "I thought I wouldn't see you until after work," she said.

"I didn't want to bother you while you are working," he said. "I came back to look at some of the art. And maybe to bother you just a little bit."

They chatted for a few minutes until she excused herself to go back to her duties, confirming their evening dinner plans as she walked away.

He wandered in the direction of Calder's mercury fountain, not wanting to look too interested in *Guernica.* The security guard and one of the workmen exited the nearby office. The guard walked in the opposite direction, toward the door upon which the Fuhrer's fury had left its mark that morning. The man he had identified as one of the movers headed toward the stairway to the upper level.

"Excuse me." Heinrich got the man's attention as he walked past. "Are you the man with the moving truck?"

"Oui," Lipp responded, hesitating.

"I was just wondering," Heinrich said, trying his best to sound like a curious tourist. "How do you move a painting that large?" He pointed at *Guernica.*

"Roll it up just like you would a carpet," Lipp offered, "unless the artist has other ideas. We'll have to see what he says, but that's how I'd do it."

"Will he be here soon? I'd like to meet him," Heinrich continued.

"He won't be here before the pavilion closes."

"*Danke.*" Heinrich gave his best imitation of being disappointed.

"We have a suspect in the shooting at Expo '37," Ormonde said, pouring a thin stream of coffee into a small demitasse.

Gaudin had stopped at the 16th precinct to see if there was any new information on the investigation. He was working on a follow-up story for the morning newspaper, and Ormonde seemed a likely place to start. Plus, there was always free coffee.

"Apparently a group of Catalonian secessionists were at the rally," Ormonde said. "One of them was the brother of the director of the Spanish exhibit, Renaldo. I met him at the pavilion. He claimed he spent a lot of time there with his brother and just happened to be there Saturday, but the security guard said he'd never seen him before he showed up in the director's office this morning."

"Lots of people pass through the pavilion," Gaudin offered. "Maybe the security guard just never saw him."

"I interviewed the security guard," the detective said with a tinge of humor. "He doesn't have a life. He spends all his time at the pavilion. He comes across as a toady. It's not likely he would miss someone related to the director."

Gaudin nodded.

"There has been talk over the wire about the Catalans and Franco cutting a deal to give Catalonia its independence and end the war," he said. "Maybe things got a little heated at the rally."

"That's what we're thinking," Ormonde said. "We are watching Puig-the-younger and a couple of his friends. They have staked out the freight entrance to Expo '37 and we have them staked out. Please don't write anything without checking back with me first. I don't want them to know we have them under surveillance."

Gaudin nodded. "Any sibling rivalry between the brothers that might explain what happened?"

"It appears that the injury to the director was an accident caused when the crowd panicked," Ormonde said. "The Puig family is quite involved in Catalonian politics, but we have nothing that would lead us to believe that the elder brother was the target."

Gaudin's follow-up question was interrupted by the telephone on Ormonde's desk. The conversation between the detective and the person on the phone was unrelated to the reporter's task and took Ormonde in pursuit of a different crime. Gaudin finished his coffee and decided to check with the hospital on Jose Puig's condition. As Ormonde hung up the phone, stood and slipped into his coat, the reporter asked to use it.

"Just leave ten francs on the table," Ormonde joked.

Gaudin gave him the universal "screw you" salute and dialed the hospital. There was no change in Director Puig's condition.

SATURDAY EVENING, NOVEMBER 27, 1937

"They say this is the intellectual hub of Paris," Heinrich said, keeping his voice at a conspiratorial level, just above the hubbub in *Café du Dome*. "But it's really where all the spies hang out, so be careful what you say."

Monique giggled in response, the effect of her second glass of champagne apparent.

The waiter came and Heinrich ordered for them, including another round of champagne. She sat across from him—the world, through her eyes, a golden haze.

It's the lighting, she thought, and it was, as the saffron glow of the café's lights turned Heinrich's blonde hair into a halo. But it was also the romantic whirlwind unlike any she had experienced in her seventeen years. Mesmerized by his good looks and confident demeanor, Monique had felt elegant on the arm of the handsome uniformed German. She also felt invincible against the stares of passersby on the streets of Montparnasse and the other café patrons.

He had finished first in his class, starred in football and joined the Luftwaffe at age twenty. Now, four years later, he was about to become a captain. Like General Goering, he had never piloted a plane. His interest was in administration and politics, not dropping bombs.

Monique sat, spellbound, as Heinrich told her of his life.

"And what of you?" he asked, a twinkle in his blue eyes. "How have you come to be sitting in this den of intelligentsia? Are you a spy sent to bewitch a poor boy from Dresden into telling you all the secrets of the German military?"

Amid the tinkle of her laughter, and denial of his allegations, their food arrived. Heinrich slid around the circular booth until he was sitting next to her, their thighs touching.

"May I?" he asked, picking up his knife and fork. He cut her *boeuf bourguignon* into small bites. "There," he said, when he was done. "Shall we toast to all things French: cuisine, champagne, and you?"

He did not slide back to his side of the circular booth.

She told him of the almost-eighteen years of her life during dinner: growing up in Montmorency just north of Paris, she had moved to the city at thirteen to attend academe. She loved to write and hoped to attend Institut de France and follow in the footsteps of Roger Martin du Gard who, earlier in the year, had won the Nobel Prize for literature.

"How did you come to be a guide at the Spanish pavilion?" Heinrich asked as they sipped calvados, a potent apple brandy ordered by Heinrich after their plates had been cleared. The brandy was a new experience for Monique.

"Luck, really," she said, slurring her words slightly. "The opening of the pavilion was delayed because Miro hadn't finished *The Reaper*, and a couple of guides who had been hired bailed out because of the delay.

I knew one of the other guides and they told me about the openings. I applied and they hired me right before it opened."

"So, what will you do after it closes tomorrow?"

"Not sure. Maybe go to America."

Her answer caught Heinrich by surprise. He had envisioned weekend liaisons in Paris.

"Well," he said, covering his disappointment, "Let's have one more to toast to your future."

After their toast, she snuggled against him under his arm which was wrapped around her shoulders. They sipped in silence until Heinrich asked, in a just-making-conversation manner, "What will happen to all the beautiful art work when they tear down the pavilion?"

"For now, it's going to my uncle's warehouse," she said.

"Your uncle?"

"Antoine Lipp. He owns a moving company. He has a contract to move all the art. He will store all the art in his warehouse until there is an agreement on where it's all supposed to go. There's an argument about who has the right to one of the big paintings."

"How did your uncle get a contract to move the art?"

"I told the director about him and they got together."

"You continue to amaze me," Heinrich said, pulling the young woman even closer to him. "Beautiful, a talented writer, and a head for business too."

Picard arrived a few minutes after 8 p.m. Jardin du Trocadero was eerily quiet, and there was no sign of Lipp or his truck.

He waited, shivering in the evening chill.

By eight-thirty he was sure something had gone wrong.

Again.

He had moved to Paris fresh out of university. The lure of a career in private security had beckoned: good pay, snappy uniforms, position of authority, Parisian women. It promised to be a paradise for a young man, and, with France turning more and more of its attention to national defense, there were fewer gendarmes available for private work. Local security jobs were said to be plentiful.

Reality had not fulfilled the promise.

Picard applied for numerous jobs. After being turned down several times he went to a private academy for additional training, but still no job had come his way. Others had been hired, but not him. That was the way of Paris in 1937. If you didn't have connections you weren't likely to get a job, and Picard didn't have connections. He washed dishes at a restaurant and worked in a warehouse to make ends meet. Finally, he landed the job at the Spanish pavilion thanks to an acquaintance at the academy who had been hired for the position but then got a permanent job with a security firm before the pavilion opened.

Picard had thought it was his dream job. Eight months later he found it boring, with long hours and meager pay. Now only one day remained before the Exposition ended. His job would last a few more days while everything was being removed from the pavilion, but beyond that was unemployment, or back to washing dishes.

He considered returning home, to Toulouse, when the Exposition ended. It would be humiliating (*better humiliated than hungry*, he thought), but he had discarded the idea because of fear that he would soon be conscripted into the military. Had he been totally honest, Picard would have had to admit that he was afraid of the soldiers at the adjacent German pavilion. Bulging with weapons, wearing their metal helmets, marching in goose step—to him they appeared invincible.

The specter of war between France and Germany grew daily. The Nazis were supporting Franco in the Spanish revolution, and there were daily news articles about the German government using Spain as a training ground for its military. France had responded by increasing its military strength.

Better to stay in Paris and lose myself in the crowd, he concluded.

Picard unlocked the main entrance and carefully let himself inside. He turned on the lights and checked to make sure everything was in order. *The Reaper* and *Guernica* were in their proper places. He went to the office and looked up the number for Lipp Moving. He called but there was no answer. He waited ten minutes and called again with the same result.

At nine he left. His American dream had disappeared over the horizon and, again, Picard felt hopeless.

SUNDAY, NOVEMBER 28, 1937

Zephyrs of damp air on the back of a Mediterranean warm front gave the last day of Expo '37 the feel of springtime. The crowds came early, dressed in colorful clothes and bright smiles. The festive aura amplified Monique's dreamy euphoria as she glided down the esplanade toward the Spanish pavilion, still feeling lubricious from a night of lovemaking.

Neither the sight of Monique nor the high spirits of the crowd were an antidote for the dour mood of Picard, however. The early arrival of Dr. Goma was a further reminder that he no longer was in control. He spent the morning behind the pavilion, chain smoking and wishing his headache would go away.

The crowd thinned as lunchtime approached. Musical instruments could be heard tuning on the esplanade as a band prepared for the closing ceremonies, and Picard, tired of his self-imposed isolation, wandered toward the sound. Bleachers that were not there the day before had been erected in a horseshoe, facing a large stage draped in bunting. Several rows of chairs on risers waited for the notables who would bask in the closing glory of one of the largest events ever orchestrated by man. Seven months in duration, and attended by thirty-one million spectators, Expo '37 had been a resounding success despite a lingering worldwide depression and ominous war clouds hanging over Europe.

Heinrich stepped on to the podium just as the last dignitaries were being seated. He hurried to take his place behind Goering.

"I was worried that your sense of duty had slipped below your belt buckle," Goering whispered out of the side of his mouth, a bemused look on his face.

Heinrich looked straight ahead, without change of expression: "It took time to get the information."

Goering nodded, still smiling.

As the closing ceremony droned on Heinrich scribbled a note and slid it under Goering's elbow.

"All art to be moved to local warehouse tonight or tomorrow, including *Guernica.* Plan is in place to satisfy the Fuhrer."

Goering signaled for Heinrich's pencil, then turned the note over and wrote on the back: "We're leaving after Speer receives his award. You stay and carry out the plan. Mind your belt buckle!"

Heinrich took the note from Goering, read it, and handed it back to his commander. He nodded and allowed himself a half smile. Monique's address was tucked safely among his papers, and he planned to hang his belt buckle in her boudoir again before he returned to Germany.

Picard walked back to the pavilion, bored with listening to speeches and applause that pounded on his ever-throbbing head. The noise and the music faded as he walked, hoping that he might see Monique. Without a ticket to America to give her, he did not expect to see her again after the Expo closed.

He entered the nearly-empty second level. Standing, facing the opposite wall, was Antoine Lipp, writing on a clipboard. Blood rushed to Picard's cheeks as he strode to Lipp and said, in a louder than necessary voice, "Where were you last night?"

Lipp, a full head taller and thirty years older than the security guard, put his index finger to his lips. "Not so loud," he whispered. He put his arm around Picard and guided him like a child to a corner, out of earshot of any spectators.

"There was a change of plans," he said softly. "I convinced Mr. Dreyfus that it was not a good idea to move *The Reaper* before the Expo closed. It would reflect poorly on Mr. Miro and be considered an insult by the Spanish government. Apparently, you have no telephone, so I could not reach you to tell you of the change."

"I was here last night. Why didn't you come and tell me, or send someone?"

"No one would question a security guard checking on his pavilion in the evening," Lipp explained, "but a security guard meeting a moving agent could raise some questions as to why they had chosen such an odd time and deserted place to meet. Do you understand?"

Picard's angry face faded to a scowl as he struggled to comprehend Lipp's meaning.

"Perhaps this will help you accept my apology." Lipp handed him a fat envelope. "It's from Dreyfus. I trust you will see that it gets into the right hands." The envelope was delivered with a sly smile.

Picard could feel bank notes inside the envelope. Now he understood. He quickly stuffed it in his jacket pocket.

"Thank you. I will," he said.

Picard descended the stairs to the main floor, looking for Monique. Not seeing her, he went directly to the office and knocked. There was no answer, so he let himself in and locked the door behind him.

He spread out eight bank notes on the desk. He had never seen anything like them, but there was the number 100 on each one, and the words "United States of America." *Lipp is an honest man,* he thought. *The change in plans eliminated the extra pickup charge so I got the full eight hundred. I would not have thought of that.*

He placed the bank notes back in the envelope and wrote a note to Dr. Goma whom, he assumed, was still at the closing ceremony. "I am feeling very ill," it read. "I am going home. I will try to be in tomorrow."

He left the note on the desk and left the office to search for Monique to tell her the good news. The only tour guide he found informed him that Monique and the other guides had been sent home with their final paychecks. Dr. Goma did not feel the need for multiple tour guides in the final hours.

Picard considered the situation for a moment, then returned to the office and found the file cabinet where employee information was kept. He wrote down Monique's address and left.

SUNDAY EVENING, NOVEMBER 28, 1937

Trucks began lining up at the freight entrance an hour before Expo '37 was scheduled to close. At six thirty, the gendarmes shooed the last of the spectators out of Jardin du Trocadero, and more than a hundred trucks and livery vehicles spread out across the promenade to gather up the array of technology, industrial showmanship, futuristic fantasy and artistic excellence that had dazzled the world.

On the corner of Rue le Notre, a block from the entrance, Edgardo had set up their observation post before the closing ceremonies had even begun. He had insisted, over the grumbling of his cohorts, "in the event someone tries to remove *The Reaper* prematurely." In the five hours they had been watching no vehicle had been let into or out of the Exposition campus. The sullen silence of Antonio and Renaldo was testing Edgardo's temper, barely contained under the best of circumstances.

Now, as daylight waned, the trucks that were lining up appeared virtually identical. Nearly all were of the same shape and size, and differences in their drab colors became indistinguishable under the street lamps. Those with markings, like Lipp's trucks, that might otherwise allow them to be identified, were incomprehensible in the dim light. By the time the trucks were allowed to enter the Expo '37 campus, it was apparent to Edgardo that it would be impossible from their vantage point to identify which of the trucks were coming from the Spanish pavilion.

Angered at his own failure to anticipate this problem, Edgardo ordered the reluctant Antonio to find a vantage point inside the campus where he could both watch the Spanish pavilion and signal them when trucks left. Rebuffed by the gate guards, Antonio returned to the car, and Edgardo, incensed by what he viewed as a halfhearted attempt, berated the older man with a profanity-laced tirade that ended with a punch to the side of his head. A trickle of blood ran out of Antonio's ear as he cowered in the front seat.

"Did he just hit him?" a plain-clothes gendarme, sitting in an unmarked vehicle parked three cars behind Edgardo's Citroen, asked.

"Something just happened," said the other. "But our guy is in the back seat and it didn't look like he was involved."

"So, we just wait?"

"We wait."

Minutes passed in the stationary Citroen before Edgardo broke the uncomfortable silence by announcing his need to relieve himself. Renaldo and Antonio watched as he approached the guards and was summarily turned away in his attempt to convince them to let him into the Expo to use a toilet.

When Edgardo was out of sight, Renaldo was the first to speak.

"Are you all right?"

"I'm fine," was the less-than-truthful answer. "When this is done, I will take care of the great Edgardo."

Renaldo nodded, but he knew that Antonio was no match for the ruthless soldier. "Perhaps it won't be necessary," he offered.

When Edgardo returned, Renaldo offered to get food for the group. He took orders from the other two, and sauntered away from the car, relieved to stretch his legs and be away from the menacing Edgardo. He hoped that Antonio would not do or say anything that would set Edgardo off while he was gone.

He placed an order at the first restaurant he came to and asked if there was a public telephone. The closest one was on the corner of Rue de Passy and Rue de La Tour, a block away. He paid for the food and excused himself, indicating that he would return in a few minutes for it.

Luckily the phone booth was empty. Renaldo stepped inside, fished the card of Detective Ormonde out of his pocket, and dialed the number.

"This is Renaldo Puig," he said. "I met you this morning in the Spanish pavilion at Expo '37. I have information about who shot the person at the demonstration earlier this week."

Renaldo paused as the person on the other end scrambled to find a pen and paper.

"His name is Edgardo Vivas. He is billeted at the Hotel d'Albion. Right now, he is sitting in the driver's seat of a green Citroen parked on Rue le Notre a block from the freight entrance to Jardins du Trocadero. He has a gun, the same one he used to shoot the man at the demonstration. A man named Antonio is in the car also. He had nothing to do with the shooting."

So, the great Pablo Picasso has come to supervise the removal of his painting. It is too bad he will be disappointed.

Through night-vision binoculars, an innovation recently developed for the German military, Heinrich watched the Spanish pavilion door through which Picasso had disappeared just moments earlier. His contempt for the avant-garde art movement, of which Picasso was the acknowledged if uncrowned leader, was nurtured by the German high command which preached that such art reflected the morally bankrupt liberalism that infected much of Europe. A policy created personally by Hitler, a self-professed art expert, it quickly became Nazi party dogma.

Heinrich saw those branded "liberal" by the Nazis, Picasso included, as weak and stupid and soon to be crushed under the bombs and the boots of the Reich. As his thoughts dwelled on war, he realized that his pulse was racing and he had broken a sweat.

Heinrich took a deep breath to regain composure.

Goering's official order, carefully leaked to members of Hitler's staff, was to have *Guernica* destroyed. The secret order he had given Heinrich, however, was to destroy a painting that Hitler would believe to be *Guernica* but, in fact, was not. Picasso's mural was to be secretly shipped to Goering's villa in Bavaria. Goering had inferred, without specifically so stating, that because of its similarity in size the painting to be destroyed was *The Reaper*.

In a boozy, sex-addled conversation the previous night with Monique, the two had mused about the value of the two huge paintings at the Spanish pavilion. They were both certain that each of the paintings was worth more than either of them would earn in ten years, maybe a lifetime. Playfully, through their intoxicated haze, they talked of how they would steal one of the paintings, sell it, and live richly and happily ever after.

By morning, Heinrich had chosen to ignore Goering's implied suggestion.

If I am going to steal Guernica *and make it appear to be a rolled-up carpet, there is no reason I can't do the same for* The Reaper. Heinrich reasoned. *Everything else will burn in Lipp's warehouse. The Fuhrer will think* Guernica *burned. Herr General will think* The Reaper *burned. I will be the only one to know the truth.* Heinrich might have disdain for Miro and avant-garde art, but he had high regard for the millions of reichsmarks it would put in his pocket.

"It's really quite simple," he told Monique before they parted. "We will roll it up like a carpet and store it in your uncle's warehouse. You will tell him it's a carpet and he will store it for you at no charge as a favor for getting him the Spanish contract. When the time is right, I will ask General Goering to help me find a buyer for it, and we will be rich."

Thinking that he was still joking, Monique was happy to declare her support for the plan, unaware of the Goering-ordered plan that included the burning of the warehouse.

The ground level main doors were propped open and workmen were beating a path between the pavilion and the trucks parked nearby, carrying out furniture and miscellany, returning with tools or packing boxes.

Heinrich changed his location to maintain a clear view of the open doorway as more and more trucks filled the concourse. His watch ticked toward eight o'clock and nothing that resembled a rolled-up carpet had yet left the pavilion. Another truck backed into the line in front of the pavilion, completely blocking Heinrich's view of what was coming out of the pavilion.

Inside the building, workmen were loading furniture onto carts. Hand dollies stacked with boxes were being wheeled about. One man was removing pictures from the walls and stacking them on a pallet. Two men were attending to *The Reaper*, one of them on a ladder. Three more men, including two in suits, were fidgeting around the Picasso painting. Hurry was the order of the hour.

To Gaudin, whose press credentials gave him access to the grounds of the now-closed exposition, there was a sadness to all the activity. Tomorrow there would be nothing but forlorn, empty edifices. In a week, even those would be gone. The great fair, which had arrived with such anticipation and fanfare seven months earlier to display the greatest and best that man had to offer, would be disassembled in less than a week. The reporter marveled at how fragile were the things made by man; how fleeting his grand accomplishments; what little meaning there was in the word "new."

He entered the pavilion through the open main entrance looking for Picard. A single gendarme stood apart, watching the activity.

"I am looking for Francois Picard, the pavilion security guard," Gaudin said, showing his press card. "Is he here?"

"He left. He wasn't feeling well," the gendarme responded.

Gaudin explained that he was doing a follow-up story on the riot and shooting.

"I'm afraid I can't help you. I'm just here to keep the peace while that painting is removed," said the gendarme, pointing toward *Guernica.*

Reporter's intuition went off in his head like a bell. "Is there some sort of problem?" he asked.

A new story unfolded for Gaudin as the gendarme explained the dispute over the painting. He had remained behind when the rest of his squad left, mostly to keep the animated little man who was standing in front of the painting from doing anything contrary to the "peace" agreement that had been reached.

The nervous little man, he explained, was the curator of a museum where, allegedly, the painting was to be delivered. "The other man is the director of this pavilion, Dr. Goma, and the big fellow with them is the mover who is going to remove and store the painting until someone determines whether Picasso or the museum gets the painting."

Gaudin thanked the officer and joined the group of three, temporarily interrupting a heated discussion. He introduced himself, which immediately triggered a flurry of claims, accusations and threats from the museum curator, directed first at the absent Pablo Picasso, and then at Antoine Lipp, who stood there with a bemused look on his face, looking down at the little Spaniard.

"Let me get this straight," Gaudin interrupted after a few minutes. "Picasso was commissioned by the Spanish government to do a painting but didn't get paid for it. That same Spanish government promised the painting to you, or rather, to your museum.

"And you," he continued, turning to Dr. Goma, "as the newly appointed director of the pavilion, are the representative of the Spanish government."

Goma nodded reluctantly.

"So, it would appear that the outcome is in your hands," Gaudin continued. "Is the Spanish government going to pay Picasso?"

"I will arrange to have Senor Picasso paid," Dr. Goma said, without hesitation. "Until the payment is made, Mr. Lipp will keep the painting securely stored in his warehouse."

"How much is owed to Monsieur Picasso?" Gaudin asked.

The question caught Dr. Goma off guard. "I…I am not at liberty to divulge that information," he stammered.

"Do you *know* how much Picasso is owed?" Gaudin pressed on.

Another pause. "Yes. Yes I do."

Gaudin knew a lie when he heard one.

"Monsieur Picasso's works are not inexpensive. Is it more than 100,000 francs?" Gaudin continued.

"I…I am not at liberty to disclose that information," the pavilion director repeated, wishing with all his heart that he had never accepted this appointment.

"Is it more than 200,000?"

Goma became increasingly flustered and by the time the reporter was done it was clear to everyone that Director Goma had no idea how much the Spanish government owed Picasso, and, even worse, had no idea how or if he was going to arrange the payment.

"One more thing," Gaudin concluded.

Dr. Goma sighed, thankful that the questioning was about to end.

"It is commonly known that the Spanish government is in dire financial circumstances and struggling to support the war. Do you honestly believe that the government is going to pay a huge sum for a painting when its soldiers are going hungry and don't have enough bullets to defend themselves?"

Goma had not thought of the issue in those terms. Even Mendez was stunned into silence.

"Well, do you?" repeated Gaudin, breaking the uncomfortable silence.

"I, um, I...don't make policy for the Spanish government," Goma sputtered. "We will try our best to convince the government to pay Senor Picasso."

"Merci." Gaudin turned and walked out of the pavilion. He knew that the *Paris-Soir* wouldn't give the story much play since its sympathies lay with the Spanish government, but he could sell a much larger story to one of the art newspapers.

Both Spaniards looked deflated as they watched the reporter walk out of the pavilion.

"We must call Ambassador Araquistain!" Mendez said, finally finding his tongue.

Lipp had listened with interest to the inquisition of Dr. Goma. He stood for a moment, thinking, then giving a small nod in response to an internal decision made, he went to join the two workmen dismantling *The Reaper*.

Trucks continued to trickle onto the exposition grounds and disassembly of Expo '37 continued its frantic pace. By eight-thirty the first trucks began leaving, beds sitting low on their tires as if in tribute to the valuable treasures they carried.

A fourth freight truck, this one with no markings, pulled in front of the Spanish pavilion, unnoticed by Dr. Goma or Mendez who sat dejectedly in the director's office.

"I do not believe they are going to pay Picasso," Goma sighed. "I think the only hope is that Ambassador Araquistain can convince him to donate the painting."

Goma had spent the last hour on the phone, first with the ambassador, then with government officials in Valencia and Barcelona, then again with Ambassador Araquistain. Nothing that had transpired left him with any confidence that Picasso would be paid for *Guernica.*

"That greedy son of a snake wouldn't make a donation to his own mother," Mendez railed.

"Nevertheless, Ambassador Araquistain has said he will try to reason with him. Perhaps he will have a change of heart," Goma said. "The ambassador also suggested that it might be better if you were not here when Picasso returns to oversee the removal of the painting."

Goma expected another tirade, but Mendez just sighed in an admission of defeat.

The unmarked truck disgorged three large rolls of carpet which were then unrolled on the main floor of the pavilion.

Picasso and Lipp stood at the side of *Guernica,* watching the men at work.

"Thank you for bringing the carpet," Lipp said

"Thank you for the call," Picasso replied. "I appreciate your honesty."

"I would prefer not to be responsible for your painting," Lipp responded. "Monsieur museum director appears to be capable of some rash actions. It is safer in your hands, particularly if he doesn't know you have it."

Picasso nodded.

Two of Lipp's warehousemen made repeated trips from the second floor, bringing unframed posters and wall hangings and carefully laying them on one of the unrolled carpets.

Each time they descended the stairs they were careful to stay clear of two other men on the staircase landing removing *The Reaper* panel by panel. Each panel was delicately transported to the main floor, wrapped in blankets supplied by the Lipp Moving Company, and stacked flat: three long panels, three short panels.

Director Goma stayed in his tiny office waiting for the Ambassador to call, busying himself with packing the contents of the director's desk and file cabinet.

Unnoticed, Picard, still dressed in his disheveled uniform, a fresh bandage swathing his injured head, reentered the pavilion and stood by the main entrance. He watched as the last panels of *The Reaper* were taken down, wrapped and stacked. He was momentarily embarrassed, realizing for the first time that *The Reaper* wasn't painted on the pavilion wall. *So what,* he thought, shaking off his momentary mortification, *I'm going to America.*

He made his way to the director's office and slid through the half-open door. He cleared his throat to get Goma's attention.

"I'm feeling much better and can finish up here and lock up when they leave," he said. To his surprise there was no objection. Goma put on his suit jacket, took one last look around the pavilion, and walked toward the entrance, his shoulders bowed with the weight of knowing that his one day as director of the Spanish exhibit at Expo '37 had been a total and utter disaster.

Heinrich parked the motorcycle on the southwest corner of the German pavilion next to a uniformed soldier, still standing where Heinrich had left him an hour earlier with orders to watch for activity at the Spanish pavilion. Four large straight-trucks and two vans were parked in a row in front of the main entrance. Both vans and two of the large trucks were backed in, their grills facing the Germans' vantage point.

"Have any trucks left?" Heinrich asked. "Have they loaded any large objects looking like a rolled-up carpet?" He continued, not waiting for answers to his initial question.

Heinrich dismissed the soldier after being assured that no one had left and no carpet had been loaded. "Return to your other duties but do not leave the pavilion until I return," he instructed the soldier. "We will start the training mission at 0200 hours. You will need to change into night gear. See to it." He took from his pocket a tin of black greasepaint, standard issue for night operations, and flipped it to the soldier who caught it with one hand, saluted with the other and spun on his heels all in one movement, then strode smartly back to the monolithic German hall.

Heinrich was dressed in mottled grey-and-black night camouflage. The nimble Zundapp DB250 that had been arranged for him by the chief of security was also dark grey, its engine muffled to emit only a muted purr rather than the usual raucous cacophony of a motorcycle engine. He would be able to move in and out of the sporadic dark and light patches of nighttime Paris with minimal chance of being seen or heard.

The first stage of his plan didn't require invisibility, only a modicum of discretion so as not to draw attention to himself. The busy Parisian evening traffic would provide him that cover while the motorcycle gave him the ability to move nimbly and quickly through the traffic at a reasonable distance from the moving truck. Once he located the warehouse he would survey the area to determine the best avenue of escape.

Later, when he returned to scope out the warehouse security measures, and when he and his squad commenced the mission, he would need to be invisible.

He had told the four soldiers that were to accompany him that Reich Marshall Goering had purchased two expensive rugs while in Paris. They were being stored at a warehouse, awaiting shipment to Germany. Rather than wait for delivery, Goering had decided to use the opportunity for a training mission that was meant to approximate the clandestine extrication of a person or object from a heavily guarded facility.

They were, Heinrich emphasized, being given the rare opportunity to participate in a "live" urban training exercise: live ammunition and live hostile security guards. It must take them no more than ten minutes from the time they entered the warehouse to subdue the guards, locate the rugs and exit the warehouse.

The unwary warehouse security personnel would be no match for a squad of crack SS troops trained in night combat. Secretly Heinrich hoped there would be some resistance so his handpicked squad would be afforded the opportunity to use the hand-to-hand assassination techniques for which they had been meticulously trained. Violent suppression of resistance, covertly carried out, would be looked upon favorably by Goering. It would once again prove Heinrich's proficiency and give the Reich Marshal one more reason to appoint him commander of Goering's elite special operations team.

After *Guernica* and *The Reaper* were removed, the warehouse would be burned to complete the ruse. Their training in incendiary techniques would assure that nothing would be left of the warehouse or its contents, including the security guards. Except for Goering and Heinrich, the world would believe that *Guernica* and the entire contents of the Spanish exhibit were totally destroyed. And only Heinrich would know of the survival of *The Reaper*.

The two "carpets" would be stowed under the seat of a troop truck leaving for Berlin in the morning, part of a column of trucks filled with the contents of the German pavilion. One of the four soldiers chosen for the mission by Heinrich would be driving the truck, while Heinrich himself would be riding shotgun, prepared to dissuade any border personnel who might prove uncharacteristically curious. The other three mission operatives would be seated amongst the rows of armed Wehrmacht sitting on the bench seats in the bed of the troop truck. The soldiers would have no idea that they were acting as camouflage for the two paintings, but their presence should be enough to discourage the French border authorities from looking too closely at the truck's contents.

Once the soldiers were delivered to Berlin-Tegel Airfield, Heinrich and the driver would stop at a warehouse and unload one of the carpets under the guise that Goering wanted that carpet for his Berlin apartment. They would then make the two-hour trip to Carinhall,

Goering's villa in the Schorfheide Forest northeast of Berlin, where they would unload the carpet into which *Guernica* had been rolled.

The mission, for obvious reasons, was top secret. They were never to speak of the mission or their involvement. Once completed, as far as they were concerned, it had never happened. Their reward would be assignment to Goering's personal clandestine unit, an assignment that would give them the prestige and perks that came only to the highest ranking of the Nazi SS.

Failure in any aspect of the mission, including even the slightest breach of the code of silence, would result in consequences that would be disagreeable, dishonorable and, perhaps, deadly.

The steady stream of workmen, like an army of ants, continued their back and forth parade under the watchful eyes of Lipp, Picasso and Picard.

And Heinrich.

And Edgardo.

Edgardo had left his two companions in the waiting Citroen. Using the fading light to his advantage, he slipped through the ring of security that encircled the Expo grounds. Staying carefully in the shadows, he had located a vantage point from which he watched the loading.

He was also watching Heinrich. *Who is the man in camouflage* and *why is he so interested?* Of one thing he was certain, the presence of another observer was not in his, or the revolution's, best interest. *That bastard, Franco, has sent someone to steal the painting so he won't have to make a deal with us to free Catalonia,* Edgardo fumed.

In the evening darkness, with the scene backlit by lights from the pavilion, it was difficult to see exactly what was being loaded into which vehicle, but it appeared to both outside observers that the bulk of the pavilion's contents was being loaded into two large trucks with "Lipp Moving Company" dimly visible on the doors.

Heinrich watched as two rolls of carpet were loaded into one of the Lipp trucks. He exhaled. Having them both in the same truck eliminated the one flaw in his plan—that the paintings would be in separate trucks, each going in a different direction. He walked toward his waiting motorcycle.

Edgardo watched. The camouflaged figure's immediate reaction to the loading of the two carpet rolls confirmed Edgardo's own belief that the large Lipp truck was carrying *El Segador.* Distracted, he failed to see the flat panels being loaded into one of the smaller trucks. The rear doors clicked shut and Antoine Lipp slid into the driver's seat, started the engine and pulled smoothly away, leaving a gap like a missing tooth in the line of vehicles. The van headed for the exit, quickly blended into a string of taillights and passed through security.

Minutes later, the other trucks followed. In the passenger seat of the last truck, identical to the others except for its lack of markings, sat Picasso.

Heinrich was ahead of the trucks, having already passed through security, sitting astride the motorcycle just outside the gate, the engine purring quietly.

Two blocks ahead, on the opposite side of Boulevard Delessert, three black police cars sat nose to tail, waiting. The Citroen sat empty, one block further down the street on the opposite side.

"What do we do now?" The gendarme in the lead car spoke into a microphone attached to the dashboard by a circular cable.

"Wait to see if any of them return," came the crackling voice of Detective Ormonde. "I'll call Hotel d'Albion and see if Vivas and Puig have checked out. If they haven't, and if no one returns to the car in fifteen minutes, squads 37 and 49 should immediately go to the hotel and wait for them."

The surveillance officer acknowledged the order and put the microphone back on the hook.

Time passed at the pace of a slug. The officer looked at his watch. It had been three minutes since he looked the last time.

Ormonde's voice came back over the radio: "Officer Richebourg? Neither Vivas or Puig have checked out, nor has the other fellow, Antonio Cervantes. Anyone return to the car?"

"No." Richebourg responded. "I'll wait another ten minutes and if no one shows up I'll have the other two squads go to the hotel and wait there."

A few minutes later a figure materialized out of the darkness, walking toward the Citroen. He stopped, looked around, and stood for a few moments. Then he opened the driver's door.

"That's him!" Richebourg said into the microphone. "Move in."

Richebourg swerved into the driving lane in front of a moving truck. The two trailing squad cars turned on their flashers to force the line of traffic to make way as they lurched out of their parking spaces.

Gaudin was busily pecking away at his typewriter, finishing the story about the dust-up between Picasso and the Spanish government, when his editor shouted. "Are you about done with that story?"

"Almost."

"Wrap it up! There's been gunfire at Expo '37 again. Call your friend Ormonde to see what the hell is going on now! We'll have to squeeze it into the front of the second section."

Merde! thought Gaudin.

Paris was quiet. The early winter winds had died. The moon had sunk low in the west, and the sun was several hours from heralding a new day. Traffic had finally tired of the City of Lights and only a few cars carrying people to their wee-hour-in-the-morning jobs dotted the street.

Two lovers, bundled up against the cold, walked along the Seine. A faint glow in the sky could be seen to the east. Soon sirens could be heard in the distance, piercing the City's early-morning calm. The glow grew.

"Must be a big fire," he said to her. "Somewhere up in the warehouse district, I think."

MONDAY, NOVEMBER 29, 1937

"You're going to make me a captain," chuckled Ormonde, lifting his coffee cup in a toast as he and Gaudin celebrated solving the murder of Andres Duron. The Monday morning edition of *Paris-Soir* lay on Ormonde's desk, Gaudin's front-page article on full display. The headline read: "Murder Suspect Arrested at Expo '37," followed by a second headline: "Two Shot in Gunfight as Gendarmes Apprehend Suspect."

By Pierre Gaudin
Staff Writer

Edgardo Vivas, a Spanish national and the man suspected of pulling the trigger in a fatal shooting at Expo '37 last Wednesday, was arrested by gendarmes Sunday outside Jardins du Trocadero just hours after the close of the Exposition.

In response to a tip received from an unidentified source, gendarmes trapped Vivas while he was loitering on Boulevard Delessert just blocks from the freight entrance to Expo '37. When confronted, Vivas responded with gunfire and fled the scene on foot. He was apprehended after a short chase.

Duron, a native of Tarragona, Spain, was one of several speakers at a rally protesting German support of the anti-government military insurgents in the on-going civil war in Spain. Duron died at Hospital Ste. Perine Saturday evening.

"Based upon information that we received that led to the arrest, and the recovery of the gun, Vivas has been charged with the murder of Andres Duron," said Detective Robert Ormonde, who was in charge of the take-down.

Gendarmes recovered the handgun, believed to have been discarded by Vivas during the chase. The gun is believed to be the gun used in the Duron shooting. The weapon is also being tested to determine if it fired the bullets that struck two other people who were in the

> vicinity of the arrest. Positive identification would likely lead to more charges being filed against Vivas.
>
> Georges Papedoux, a truck driver who was hauling material from the Exposition, was slightly injured when a shot fired during the arrest of Vivas grazed his shoulder. He was treated at the scene and released.
>
> More seriously wounded was a person who had not been identified as of the time this edition went to press. A male believed to be in his early thirties, he was listed in critical condition at Hospital Ste. Perine.
>
> The shooting last Wednesday that led to the arrest is believed to have stemmed from a clash between two groups of Spanish nationals with opposing views on the civil war that has wracked Spain for the past eighteen months. Vivas, whose last known address is in the Spanish city of Sitges, is purportedly a supporter of Catalonian secession from Spain, whereas Duron was a supporter of the Republican government.

Adjacent to the article was a short story about a dispute over ownership of the painting *Guernica* between its artist, Pablo Picasso, the Spanish government and a museum curator.

"Just don't forget your friends when you ascend to high places," Gaudin said in response to Ormonde's facetious jest.

"Never," Ormonde asserted, again raising his coffee cup in toast to his friend.

"Have you squeezed a confession out of Vivas yet?" Gaudin asked.

"He's a tough buzzard. Ex-military. Claims he was here for the close of the Expo and was waiting for a friend. Claims to know nothing about the gun."

"Did he identify the friend?"

"A fellow named Antonio Cervantes," Ormonde answered. "We've confirmed that they shared a hotel room at Hotel d'Albion the past several days. Cervantes checked out Sunday night, and we haven't located him. Pretty good chance he's already across the border in Spain."

"So, his alibi has disappeared," interjected Gaudin.

Ormonde cocked an eyebrow.

"It may be more of a loss for us than for Vivas," he said. "We knew about Cervantes from our informant. When we had them under surveillance, Vivas pistol-whipped Cervantes over some disagreement. The informant said Cervantes had nothing to do with the shooting. He may not have been such a good alibi for Vivas."

"What about the informant?" asked Gaudin. "Can he lead you to Cervantes?"

"He's in the wind," Ormonde replied. "He was at the same hotel as the other two. He also checked out Sunday night. My guess is that he's also back in Spain."

"Do you know who he is?"

"He identified himself when he called to tip us off," Ormonde acknowledged, "but I can't tell you. If he's back in Spain, as I expect, and if it were to become known that he ratted out Vivas, I think he'd be dead in twenty-four hours. Hard for a corpse to testify."

"Will he come back to testify against Vivas?"

"I don't know," Ormonde said. "He's got some ties here, so I'm hoping he will."

"If he doesn't, where does that leave your prosecution of Vivas?" Gaudin continued to press the issue, trying to find something newsworthy for the evening newspaper.

"Circumstantial," replied Ormonde. "We have the gun. When we get the report back, I'm certain it will prove to be the gun that killed Duron. I'm hoping it also has Vivas's fingerprints on it, but I doubt that it will. He's too sharp. When we arrested him, he was actually walking down the sidewalk as cool as you please, like he didn't have a care in the world."

"Did anyone see him toss the gun?"

"No such luck," the detective continued. "We found it about a block from where we arrested him, under some bushes, about twenty meters from where the unidentified fellow was shot."

"Still don't know who he is?"

Ormonde shook his head.

"He had no identification," Ormonde explained. "He was wearing night camouflage, and was apparently sitting on a motorcycle parked about a block from where we first saw Vivas. He was shot twice in the back at close range. We found him folded over the handlebars of the tipped-over motorcycle.

"We checked with other law enforcement agencies, thinking he might be attached to Interpol or some other agency because of the way he was dressed, but no one is stepping forward to claim him. One thing is certain, though. He wasn't an innocent bystander who was accidentally shot. The shooting was intentional."

"There's something going on here that we're not seeing," opined Gaudin.

"Now you're starting to think like a gendarme," Ormonde laughed.

"Seriously," the reporter continued, "why was Vivas waiting outside the freight gate, and what was this camouflaged motorcycle guy doing there? There's something missing from this equation."

They sat for a minute, sipping coffee and pondering the missing piece of the puzzle, oblivious to the constant hubbub around them.

"Yesterday, you mentioned it might have something to do with some art work," Gaudin recalled. "Was that a hunch, or did that information come from a source?"

"A little of both," Ormonde responded. "When I was at the Spanish pavilion yesterday I overheard a telephone conversation that related to removal of art work from the exhibit. The informant was part of that phone call. I just put two and two together. I don't think it's a coincidence."

"What if Vivas was waiting outside the Expo to assassinate the man on the motorcycle?" Gaudin asked.

"Certainly a possibility," the detective admitted. "It still doesn't explain why the man on the motorcycle was there, though. We can pass a picture of the man around the Expo and see if anybody recognizes him. Not likely we'll come up with anything now that the Expo is over, though."

"What about the staff at the Spanish pavilion?" Gaudin asked. "I assume you got their contact information when you were there."

"We are about to start interviewing them," Ormonde responded. "I'm going to have them bring in the security guard first so I can question him. He was real jumpy when I talked to him at the pavilion.

I think he may have been covering something and I'd like to know what it is."

Halfway across the city, Picard had given up trying to sleep. It had been a fitful night, his mind see-sawing between the fear of a knock on the door that would lead to his arrest and the excitement of going to America.

The grey light of dawn sifted through the windows of his flat as he carefully unwrapped the gauze from his head. The large bruise over his right eye, and the smaller one just below his cheekbone, were transforming from purple to yellow. A small cut on his ear was caked with blood. It must have broken open as he tossed and turned during the night. With his fingers he searched for another cut on his scalp. When he found the stitches he jerked in pain.

This will be a terrible picture for a passport, he thought as he looked at his discolored visage in the mirror.

He peered into the mirror for a few more minutes, carefully dabbing at the injured ear. He would buy makeup to cover the bruises as best he could, and then go apply for a passport. Then he'd buy two tickets on the next boat to America. He would personally visit Monique this evening to deliver her ticket.

Satisfied with his plan for the day, Picard sat down at the tiny wooden counter that served as both desk and dinner table and, for the third time since he'd gotten back to his flat the prior evening, counted the hundred-dollar bills. The count hadn't changed. There were still eight $100 U.S. bills. To Picard it was a fortune. The guilt of how he had amassed such a fortune did not weigh heavily on him, but the prospect of being caught did.

He had watched as the disassembled panels of *The Reaper* were loaded into a Lipp Moving Company van, and as it inched its way toward the streets of Paris. Then he heard gunfire, and brake lights lit up the concourse as the cordon of trucks came to a halt. He was sure his fraud had been discovered. He ran in the opposite direction from the gunfire, crossed Pont d'lena to the Metro station at the base of the Eiffel Tower and caught the first bus. That it was going in the wrong direction was not important. Getting away from the scene of his crime was all that had mattered to Picard.

At nine he left his flat, caught the Metro at Mairie d'Issy, then switched to Line No. 4 at Montparnasse where he purchased a tube of makeup at the *pharmacie* just outside the station. The pharmacist assured him that it would match his skin color and cover the bruises.

He exited at St-Michel and walked across the bridge to the Palais de Justice. Signs pointed him to the Office of Passports. He stopped at a public bathroom where he gingerly dabbed makeup over the discolored parts of his face. He peered in the mirror, deemed his makeup application acceptable, walked out of the restroom and came face to face with French bureaucracy.

"It will take at least three months for your passport to be issued," he was told by a clerk standing behind a well-worn wooden counter. Iron bars separated him from the clerk, probably there to keep away a citizenry incensed at the incompetence of their government.

Picard's shoulders sagged, then hunched as his headache, still lurking from the concussion, thundered back to life. Despite the pain, and not knowing what else to do, Picard filled out the passport application, paid the twenty-franc fee and left the building, furtively looking right and left as paranoia swept over him. He stood shivering at the Metro station, fearing arrest at any moment.

Once on the bus, feeling safer, Picard's anxiety subsided, leaving room for jumbled, painful thoughts. *The lease on my flat runs out in December. Three months will use up a lot of my money. Could I even find another place to live for two months?* His fortune, so large an hour ago, now seemed so meager. *I might have to go back to Toulouse to live with my family. Should I have put my parents' address on my passport application? How will they know where to send it to me if I've moved? If I tell my parents that I'm going to America, they will want to know where the money came from to pay for the ticket, and what I will do when I get there. They will try to discourage me; tell me to stay in Toulouse and marry a nice girl; give them grandchildren. If I stay in Paris will I have enough money left to buy a ticket to America? Are the retail boutiques hiring more security for the Christmas season?*

Hands shoved into his coat pockets, shoulders slumped, his gait slow and shuffling, Picard's depression was in plain view as he walked from the Metro stop by his apartment building.

"Picard! Francois Picard!"

He turned to look for the source of the shout. His quandary turned to dread as two uniformed gendarmes crossed the street, coming toward him.

"Are you Francois Picard?" one of them asked.

He nodded, his mouth too dry to respond.

"Monsieur Picard, we'd like you to come with us to answer some questions about a shooting that took place last night at Expo '37," the officer said as he stepped up on the curb. Even in his addled state, Picard recognized the difference between a request and an order.

"I've, I've already talked to you about that," Picard stuttered. "I don't know anything else."

He felt flushed, dizzy. Sweat began to trickle down his back.

"We need to talk to you about a shooting that took place on Sunday just outside Trocadero du Jardin," the gendarme continued. "Not the one that happened last week. We need you to identify the people involved in the shooting."

"The shooting was last Wednesday," Picard said, not understanding.

"There was another shooting last night," the officer explained. "We think it may have been related to the shooting last week. That's why we need your help."

Picard exhaled loud enough for the two officers to hear.

"Can you come with us now?"

"Uh. Yes. Uh. I guess I can," Picard stammered, relief slowly materializing with the realization that they had not come to arrest him for the theft of *The Reaper.*

"Run a check on Picard. See if he has a criminal record."

The officer nodded. "He's in interrogation room two," he informed Ormonde. "He's pretty nervous. Almost soiled himself when he saw us."

"We'll let him sit and stew a bit," the chief detective said. "Let me know right away about his record."

The officer left and Ormond scribbled a few notes on a pad of paper, then slipped the photos of Vivas and the man on the motorcycle under the top page of the pad. He dialed Hospital Ste. Perine, waited for the hospital administrator to come on the line, and then verified that both Jose Puig and the man on the motorcycle were still in intensive care. Puig's condition hadn't changed. It was too early to tell if the motorcycle man would survive.

He took a bite of the sandwich that was lying on his desk, poured fresh coffee into the thimble-sized cup, picked up his pad and ambled toward the interrogation room. He stood and watched Picard through the two-way mirror. The bandage was gone, but he was the same nervous, twitchy fellow.

Maybe it's just his demeanor. Or maybe he has something to hide.

"Monsieur Picard. Nice to see you again," Ormonde assured him as he entered the interrogation room. "Thanks for coming in."

"Sure. Could I get a glass of water?" Picard rasped.

"Of course."

To Picard it seemed like an eternity before Ormonde returned to the room, a glass of water in his hand.

"There was another shooting?" Picard asked after draining the glass.

"Yes. That's why we asked you to come in," Ormonde responded. "We think there may be a connection with the shooting last week. How are you feeling, by the way?"

"I'm fine. Still a little headache, but otherwise I'm fine."

"And how is Director Puig?"

Picard was caught off guard. He hadn't thought of the director since he had left the hospital four days ago.

"All right, I guess," he said.

"I was wondering," Ormonde continued. "How did a French security guard end up being in charge of the Spanish pavilion?"

"I...um...there was no one else to take charge," Picard responded.

"What about an assistant director, or the director's brother?"

"Director Puig was in control of everything. There was no assistant director. He never wanted anyone else to know what was going on," Picard answered.

"Why was that?"

"Because he was an unpleasant little man who thought he was better than everyone else," Picard said, his dislike for the director bubbling to the surface.

"So, you're not particularly sad that he's in the hospital in critical condition."

The statement jolted Picard.

"I wish him no harm," he said, "and a full recovery. Hopefully he will recover as a nicer person."

"What about his brother, Renaldo?"

"I don't know anything about him," Picard said honestly. "The only time I saw him was the day after the shooting."

"Why would the director's brother be interested in the art work at the Pavilion?"

The question made Picard's stomach contract. The momentary hesitation before he answered let Ormonde know that he had hit a nerve.

"He said he was trying to make sure his brother's wishes were carried out," Picard answered. "I didn't believe him. I think he may have been trying to steal something."

"What made you think that?"

"The way he acted when I caught him in the director's office going through papers," Picard answered, warming to the task. *No better way to take the focus off me than to shift suspicion to Picard's brother.* "He was nervous. He talked like he was trying to cover up something."

"You're very observant."

Ormonde's flattery brought results.

"I am a graduate of the academy." Picard said, puffing up at the assumed importance of this announcement. "I am trained to be observant."

Ormonde nodded.

"So, you think he was trying to steal artwork at the pavilion?"

"Maybe. It's possible," Picard answered, hoping his answer had not sounded too eager.

"And what do you think he was trying to steal?"

"I don't know."

"Can you identify this man?" Ormonde pulled the picture of Edgardo Vivas from beneath the top sheet of his note pad.

Picard looked at the photograph and slowly shook his head.

"No. I don't recognize him."

"Please look again. Tell me if you ever saw him around the pavilion."

Picard again stared at the picture.

"I don't think so," he said.

"What happened Sunday afternoon when the gendarmes were called to the pavilion?" Ormonde asked, changing the subject to keep Picard off balance.

After another hesitation, Picard answered: "Pablo Picasso showed up at the pavilion to take back his painting. He said that he hadn't been paid by the Spanish government so it still belonged to him. Before Picasso showed up a new director had arrived from the Spanish Embassy, along with a fellow named Mendez who is the director of some museum. There was an argument between Picasso and Mendez about who was entitled to the painting. It got physical, and I called the gendarmes to restore order."

"So, what did you do with the art work?"

"I didn't do anything with it," Picard denied quickly. "Director Puig had hired a moving company to remove it after the exposition was over. As far as I know, that's what happened."

"Could Director Puig's brother have hired the mover?"

Picard thought for a moment. "I suppose that's possible."

"You didn't hire the moving company?"

"No."

"Did you have any contact with the moving company?" Ormonde continued.

"Not really," was Picard's instant reply. Then, thinking better of his denial: "I did talk with the mover to help coordinate removal of the contents of the pavilion, but that was all."

"Who was the moving company?"

"Lipp. Lipp Moving Company," Picard said.

Ormonde paused for a moment, thinking.

"Wasn't that the company whose warehouse burned Sunday night?"

"What! Really, is that true?" Picard's shock convinced Ormonde that the security guard knew nothing about the fire.

"Let me check to make sure," Ormonde said.

He left the room, looking for a phone to use. At the desk of the officer who was checking Picard's criminal background, Ormonde stopped and held out both hands, palms up, questioning.

"He's clean," the officer responded to the gesture. "Are you getting anything out of him?"

"The plot is thickening," the detective replied. "It appears someone may have been trying to steal art from the Spanish pavilion, maybe a painting by Pablo Picasso. Now it appears that a warehouse owned by the company that moved the contents of the Spanish pavilion burned to the ground last night. A coincidence perhaps?"

The officer nodded in recognition of Ormonde's sarcasm.

"See if you can get me an inventory of the art work that was at the Spanish pavilion," Ormonde said. "Try Lipp Moving Company first. That's the company whose warehouse burned. I'll ask Picard if he knows where a copy might be, as well. Also, Picard says he graduated from the police academy. Couldn't have been more than three or four years ago. Check that out, too."

Back at his desk, Ormonde dialed the phone. Gaudin answered.

"There was a fire in the warehouse district last night," Ormonde said, skipping the usual pleasantries. "Can you check the name of the company whose warehouse burned?"

"Sure. How soon do you need it?" the reporter asked.

"Right away," Ormonde responded. "I'm in the middle of interrogating Picard, the security guard. I think the warehouse that burned belonged to the same company that removed all the art from the Spanish pavilion. I may have found that missing link we were talking about."

"Hang on. I'll be right back."

The reporter was back in less than a minute.

"Lipp Moving Company," he said.

"Bingo!"

"I was right," Ormonde said as he reentered the interrogation room. "It *was* Lipp Moving Company. Their warehouse burned early this morning. Fire Department is still looking into the cause."

Picard sat, stunned and confused.

Ormonde waited. When Picard didn't volunteer information, he asked: "Do you have an inventory of the art work that was in the pavilion?"

"No...No," he said quietly.

"Were there many pieces?" Ormonde asked.

"Several hundred."

"I'm just talking about art that would have substantial monetary value," Ormonde clarified. "Not posters or copies. Probably original works. How many of those would there be?"

Picard thought for a minute.

"Maybe ten," he said. "No more than that."

"Can you give me a list from memory?"

"Two works by Picasso," Picard started. "A large painting named *Guernica* and a sculpture that actually sat outside the pavilion. Those are what he came to get on Sunday.

"Another sculpture, tall. It looked like an upside-down umbrella. It was right beside the main entrance. It was done by a sculptor named Perez. There was another sculpture made of metal that sat on the main floor. It was kind of a fountain, only it used mercury instead of water. A man named Calder did it. He's American."

Ormonde scribbled notes on his pad as Picard continued to recount the list of major art pieces.

"Is that it?" he asked when Picard stopped. "There are eight?"

The security guard tried to think. He had intentionally omitted *The Reaper* from the list. *Should I add it? Will they discover it if I don't? Can they tie it back to me? More likely that they'll find out about it anyway and it will look like I'm covering up something.* The Reaper *shouldn't have been in the warehouse anyway.* He opted for full disclosure.

"One more," he said. "A big painting at the top of the stairs. It looked like it was part of the wall. I almost forgot about it. It's called *El Segador. The Reaper.* It was a painting by Joan Miro."

"That's nine," Ormonde stated. "Are you sure that's all?"

"I think so."

A gurgling sound emanated from Picard's stomach.

"Could I get something to eat?" Picard said, embarrassed. "I haven't had lunch."

"We're about done," Ormonde said. "Just a couple more questions. Were you at the pavilion when the art work was removed?"

"I was there for part of it."

"Who else was there?"

"The new director," Picard said. "Dr. Goma. Mendez, the museum curator. They left before the loading started. Lipp, I think his first name is Antoine, and several of his workmen. Picasso and two or three of his workmen…"

"Picasso was there?" interrupted a surprised Ormonde.

"Yes," Picard nodded, "Lipp asked him to come and help move some of the larger pieces. He came after Dr. Goma and Mendez left."

"Who else?"

"That's all," Picard said, omitting the presence of the American's representative. This time he elected against full disclosure.

"Did you supervise the removal of the art work from the pavilion?"

"Yes…no, not really. I was there for the first part of it, but left before they were done," Picard answered. "Lipp was in charge. And Picasso."

"Why did you leave? Wasn't it your duty to lock up the pavilion after everything was removed?"

"There was no reason to lock it," Picard said, defensively. "It would be empty. The main door was broken and couldn't be locked. Workmen would be coming to start demolition. Besides, I wasn't feeling particularly well." He tapped the side of his head, then winced at his mistake.

Ormonde paused for a moment to allow time for Picard's pain to subside.

"If you think of any more art work, or of anyone else who was at the pavilion after it closed on Sunday, please call me," he said, handing him a business card. "You aren't planning on going anywhere, are you."

"Uh. I might go and see my parents in Toulouse," Picard said. "Why?"

"In case we need to ask you more questions," Ormonde answered, a slight edge to his voice. "If you do decide to go to Toulouse, or anywhere else outside of Paris, please let me know. Okay?"

Picard nodded, trying not to look annoyed.

"Say!" he said suddenly, his mood changing. "I'm out of a job. Could you help me get a job with the department?"

"I'll see if we're hiring," Ormonde parried, knowing full well that Picard could not be a gendarme unless he joined the military.

"Thanks." Picard said. "Can I go now?"

"One last thing," Ormonde said. "Can you identify this person?"

He handed the now-standing Picard the photo of the man on the motorcycle.

Picard did a double take.

"I think that's a German officer who was with Hitler when he toured the pavilion Sunday morning."

This time it was Ormonde's turn to sit down.

From the moment Picard identified the shooting victim as a German soldier, Ormonde knew that he had lost control of the case. The events of the last days of the Expo, which had threatened to evolve into an international incident, now had risen to full international disaster status. Herr Fuhrer would not take the shooting of one of his soldiers lightly. Although technically not an act of war, the finer nuances of international law and diplomacy were generally lost on Hitler, and this might be just enough to provoke him. The tense relationship between Germany and France exacerbated the matter.

Ormonde was tempted to withhold the information for twenty-four hours. It would allow him time to continue the investigation without the intervention of the Interior Department and its covert police force, commonly referred to as the "RG," but he knew that any delay would be frowned upon by Interior and would likely be interpreted by the Germans as a cover-up. Still, he hesitated. It made Ormonde nervous whenever he had to deal with France's central intelligence agency.

Eventually, duty overrode his instincts. He dialed RG headquarters in Interior Ministry, identified himself and explained the reason for his call.

"He was shot on Sunday night," Ormonde said in response to a question from the inquisitor on the other end of the line. "We think he may have been shot by the same person who shot a protester last Wednesday. We just found out that he is a German soldier—the man shot last night, not the protest speaker."

Within hours the police headquarters of Paris's 16th Arrondissement was infiltrated with RG operatives, Department of Interior bureaucrats, and even a representative from the office of president of the Council of Ministers, Leon Blum. Ormonde and the other officers involved were debriefed. Ormonde was informed that the German soldier had been identified as Luftwaffe Captain Heinrich Kallenbach. The Germans weren't giving any more information and that included any reason why Captain Kallenbach would have been sitting on a motorcycle Sunday night, a block outside the entry to Expo '37, wearing night camouflage and no identification.

Ormonde confirmed, for the third or fourth time, that he would not talk to any German authorities, and that he would make sure that all communications of that sort coming into the 16th Arrondissiment station would be forwarded to RG for response.

As of 6 p.m., Monday, November 29, 1937, Detective Robert Ormonde was no longer involved in the investigation of the murder of Andres Duron, nor the shooting of Heinrich Kallenbach, nor did he any longer have custody of Edgardo Vivas. It was as if his office had been swept clean of any trace of the work that had dominated his last ninety-six hours.

Vivas will wish he hadn't shot the German, Ormonde thought. Interrogation by the RG was quite different from that conducted by Parisian gendarmes—quite different in an unpleasant, gruesome, painful way. *Maybe they'll be able to get the witnesses back here from Spain so that the bastard will get convicted.*

Disappointed, but with the confidence of knowing that he and his men had done a good job, Ormonde walked out of the police station. Walking up the steps was his favorite crime reporter.

"Let's go have a beer," he said to Gaudin.

Without hesitation, Gaudin did a U-turn and the two headed for a nearby *taverne,* a hangout for off-duty gendarmes.

Over bottles of Karlsberg they exchanged the tales of the day. Ormonde was predictably deflated by having the investigation removed from his jurisdiction.

"Why don't you investigate the Lipp fire?" Gaudin suggested. "The Fire Brigade just released its findings. It was intentional. That would keep you close to the case and give you a reason to keep snooping."

"You have such a way with words," Ormonde said in mock offense. "Is that what you think I do? Snoop!?"

Gaudin recognized the gemdarme's comment for what it was. "I snoop. You investigate," he corrected, with a lift of one eyebrow. "Really," he continued. "It would keep you involved."

"And keep your information pipeline open," Ormonde added, completing Gaudin's thought.

"That, too," the reporter said, with a grin.

"You know it's not that easy," Ormonde continued. "The fire wasn't in my Arrondissiment so it's officially outside my jurisdiction. I'd have to get a special assignment from the Prefect's office, and you know how much we love it when someone comes in from outside to take over our investigations."

"But this is a warehouse fire, not a murder," argued the reporter. "And you already have a wealth of information."

"It's arson, not just any warehouse fire, but I'll call the Twelfth tomorrow and see what their chief detective says. If it's okay with him, I'll ask the Prefect for the assignment."

TUESDAY, NOVEMBER 30, 1937

Paris-Soir had scooped the competition, and Pierre Gaudin's name was on everyone's lips the next morning.

"Man Shot at Expo '37 Identified as German Military Officer" read the headline. Under Gaudin's byline, the story unfolded:

> Paris police have identified the man shot outside Expo '37 late Sunday as Heinrich Kallenbach, a captain in the German Luftwaffe. Kallenbach, still in critical condition at Hospital Ste. Perine, was shot during the arrest of Edgardo Vivas, the man charged with the murder of Andres Duron, a Spanish national who was shot Saturday while speaking at an anti-war rally. Duron was protesting German involvement in the Spanish civil war.
>
> Police have confirmed that the gun found at the scene of Sunday's shooting was the same gun that was used to kill Duron. German officials have refused to comment on the reason for Kallenbach's presence at the site of the arrest.
>
> Gendarme Detective Roberto Ormonde, who was in charge of the investigation, said that Kallenbach was not involved in the arrest of Vivas, although his presence at the site of the shooting raised several questions. Kallenbach was riding a motorcycle and wearing garments that appeared to be night time camouflage at the time of the shooting. He was not carrying any identification.
>
> "It does not appear to have been an accidental shooting," Ormonde said. "Captain Kallenbach was shot twice in the back at close range." According to Ormonde the Central Directorate of General Intelligence has taken over the investigation into the shooting.

Vivas, who remains in custody for the murder of Duron, has not yet been charged with the shooting of Kallenbach.

In a related story, the other person wounded during the arrest of Vivas on Sunday evening, Georges Papedoux, was a driver for Lipp Moving Company, the company hired to move and store the contents of the Spanish pavilion following the close of Expo '37 Sunday. The Lipp warehouse was consumed by fire early Monday morning. Papedoux is the son-in-law of the owner, Antoine Lipp.

Lipp could not be reached for comment, but a spokesman for the Lipp family expressed gratitude that Papedoux was not more seriously injured, and said that the family was trying to assess the extent of its loss as a result of the fire.

The Paris Fire Brigade is investigating the cause of the blaze.

"Monsieur Lipp, I am a reporter for the *Paris-Soir*. I'd like to talk to you about the fire at your warehouse."

Antoine Lipp looked directly at Gaudin. "I have nothing to say." He was clearly upset.

"I am writing a story for Wednesday's paper that says fire inspectors found that the fire was intentionally set," Gaudin pressed on. "Do you really want the story to say that the owner had no comment?"

"I have comments!" Lipp bellowed. "Who would set such a fire and ruin a man's livelihood? Who would destroy a business that I spent thirty years building? What reason could someone have to do such a thing? Tell me that!"

"So, you don't dispute the finding that the fire was intentionally set?"

"How could I dispute it?" he shouted, his anger unabated. "These people are professionals. They should know if it was intentional or not. If they say it is, then it is!"

"Is there anyone who might want to hurt you? Drive you out of business?" Gaudin asked.

"I have no enemies," Lipp responded. "I have competitors, but they are good and honorable men. They would not do a thing such as this."

"The fire occurred on the same night that you removed the contents of the Spanish pavilion from Expo '37. Do you think that is a coincidence?"

"I don't know from coincidence," Lipp said.

"I mean, do you think that the fire and the contents of the Spanish exhibit may have been connected somehow?" Gaudin rephrased.

"I never thought of that," he said after what appeared to Gaudin to be a staged pause.

"Even though your son-in-law was shot as he drove one of your trucks leaving the Expo?" Gaudin went on, trying to test the edges of Lipp's credibility. "Despite that, you never thought there might be a connection?"

"He was shot by the police," Lipp responded, without hesitation this time. "It was an accident. He was in the wrong place at the wrong time. He's good at that."

To the best of Gaudin's knowledge the source of the shot that grazed Lipp's son-in-law had not been identified. Maybe Lipp knew something he didn't. He let it pass for the moment.

"There was a dust-up at the Spanish pavilion on Sunday between Pablo Picasso and a museum curator, Sergio Mendez. Were you there?"

"Yes. I solved the problem," Lipp said proudly.

"How did you do that?"

"I persuaded Picasso and Mendez that the best thing was to let me take the painting and keep it until it was determined whether Picasso was going to be paid," said Lipp, imagining himself being described in the newspaper as a great statesman.

"Do you think that anyone involved in that disagreement might have had something to do with the fire?"

Lipp paused again: "Mendez could have done it I suppose. He was very angry."

"Not Picasso?"

"He would have no reason," Lipp responded. "He helped remove some of the paintings Sunday night. My men have limited experience in dealing with art as big as some of what I had to remove. Picasso has experience so I called and asked for his help. I even agreed to let Picasso take his own art work back to his studio for safekeeping, on the promise that he would deliver it to the Spanish government if they paid him."

"Could that have made Mendez even more angry?" Gaudin speculated.

"If he found out about it, it probably would have."

"Angry enough to set fire to your warehouse?"

"Maybe," Lipp agreed.

Gaudin fed Ormonde the information from his interview with Lipp, but the detective was still obsessing over the shootings.

"Why was Hitler at the Spanish pavilion Sunday morning?" Ormonde mused out loud, not expecting an answer.

"Beats me," Gaudin responded. "Didn't you ask the security guard?"

"I was so shocked when I learned that the shooting victim was a German soldier, I forgot to ask. Not very professional," admitted the chief detective.

"That was quite a revelation," Gaudin jumped in, trying to justify his friend's oversight. "Just when we thought the international incident had gone away. BAM! There it was again. I probably would have forgotten my own name."

Ormonde appreciated his friend's effort. He poured each of them freshly brewed coffee and sat without speaking, pondering the situation through the steam rising from his cup.

"Maybe you should go ask him," Gaudin said matter-of-factly, breaking the detective's trance.

"Go ask who what?"

"Go ask our favorite security guard why Hitler was at the Spanish pavilion," Gaudin said. "I'd be willing to bet it's connected to the reason Herr Kallenbach was sitting in his camouflage outside Expo '37."

"I can't do that. If the RG finds out that I'm still snooping around my head will be on the chopping block."

"They're investigating the shootings, right?"

"Correct."

"They're not investigating an art theft…or an arson." Gaudin tantalized the detective.

"Riiiight," Ormonde responded, drawing out his answer, seeing where Gaudin was heading.

"You suspect that this all had something to do with someone trying to steal Spanish art," the reporter continued, "and that the fire resulted from that, so investigate the arson."

"I'm not authorized to investigate the fire…uh…the arson," Ormonde corrected himself. He was still awaiting a return call from the chief detective from the Twelfth.

"OK, so you suspect that someone was trying to steal art from the Spanish pavilion," Gaudin modified his proposition.

"Close enough," Ormonde responded.

"And you always thought the security guard was involved, or at least knew something, right?"

"You're very clever," Ormonde said to his friend, "but no one has filed a claim for any lost art work so there can be no official investigation. The RG would see right through that. It may be enough to keep me from losing my job, but I'd still be severely reprimanded, and at this stage of my career, I don't want to do anything that might jeopardize my pension."

Gaudin nodded, resigned to his friend's plight. He deliberately set down his coffee cup and looked up with a bemused smile: "But there's nothing to prevent *me* from asking the question."

"United States Reduces Immigration Quotas." The headline in *Petit Parisien*, lying on an adjacent table, fairly screamed at Picard. He picked up his espresso and éclair and moved to read the article, thinking *surely not France.*

But, indeed, it was France, along with every other country in the world. The United States was reducing immigration quotas beginning in 1938, and the new quota for France would be less than four thousand.

Picard suppressed a cry of anguish. What had he done to suffer this curse? Evidence was mounting that someone, somewhere, did not want him to go to the United States. He sat, holding the handle of the espresso cup between thumb and forefinger as it grew cold. *What next?* he wondered.

The answer was waiting in the form of a letter from his mother when he returned to his flat. It contained the usual pleasantries and well wishes, news of the family and, by the way, he had received a letter from the French Army. He was being conscripted. The letter was enclosed.

"Report for examination on January 6, 1938," it said, "and be prepared for immediate assignment."

He recoiled as though the letter was on fire. It fluttered to the floor.

When Picard allowed himself to admit the truth, he was afraid of the Germans and he was afraid to die and the two seemed inextricably entwined. He knew in his soul, as did most of the citizenry of France (except for the politicians who seemed to be oblivious to what was happening), that war was inevitable. He did not want to be in the army. The past week had only served as confirmation.

He coiled up in a fetal position on the flimsy mattress in his tiny, cold flat, pulled his thin blanket and coat over him and waited for the chill to go away. He dreamed of bombs exploding, body parts in flight, blood spattering, staccato hammering of machine guns. The machine gun fire dissolved into sharp knocking on his door as he woke up from the nightmare.

"What? Who is it?" Picard's shaky voice came from under the covers.

"Francois Picard?"

"Uh. *Oui.*"

"My name is Pierre Gaudin. I'm a reporter. I'm doing a story on the events at the Spanish pavilion. I'd like to talk to you, if that's all right with you."

"Just a minute." Picard splashed icy water on his face to rinse away the fear, and ran this hand through his sweaty hair as he answered the door. The nightmare lingered in his mind. It was a relief to have another human being in the room.

Gaudin entered the dingy apartment. A rumpled cot was pushed against one wall. A rickety wooden bench with one chair sat on the opposite wall beneath the only cupboard. Clothes hung on two hooks near the bed. Another pile lay on the floor. Through the only other door in the room he could see the toilet and a sink. A small ice box and an electric hot plate completed the furnishings.

The reporter stood until Picard motioned him to sit at the bench. Picard hung his coat on a hook and took a seat on the bed.

"Do you remember me? We met at the Spanish Pavilion last Saturday, after the shooting and the riot," Gaudin said.

Picard straightened the twisted blanket, staring at the man, trying to remember him. "I'm sorry, but I don't remember. Where did we meet?"

"In your office…the director's office. You had a bandage on your head. I'm glad to see you are recovering," Gaudin answered. "I'm writing a follow-up story, about the second shooting on Sunday. I have been told that you were the person who identified the shooting victim as a German Air Force Officer who was in the Spanish pavilion on Sunday, in the company of Adolph Hitler."

Picard nodded.

"Can you tell me about Hitler's visit?"

"It was short. He wanted to see the paintings," Picard responded. "He went crazy…" Picard stopped in mid-sentence. "Why don't you ask the Germans?"

Gaudin was caught off guard by the shift in the security guard's response. "They're not talking," he said, "except to accuse the French government of complicity in the shooting." Gaudin realized he had given away more than he had gotten.

"Hitler was at the pavilion Sunday, but there is a lot more to it than that," Picard said. "But if I'm going to give you the information I want something in return. Your newspaper—it's very powerful, isn't it?"

"I'm not sure what you mean," Gaudin responded, puzzled by the tack the conversation had taken.

"People at your newspaper know people at high places in government, right?" Picard continued.

"Yes, I suppose they do."

"I want a harmless little favor," Picard continued. "It won't hurt anyone. It will only benefit me, and my girlfriend."

"What is it?" Gaudin asked.

"I want your newspaper to expedite passport applications for us."

Gaudin thought for a moment. He had been prepared to negotiate a payment, but this was a first. "I'm not sure we have the connections do that," he said.

"I assume that some newspapers in Paris have those connections, if not yours, another one. I'll find one and give them the story."

Gaudin didn't like being played, but he didn't want to let a story get away either.

"Before you go to another newspaper, let me find out if we can speed up a passport," he said. "If we do I'll let you know, and then, if the story proves newsworthy, we will expedite your passport."

"And my girlfriend's."

"Yes." The reporter started to ask another question, but Picard held up his hand to signal stop, exercising his newfound power.

"No more questions until I get an answer," he declared, a surprising tone of authority in his voice. The nightmares seemed far in the past.

Gaudin got up to leave.

"Why do you want your passport application expedited?" He slipped in the question just as he was reaching the door. "It might help me convince the newspaper ownership."

Picard thought for a moment. "It's really none of your business," he finally said, "but if you must know, I have a job waiting for me in the United States, and I was told today it will take at least three months to issue a passport. If I can't get to the United States by the end of the year, the job will not be available."

"We've paid money for stories. We've gotten criminal charges dropped and sentences reduced, but this is a new one." The publisher of *Paris-Soir* was nonplussed by Gaudin's request.

"He says he has a job waiting in the United States, but it will be gone if he can't get there by the first of the year," Gaudin explained. "Apparently it takes three months to get a passport these days."

"This could be a big story," the newspaper's editor chimed in, repeating words uttered only minutes earlier when Gaudin had first disclosed Picard's demand. "It may shed light on the shooting of the German soldier and what he was doing, or, even better, force the Germans to come up with some answers."

The publisher stroked his chin thoughtfully, nodding. By mid-afternoon Gaudin was back in Picard's dreary apartment.

"Do I look like a fool!?" Picard said, irritated.

The reporter had underestimated the security guard, thinking that he was naïve enough to divulge the story without having to make a commitment.

"I said we'd help you *if* the story was worth it," Gaudin said, still negotiating.

"I'll be the judge of that," Picard snapped. "You get the story when I—*we*—get our passports, or I'll take it elsewhere."

"Or," Gaudin, replied, "I could tell Detective Ormonde that you are planning to leave the country, in which case your passport application might get lost in the bureaucracy…forever."

Picard looked like he'd taken a left hook to the gut.

"There has to be a little trust on both sides," the reporter restarted the conversation. "I found out that we could expedite your passport, and I set the wheels in motion to do it. It will take about a week. In a week, your story will be old news and worthless. You need to trust me enough to give me the story. Do that and you'll have your passport in a week. If not, then I'm leaving and you can try your luck with another newspaper."

Picard realized he had played his hand. He doubted that anyone could make the wheels of bureaucracy move any quicker, and if Ormonde found out he was planning to leave the country he had no doubt that the detective would stop him. And on January 6, he'd be in the army.

"That seems fair," he said, nodding.

"So, tell me about Hitler's visit to the Spanish pavilion last Sunday."

"The German that was shot later, and another German soldier, showed up at the pavilion about 7 a.m. to announce that Hitler wanted to tour the pavilion before it opened to the public," Picard said. "He said that Hitler wanted to see the art work. At the time I thought they were security guards from the German pavilion, but when they showed up an hour later for the tour I realized that they were regular German military. The guy who was shot..."

"Captain Heinrich Kallenbach," interjected Gaudin.

"Captain Kallenbach...was also part of the group that came back for the tour. He acted as an interpreter. When Hitler saw the Picasso painting he went berserk. He yelled and waved his arms and stormed out of the pavilion. He slammed the front door so hard that it broke. He screamed something at General Goering before he left..."

"Goering was there, too?" exclaimed Gaudin, surprised by the disclosure.

"Yes. He stayed and looked at the art after Hitler left. He was actually quite nice, made light of Hitler's tantrum. In fact, I think the fellow that was shot might have been part of Goering's entourage because he also stayed after Hitler stormed out. Anyway, when Hitler was ranting at Goering I heard him say the word 'zerstoren' which, I believe means "destroy." I don't speak German, but I think Hitler told Goering to destroy Picasso's painting."

WEDNESDAY, DECEMBER 1, 1937

"We can't print this story."

The statement crashed down upon Gaudin like a wall of bricks.

Sebastien Maistre, publisher of *Paris-Soir,* sat across the desk, trying to get the few strands of his comb-over to stay on top of his head.

"Look, I want to print this as much as you do," he counseled Gaudin, "but this is a matter of national security. When I arranged to get the passports expedited for your source, I had to promise to provide any information we learned to the RG. My friend, the secretary, has instructed me to keep the story under wraps until the information you learned is transmitted through proper channels. There is fear that if the Germans are first confronted with this in a newspaper story it will force them to retaliate, if only for propaganda purposes."

"Do we get *anything* out of this?" Gaudin pleaded. "For uncovering the story, I mean."

"When the government feels that it is safe to let this become public, I have been assured we will be the first to know and will be given at least twenty-four hours to release the story before any other media is informed," Maistre said, "Other than that, maybe a plaque on the wall someday, or the leverage to ask for another favor in the future."

"You mean *if* the government feels it's ever safe," retorted Gaudin, his anger and frustration barely contained.

He took his disappointment to the friendly confines of the 16th Arrondissiment station and the coffee pot of Detective Ormonde.

"So they have you throttled, just like me," Ormonde commiserated. "Damn Intelligencia! Damn!"

Gaudin agreed with a few expletives of his own.

"Even after I confirmed Picard's story with the tour guide, they wouldn't print my article," he lamented. "This is the kind of story that comes along once a decade. It's *Prix Goncourt* stuff, maybe, and I can't get it printed."

"And I can't investigate it."

"Are you still keeping an eye on Picard?" Gaudin finally asked, breaking a lengthy silence.

"No," Ormonde responded in resignation, "No reason anymore."

"What about the other suspect, Mendez, the museum curator?" Gaudin probed, hoping for something.

"His alibi checked out. He couldn't have set the fire."

They looked at each other in mutual exasperation.

"Merde," they said in unison.

The story that appeared in the *Paris Soir* that morning wasn't going to win Gaudin a Pulitzer.

Warehouse Fire
Ruled an Arson

A warehouse fire that destroyed much of the art work that was contained in the Spanish pavilion at Expo '37 has been ruled an arson.

A fire report released late Tuesday by the Paris Fire Brigade said that the fire had been intentionally set.

Paris Fire Brigade Commander, General Gerard Mitterand, when asked about the report, said that the existence of a flash point near the door of the warehouse was clear indication that the fire was not accidental.

"Clearly, this is a case of arson," Mitterand said. "It was an old, wood-frame building. It went up very quickly. By the time fire crews arrived the building was completely engulfed in flames. There was not much to be done accept to contain the fire so it didn't spread to other buildings. The Fire Brigade did a remarkable job to keep it from spreading."

The warehouse contained hundreds of items being stored for customers, including the contents of the Spanish exhibit from the Expo '37.

Antoine Lipp, owner of the building, expressed outrage when informed of the findings. "Who would do such a thing?" he raged. "Who would ruin a man's livelihood by setting such a fire, ruin a business that I have spent thirty years building?"

When asked of the extent of the loss, Lipp said, "We haven't even started to assess the amount of the loss."

Spanish ambassador, Luis Araquistain, called the fire a national tragedy for Spain.

"Loss of treasured art is an unspeakable disaster," said the Ambassador. "These cannot be replaced. The entire nation is in mourning."

WEDNESDAY EVENING, DECEMBER 1, 1937

BARCELONA

Renaldo Puig sat, his elbows on the table, his head in his hands. The bare bulb hanging from a single strand of wire cast a yellowish pallor on the peeling, discolored walls of the cheap room and on the agonized recesses of his memory.

Antonio had held the lantern as they looked among the rolls of carpet in the Lipp warehouse for the one containing *El Segador*. Then there were sirens and dogs barking and Antonio ran. Renaldo followed, falling over something in the dark, gashing his ankle, limping after Antonio. He could see Antonio running ahead, the lantern swinging wildly, then pushing the door open at full speed, but the door swung back with equal ferocity, knocking Antonio off balance, sending the lantern flying. Flames spread from the shattered lantern. Renaldo limped to the door and helped his stunned comrade to his feet and out the door. He went back and hastily stomped on the flames, then hobbled back out the door. Antonio was already climbing over the fence twenty meters ahead. An eternity passed before Renaldo joined him on the other side.

They sat in the car, not speaking. The sirens faded. The dogs still barked. Renaldo started the car and slowly drove away.

We will try again, tomorrow, he thought.

But there was no tomorrow.

By the next day, Lipp's warehouse had burned to the ground.

Edgardo would have gotten El Segador from the warehouse. He would not have panicked, would not have been a coward. Like Judas Iscariot, he had turned Edgardo in to the police. He had turned against the one man who could have delivered the painting and independence for Catalonia. He had failed his country. He had failed his brother who lay in a hospital in Paris with this throat slit and his life hanging by a thread.

Renaldo lifted the gun from the table and pulled the trigger.

FRIDAY, DECEMBER 4, 1937

PARIS

The German soldier sitting outside the hospital room door stood and touched his helmet.

"Mademoiselle," he acknowledged in a clipped accent.

Monique responded with a curt nod and entered the hospital room. It was the fourth day in a row she had come to visit Heinrich. On her first visit, the sentry had refused to allow her to enter Captain Kallenbach's room, but she pleaded, explaining that Kallenbach and she had met at Expo '37, and that she was his only friend in Paris.

I wish I had a friend in Paris like you. What harm can it do? If the captain recovers, perhaps he'll remember that I let her visit him. Perhaps she'll introduce me to a friend of hers.

So, he relented.

At first Monique just sat by Heinrich's bedside as he lay unconscious, tubes running from his nose and mouth, a mask covering his face, pumping oxygen into his lungs.

At the second visit she talked to his inert body, telling him more about herself, about Paris, about working at the Spanish pavilion. She squeezed his hand. He squeezed back, trying to convey his thanks for her presence.

On the third day Kallenbach was awake, able to sit up in bed and feed himself. The tubes had been removed. She stayed until the nurse came in to give him his meds and informed her that visiting hours were over. She kissed him goodnight and left.

Today, he was out of his room, undergoing some procedure.

On the fifth day he was gone.

Picard's bravado slipped quickly away as he stood outside the door to apartment number 3 at 472 Rue Cambron.

He had left Palais de Justice with a new passport in his pocket, two tickets to America on the *Ile De France*, and a lightness in his step. But now, with his hand poised to knock on the door to Monique's apartment, he balked. He wiped his sweaty palm on his pants leg and raised his hand again, then lowered it and, with shoulders slumped, stuffed it in his pocket and turned to leave.

She would not have come with me, anyway, he was thinking as he descended the stairs.

I can get a refund for the ticket.

"Francois, what are you doing here?"

He looked up to see Monique ascending the staircase toward him.

"I…looking for you…I have that ticket…your ticket to America."

The pensive look on her face was not what Picard had hoped for.

"I…ah…you…ah…we talked about it. I said I'd get you a ticket to America. You…agreed."

He held out the ticket to her.

Monique took it from his fingers and looked at it, slowly revolving it from front to back to front. Her expression gave no indication of what she was thinking. Picard held his breath.

"That's very sweet of you," she finally said, "but I can't accept this."

"But…you said…"

"Would you like to come up for a minute?"

Obediently Picard followed her up the stairs and into her apartment: two rooms, much nicer than his, decorated in whites and yellows, bed made, no dirty dishes or clothes on the floor. She offered to make tea, but he declined. She did not offer him a place to sit.

"I can't go to America," she said. "Someone, a friend, has disappeared, and I have to find him."

"But the ship doesn't sail until after Christmas, more than three weeks," Picard said. "I could help you find your friend."

"If I find him I'll have to take care of him. He's been injured."

"I've been injured," Picard responded, touching the now-discolored bruises on his face.

"I know. I'm sorry," she said. "You look like you're healing."

"Is this friend your boyfriend or something?"

Monique busied herself straightening pillows on a wrought-iron settee. "No. Well, sort of. Not really," she said. "It's…different."

"There's going to be a war, you know," Picard countered. "You could be injured. Or worse."

Monique paused.

He pressed on. "What if you can't find this *friend*? Then what? You'll have no friend *and* you'll be here by yourself with a war going on around you."

"I have my family."

Sensing he had lost the momentum of the conversation, Picard awkwardly backed toward the door. "You keep this ticket," he said, placing it on the table as he opened the door behind him. "The ship leaves on the twenty-ninth from Marseille."

WEDNESDAY, DECEMBER 29, 1937

MARSEILLE

She is not coming.

Picard's gaze swung from one end of the quay to the other. He had prayed that Monique would suddenly appear, waving to him, a bright smile on her face, but he knew it was a hollow hope. Slate skies and a stiff breeze turned the Mediterranean an angry greenish-black, flattened the whitecaps, sprayed mist into the frigid air. As the time for boarding grew close, the ache in his chest grew.

The queue leading to the gangplank stretched down the quay past the ticket shack. Picard withdrew farther into his thin coat. He pushed the cardboard box along with his foot as he shuffled forward, hoping the cord that held it together would not break. Everything he owned was in that box, or in the canvas bag that hung over his shoulder. His passport and his ticket stub were held tightly in his hand, and his money, what was left of it, was safely tucked away—some in his pocket, some in his shoes, some carefully folded and slid into an opening which he had cut into his belt.

He looked again at his ticket stub. Steerage on the *Ile De France*, a decades old liner that looked its age as it squatted by the dock, blocking the wind and calming the water beneath the oil slick it created. Neither the condition of the ship nor the lowly state of his accommodations occupied Picard's thoughts, however.

He recounted his money in his head. He had about fifty U.S. dollars in his pocket, one hundred dollars in each shoe, and another one hundred in his belt. He had spent over twelve thousand francs in less than a month—a sum that he could not have imagined owning, much less spending, just two months ago. He had bought passage to the United States, paid for his passport, purchased some new clothes, paid all of his bills and wasted part of it buying a ticket for Monique. Mostly, though, he had squandered it playing big shot with his few friends. But it didn't matter.

Just get me across the Atlantic. In a week I'll be in America, and I'll soon be rich, he thought.

Picard reached the end of the gangplank, picked up his box, and shuffled up the incline with the rest of the steerage passengers. As he stepped on the deck of a ship for the first time he looked back, first at the quay in search of Monique, and then at the city of Marseille.

Au revoir, France. I shall come back someday a rich and important man.

He walked in the direction the steward was pointing, toward the door that led to the bowels of the ship.

The cord on the box broke.

1938

MONDAY, OCTOBER 3, 1938

PARIS

The front-page headline in the morning *Paris-Soir* read:
"PRIME MINISTER DALADIER:
'SUDETENLAND TO GERMANY
ASSURES PEACE,' CROWD CHEERS"

But Monique was not cheering. She was sitting on the witness stand: small, intimidated.

"You say you visited this German soldier at Hospital Ste. Perine five times?" the insurance company's advocate repeated, derision in his voice.

"Yes. But he wasn't there on the fifth visit."

"What was your interest in visiting him?"

"I…I…I guess I was being a good Samaritan. He…"

"Hadn't you had a liaison with him before he was shot?" It was an accusation, not a question.

"We had lunch once…"

"And was the *lunch* at your apartment or in some hotel room?"

"No, it…"

"You did much more than just eat lunch with Captain Kallenbach, didn't you?"

"No, I…"

"Objection!"

"I'll withdraw the question, Your Honor," the lawyer said, speaking directly to the judge as if Monique had ceased to exist. He had made his point. He didn't need the answer.

"And when you went back to visit him the fourth time, he was gone?" He turned back to Monique.

"Yes."

"And you claim you've never talked to him since."

"No. Yes. I tried to find him, but I couldn't," Monique said quietly. "He probably went back to Germany."

Monique had tried to find Heinrich, but the German embassy

refused to acknowledge that he existed and, much to her surprise, the French bureaucrats were uninterested in helping her. After two unrewarded visits to agencies she thought might be of help, she had been visited by an RG investigator who had accused her of being a German spy. Since that visit, Monique thought she was followed whenever she left her apartment.

Two weeks earlier she had been subpoenaed to testify on behalf of her uncle, Antoine Lipp, in his trial to collect insurance for losses caused by the warehouse fire. She had dutifully appeared, answered the questions posed by Lipp's lawyer, and now was the target of the frightful cross-examination by the insurance attorney, a man who wildly gesticulated with every question and had the face of a weasel.

"So, you claim that this German soldier, with whom you had *lunch* one time, and whom you visited in the hospital multiple times, during much of which he was unconscious, confided in you about plans to rob and burn your Uncle's warehouse."

"Objection," Lipp's attorney interjected, "Mischaracterization of the evidence."

"How so, counsel?" the Judge inquired.

"I believe the evidence was that he was unconscious only during her first visit to the hospital."

"Over-ruled. Answer the question, please."

"It wasn't that way," she answered.

"Oh, really!" the insurance attorney responded sarcastically, his black eyes peering down his long nose at the frightened witness. "What way was it?"

"At first he wouldn't say anything," Monique answered. "But during my third visit I asked him about Herr Hitler's tantrum when he saw *Guernica*. He said the reason he was still in France was that General Goering had ordered him to destroy one painting and steal...he used the word 'commandeer'...another of the paintings for Goering."

"So, he was on this supposed mission when he got shot?"

"I assume so," she said. "He didn't tell me that, but I assume that is why he was there."

"When did he tell you he was planning to destroy the painting by burning it?"

"I think it was during the same conversation about Hitler's tantrum. He used the word 'incinerate.'"

"But he couldn't have *incinerated* the painting, could he?" the lawyer raged, driving home his key point. "The *incineration* happened early in the morning of November 26. Captain Kallenbach was shot in the early evening of November 25th, so he couldn't have set the fire, could he?"

"No," was the meek answer.

"By the time the fire occurred, Kallenbach was at Hospital St. Perine in intensive care, wasn't he?"

A small "yes" was all she could reply.

"And you never mentioned this conversation to your uncle, Antoine Lipp?"

"No, by the time Heinrich told me, the warehouse had already burned."

"So, as far as you know, your uncle could have set fire to the warehouse!"

"Objection!"

Monique rummaged through her purse for the correct change as she stood at the St-Michel bus stop. She had been unable to look at her uncle as she left the courtroom. Contempt for her could be seen on his face and, worse, within days her entire family would know of her indiscretion with the German soldier.

Too late to return to work at the shop where she now sold women's clothing, Monique got off the bus one stop early. She sat at an outdoor table under the late summer sun and sipped espresso. As usual, she felt like she was being watched. *I need to get away,* she thought.

As she dug for francs to pay for the espresso, her hand felt thick paper on the bottom of her purse. She pulled out the forgotten steamship ticket. *Ile De France. Departure: December 29, 1937, 9:00 a.m.* She sighed and looked for a waste bin to discard it. Seeing none, she laid it face down on the table and, as she finished her espresso, began to read the fine print on the back of the ticket.

"May be redeemed for equivalent ticket within twelve months of departure date," it read.

2009

SUNDAY, MAY 17, 2009

SAINT PAUL, MINNESOTA, USA

"You could buy a third-world country."

"I'd rather have the painting."

Dirty plates, remnants of crusty bread and half-empty glasses of yellow wine cluttered the table around which the three sat. Most of the lunch crowd was long gone, and the clink of silverware and glasses being gathered by busboys punctuated their discussion of Vincent van Gogh's *Portrait of Dr. Gachet* and its sale at auction two days earlier.

"Who bought it?"

"Some Japanese guy. Eighty-two-and-a-half million dollars. That's crazy," said the one named Louis.

"That makes two of them," said another, the only one of the three who didn't look like a hippie leftover from the seventies. "The buyer *and* van Gogh." With black curly hair, deep brown skin, black eyes and the fluid movements of an athlete, Hamilton Blethen was an anomaly in the Twin Cities art scene.

"You think you'll ever sell a painting for seven figures, Ham?" Louis asked.

"I'd be happy to sell one for two figures so I could pay the electric bill," Blethen replied. "I'll be like van Gogh. My paintings will be valuable after I die."

"Yeah. He only sold two paintings," said the third member of the group, a skinny kid with pale skin and stringy black hair.

"That's probably why he shot himself," was Blethen's caustic response. He stood up and downed the last of his wine. "Got to go take Barca for a walk," he announced as he picked through his billfold, coming up with a ten and four ones which he tossed on the table. "That should cover my part."

Blethen had gotten Barca seven years ago as a puppy just after returning from studying in France. They'd been inseparable since. His friends chided: "If it wasn't for Barca you'd probably be married with kids. Now everybody thinks you're a gay painter with a dog."

But Blethen had found Barca to be more reliable than women—never questioning, always adoring, and never abandoning him.

The big golden retriever greeted him with his usual enthusiasm, the tempo of his tail beating against the wall accelerating as Blethen took his leash off the hook. A long walk in the Cathedral Hill neighborhood gave Barca a chance to burn off energy, and Blethen time to worry. After the nearly-finished Vermeer sitting in his studio there were no more projects in the pipeline, and he dreaded the prospect of once again trying to live off the sale of his own original work. That prospect was the real reason he had delayed completing the Vermeer, even though finishing would mean payment and payment meant he could stop the dunning calls and letters he received daily.

He had been hired to paint a copy of *Girl with a Pearl Earring* for a high-end jewelry store in a toney Cleveland suburb. The customer had become anxious because of his lack of progress and was threatening to reject the painting if it wasn't finished and delivered before the date of their grand opening.

Blethen convinced himself that the reason his ninety-nine-percent complete pearl earringed girl had sat on the easel for the past two weeks was because he had failed to capture Vermeer's mastery of light. He had not been able to conjure a means of fixing his perceived problem, and he didn't have time to start over. He walked back and forth in front of the fifteen-by-eighteen-inch oil-on-canvas—a winsome lass with a funky blue-banded hat and a pearl earring staring back at him. Ordinarily he would have ignored the phone ringing in the other room, the living area of his three-room apartment, but lacking artistic inspiration at the moment, he ambled into the other room and answered.

"Mista Blethen? This is Arthur Kincaid," said as if the declaration should have brought instant recognition. "Ah wish to retain your services."

"What services are you looking for?" Blethen responded, after a pause.

"Your services as a painter. Have you evah painted a Miro?"

"I don't do contemporary. Not much of a fan of avant-garde.

Besides, virtually everything Miro did is available in poster form and sells for ten bucks. You could…"

"The key word there, Mista Blethen, is, *virtually*," Kincaid interrupted. "There ah many paintings done by Miro that have nevah been copied. I would like you to paint one of them for me." Kincaid's Gloucester-fisherman accent pinpointed his New England ancestry, but even with that clue the name Arthur Kincaid didn't resonate with Blethen.

"Which painting do you want painted?" he asked.

"*El Segador.*" Kincaid paused, waiting for recognition. Hearing none, he continued: "Miro was commissioned by the Spanish govament to paint it for the 1937 Paris World Exposition. In English it is commonly known as *The Reaper.*"

"I'm not familiar with it. Where's the original?"

"That is the challenge, Mista Blethen. There is no original. It was destroyed over seventy years ago."

"That will make it difficult." Blethen said, suddenly wary. "Why do you want me to paint it?"

"My reasons are my own, Mista Blethen, and of no concern to you. You come highly recommended, both for the quality of your work *and* your discretion. I assure you that I am willing to pay you well for both."

"Wait. Wait." Blethen said, buying time to weigh what sounded like a bald-faced proposition to paint a forgery. "I vaguely remember something from a class years ago. Wasn't that painting lost, or something, during the Spanish civil war?"

"I'm not really interested in the history of the painting. I just want you to paint it for me."

Blethen continued to roll the name Arthur Kincaid over in his mind. "I'm not sure…."

"Is one million dollars enough to overcome your hesitancy?"

Blethen stared at the phone.

"I…I'll have to do some research," he finally rasped. "I assume there are photos?"

"Only a few, and they are in black and white."

"What if I can't find enough information to make an accurate copy?"

"I'm calling you because I've been told you are, perhaps, the only one who is capable of doing so. You will, of course, be paid upon delivery of your work."

"Ah, wait a minute. I'll have expenses. I'll need an advance for expenses."

"Mista Blethen, you sound reasonably intelligent. I am sure you won't embark on this journey if you don't feel you are capable of creating a perfect replica of *The Reaper.*"

"Uh, give me a couple of days to see if it's possible, and I'll get back to you."

"I will call you back on Monday, a week from tomorrow, at eight a.m. In two or three days you will receive a package. It will contain a picture of Miro painting *The Reaper,* and, Mista Blethen, you are to tell no one of this conversation or our little arrangement. Do you understand?"

"That is always my policy. If you don't want me to tell anyone, I don't."

Even if it hadn't been Blethen's policy before, the edge in Kincaid's voice confirmed that it was now.

"Good day, Mista Blethen." Click.

Holy shit!

Blethen had built a reputation by painting copies of old masters for wealthy people, restaurants, or other businesses, such as the jewelry store. His customers wanted to hang something on the wall that exuded wealth, status, and old-world elegance. Usually, for the individual customer, it was all about the intrigue of having a Rembrandt or a Caravaggio hanging on the wall. Is it real, their friends would wonder? How much is it worth? Where did you get it? Those were the questions the client wanted asked, and Blethen was extremely good at copying other artists' work. At least two of his paintings were hanging in major museums, part of collections on loan from his clients. The museums and the public believed them to be originals, not questioning the veracity of their donors.

If asked, Blethen was not sure how he would respond, but no one had asked, and in keeping with his personal code, he hadn't volunteered. Silence, he had learned early, like brushes and canvas, was a tool of the trade of an art copier. Word traveled fast in the art community and, if an art copier was indiscreet, the client lost face and the artist's phone stopped ringing. He could end up painting CD jackets for a living.

Kincaid's call pushed *The Girl with a Pearl Earring* down Blethen's priority list. Right now, he needed to scratch the itch created by the name Arthur Kincaid. He leashed Barca and headed for the public library.

The painter and his dog were frequent visitors. Barca lay quietly by the chair with only the occasional thump of his tail on the wood floor to break the library's code of silence, while Blethen pored over a compilation of the works of an artist whose work he had been asked to copy. This time, however, it was not the artist but the client whom he needed to research. With the help of the reference librarian on duty, he gathered a stack of newspaper and magazine articles about Arthur Kincaid. As he perused them, they began to paint their own picture.

Kincaid was born in Portsmouth, New Hampshire; Ivy League educated; inherited daddy's newspaper; built it into a media empire; influential politically; wealthy. He was appointed to a presidential commission, then was the target of a House investigative committee on media ethics and resigned his commission. Several years later he was nominated, and subsequently rejected, as ambassador to Portugal. Several articles connected him to a sex scandal that brought down a United States Senator, the same one that had been his primary adversary in the ambassadorial confirmation hearings. A few articles spoke of philanthropic efforts and provided photos: a big man, maybe six-four or six-five, two hundred fifty pounds or more, mostly bald. No close-ups. No good look at his face. There was reference to other alleged scandals and questionable business dealings, but nothing about spouses or children. There was also no mention of art collecting.

A librarian stopped to pat Barca on the head and tell Blethen that the library would be closing in ten minutes.

Back at the studio, Barca leaned against Blethen to emphasize that it was dinnertime, then sat patiently as a scoop of nuggets was poured into his bowl. "Go," was the signal, and the food was gone in less than a minute.

Blethen opened a beer and a can of sardines and turned on the Twins game just in time to see the locals take a 2-0 lead. He washed dishes left over from breakfast, got down on the floor to wrestle with Barca, and listened as the Twins lost to the Yankees 3-2 in ten innings, all the while thinking about Kincaid. The omissions were as telling as the information contained in the articles, and Blethen's sixth sense shouted, *Forgery! But a million dollars? What could it hurt to do a little research to see if painting* The Reaper *was even possible?*

For an art copier of Blethen's talent the line between a copy and a forgery was the width of his signature. A close look at the edge or back corner of a copy would disclose that this "Lautrec" was painted by Joe Bergeron, or that "Vermeer" by Hamilton Blethen. A forgery, on the other hand, bore no evidence of the actual painter. And while those who copy others' masterpieces live in relative obscurity, the names of the great forgers—Eric Hebborn, Elmyr de Hory, Han van Meegeren—were almost as well-known as those of the great painters themselves, both because of their unique talent and their propensity for violent, sometimes self-inflicted, deaths.

Another significant difference between a copier and a forger was in the forefront of Blethen's thoughts: a forger can make six or seven figures for a work; an art copier struggles to pay his rent.

MONDAY, MAY 18, 2009

A cold, wet nose on a bare shoulder was his wake-up call.

"Hey, buddy. Gotta go out?"

Barca pushed his nose further under Blethen's arm as his tail kept rhythm against the mattress. Before he had finished stretching,

Blethen's thoughts turned to Kincaid and *The Reaper,* and stayed there as both he and Barca did their morning routines. A rummage through old boxes in the hallway closet located his little black book from college and a phone number for Allison McKenzie, an old girlfriend who had become a writer for the *Boston Globe.* It was a long shot.

"You've reached Allison Long's mobile phone. Please leave a message and I'll get back to you as soon as possible. *She got married,* he thought. *How long since we've talked...four, five years? I wonder if she's still at the Globe?*

Beep.

"Allison. A voice from the past. Ham Blethen. Please call me. If you're still at the *Globe*, I'm looking for some information about one of your local characters, a man named Arthur Kincaid." He left his number.

Blethen closed the connection and punched in a more familiar number.

Jim Benson was chair of the department of fine arts at a small liberal arts university in Saint Paul. He and Ham had met at a Degas exhibit and found common interests in good wine and European art. A friendship had grown, partly fueled by Benson's admiration for Blethen's painting skills and partly by his curiosity about the life of an art copier.

"Jim? Who've you got in your department that's an expert on the Modernism movement in the early twentieth century?" Blethen asked.

"There's a grad student who's had a couple of articles published on the era," Benson said. "I don't know if she's an expert, but she's certainly knowledgeable. Why do you ask?"

"I want to hire someone to do some research for me. I'm more interested in the historical perspective than about any particular painting or painter." Blethen lied, purposely diverting attention away from the real reason for his inquiry. "How do I get in contact with her?"

"I would want to contact her first and see if she has an interest. What do I tell her?"

"Tell her I'd like to have coffee with her to discuss Modernism and the Avant-Garde art movement in the first half of the twentieth century. And that there may be a paid research project in it for her."

"I'll talk to her. I'll have her call you if she's interested. Her name is Toni Shapiro. Can you tell me what it's about?"

"Just a potential gig. Can't give you any details. Sorry. But, hey, I'm trying to employ one of your starving students. Isn't that enough?"

"Have you done anything new recently?" Benson skipped right past the attempt at humor.

"I'm just finishing up a Vermeer. Would you like to stop for a glass of vino and take a look?"

They set a date for Sunday night, and Benson reconfirmed he'd be in contact with the grad student. "Hang on to your hat if you do meet with her," he added. "She's a real firecracker."

WEDNESDAY, MAY 20, 2009

Blethen wasn't sure whether Jim Benson was referring to the color of her hair or her personality, but his assessment was spot on. Toni Shapiro turned out to be Antoinette Chapereaux, and she cantered into Starbucks like a young colt, all legs and long strides with a bright orange Afro right out of the sixties, freckles and green eyes, dressed in jean shorts, a tee shirt that read *Liberte, Egalite, Fraternite*, a baseball cap and an over-sized bag slung haphazardly over her shoulder.

"That's just the way it is," she explained after introducing herself, not waiting for a question. "I'm a little sensitive about the hair when I first meet someone. Sorry. People keep asking me if it's mine, or if it's a wig, but this really is its natural color. I've given up trying to straighten it. It just likes to frizz."

He found it interesting that she talked about her hair in the third person, but eventually they got her hair issues, the spelling of her name and the usual preliminaries out of the way. She did most of the talking, in staccato bursts: born in Narbonne, France, twenty-six years ago; moved to the United States when she was eleven; got her bachelor's degree from Princeton; was in her third year of a doctoral program in art history; liked caramel macchiatos but couldn't afford them; loved to do research.

She gave the impression of being in constant motion even when she sat still drinking the macchiato Blethen bought her, papers spilling out of her bag.

They talked Spanish art long enough for a second macchiato, and for her motor to wind down, but when the conversation veered toward the research project she again launched into hyperdrive, spewing questions with Gatling gun rapidity: Why was he interested in early twentieth century Spanish art? What was the purpose of the research? Did he want her to focus on any specific movement? Was there a particular artist? Did he know that parts of Catalonia were actually in France? When did he need the paper? How much was she going to get paid? Did she need to limit it in length? What did he do for a living?

Eventually they agreed on an hourly rate. Blethen handed her a memo he had prepared on the scope of the research, and they agreed to touch base on Friday for a progress report. They exchanged phone numbers, and, with all macchiatos vanquished, she bolted out of her chair and raced out of Starbucks.

Blethen exhaled. He was exhausted. He hadn't spent that much time listening since he'd had five lecture classes in one semester. *Firecracker, indeed.*

He returned to his studio and *The Girl with a Pearl Earring*, staring at her for the better part of an hour, but his thoughts kept straying and brush never touched canvas. Finally, he and Barca went for a walk.

"Women," he complained to his four-legged confidante. "What the hell is it about them that always screws up my world? I just pissed away an hour thinking about her instead of painting. She really does have an unusual look, and she's smart as hell."

Barca stopped and looked up at him with a look that Blethen was sure meant "Not again, dumb shit."

"Just to paint her," he said, defensively.

Barca lifted his leg and peed on a lamp post.

Blethen sorted the mail, tossing bills into a shoebox with others that had accumulated over the past months. With anticipation he slit open a large manila envelope with a Barcelona postmark and pulled out a copy of a faded picture of a dark-haired man on a stepladder. Behind the ladder was an unfinished painting. "*The Reaper*" was handwritten on the border of the copy.

Guessing at the height of the man and the ladder, Blethen judged *The Reaper* to be about twenty feet tall. *Where am I going to find a canvas that big,* he wondered.

After studying the picture, Blethen squeezed the edges of the envelope together and drew out another piece of paper; an article from an English-speaking Italian newspaper, *Corriere della Sera,* dated 2007. "Suspected Art Forger Murdered," read the headline. The painter, an American, had been beaten, tied to a chair and his fingers had been cut off. He'd bled to death. In the margin of the article was another handwritten note: "Loose lips!"

Blethen's bladder contracted in concert with the chill that raced up his backbone. He refolded both pieces of paper and warily slid them back into the envelope.

There were two phone messages from Allison McKenzie-Long and one from Jim Benson on his voice mail. He tried to stop his hands from trembling as he dialed Benson's number. "Your description of her was right on the money," Blethen said to Benson's voicemail. "She's very smart, and she talks like a string of firecrackers going off, with hair color to match. I hired her."

Then he called Allison.

"Allison Long."

"Hi, Allison. Ham Blethen. How are you?"

"Hamilton Blethen! How's my favorite art forger!"

"Whoa. Don't kid about stuff like that, Allison. I just read a newspaper article about an art forger that got whacked in Italy, and it makes me a little nervous. I'm just a humble art copier."

She laughed. "How are you, Ham? Is the world treating you well?"

"Well enough. I see you got married."

"Yes."

"Any kids?"

"No," she said, "but since you know I'm married you didn't call to ask me out, and I know you didn't call me to talk about married life, so what's up?"

"Do you still work for the *Boston Globe*?"

"Yes."

"I'm looking for information on one of your east coasty types. His name's Arthur Kincaid. Ring any bells?

"Kincaid. That's old money. Media empire. Arthur, I think, is second or third generation."

"I've done some research at the local library," Blethen said, "but I need more than what I'm finding here. What I'm looking for is this guy's reputation, how his peers consider him, can he be trusted? Are there any stories or rumors that might lead one to believe he's not a straight shooter? Does he pay his bills or stiff his creditors? Is he dangerous? Stuff like that doesn't come across in newspaper articles. You must have some old beat reporters there, or in your Washington bureau, who remember when this guy was a big deal there."

"Customer?"

"Maybe. Can you help me out?"

"Sure. I'll ask around. See what I can find."

Blethen gave Allison the information he had about Kincaid, leaving out the man's penchant for collecting old newspaper clippings.

"I need this pretty quickly," he added. "I've got to make a decision by Monday on whether to take this guy on as a client."

"I'll check with a couple of the older news guys and see what I can find out."

"I love you, sweetheart. Always have."

"You are still full of B.S., Ham," she laughed. "I'll do it for old time's sake, but if I come up with something you owe me a bottle of 1987 Lafite."

"Allison, if everything works out, I'll buy you a case and deliver it personally."

The good-natured banter with his long-ago girlfriend tamped down Blethen's anxiety. He poured himself a glass of cheap wine and sank into his ratty, overstuffed chair, recalling the good times he'd shared with Allison. But his thoughts kept wandering to *The Reaper,* and Kincaid, and a million dollars, and the short life expectancy of art forgers.

He needed to get out of his own head. The bars on Grand Avenue beckoned.

THURSDAY, MAY 21, 2009

Barca sat with his chin on the bare leg of Blethen's overnight guest, his big brown eyes gazing upward hopefully, trying his best to beg the young woman out of her breakfast.

"Don't look at me like that," her admonition to Barca betrayed by the lilt in her voice. "Is it okay if I give him something?"

"Camel's nose under the tent," Blethen replied as he stuck his fork through another piece of pancake and braunschweiger.

"What?"

"Camel's nose under the tent," he repeated. "If you give in to his begging, pretty soon he'll be climbing in your lap and eating off your plate. Next thing you know, he'll be sitting in your chair and you'll be on the floor. You know, you give him something and it's like a camel's nose under the tent. It's just the beginning."

The puzzled look on her face indicated she neither knew nor understood.

"Barca, mind your manners," Blethen said, discreetly rolling his eyes. With an exaggerated sigh the big dog lay down at her feet, long nose glumly thrust between his paws.

Blethen named him Barca after an obscure historical figure, Hamilcar Barca, Carthaginian general and father of Hannibal. Since he first read the name in high school history Blethen had been enamored with it. He even speculated about changing his own name, if for no other reason than to spite his mother, but naming his dog Barca proved to be a lot easier and less expensive. Like his historical namesake, Barca had proven to be steadfast in his devotion, making Blethen wonder if the big sigh was because Barca's begging had failed or because another of his master's liaisons had lasted one night.

His overnight companion dispatched, Blethen wandered into his studio to make another pass at *The Girl with a Pearl Earring.* Crisp spring sunshine beamed through the south-facing windows, reflecting off dust particles sent airborne by Blethen's movement. He tried to force himself into "the zone" but couldn't make it happen.

He gave up, ambled into the living area, opened a beer and turned on the Twins' game.

Baseball had been his passion before painting. When Blethen was pitching at his best he could tune out all sound and movement and focus solely on the catcher's glove. That's what baseball players called being "in the zone." When he was there the game was effortless. He could throw all his pitches exactly where he wanted, wherever his catcher called for the ball. The fans disappeared. His teammates disappeared. The batter disappeared. It was only him and the catcher's glove.

A year playing junior college baseball got him noticed by a Mets' scout. They offered him a try-out and a contract. During his two years in the minor leagues he found the zone from time to time, but not often enough to overcome his personal baggage. The freedom, the money, the women and the booze were too much for a nineteen-year-old. He was in and out of trouble more often than the bullpen, and by twenty-one was out of baseball.

Then Blethen learned that "the zone" was not unique to baseball.

After three years in the army, with no prospects or focus in his life, Blethen went back to college. For no particular reason, other than that it didn't sound too difficult, he enrolled in a painting class. He liked the mental creativity it allowed him, but the physical act of painting was a struggle, complicated by his competitive nature. To his unpracticed eye, his efforts didn't measure up to the work of the other students. The harder he tried, the worse his paintings got.

One day it all changed.

The crusty professor assigned a class project: duplicate Mars's hand from Botticelli's classic, *Venus and Mars.* Blethen painted as if in a dream, every stroke perfect. Texture and color flowed from his brush. The professor summoned the other students to see it, then waxed eloquently about the perception, knowledge and dedication it takes to do even a small piece of a master, referring throughout his monologue to Ham's Botticelli-like hand.

Later, over coffee at the student union with classmates, Ham realized that all sounds and sites had faded from his consciousness while he was painting the hand. He had been "in the zone" for the first time since walking off his last pitcher's mound.

He went back to the classroom that evening, and in the solitude once again induced the trance-like state. He painted the face of Mars. The next day the professor went bonkers, declaring Ham one of the next great painters. Unfortunately, the prophecy fell short. Even when in the zone Ham wasn't able to create the same depth, intensity or mystic quality in his own, original work.

Today the zone eluded him. He couldn't block out *The Reaper* and Kincaid. With the Twins comfortably ahead of the Brewers, and the sun warming the day into the high sixties, Blethen hooked up Barca and they walked the two miles to the library to learn more about *The Reaper.*

Dappled sunlight on Summit Avenue drew his thoughts back to Vermeer and the Dutch artist's mastery of light, which in turn had him picturing Toni Chapereaux in the portico of a south-facing grand mansion, her shoulder leaning against a gothic pillar, a light breeze causing the sun to shimmer in her flaming hair, her freckles disappearing and reappearing as the sunlight danced between the leaves overhead.

FRIDAY, MAY 22, 2009

He met Toni at Starbucks. Amid the coffee shop cacophony and caramel-flavored macchiatos, she orally downloaded a stream of the results of her research in her usual manic manner: "Joan Miro was born in 1893 in Barcelona died on Christmas day 1983 in Palma de Majorca lived in Paris in exile with other Spanish artists who were on the losing side of the civil war spent much of his life in Majorca did not return to Spain until Franco fell from power in the seventies one of the pillars of Cubism Abstract Expressionism and Surrealism…" (breath) "…his disdain for traditional painting was summed up in his description of his own work 'assassination of painting,' became popular in the United States in the 1930s the National Gallery of Art in Washington D.C. has a large permanent Miro exhibit The Miro Foundation in Barcelona houses the largest number of his works his studio in Palma de Majorca is now a museum…" (breath)

As he listened, Blethen flipped through a pile of papers attached to her report. A copy of a photo with Miro standing on the floor beside a stepladder in front of a painting that appeared to be the same as the one in the picture from the manila envelope. It jumped out at him. He casually turned the page to avoid showing interest.

"One of his paintings, *La Caresse des Etoiles*, The Caress of the Stars, sold for seventeen million," she continued.

That got Blethen's attention. *Maybe a million isn't enough,* he thought.

Other than the photo, there was no mention of *The Reaper* in her report—no surprise since his own research had turned up a remarkable lack of interest or information about the painting or its disappearance. He had purposely omitted any mention of it in his memo to Toni.

"I'd like more detailed research on Miro's painting in the 1930s and '40s," he said. "I want a sense of his style during that time. What mediums was he working in? What were his themes? What colors did he favor? If there's a monograph of his work from that period in the university library, bring it with you."

They agreed to meet on Sunday.

Blethen wished he had someone to talk to to help him think through the conundrum he faced. As he stood in front of his stove watching bubbles form on the topside of the pancakes he was making for dinner he tried once again to focus: *Kincaid hired the dead forger to paint* The Reaper, *and killed him because he didn't keep his mouth shut? What other reason could there be for him to have a copy of a two-year-old newspaper article about the murder of an art forger?*

That conclusion, alone, should have been enough to convince Blethen not to paint *The Reaper,* but he'd spent several hours diluting the afternoon coffee with evening wine, and a million dollars kept waltzing with the alcohol. *I'll never get another chance like this,* he thought. *So it's a forgery. Not the first time. So what's the big deal?*

And then there were the questions.

Why is there so little information on this painting? Why is there so little information about its disappearance? When a famous painter's work disappears it usually makes big headlines. Why not in this case? Why is an old rich guy with no apparent history of art collecting willing to pop for a million dollars for a copy of a painting that disappeared in 1937? Obvious answer: he's going to make many millions. Other obvious answer: he doesn't plan on paying for it.

Through the burgundy haze Blethen was sure of only two things: he didn't know what he was going to do, and he was running out of time to do it.

SATURDAY, MAY 23, 2009

It was only a small headache, but to have a jangling phone introduce him to his hangover was irritating, particularly at six a.m. when there was only silence on the other end when he answered.

The call with no caller was prophetic of Blethen's entire day, interrupted with phone calls.

Allison called. Arthur Kincaid was not someone to mess with. According to her sources, his ruthless streak extended well beyond taking down a U.S. senator who had crossed him. There were numerous business partners and competitors that had been left financially and reputationally broken in his wake. One had committed suicide. There was suspicion that Kincaid had ties to the Irish Republic Army. Or to the Mafia. Or both. About five years ago there had been a dust-up between him and some Las Vegas casino interests. Although there was nothing that was proven illegal, nor any known violence, Kincaid had been out of the spotlight since.

"My advice would be to pass on this guy," Allison said. "It seems like everyone who deals with him gets hurt."

Jim Benson's call came in shortly after noon. Since they both had to meet with Toni Chapereaux he had invited her to Ham's Sunday evening to have their meetups and see the Vermeer. Was that all right? Although it presented a problem, Ham said "sure." He didn't want Benson to know about his interest in Miro, much less *The Reaper,* and he hoped Toni hadn't said anything. He hadn't told her to keep her research secret. He would have to figure out a way to meet with her separately to discuss her research.

He was still thinking of Toni, wondering if she and Benson had something going on, when the phone rang again.

Elaine Ravalo was an aging socialite with too much time on her hands and lots of her husband's money to spend. Blethen had copied two Gainsboroughs for her, and now she wanted a third. She also wanted a face-to-face meeting, a risky proposition he had learned when delivering the first Gainsborough.

In a baritone voice dripping with innuendo, Mrs. Ravalo had made it clear she was at least as interested in the artist as in the painting, *River Landscape with Rustic Lovers.* Exposed cleavage and no sign of underwear under her silk wrap had made the delivery awkward until she handed him a check with one hand and groped him with the other. Never wanting to disappoint a client, Blethen had obliged, and a few months later it appeared the accommodation had paid off when she ordered a second painting.

On an idyllic afternoon, without the encumbrance of paint brushes or clothes, Blethen had allowed himself a moment of vulnerability. As they lay exhausted, entangled in the sheets on his messy bed, Elaine asked about his family, and for one of the few times in his adult life he talked about his mother.

"The last time I saw her I was four, standing next to my Grandma, holding a grocery bag with my clothes in it, watching her walk away," he said. "She had red hair and was wearing a yellow blouse. Got in a car and drove away. That was it, the last time."

"She just left you?"

Blethen nodded.

"Did you ever try to find her?"

"Why would I? Only time I ever heard from her was a card when I graduated from high school. It said: 'Congratulations' and it was signed 'Magnolia.' I didn't even know who it was from because that wasn't her name, but my Grandma said it looked like her writing. It didn't even say 'love' or 'mom.' Just 'congratulations.' I threw it away."

"What about your father?"

"Never knew him. I don't think my mother knew him either. I wasn't a love child. I was a drugged-up orgy child. She didn't want me. Drugs were more important." As he talked the edge in his voice grew sharper.

"Did your Grandma raise you?"

"No. She was too broke. I ended up in foster care."

"So, other family?"

"I talk to my Grandma once in a while. She's my only family. I never got adopted. Nobody wanted a brown kid in a white world."

Making himself vulnerable to someone like Elaine was a mistake. She immediately transformed into the role of lover-mother: hovering, instructing, touching, obligating. It took several weeks and awkward moments for him to extract himself from her motherly/loverly clutches. When he'd finished the second painting, he thought he'd never see her again. That had been more than a year ago. Now, she wanted a third Gainsborough, the portrait of Georgiana, Duchess of Devonshire that Gainsborough had painted in the mid-eighteenth century. Elaine wanted her face in the portrait, not that of the Duchess. This would, she opined, require numerous sittings at his studio.

His first instinct was to turn her down. He really didn't want to become embroiled with her again. On the other hand, another commission in the pipeline gave him options.

I could turn down The Reaper, he thought. *Or negotiate a higher price.*

Blethen increased his fee for the third Gainsborough fourfold, with half up front. *Lust hath its price,* he reasoned.

She didn't blink. Lust was willing to pay.

He suggested lunch at a private club where her husband was a member to go over the details. A *relatively safe place,* he thought, *to keep her libido in check.*

SUNDAY, MAY 24, 2009

Benson brought wine.

"I thought you were coming over to drink mine," Blethen said as he took the bottle of '06 Mondavi reserve cab from his friend.

"Thought we might need a spare."

"Let's drink the spare first. Looks better than anything I've got."

They were complimenting the wine and discussing Blethen's rendition of *The Girl with the Pearl Earring* when the front door buzzer went off, announcing Toni's arrival. "Oooh. Nice," she said of the wine. "What a beautiful dog" when Barca came into the studio to check out the new intruder. And, "Really? You painted this?" when she saw the Vermeer.

"That's what I do," Blethen said. "I paint replicas of old masters. This one is for a jewelry store in Ohio."

"Isn't that forgery?" she blurted, her elfin face pursed in concern.

"No, no," Benson interjected. "He signs them with his own name. Everyone knows it's a copy. Everyone knows it's not the original."

She leaned toward the painting, studying it. "I didn't even know that was a job, painting copies of other people's work.

"There're only a few of us," Blethen said, trying not to sound defensive.

"You've got to be a really talented painter to do what Ham does," Benson chimed in.

They held their breath, as if the future of the painting depended upon Toni's approval.

The tip of her tongue appeared between her teeth as she peered at the work, looking for some discerning evidence that would distinguish it from the real thing. She gave a small nod. "This is really good," she said.

In Blethen's mind, he had just been given permission to finish the work.

They spent the next hour debating the authenticity of Johannes Vermeer's paintings, scratching Barca's ears and drinking a second bottle of wine. As their glasses ran dry, among not-so-subtle hints from Blethen that he needed to talk to Toni privately, Benson reluctantly left.

"What have you got for me?" Blethen asked, and Toni provided a rapid-fire account of Miro's work in the 1930s and 40s. Together they looked through a book she borrowed from the university library, a compilation of some of the Catalan painter's works from the era, lingering over *Aidez L'Espagne*, a 1937 work by Miro originally meant to be a postage stamp design. It featured a Catalan peasant against a blue background wearing the traditional red cap of a reaper, with a large yellow fist raised in revolt. According to the note that accompanied the picture the painting had become an emblem of resistance for the Spanish republican government in the civil war that wracked the country from 1936 to 1939. Confident that he could now approximate the colors of *The Reaper,* Blethen paid Toni for her research.

"I'd like to hang on to the monograph for a couple of days," he said, referring to the book of Miro paintings.

"No problem," she said, accepting the check. "Could I ask a favor? Could I look at some of your original work before I go?"

"Uh. Sure. Why?"

"I'd really like to see something you've painted that isn't a copy of someone else's work."

"It's not that good." He shrugged, moving a light stanchion and a stepladder out of the way as he worked his way behind a bench where several canvases were leaning face-first against the wall. He looked at several before pulling out a three-by-four canvas, an urban landscape dominated by a suspended bridge with a city skyline in the distance. He propped it against the bench so she could view it.

"I did this several years ago during my 'city' phase," he explained with air quotes.

Toni tilted her head from side to side, not saying anything.

He lifted a tarp and removed a second, smaller canvas: a woman wearing a floppy fedora and oversized scarf, holding a leash, attached to a dog that resembled a greyhound, in one hand and a walking stick in the other. The painting was impressionistic in style.

"I like this one," she said.

"I did it while I was studying in Paris. Had a couple of offers for it, but I was never so desperate that I had to part with it. It's one of the few I actually like."

"The woman?"

"Someone I saw walking a dog in Luxembourg Garden. She just exuded elegance."

Toni gazed at the painting. Vertical frown lines formed between her eyebrows as she slowly moved her head from side-to-side. Finally, she turned. "I should be going."

"Before you do, could I ask *you* for a favor?" Blethen said.

"Sure."

"When we met at Starbucks last week I thought of this painting," he said, nodding toward the woman with the greyhound. "You're like her, unique…"

"It's my hair," she interrupted.

"No. Well, yes, that may be part of it," he said as he moved the stepladder to the center of the studio, "but I'm talking about more than that. When I saw you studying the Vermeer with the early evening light creating shadows and movements and your expressions changing, I thought, ah, um, I'd like to paint you."

"I'm not elegant. I'm a klutz and…"

This time Blethen interrupted: "Elegance you can buy and wear. You have something that you can't get at a store—enthusiasm, positivity that fairly comes out your pores. I'd like to try and capture that on canvas."

She looked embarrassed by the suggestion. "I'm flattered, but…"

"Humor me for just a little bit," he interrupted. "Let me set a scene. If you don't like it we'll stop."

Her nod was barely discernible. "Okay," she said in a small voice.

She let him take her hand and guide her to the stepladder, motioning her to sit, then move her a step higher so she could extend her left leg and rest her foot on the first step, giving her leverage to hold her position. He stepped back and studied the pose, his thumbs hooked under his chin, his fingers steepled over his nose. He stepped forward and, placing a hand on each of her hips, gently turned her so she was sitting on the ladder at a forty-five-degree angle. He stepped back, adjusted the light standard and turned down the wattage to soften the shadows. Again he approached the ladder, took her right hand, and placed it on her bent knee.

"Put your left hand on the back of your neck," he said, a softness in his voice. "Raise your elbow a bit."

As if in a dream, she touched the back of her neck, imagining the fingertips were Blethen's and not hers.

"There. That's good," he said.

He placed his foot on the bottom rung of the ladder and, careful not to brush against her, leaned forward, gently tilting her head to the left. He could feel her arch her back slightly, and the heat of her skin through the thin tee shirt, as he placed his hands on her shoulders and rotated them slightly.

"Think of your happy place," he said as he backed away and picked a thirty-five- millimeter camera from his workbench. A faint smile made her face luminous, and Blethen quickly snapped photos.

"Perfect," he said as he put the camera back on the bench. He offered his hand to Toni. Carefully she stepped down from her perch, then turned into him and, looking up, offered her lips.

MONDAY, MAY 25, 2009

He opened one eye. Red digits glared 3:38 a.m., seven minutes since the last time he looked. His mind wouldn't stop spinning. Less than five hours until Kincaid would call. Less than five hours to figure out what he was going to do. He knew he could reproduce *The Reaper*. That wasn't the issue. Twelve hours ago he had been prepared to cross the line from copier to forger. Then he saw the look on Toni's face. Any respect she had for him as an artist was gone the moment she thought he was forging the Vermeer.

Dammit! Women sure as hell complicate everything. Barca stirred on the other side of the bed. Blethen reached over and stroked the dog's soft fur. *Oh, buddy.* He sighed. *This one might be worth it.*

2:00 P.M.

BARCELONA

"Will Señor Kincaid be joining you, Miss Magnolia?" the starched *maître d'* asked.

"No, Juan Carlos. Señor Kincaid is tending to some business. I will be having lunch alone today."

He took her shopping bags and signaled a bellboy to have them taken to her room. She followed him through Restaurant Drolma, nearly empty because of the late hour, to her regular table next to a window looking out on Passeig de Gracia, a lovely tree-lined boulevard that traversed the Eixample, the historic district of Barcelona.

"Would you like me to prepare something tableside for you? A fig and black truffle salad, perhaps?" He pulled out her chair with a flourish, snapped the folded linen napkin to open it and deftly laid it across her lap in a perfect triangle.

"That would be fine. May I see the wine list, please?"

She sipped Segura Viudas Cava, nibbled on the salad and people-watched as Barcelonans strolled in the warm afternoon sun. It was not often that she took the time to enjoy the fashionable district just outside the old city walls, with its Gaudi architecture, tree-lined boulevards, world-class shops and great restaurants, Drolma being the best in her opinion.

But today she felt the need to take some time for herself and clear her mind of the uncertainty caused by Kincaid's declining health.

Magnolia Kanaranzi wasn't her real name.

A black-robed judge with a sharp voice and a gavel as an exclamation point had told her it was her last chance. "I can put you back in jail again for a long time," he said, "or you can get out of town, out of Minnesota, and never come back. Your choice." She chose get out of town. She threw everything she owned in a duffel bag and, with three dollars in her pocket, begged a ride at a local biker bar with a bedraggled cowboy headed for Sturgis, South Dakota, who said he'd be happy to "give her a ride" anytime, anywhere. She really didn't care who he was, or where he was going, or that she might have to fuck him to get there. She'd had worse.

She wasn't going back to prison.

She had been stoned or drunk for most of a decade, burning through a dozen jobs in the early years. Sometimes she was fired. Sometimes she just wandered off and never returned. By the last year or two she was selling dope and her body, and living on the streets or with anyone who'd have her. Along the way she got pregnant, had an abortion, got pregnant again. She tried being a mother, but learned she had neither the instinct nor the interest. She left the kid with her mother.

Inevitably she got caught up in the legal system: prostitution, possession, public drunkenness, petty theft. She went through treatment several times. It didn't take. She didn't care. In the rare moments when she was straight she hated herself, hated what she'd done, hated what she'd become. Then she'd revert to drugs and alcohol to forget. The cycle between moments of sobriety became longer and longer.

She straddled the throbbing Harley as it rumbled west in the summer of 1976, one of a hundred bikers with a single destination, the Sturgis Road Rally. It was a fitting parable of her life, roaring ninety miles an hour down a dead-end life with people she didn't know to a place she didn't care about, stoned.

Then she saw the road sign: exit left to Magnolia, turn right and go to Kanaranzi. The motorcycle herd roared past the sign, relentlessly headed west down I-90 toward Sturgis. With the drug-induced fog in her brain and the wind in her face, she repeated the message on the sign. She liked the sound of it. Mag-no-li-a Kana-ran-zi. To her it sounded like Italian royalty. Maybe she would be a duchess. By the time the sign was five miles behind her she had changed her name. She spent the next several hours on the back of a Harley, glued to the back side of a man she didn't know, making up stories about a woman she wasn't. When the herd paused on its westward trek she went into the first available bathroom and peered at herself in the mirror. She splashed water on her wind-burned face, pulled back her wind-ratted hair and decided that she looked Italian.

She forgot most of the stories by the time they hit Sturgis, but the name stuck.

Juan Carlos appeared at table-side and refilled her wine glass. "Can I get you anything?"

She declined.

"Are you all right?" he asked, an old friend detecting a sadness in her eyes.

"Just a bit melancholy," Magnolia said, taking her napkin and dabbing a tear from her cheek as Frank Sinatra's voice intoned the words of *My Way* in the background. Juan Carlos quickly scanned the nearly empty dining room. Detecting no need for his immediate attention, he sat down across from her.

"Is there something I can do to help?" he asked.

"You are so kind, but not this time," she said. "It's just some things from my past I have to deal with."

"I always think better when I exercise," he said. "It helps clear the mind. Perhaps a walk on such a beautiful day would make you feel better."

"That's a good idea. I'll just finish my wine."

"There's a lovely little *botiga* that sells silk scarves just around the corner. Perhaps something for yourself would lift your sadness," the *maître d'* suggested. She nodded. "And if the things you have to deal with are too troubling, I know someone who can help." He handed her a business card.

Rising, he smiled as he withdrew, pleased that he had been able to give a small bit of comfort to one of his favorite patrons.

Magnolia looked at the card: "Henri Hawke" was the name on it. She put it in her purse.

As she lingered over her wine, Sinatra's voice crept back into her consciousness crooning something about regrets. She'd had many. She had come to terms with all of them except one. Soon that would be resolved, too, in the only way she knew how.

9:07 A.M.

SAINT PAUL

Blethen woke with a start. *Sonofabitch!* He'd overslept and missed the call. *Dammit!* He bailed out of bed and frantically checked his voice mail for messages. There were none from Arthur Kincaid.

"Why the hell didn't you wake me up?" he yelled at Barca, then immediately regretted it when the big dog's brown eyes saddened. Blethen stooped and gave Barca a hug to compensate for his own stupidity.

Is this the right day? It is Monday. What the hell? He checked his messages again. It seemed to be functioning properly. Coffee percolated as he brushed his teeth and washed his face, skipping his usual morning shower in fear of missing Kincaid's call. Again, the thought *what-in-the-hell* as confusion coursed through his brain. He poured a cup of coffee and settled into his overstuffed chair.

The clock ticked toward ten and he turned on the television to see if some cataclysmic event might explain the missing phone call. There was none. He called Jim Benson.

"Sorry I booted you out last night," Blethen said. "I needed to talk to Toni about her research."

"I got the picture. Did *you* do any research after I left?"

Blethen ignored the innuendo. "Would you do me a favor and call me. I'm not sure my phone is working."

Benson called. The phone worked and so did his voice mail. By noon Blethen was sure he wasn't going to get a call from Kincaid. *Is this some kind of joke? Some prank? Wasting my time. Who the hell would do this?* He sorted through possible culprits: practical jokers among his friends, other artists. At lunch Louis had asked if he thought he'd ever get a million-dollar commission and the next day he'd gotten the call. *But the envelope had a Barcelona postmark. The newspaper clipping was from a two-year-old Italian newspaper. That is way beyond Louis's capacity.*

Barca interrupted the analysis by sticking his nose in Blethen's crotch, looking up expectantly. It was after noon and he hadn't been let out. They walked to a local photography store he often used and dropped off the film from the previous evening. Ordinarily it would take a week to get the pictures back, but Blethen convinced the manager that it was an emergency. They would be ready by Wednesday.

As they walked, Blethen half-expected someone to jump from behind a tree or a door and yell "Gotcha" but it didn't happen, and by the time they returned to the studio his ire had subsided. At least he didn't have to make a choice between a million dollars and being a forger.

That evening he put the final touches on the Vermeer. A few brush strokes on her cheek and turban had deepened the shadow and, in response, the girl's face had organically grown brighter, more luminous. He accomplished what had been eluding him for weeks.

Blethen poured a glass of wine and lit a cigar, a little victory ritual he had adopted to celebrate the completion of another painting. On the edge of the stretched canvas he wrote "copy by HBlethen" in charcoal, then carefully dabbed clear fingernail polish over it.

He put it in the oven where it would age centuries in less than twenty-four hours.

The phone rang in his living quarters as he closed the oven door. He checked the clock as he picked up. It was just after 1 a.m.

"Hello?"

The line was open. He could hear someone breathing on the other end, but there was no response.

"Hello," he repeated.

The person on the other end hung up.

5:00 P.M.

BARCELONA

Magnolia knew Kincaid would be on the phone or holding a meeting, so, taking the *maître d'*s advice, she exited Drolma and, in the soft late afternoon light, strolled past shops she had earlier browsed. Turning left at Plaza de Catalunya, she ambled down Las Ramblas toward the waterfront, stopping to enjoy the mimes that silently plied their craft on the wide promenade. Wandering into La Boqueria to indulge in the smells and colors of the brightly-lit food market, Maggie stopped to taste samples at the mushroom stall, then continued southward until she reached Monument a Colom, a commemoration of Columbus's return from America in 1493; impressive until you realize that the statue of Columbus atop the ornate column is pointing in the wrong direction—toward Italy, not the New World.

Juan Carlos had been right. The walk amongst the tourists and the sounds of the city had restored her. She looked at her watch. Kincaid would be done with business and ready for dinner. She caught a taxi back to the hotel.

The shopping bags were sitting inside the penthouse door, having been dutifully delivered.

"Arthur?" she called as she entered the living room. He was lying on the couch, his eyes unblinking, his mouth open, dried saliva on his cheek and neck. His skin was the color of ashes.

"Arthur!" she screamed as she rushed to him and put two fingers on his neck. There was a pulse.

"Arthur." She tried to shake the big man, but there was no response. She put her ear to his lips and felt, more than heard, shallow breathing. She raced to the bedroom and called the front desk. "I need an ambulance. Mr. Kincaid is unconscious. Hurry!" she shouted. She returned to the living room and put her hand to his forehead. He felt cold. She retrieved a blanket from the bedroom and covered him.

"Oh, Arthur. Not this soon," she said aloud.

Arthur's cancer had been a specter in their lives since his diagnosis over a year ago. Chemotherapy had provided hope, but it was temporary. The tumor marker numbers had been up at his last exam and another round of chemo was prescribed, but he had business in Europe that couldn't wait and Kincaid had persuaded the doctors to postpone treatment until he returned.

Had he been arguing for his own death? she wondered. *Did he know his time was up?*

She sagged to the floor beside the couch and took Kincaid's cold hand in hers. "Oh, Arthur. Did you make the call?" she whispered to his unhearing ear. "Is he going to paint *The Reaper*?"

WEDNESDAY, MAY 27, 2009

"He's had a stroke. He needs you to come to Barcelona as soon as possible."

The emergency room doctor had told Magnolia that it wasn't Kincaid's cancer that had felled him, but *un accidente cerebrovascular*, a stroke. She called Arthur's personal attorney in Boston, Byron MacMillan. MacMillan was the linchpin of Kincaid's business interests.

He controlled the money and he knew where the skeletons were buried. As much as he detested taking orders from Magnolia, he confirmed he would be in Barcelona by Monday morning.

MacMillan had been her nemesis from the beginning, seeing her only as a gold digger. She thought that her unwavering loyalty to Kincaid for thirty years, and her growing understanding and involvement in his business enterprises, should have proven she was much more than a bimbo looking for a pay day. But he had not relented.

She had learned to tolerate MacMillan's bluntness and accusations, even as they had become more frequent and caustic recently as Kincaid began to rely more and more on her. She knew a day would come when she and MacMillan would have a confrontation from which only one of them would survive. She had not expected it to come this soon.

Kincaid oscillated between long stretches of sleep and short periods of consciousness, hooked to a profusion of tubes and medical gadgets. Thus far, he had been unable to speak.

Magnolia sat at his bedside, worried, and wondering if he had made the call. She had pressed the doctors for the time the stroke had occurred, but the best they could do was to estimate, from the dried spittle on his cheek, that it had happened at least an hour before she found him. As she prayed for Kincaid to recover sufficiently to give her the answer, her thoughts drifted to when they had met.

Magnolia forgot the cowboy with the Harley from the moment her feet touched dirt in Sturgis. In her ever-addled mind she was no longer a drunken, law-breaking druggie. She was Italian royalty, too good for the greaser she had ridden behind for six hundred miles. She was free to be whoever she wanted to be.

But nothing changed. She hopped from bar to bar, from party to party. Over the course of the week she met scores of people; drank, smoked, screwed and snorted with many of them; and told fictional stories of her past as an Italian duchess. She gave little thought to what she said or to whom. After all, she would never see these people again, and no one really cared.

Then one morning she woke up and the rally was over. She was dumbfounded, not having anticipated that it would end or what she would do next. She tried to catch a ride with several late-departing bikers, but after looking in a mirror at a local gas station she realized why they'd declined. She looked like shit. She hadn't bathed since the night she bunked in with a lesbian waitress and hadn't changed her clothes since she'd left Minnesota.

Somewhere along the way, she borrowed or stole money from someone because there was over a hundred dollars in her pocket and she was sure she hadn't turned a trick. *Magnolia Kanaranzi didn't do tricks!* She counted the money, then stuffed it back in her pocket. She was going to get cleaned up, but first she needed a drink. She walked several blocks before she found a liquor store. She bought a half pint of Wild Turkey and headed for the closest motel.

"Sixty-nine dollars," the motel clerk told her.

"But I only need it for a couple of hours to clean up and take a nap," she pleaded.

"Sixty-nine dollars," he repeated. She argued, but the smell of liquor on her breath and her disheveled state weren't persuasive. Her new life was turning out to be her old life.

"What time is check out?" The voice came from behind and above her head. She turned and looked up at a large man, clean, expensive clothes, receding hairline. He didn't look like a biker.

"Eleven o'clock. Fifteen minutes from now," the motel clerk answered.

"How much would it cost me to extend my check out time a couple hours?" the man asked. Magnolia was annoyed by the intruder.

"If you're out by one o'clock, I'll give it to you for twenty bucks."

The man reached in his pocket, pulled out a money clip and removed a twenty.

"Here," he said, handing a surprised Magnolia the key. "It's room number eight. There are still a couple of clean towels in the bathroom."

He was sitting in the driver's seat of a large red and chrome flatbed truck in the motel parking lot when she came out of room number eight an hour and a half later. His arm, encased in a starched and pressed long-sleeved shirt despite the heat, rested on the sill of the rolled down window. A large ring was on his left hand. Magnolia could see the silhouette of another man sitting in the passenger's seat. In the bed of the truck were two shiny motorcycles.

"Would you like to have lunch?" he asked.

She hesitated. She had never done a threesome. Then she remembered that Magnolia Kanaranzi didn't do tricks.

"No, thanks."

"Do you have anything left from the money I loaned you?" the man asked.

Magnolia was stunned. She hadn't remembered him.

"Yes. I have some," she said. "Do you want it back now?"

"No. But in case you ever can pay it back, here's my card. I didn't have one with me the other night, and you probably don't remember me."

She reached up and took the card. "Arthur Kincaid. Communications Consultant."

He started the truck.

"Art," Magnolia shouted. "How much did I borrow?"

"It's Arthur," he replied, "and it was two hundred dollars."

"Thanks," she said. "I'll send you the money as soon as I can."

Kincaid nodded. "Are you sure you don't want to have lunch with us?" he said. "We're just going over to the Best Western."

She hesitated.

"No strings attached?" she said.

"Same strings as the loan," he said.

"Okay," she said.

Kincaid and his friend were on a month-long tour. Sturgis was their first stop, then the Grand Canyon, then the California coast. Magnolia went with them as far as Las Vegas. Enroute, Kincaid called someone he knew and arranged a job for "Maggie" as a hostess at a casino. "Why would you do that? You don't know me," she said.

"No, I don't. But I see someone with a lot of moxie who just needs a little help."

She looked at him. "Where'd you get that idea?"

"I watched you turn down two hundred dollars to screw some guy in that bar, and then try to borrow it from him. I figured anybody with that much moxie deserved the two hundred dollars."

"I was stoned."

"Maybe so, but I'm impressed by entrepreneurs, even when they're stoned."

Part of Magnolia's new job was a requirement that she go through an outpatient program for addiction.

"Don't screw this up, Maggie," he'd told her just before he left Las Vegas. "This is your chance to start over. You're smart and you have good instincts when you're sober. You have a lot to offer someone. Make this work, Magnolia Kanaranzi, and you never know what your future might hold."

She had hung on to that speech. The way he had said it stirred memories of her own childhood when she was bright and energetic and full of potential. It was the first time in years someone told her she was worth something.

She kept the job. She got clean. She rented her own apartment. She turned thirty. She had a boyfriend but felt neither the need nor the desire to live with him. She hired a shrink to deal with her past. It was painful. Too painful, at times, for her to deal with. At those times she would call Kincaid. The calls were never long, never romantic, but they always got her past the crisis.

Magnolia hadn't needed to make one of those calls for months. She had been made a pit boss which meant she could pay her bills without skimming from the house. She worked long hours, so her social life suffered, but she really didn't care. She liked being independent and sober.

Then Kincaid showed up at one of the blackjack tables where she was supervising.

"Magnolia Kanaranzi. Italian royalty, I believe."

She spun to see Arthur sitting at the table, a broad smile on his face. It had been nearly three years since he had left her in Las Vegas. The ring of tables prevented her from rushing to hug him. Instead, using the emotional control that she had learned on the street and refined in the pit, she called the floor boss to cover for her, ducked out of the ring of tables, walked over to where Arthur Kincaid was sitting, stood him up and gave him a full body hug. Her head barely came to his chin.

"This man," she announced to anyone within earshot, "is my guardian angel." Tears welled up in her eyes.

The reunion was joyous. They caught up with what each had been doing. It became apparent that Kincaid had been keeping track of her from afar. She told him that she had been clean for twenty-six months. He told her that he had inherited his father's newspaper and was building a media empire.

"I want you to leave Las Vegas and come to Boston with me," he said.

She was shocked. They had never had sex. They hadn't even kissed. The most intimate thing they'd ever done was hug an hour ago.

"Are you asking me to marry you?"

It was Kincaid's turn to look surprised.

"No. I'm asking you to come to work for me."

"That's a relief," she said. She meant it. Arthur may be her guardian angel, but she was not ready to give up her newly found independence. "I love you, Arthur, but not in that way," she said.

"That's good," he said, "because if we were romantically involved, I couldn't hire you. In my world, business and romance don't mix."

She thought for a minute. "What would I be doing?" she asked.

"In the beginning, you would serve as my personal assistant, travel with me, be an extra set of eyes and ears, take care of details. Over time you'll learn my business and, if you show the aptitude, become more involved."

"Are you sure you want to do this?" she asked. "You don't know me. I could turn out to be a huge embarrassment. How do you know I can even do what you're asking?"

"When I met you in Sturgis you were a wreck, but you still showed control and the brass to try and make a deal," he said. "I had a good feeling about you. When we ran into each other a second time in that motel I knew that it had to be more than just coincidence. I tried to give you a chance. You took it, and look at you now. You're clean. You're successful. You're strong and independent. You even legally changed your name."

"How did you know that?" Magnolia asked, surprised by what she had thought was a well-kept secret.

"I know a lot about you, Maggie. I've made it my business to know you. I know about your past, about the drugs and the alcohol and the run-ins with the legal system. I know that you have fought your way out of that on your own. It's made you stronger. I know that you are in the perfect position to accept a new challenge. And I know that I will never have to question your loyalty."

She fought back tears. *What did this man see in her that she couldn't see in herself?*

"When do you want me in Boston?" she asked.

Kincaid's cancer had been denied, battled and finally accepted. Arthur and Magnolia knew it would end his life at some point, and they had been slowly, sometimes painfully, preparing for it. The stroke, on the other hand, had come without warning. Now he was on life support, too weak to be flown to the United States for treatment. The doctors seemed reluctant to do anything more than keep him comfortable—perhaps because of his frail condition, perhaps because of his cancer, perhaps because of the shortcomings of Spanish medical services. Perhaps because nothing could really be done.

To complicate matters further, Magnolia had confirmed with the hotel operator that Kincaid had not made a call to the United States on the day of the stroke. Now, she was faced with the prospect of having to deal with MacMillan on the issue of the painting. It would only serve to convince him that he had been right all along: she was nothing more than a gold digger.

MAY 27, 2009, NOON

SAINT PAUL

He decided to leave the Vermeer in the oven until after lunch, if for no other reason than to have an excuse to end the lunch meeting with "Mrs. Robinson." That was the nickname Jim Benson had given Elaine Ravalo a year ago when Blethen had confided in him about their ribald affair.

"Just like Dustin Hoffman and Anne Bancroft in *The Graduate*," Benson had said. Thinking the reference was comical, Blethen started referring to her by that name, except when he was talking to her. Then he called her Elaine.

His arrival at the exclusive club exactly at noon caused a momentary stir. Blethen was the only person of color in the room who wasn't in wait-staff uniform, leaving them unsure whether to have him wait for Elaine who was, of course, fashionably late, or to seat him. The *maître d'* quickly assessed the situation and, deciding that it wouldn't do to have him standing by the entry as club members and their guests arrived for lunch, seated him in the farthest corner of the mahogany-paneled dining room.

Finding the consternation his presence caused both sad and comical, Blethen waited as the clock ticked. He was actually pleased with the location of the table. At least it wouldn't make him and Elaine the center of attention he thought, but neither the table's location nor the prospect that she would be seen by friends of her husband deterred Elaine.

"Dahling, Hamilton," she bellowed as she swept through the dining room to their table, drawing disapproving stares from the stiff-necked patrons. Blethen rose and braced himself as she bore down on him, the *maître d'* three steps behind. She engulfed him in a bear-hug. "So wonderful to see you again, dahling," she said, her voice only a few decibels lower even though she was speaking into his ear.

"May I get you something, Mrs. Ravalo," the now-obsequious *maître d'* asked as he pulled out her chair.

Over glasses of Chablis, Elaine oozed over both Blethen and the young waiter who served them, even though the waiter's Y chromosome appeared to be somewhat underdeveloped. She was aware of the whispering from the patrician luncheon crowd, and she punctuated her conversation with booming laughter and touchy-feely attentiveness, as though to purposely bring attention to her lunch with a handsome, dark-skinned man roughly half her age.

Both embarrassed and peeved at being used in this fashion, Blethen, nevertheless, managed to eat lunch and conduct business.

With the baking Vermeer as his excuse, Blethen terminated the lunch after two hours. He left with a hefty four-figure check and an appointment for her first sitting as Elaine, still seated at the table, ordered a fourth glass of wine while pawing at the flustered waiter.

Over centuries, as oil paintings age, they develop fine cracks in their paint called craquelure. Art forgers invested thousands of hours developing a technique that enabled them to duplicate craquelure in just a few hours. The process was a well-guarded secret until a forger named Eric Hebborn broke the code of silence by writing *The Art Forger's Handbook,* making the craquelure duplication process, and a whole lot more, public knowledge. There was much speculation that the book was also the reason for his violent death.

Perhaps it was over-kill to put craquelure in a copy, but for Blethen it was a matter of professional pride to deliver a painting that was as close to the original as he could make it. He created craquelure in all the old masters he copied, and it set him apart from his competitors.

As *Girl with the Pearl Earring* cooled and the paint fissured, Blethen consigned it to old age by dusting the painting with the ashes saved from his victory cigar. When completely cool, he blew off the excess ashes and then lightly brushed the painting with a soft, horsehair brush. Once the client framed the work, covering his name, it would take more than a visual inspection to distinguish Blethen's *"Girl"* from Johannes Vermeer's three-hundred-twenty-five-year-old original. He packaged the canvas and called UPS for a pickup, then left a message for his client telling them their painting was on its way.

Elaine's check put Blethen in an optimistic mood. Completing the painting gave him a sense of contentment. Today he'd hit the daily double, so, with the check in his pocket and the Vermeer nestled at the UPS pickup spot, he put Barca on his leash and they went for an evening s and s ("stroll and sniff" for those who don't speak "Barca"). He deposited the check via the twenty-four-hour ATM, and, with cash in his pocket and a spring in his step, they meandered down Grand Avenue, stopping only at the pharmacy to pick up the photos, until drawn to a cluttered storefront by the aroma of fresh coffee. Barca dutifully sat by the open doorway as Blethen went in to investigate. Ten minutes later he came out with iced coffee, a biscotti and the vinyl soundtrack from *The Graduate.* He shared the biscotti with Barca as they reversed course and headed back toward home, stopping only to pick up a six-pack of Heineken.

As they listened to Simon and Garfunkel, Blethen sipped a Heineken and scratched Barca's ears, whose head lay on his master's lap. It was a rare night. He was happy to be home, just Barca and him. Today he liked his life. He was lucky enough to have his hobby as his profession. It had its economic ups and downs, but generally it provided enough money to support his simple lifestyle. He had friends who he enjoyed and who, at least, tolerated him. He did what he wanted, when he wanted. His roommate was loyal, loving and always happy to see him. They never had to "talk." The only games they played were fetch and tug-of-war. He didn't care that there was no call from Kincaid. Truthfully, he was happy to be relieved of the million-dollar temptation.

If, at age thirty-eight, his life couldn't get better, then why did his thoughts keep drifting back to Toni Chapereaux? He puzzled over the enigma.

THURSDAY, MAY 28, 2009

Blethen called her. "Want to have lunch?"

They met in Minneapolis at the Monte Carlo, a place with a Miro painting on the wall by the hostess stand, frequented by Blethen because of its bourbon selection.

"I thought you'd enjoy the art in light of your research," he said to Toni, referring to the Miro as she joined him. "Doesn't look like my deal to paint one of his works is going to work out, though."

"You mean you paid me for no reason? I'm sorry."

"Money well spent," he said. "Otherwise, we wouldn't have met." She smiled.

"Can I ask which of his paintings you were being asked to do?"

"It's called *El Segador, The Reaper* in English." He didn't see any harm in telling her now that the potential gig had disappeared.

Over a pair of rare steak sandwiches, they spent the next hour looking at the photos that Blethen had taken in his studio. Eventually they chose three that he would use as his guide to recreate on canvas the intangible cachet of his lunch date.

"I'm really honored that you're going to paint me," Toni said, "Can I ask what style you're planning to use?"

"Because you liked the French woman in the park, I'm leaning toward impressionism, maybe in the style of Renoir, but I'm not positive. For me, style tends to naturally evolve. Usually when I start out with a specific style in mind the content of the painting changes it before I'm done. Maybe that's why most of my original stuff is crap."

"There was nothing crappy about the woman and the greyhound," Toni responded, not surprised by his negative assessment of his own work. With a pixie smile, she tilted her head and held up both hands, palms up, making Blethen laugh. "And this one won't be crappy either. How could it be?"

"You're right. With you as model, it will be the next *Mona Lisa*—with orange hair." They both laughed, drawing the attention of the handful of late lunch patrons. *What is it about her,* he thought. *I'd be embarrassed if I were with Elaine, but I'm not with Toni.* He wished lunch wouldn't end.

He invited her to go to the Twins game with him. "The Red Sox are in town," he said, but she demurred.

"This is my social outing for the day. I need to study. Paper to write, laundry to do."

"I usually play second fiddle to laundry," he replied with a grin. "How about if I come to your place tomorrow night and bring Chinese? You have to eat, and that way you won't have to take the time to fix anything. I promise I won't stay long."

"Why Mr. Blethen, did I just see a trace of domesticity?"

"Guilty as charged," he said.

They parted in the parking lot with a full body hug and a lingering kiss. Blethen knew he wasn't going to accomplish anything productive the rest of the day with that memory lingering. He went back to St. Paul and took Barca for a walk.

As Barca sniffed at yet another tree, he punched number one on his speed dial. It rang several times before a warm old voice, filled with good memories and the aroma of fresh bread and cookies, answered. "Hello," the voice said.

"Hi, Grandma. It's Ham. Let me be the first to wish you happy birthday."

"Why thank you, Hamilton, but my birthday isn't until next week. How have you been?"

"Just fine, Grandma. How about you?"

"I'm fine dear," she said, her standard response. "It's so nice to hear your voice. Tell me what you've been doing recently."

"Pretty much the same. Selling a few paintings. Making a living. I was wondering when it might be convenient to come and see you. We could spend the day together. I'll take you out to dinner to celebrate."

"That would be very nice, dear," she responded. "When would you like to come?"

"How about a week from Saturday?" It would give him time to buy her a gift.

"You can help me plant some flowers," she responded. "That nice

Mr. Adams said he would take me to the nursery next week to buy annuals. Saturday will be a perfect day to plant."

"That's great, Grandma. I would love to help you. Is it okay if I bring someone with me?"

There was a pause.

"Of course, my dear," she said. "May I ask who?"

"I have a new lady friend. I'd like you to meet her."

Another pause…longer.

"Of course, dear. I'd love to meet her." Even Grandmas don't always tell the truth. The last "lady friend" Blethen took to meet his grandmother had turned out poorly. As they had been leaving, his Grandmother took him aside and asked, "Is this the person who you want to be with?"

Despite his affirmations that she was, it turned out that she wasn't. They had split up by the time he talked to his Grandma two weeks later.

"I didn't think she was the right person for you," she had said in her usual, kind tone of voice.

"Why? he asked, "Because she was immature?"

"That, too, dear, but mostly because she stole the snow globe that I always kept in my curio cabinet." She said it in such a matter-of-fact manner that it took Blethen a moment for it to register.

"The one that you got when you went to New York?" he shouted into the phone.

"Yes, dear," she said calmly. "I didn't think you'd want to spend your life with a thief."

With some difficulty, and a great deal of mutual hostility, he retrieved the stolen snow globe from his ex-lady friend and returned it to Grandma. She thanked him by baking fresh cookies which they jointly devoured while watching the fake snow swirl around the Empire State Building.

"This one is different," he assured her. "She's the most honest, open woman I've ever met. I'm sure you won't have to hide your snow globe. And you'll love her."

"I'm sure I will dear." Her words said one thing, but the tone in her voice was a reminder that his history with women, from the time he was abandoned by his mother, had been a series of disasters.

FRIDAY, MAY 29, 2009

He decided against Chinese takeout. Instead he found an Asian market and spent the afternoon shopping. He called Toni in the late afternoon. "Do you have a wok?" he asked.

"I do, but it's never been used."

"Great. Is it okay if I bring Barca? He's been alone a lot lately."

"Of course."

She lived in a small house in south Minneapolis with a roommate. Thankfully, he was gone for the weekend.

"He's not around much," Toni explained. "Has a girlfriend that he mostly lives with. Best of all worlds for me. We split the rent and he's seldom here."

She was dressed in shorts and a sleeveless tee, barefoot. She kissed him on the cheek, rummaged in the kitchen with him to find the wok, gave Barca a good tousling and poured sake from a pitcher sitting in a pan of hot water.

"This should keep you warm while I finish my paper," she said, handing him a glass. "You do your thing, master chef, and I'll be done in an hour or so. If dinner is ready before I'm finished, just let me know." She went into what he presumed to be her bedroom and closed the door.

Blethen happily spent the next hour chopping and stir-frying, flipping tidbits to Barca, and humming tunes by Simon and Garfunkel. Toni came out once, to refill her sake glass. Blethen, one refill ahead of her, was starting to feel a buzz. He needed to eat.

As if called by an internal dinner bell, Toni came out of her bedroom just as Blethen was stirring hot chilis into the stir fry. He refilled their sake glasses, put two Asian salads on the table and invited her to be seated. He turned the heat under the wok to low, stirred it once more, and sat.

"*Bon appétit.*" He raised his glass in toast and admired how the nipples of her small breasts stood out when she hoisted her glass in response.

"This is scrumptious," she said as she dug into the stir fry. "Just the right amount of heat."

They talked about Blethen's culinary prowess and her lack thereof; about Barca, whose long nose favored Toni's leg rather than Blethen's; and about her family in France, and how close they all were. There was going to be a family reunion and Toni was going.

Blethen got up to clear the table when they'd both finished eating. Toni, clearly enjoying being pampered, and the sake buzz, sat and pushed the remainder of her salad around the bowl, talking.

"You should come with me to the reunion. Meet my family," she said. Ordinarily, that sort of statement would lock and load Blethen's defense mechanisms but, oddly, he smiled.

"It would be fun," she said, her words slightly slurred. "You'd like my family, and you'd get to see Albi, the beautiful part of France. We could go to the Toulouse-Lautrec museums. He was born in Albi, and there are three or four museums full of his work there. Besides, if you come I won't have to spend the whole week explaining why I don't have a man in my life."

"So, you just want to use me," Blethen teased.

She sat with her chin on her hand, gazing at him, the twinkle in her eyes turning her face into mischief. "Of course," she giggled.

"It would depend upon what I've got going on," Blethen countered, turning serious, trying to process her proposition and his own uncharacteristic reaction.

"You said you finished the *Girl with the Pearl Earring*, and your Miro deal fell through."

"I've got another gig. Painting a Gainsborough for an old client." He poured more sake and tried to explain Elaine Ravalo, including her unique method of delivering payment. He emphasized his concern about having a private sitting. He omitted any mention of their raucous affair, now more than a year dormant.

"How 'bout if I help you out with yer friend, Elaine," Toni slurred.

Blethen gave a quick headshake as if he hadn't heard her correctly. "What?"

"I'll make you a deal. How 'bout if I come over and hang out during her sitting? Jus' for your protection. In exchange, you come to Albi with me."

He leaned across the table to kiss her. She wrapped both arms around his neck, her tongue was down his throat and his hand was inside her tee-shirt. Then, as suddenly as it started, it stopped. She pulled away.

"You wou'n't take advantage of a girl who's had too much to drink, wudju?"

She kissed him again, without the tongue and with less passion.

"You take yer big dog and go home, now. We'll continue thish when we're sober."

To say he had never met anyone like Toni Chapereaux was the understatement of the year.

SATURDAY, MAY 30, 2009

BARCELONA

Kincaid's condition had slightly improved. He could now utter a few words and move his right arm. He recognized MacMillan and, after a few questions from the attorney and the attending doctor, they agreed he was sufficiently aware of what was going on to conduct business. Macmillan, Kincaid and Magnolia had dealt with the most urgent issues before exhaustion overtook Kincaid and jet lag caught up with MacMillan, sending him back to his hotel for a nap.

An hour later a nurse woke Kincaid to check on his condition. When she left, Magnolia finally had an opportunity to talk to him about *The Reaper.* She retold him the story of the missing Miro painting, their plan to replicate it and gift it to her as part of his estate. It took several minutes for Kincaid's synapses to connect, but, once the story completed its journey through his damaged brain, he summoned MacMillan.

"Transfer…million dollars…to Maggie's trust to pay for…painting. *Reaper*," he said. "Make sure painting…goes…to Maggie."

"Yes, Arthur. I'll get right on it," the lawyer said matter-of-factly. "If you are still alive when the painting is done, you can give it to her as a gift and we'll tear up the codicil. Otherwise, I'll make sure she gets ownership through your estate." MacMillan didn't sugarcoat his words. It was one of the things Kincaid had always liked about him.

"This was your idea, wasn't it?" MacMillan growled as he and Magnolia left Kincaid's room.

"Arthur and I heard about *The Reaper* from Agusti Puig, the chef at the restaurant where you ate dinner last night," she said. "A relative of Agusti's was director of the pavilion where the painting had been exhibited before it disappeared. Arthur and I agreed that it provided an opportunity."

"An opportunity for you." MacMillan said. "A million-dollar expense for Arthur."

"Arthur wanted to leave me half of his estate," she responded, ignoring MacMillan's accusation. "I convinced him to just give me the painting."

MacMillan snorted. "Which you will sell for ten or twenty million dollars."

"If I sell it, or if I don't, what difference does it make to you?" she responded. "Whatever I get for the painting, *if* I ever sell it, will be a fraction of what he would have given me otherwise."

"The difference it makes to me," MacMillan said, his decibel level rising, "is that you are asking me to participate in a crime. You are asking me to broker a forged painting."

"I am doing nothing of the sort," she whispered, motioning for the attorney to keep the volume down. "Arthur is making a gift of the painting to me. *He* is telling *you* to pay a painter and to deliver it to me. What I do with it is of no concern to you."

"We'll see about that," he said, turning his back to her and walking down the hospital corridor.

Magnolia felt her jaws clench but refrained from responding to the receding back of the lawyer. She stepped back into the hospital room to check on Kincaid. His pain medication had transported him into a deep sleep, unperturbed by their loud voices.

She opened her purse and removed a business card, then picked up the phone. She dialed the number on the card.

"Office of Henri Hawke. May I help you?"

SAINT PAUL

Toni called. She was going out with colleagues from the graduate art center. "Want to come join me?" she asked. When she added, "I want to show you off to my friends," he agreed.

Blethen walked into the Artists' Quarter a few minutes after seven and squinted through the dim lighting of St. Paul's premier jazz bar. Toni was seated at a table with six or seven others. He swivel-hipped his way between the closely packed tables, through the early evening crowd, stopping at the bar to collect a beer. Toni's group appeared to be involved in a serious debate, and she didn't see him until he was standing beside her. Sensing his presence, she looked up and, with a happy smile dancing among her freckles, stood and slid her arm around his waist, then planted a kiss flush on his lips.

"This is my new friend," she announced to the rest of the table. "Ham Blethen, meet…". She introduced everyone at the table, but with his head spinning from the unexpected nature of his welcome, he didn't remember a single name. Someone grabbed a chair from an adjacent table and wedged it in the circle next to Toni's chair. Blethen sat, prepared to explain how they met, his occupation, etc., etc., but surprisingly, none of them asked the expected questions. They were far too deep into the issue of political funding of the arts, or lack thereof. The National Endowment for the Arts had again come under fire from conservative politicians and now the news media had taken up the cudgel.

Toni was among the most frequent contributors and more reasonable voices in the debate. While most of her compatriots were raging at the establishment for the current economic plight of arts, she looked at the issue from the perspective of someone who was more than just another starving student artist. When challenged, she defended her statements with facts, and, for the most part, when she spoke the others listened. Occasionally, she challenged some of her table-mates to support their loud, general diatribes with facts and reasoning. Most of them just wanted to be angry.

Blethen found himself watching, listening and admiring Toni. This young woman, whom he had known for less than two weeks, was quite special for reasons he had not expected.

"I understand you're a painter."

The question, coming from the person who had been sitting next to Toni before Blethen's chair had been wedged between them, caught Blethen by surprise. He appeared to be the youngest member of the group, tall, thin, sandy hair and the least involved in the discussion.

"Toni says you're a painter, an artist," he repeated.

"Yes. I am," Blethen replied, trying to remember his name from the introductions.

"What type of work do you do?" he asked, his voice barely audible above the din of the busy jazz club.

"I've painted a lot of things. Still lifes, landscapes, portraits. Mostly oil on canvas," Blethen said, trying purposely to be vague.

"What do you do besides paint?"

"I don't understand what you mean."

"To make a living, what else do you do to make a living? You know: insurance salesman, waiter, professional gigolo." There was no trace of humor in his voice, and the way in which it was delivered irritated Blethen.

"I just paint."

"You must really be good," he said with no intent of flattery. "I don't know anybody who makes a living just from their painting, unless, of course, they paint houses."

"I do all right, and I don't paint houses."

"Is there some gallery where I can see your work?" He continued to poke at Blethen.

Blethen wanted to tell him that he could go see his work in a museum under the name Jan Steen or Caravaggio, but he was spared by the jazz group that chose that precise moment to start its first set, drowning out everything including the disagreeable questions and the ongoing debate on artistic funding.

They ordered one more beer, listened for a little bit, and then left.

"Who was the young fellow sitting next to me?" he asked Toni.

"Todd D'Anselmo. He's in his first year of graduate study. Why?"

"He asked me a bunch of questions about what I do. I didn't tell him anything other than I was a painter. I didn't want to say anything until I talked to you."

"I don't understand," she said. "Why would you need to talk to me before talking to him?"

"Because I don't know how much you told them about me or what I do. He was really sarcastic, like he thought I was lying about making a living by painting."

"I'm not sure I've told Todd anything, but it's common knowledge in the department that I worked for you and that you're a painter, and I guess people now know that we're seeing each other socially.

"So, you haven't said anything about me being an art copier?"

"No," she replied. "It didn't occur to me that it was something they'd want to know. It's up to you to tell them as much or as little as you want about what you do."

"Okay. I just wanted to make sure I didn't put you in any compromised situation."

"Don't worry about Todd," she said, shaking her head. "He's a little creepy, but he's harmless."

On their way to Mickey's Diner for comfort food to soak up the beer, Blethen paused beside a black car with a gold bird painted on the hood.

"Smokey and the Bandit," he said. "Did you see it?" Toni hadn't.

"Iconic movie. Burt Reynolds and Sally Fields," he said. The car in the movie was called Smokey. A 1977 Trans Am just like this one. You don't see many of them anymore."

They sat at Mickey's waiting for their order and the conversation drifted to Elaine Ravalo.

"When are you going to do that?" Toni asked about the sitting.

"Monday."

"I was serious last night," she said. "I will come to your place during the sitting, if you think it would help you; for your protection, of course." Her eyes twinkled and little smile lines appeared.

"It's hard to paint when I have to continually be dodging my model," he said.

"Everything must be *hard* if your model is groping you," she laughed, very much intending the pun. "Have you ever painted in the nude?"

"What? No."

"I think it's only fair," she chided. "If your model is nude, you should be too." Her straight-faced assertion painted an entirely different picture of being chased by "Mrs. Robinson."

They laughed until tears rolled down their cheeks, causing others in the diner to look and then look away. They simultaneously started to speak but dissolved again into laughter as the visual kept bouncing and jiggling. Finally, catching his breath, Blethen said: "The sitting doesn't require her to be nude, so I guess I can keep my clothes on, but, if you're willing, I'd like you to be there."

Their meatloaf sandwiches arrived, and the conversation took a different tack.

"I'm going to visit my Grandma a week from today," Blethen said. "To celebrate her eightieth birthday. I'd like it if you'd come along."

Her shoulders sagged a centimeter.

"Oh, Ham," she said apologetically. "I can't. That's the day I'm leaving for France. I was hoping you were coming with me. I was serious last night."

"Oh, shit! I didn't realize your reunion was so soon."

They tried to cover their mutual disappointment with small talk, but the glow of the evening had fizzled. When Ham dropped Toni at her car he asked, "Are you still going to come over Monday?"

"Of course," she said.

SUNDAY, MAY 31, 2009

BARCELONA

Magnolia sat alone in the lobby bar of Hotel Majestic, her face partially obscured by a broad-brimmed hat. She sipped a glass of Albarino and watched the noisy cocktail-hour crowd.

"Would you like to order, Señora," asked the white-clad waiter.

"Just another glass of wine for now. I may have something later."

She kept her weight around 110 pounds; too thin Arthur had said. Now, with advancing age, her lack of body fat served to accentuate sagging skin, one of the tolls of her early lifestyle.

She had never thought of herself as old until Kincaid's stroke, but the suddenness of his deterioration brought into focus the thin thread by which life hangs, and the weight of trying to juggle his last wishes with her own desires forced her to confront the vagaries of time. *If we had a few more months, maybe a year, we would have had everything arranged.* But time was capricious, plus there was Byron MacMillan. It was wearing her down. She wanted to run away from it all, but she couldn't. There were things that needed to be done.

By Saturday Kincaid had recovered sufficiently to communicate, usually in a shaky scrawl on a note pad, occasionally in a raspy, slurred whisper, but before Magnolia found the right time to ask him about the painting MacMillan arrived, controlling the conversation and the purse strings. Kincaid had absolute faith in MacMillan, and she had never witnessed anything that would suggest he was anything other than Arthur's loyal *consigliere*.

In the beginning, when she was primarily an observer and companion, he ignored her. As she grew more knowledgeable about the business she would occasionally offer an idea or an opinion. He opposed her at every turn, telling her more than once that she added nothing worthwhile to the conversation and frequently referring to her as "nothing but a gold digger." His bluntness silenced her until one day she gathered the courage to complain to Kincaid about how MacMillan treated her.

"You are going to meet people in business who are bullies, Maggie, who don't like you, who don't respect you," Kincaid had said. "You need to learn how to handle those situations. You need to learn when to speak your piece and not back down; when to advocate your position and when to compromise; when to take them out of the picture, if necessary. You don't learn to do that by going into a shell."

She had always wanted to tell Arthur how grateful she was for that advice, and for all he had done for her, but she never had, and now there was no time for pleasantries or small talk or thanks—only for the things that needed to be done immediately, things that they'd both thought they had time to accomplish.

She had stood up to MacMillan, and, as Arthur started to take her point of view into consideration more frequently, she could sense MacMillan's growing hostility. Now she feared what he might do when Arthur died. She had once thought about getting a lawyer of her own but that seemed wrong as long as Arthur was still alive. He had done so much for her, taught her things, built her self-respect, made her everything that she was. To start consulting with lawyers after all that seemed disloyal, but now he was dying and her future might soon be at the mercy of MacMillan. She was sure he would show her none.

Halfway through her second glass of Albarino, a short man in an oversized suit shuffled up to her table. "Magnolia Kanaranzi?"

She nodded.

"Henri Hawke at your service." He offered a soft, well-manicured hand. His heavily pomaded hair was parted down the middle, his skin smooth and oiled. By reputation, he was one of Barcelona's most formidable criminal defense lawyers. More importantly for Magnolia, he was a fixer.

ST. PAUL

"Barca misses you."

"Oh, really? Just him?"

"Well, maybe me too. Just a little."

With that exchange, Toni accepted Blethen's invitation to dinner.

"How do you like your steak?" he asked.

"Medium rare. I'll bring a bottle of wine. And floss."

"What?"

"Floss, in case the steak gets caught in our teeth, or in case I need it in the morning."

Blethen hesitated. "I don't have an extra tooth brush," he said.

"I'll bring mine."

Dinner was delightful with no emotional hangover from the previous evening.

"Who all is coming to your reunion?" Blethen asked as they washed the dishes.

"My parents and a couple of cousins from the States. Grandpapa, all my aunts and uncles and cousins that still live in France will be there, and some relatives from Belgium, and maybe even a cousin who lives in Africa," she said. The anticipation of the family gathering made her even more animated that usual.

"Sounds like a gathering of the United Nations."

"I think there will be about fifty of us," Toni continued. "Grandpapa will be ninety this year, and everyone is making an effort to be there."

"Does he live in Narbonne?" he asked, recalling her home town.

"No, Albi," she said. "The reunion is on my uncle's farm just outside of Albi. You should come-—after you celebrate your Grandma's birthday."

The suggestion caught Blethen off guard. He hadn't been in Europe since he'd finished at The Florence Academy of Fine Arts. Going back to Europe with a little money in his pocket was an appealing idea. But meeting her family? "I'd like you to meet my new friend. He's an art forger" would not be the suggested way of making new friends or influencing potential in-laws. Just the thought made him queasy.

"Maybe," he said. "Maybe, when I get paid for the Vermeer."

"If you come we could take a couple of days and go to Barcelona." Her excitement accelerated. "We could—"

His phone rang.

"Aren't you going to answer it?" she asked. Blethen shook his head.

"Old girlfriend?" she quipped with that delightful twinkle in her eyes.

"None of my old girlfriends talk to me anymore. They're all mad because I'm out of circulation."

"Bull!" She responded with a snort. "But, really, you should come. You would love my family. Unless you're planning to spend next week reassuring your old girlfriends."

"Hmmm. Now there's a thought," Blethen replied. "Perfect way to spend the week. Calling up women I've fought with in the past to tell them I have a new girlfriend. Should lead to some really nice conversations."

Toni grinned.

He smiled back at her elfin face, perfectly framed in flaming orange curls, sprinkled with freckles, inset with emerald eyes, sitting atop a long and graceful neck that he suddenly had the urge to kiss.

"We'll see," Blethen said, "but before I commit to spending a week with your family there's a serious question that has to be answered."

Toni looked at him quizzically.

"Does all of your family have hair issues?"

She threw her dish towel at him.

MONDAY, JUNE 1, 2009

The evening was memorable, but the span between finally falling asleep and waking up was way too short. The sitting was scheduled for 11:00 a.m., and, even though Elaine was always late, Blethen had less than an hour to get prepared.

Barca did his outdoor business in a hurry, as if knowing they didn't have time to dawdle. When they got back, coffee was perking and Blethen could hear the shower running. He poured two cups and sat one on the bathroom counter for Toni, fed Barca and then picked up clothes that had been dropped in various places the night before. By the time Toni came out of the bedroom dressed in jeans and a sweatshirt, the place was back in order.

"I haven't worn this style in a long time," Blethen grinned, bikini panties hanging on the end of his outstretched finger. "Found them in the living room. I'm guessing they belong to you."

"I wondered what happened to those. I remembered them, and then they just disappeared." She took them, stepped out of her jeans and into the panties, and pulled the jeans back up. "There. Ready to begin my day as your protector."

Blethen spent the next few minutes studying Gainsborough's *Duchess*, paying particular attention to the subtlety of the lighting on her face. He positioned a chair to take best advantage of the natural light. Several potential backdrops were selected, low-wattage spotlights readied in the event the natural light failed or needed enhancement.

Earlier he had done a pencil sketch of the painting, sans face. His task for the day was to draw Elaine's face into the sketch. One day should be adequate if all went as expected, but with "Mrs. Robinson" it was almost guaranteed that the unexpected would happen, so he had blocked out two days. The actual painting of the portrait would come later when he could hole up in his studio without distractions from panting clients or a seductive girlfriend.

Entering a room was always an opportunity for Elaine.

At precisely 11:17 the buzzer signaled she had arrived. Blethen pressed the button to unlock the outer door and stepped into the hallway to greet her.

She exploded through the door and swept up the hallway in a cloud of perfume, spiked heels and white fur.

"Hamilton, dahling," she gushed. "You look absolutely yummy in your artist's garb." He didn't want to burst her bubble by telling her his "artist's garb" was pretty much what he wore every day with the exception of the paint-stained apron. He offered to take her coat.

"You can take anything you want," she offered, slithering out of the coat as she walked through the apartment door, revealing steep cleavage and a skirt too short for her age.

Right on cue Toni came around the corner from the kitchen, stuck out her hand and said, "Hi. I'm Toni."

He did quick introductions and then watched an unexpected phenomenon unfold. Elaine never skipped a beat, talking to Toni as audaciously as she did to Blethen. It was like watching Rosalind Russell in *Auntie Mame.*

Toni was swept into the conversation and, within minutes, the two of them were trading stories like they'd been friends for years. Toni seemed to enjoy the banter with the older, larger, and richer-to-the-point-of-vulgarity woman.

"You are so lucky to have this handsome hunk in your bed," Elaine said, gesturing toward Blethen. "I've been trying to get him into mine, but he must have been saving himself for you!"

Without the slightest hint of embarrassment, Toni proceeded to tell Elaine about the attributes of Blethen's butt, the first thing, she said, that had attracted her to him.

"Why Hamilton, I think you're blushing," Elaine chortled, as she turned to look at him. "Why don't you turn around and give us a look at your cute little butt."

"You are the model today, not me," he responded, trying to sound whimsical while hoping his face wasn't as red as the heat he was feeling.

"Oh, come on. Give us girls one little guilty pleasure this morning," she chided. Toni looked on in amusement.

Slowly he turned his back to them, locked his hands behind his head, counted to three, and wiggled once.

"That's all you get," he said, then added, looking at Elaine, "We've got work to do and we need to do it while the light is good. Let's get started."

"Oh, pooh," she said, faking disappointment. "You are no fun. But, then, I suppose I am paying you to paint me, so let's have at it."

Toni and Elaine hugged and said how much they enjoyed meeting each other.

"I'm going back to my place to get some things done." Toni directed her statement to Blethen, but meant it for Elaine. "See you tonight?"

"I'll call you later," he said. "I love you." Toni hesitated, the door knob in her hand, then stepped into the hallway and closed the door behind her. Blethen and Elaine moved into his studio.

Blethen explained what they were attempting to accomplish, where she would be sitting, talked about lighting and showed her the sketch he'd done.

"She's really very exceptional, you know," Elaine said, paying little attention to his lecture. Blethen smiled as he continued his preparation.

"Very self-assured. I really like her," Elaine went on. "Of course, that doesn't mean I still don't want to get into your pants. Just for old time's sake." There was a twinkle in her eye, but no seriousness in her tone. They both knew that there was no chance that would happen again.

During the course of what turned out to be a very delightful afternoon, Blethen discovered a problem he hadn't anticipated. Elaine's face was rather angular and long, while Gainsborough's Duchess had a round face. The natural light started to fade about four thirty and it became apparent a second day would be necessary to complete the sitting, not because of Elaine, as he had anticipated, but because artistic integrity required it.

After Elaine left, he called Toni and left a message, then went back to his studio to ponder *Elaine, Duchess of Saint Paul,* his name for the painting. *How am I going to modify it so the difference in the shape of their faces won't be noticeable?* he wondered. For the first time in years he felt that he was being artistically creative.

The check for the Vermeer was in his mailbox, eliminating his ready-made excuse for not joining Toni in France. She called and said she was going to spend the night getting ready for her trip. The conversation was short, her voice lacking its usual verve. Blethen and Barca went for a walk under the street lights to think about it. The temperature had dropped precipitously in the wake of a cold front, making the air sharp in their lungs. He could see their breath when they exhaled.

Barca was ready to be done with the walk after fifteen minutes. Blethen was still considering whether to make the trip, and why Toni had seemed distant on the phone, when they rounded the corner.

Sitting in front of the triplex was a black Firebird like the one that he had admired outside Mickey's Diner.

He had covered about half the distance to the car when someone tall and gaunt with the gait of a young man came out of the door of the triplex, got in the Firebird and drove off. It looked like Todd D'Anselmo, although that would have been too much of a coincidence.

Barca and Blethen stood and watched the taillights recede. Blethen heard himself exhale. Apparently, he had been holding his breath. *Why did it feel like something wasn't right?*

He checked the mail boxes, opened the inner security door and looked up and down the hallway. Nothing appeared to be out of place. His studio door was locked, no sign of any attempt to force it open. He opened the door slowly and did an inventory of the apartment and studio. Nothing appeared to be missing.

God! Ever since that Reaper call my imagination has gone crazy. He was probably just visiting another tenant. Hell, it probably wasn't even him.

He made a vow to meet his neighbors when he got back from Europe.

TUESDAY, JUNE 2, 2009

BARCELONA

Henri Hawke's office on Ronda de Sant Pau was tiny and cluttered. He moved a pile of papers off the single wooden chair across from his desk and motioned for Magnolia to sit.

"Your meeting with this MacMillan person perhaps did not go so well?" Hawke asked, knowing that if it had, she would not be sitting in his office. She explained *The Reaper*, Arthur's intention to give it to her as a gift and MacMillan's opposition.

"And, so, how would you like me to help?"

Magnolia reached into her purse and took out a check, placing it on the desk in front of Hawke. "I would like to retain your services," she said, waiting for the fifty thousand dollar amount to register with Hawke.

He glanced at the check, then looked at Magnolia and nodded. His expression showed no evidence that he was impressed by the amount of the check.

"I assume that everything from this point forward is privileged communication," she said.

"Of course."

"I need Byron MacMillan removed. Immediately."

Hawke cocked his head. "Americans are always in such a hurry," he said. "Haste brings with it risk. We will have to discuss the fee."

"I thought…"

"That is only for my silence and my participation," Hawke said, nodding toward the check still lying on his desk. "For actual services, it will cost more."

"How much more?"

"Perhaps five times that much?"

She looked around the tiny office. Other than a framed diploma, only cheap art adorned the walls. Hawke's desk looked like a leftover from World War II, metal with a formica top. There was an old water stain in the corner of the ceiling.

"You certainly don't spend it to impress your clients."

"I am the best at what I do," he said. "A low profile is advantageous. My clients are impressed by the results I give them, not by a gaudy office."

"What if I made it three hundred thousand dollars?"

With the suggestion of increasing his already sizable fee, Magnolia finally got a visible reaction from Hawke—the cocking of one eyebrow.

"For which I would want you to do a bit more, though," she added. "Set up a stock corporation for me, and a trust. I also need you to prepare a codicil to an American will and a power of attorney that will stand up in the United States. I will need the codicil and the power of attorney by tomorrow morning. The stock corporation and trust by next week. I also will need you to work out the details with the artist who is painting *The Reaper.*"

Hawke rocked back in his chair. "I will need to be paid in advance."

"That's not possible. I can pay you another fifty thousand dollars next week, but I need the power of attorney to get the rest. Once MacMillan is no longer in the picture, and I have the power of attorney, I can have the remainder to you in a week."

An hour later she left Hawke's office. Magnolia felt powerful.

Byron MacMillan was the unfortunate victim of a mugging turned deadly on the dangerous streets of Barcelona. The *Policia* had no leads. From his hospital bed the next day, with an attaché from the U.S. Embassy in attendance to authenticate his signature, a grieving Arthur Kincaid signed a power of attorney, giving Magnolia Kanaranzi full control of his finances and his business empire.

SAINT PAUL

Elaine's sitting was completed the next day. The pencil sketch would take a bit more tweaking before he started applying paint, but that could be done without her presence. Photos of her, taken from various angles while the light was good, would be used as his final guide.

By the time she left in mid-afternoon he was psychologically exhausted. He called Toni and left a message: "I'll make dinner tonight if you'd like to come over. Maybe seven? Let me know."

A long walk with Barca took them to a grocery store on Grand Avenue. Blethen bought three small steaks and greens for a salad, then stopped at the adjacent liquor store and splurged on a twenty-dollar bottle of wine. When they got back the message light on his phone was blinking. Toni would be there for dinner.

Blethen took two small salads from the refrigerator and put them on the table as Toni came into the kitchen from the studio, her wine glass in her left hand and a strange, disquieting look on her face. The look had been there since she had walked in the door a half hour earlier. She sat down without saying a word.

"*Bon appétit,*" he offered, extending his wine glass. Their glasses clinked, but the sparkle was missing from her usually-crystalline green eyes.

Long silences replaced Toni's usual nonstop chatter, and only the occasional "please" and "thank you" mitigated the thickening atmosphere that was piling up over the table like summer thunderheads.

Over the steaks, including Barca's instant demolition of the third steak, they made small talk about Elaine's sitting and Toni's day, but it was distant, brittle.

What happened? What have I done? Blethen wondered. He had thought Toni was different, but this had that Deja vu feeling of previous relationships.

"What did I do?" he finally forced himself to ask.

"Too quick," she said.

"Too quick about what?"

"The 'I love you,'" she said.

"The what?"

"You said 'I love you' when I left yesterday. Too quick," she repeated in a whisper.

He wanted to say, "I meant it" but couldn't bring himself to say it. In his mind it sounded too glib. Instead he said: "I don't understand."

"Let's clean up. Then we can talk," she said.

He had heard similar words before and they always heralded bad news. The "talk" was always about something he had done, failed to do or didn't understand, or some need that wasn't being met, or some dire thing from the past that had to be talked about. Or "I need my own space," or "It's not about you. It's about me." What he knew, for sure, was the word *talk* meant he should listen, and that it always changed the relationship. For Blethen, it was a relationship funeral march, but in Pavlovian fashion he said what he always said: "Okay, let's talk."

After cleaning the table and doing dishes in silence, Blethen refilled their wine glasses and they sat in the living room on opposite sides, him in the thread-bare over-stuffed chair and her on the couch. She talked, not in her usual staccato manner but in a measured, thoughtful way.

"Love doesn't happen in a week," she started. "Lust, excitement, passion, those things happen in a week. Love takes time. My mother always compared love to a maple leaf. It bursts from the bud in the spring, strong and virile and hopeful. As summer advances, it grows, struggling with the bad weather or bugs or disease or whatever nature throws at it. If it survives, in autumn it turns brilliant, a vibrant red-orange. That is when true love is found, when it is the most beautiful of all."

The phone rang. Blethen let it go to voicemail.

"You and I are just barely into springtime," she continued. "We feel a physical attraction to each other, but that's not love. If we think so, we're only fooling ourselves." She shifted in her seat, looking for a comfortable position, before continuing. "The physical part will diminish over time. It's then we'll find out if we're in love, if we are willing to put in the time and effort to make it blossom into something truly beautiful and lasting."

Toni rolled the stem of her wine glass back and forth between her thumb and forefinger, staring into the deep red liquid. "The really difficult part, I think, is that we each need to be willing to sacrifice and compromise and forgive for the sake of love, while at the same time maintaining ourselves as individuals. That's particularly difficult for women because we have biology and history working against us. We give birth. We are the nurturers. Historically, we have been the passive partner."

Blethen sat, transfixed by her monologue. This was a "talk" unlike any he'd ever experienced.

"I think that lust and emotion now come more easily for women," Toni continued, "because part of equality is sexual freedom. But the fact that women are slowly becoming more equal probably makes real, long-lasting love harder. A long-term relationship for two people with strong personalities is difficult because of the amount of compromise and sacrifice required, and Type A personalities aren't built for that." She exhaled and looked down at nothing in particular, thinking.

After a moment she took a sip of wine and continued: "Without the long-term relationship, lust and emotion never have time to evolve into love. To use my mom's analogy, the damage done by a summer of bugs and disease and storms is too much. The leaf shrivels and falls off. It never has a chance to become brilliant. I've thought about it a lot, and I think it takes more than just a commitment to a person. I think it takes a commitment to the concept of love, itself. You need to want to live in a state of love more than anything because you know that love is, hands down, the best state to live in."

Her eyes locked onto Blethen's. "If people can do that, then the commitment does not require sacrifice or compromise at all but is really just part of the journey that gives us time to dwell in love, savor it, suffer its hurts, revel in its highs, and bask in its moments of contentment. Only when we can look at ourselves and say 'No matter what, I want to take this journey, and this is the person I want to take it with' can we really call it love."

She put her glass on the side table, sat back and, with her chin resting on her clasped hands, she looked at Blethen, her green eyes taking on a softness he had not seen before.

Blethen had never thought about love in those terms. In reality, he had never thought much about love at all. In those fleeting moments when the subject had crossed his mind it had always been, he now realized, about lust and passion which, at the time, seemed like love to him. The idea that love was something more than that, that it had to be worked on, that it took time and effort—that was as foreign to Blethen as a loving mother.

Toni searched his face, trying to discern his reaction to her speech. His face was passive, but his mind sorted through myriads of past relationships: other women, his grandma, his mother...*Now, that was a lesson in how love brings pain.* He thought. *Come to think of it, most of my past relationships with women have brought pain...to me or to them. Was it worth the effort if all it brought was pain?*

He knew that in the past he would have said no, but something felt different this time. Was he tired of one-night stands, of days and nights by himself? Was he getting old? Or was it this unique woman sitting across from him, her legs tucked underneath her, freckles beneath blazing hair, wise in things he never thought about, unique in ways he was sure he had yet to discover.

He was trying to formulate a response when Toni said quietly: "Let's go to bed and have sex. Let's enjoy the intimacy of each other, lose ourselves in lust and passion, but let's not call it love. Not yet."

They stood, locked little fingers and walked into the bedroom.

The sex was tender, gentle, deliberate. She was the guide, the muse, the choreographer.

They lay, exhausted and sated, Toni with her head on his outstretched arm making quiet, purring noises as she slept. Blethen, on his back, stared at the ceiling. A tear slid out of the corner of his eye and across his cheekbone.

WEDNESDAY, JUNE 3, 2009

The sunlight woke him.

Blethen stretched and realized that the space next to him was empty. He lay perfectly still and listened for movement in the apartment. He heard nothing. With panic rising in his chest he bolted out of bed, slid on shorts and quickly padded to the kitchen. A note by the coffee pot read: "Wanted to get an early start, sleepyhead. Still lots to do before I leave. Hope you're still thinking about coming. Last night was great!! Toni."

Panic subsided, but a tiny sliver of pain remained to remind him of what he could have lost.

He made a fresh pot of coffee and retrieved the morning *Pioneer Press* from the front step. The front page was all about a lost Air France flight with two hundred twenty-eight people on board. The Twins had beaten the Indians 4-3. He leafed through the paper looking for the Sudoku puzzle when he remembered the call from the previous evening. Fresh coffee in hand, he checked his phone messages.

"Mr. Blethen. My name is Henri Hawke. I represent Arthur Kincaid. Please call me at your earliest convenience."

Blethen let out a "woof" and sat down, his legs unable to sustain him, as if he'd been punched in the gut. With blood pumping and mind racing, he tapped in the phone number. After six rings the call was picked up.

"*Bonjour.*" The greeting was French but with an accent.

"This is Hamilton Blethen returning the call of Henri Hawke." The background noise sounded like a bar.

"*Bonjour*, Mr. Blethen. I am Henri Hawke."

A pause.

"You called me?"

There was a muffled gulp on the other end, as if he had just swallowed something.

"*Oui.*"

Blethen waited.

"This is not a good time, Mr. Blethen. May I call you tomorrow?" The words sounded a bit slurred, but it was difficult to tell with the accent.

"Sure."

Click.

What the hell? That was weird. Everything about this is weird.

Blethen went back to the Sudoku puzzle, but he couldn't concentrate. Despite his vow to ignore the crazy phone call, thoughts of a million dollars crept back into his head.

THURSDAY, JUNE 4, 2009

BARCELONA

A week earlier Magnolia had been devastated, her world turned upside down by Kincaid's stroke. Out of that devastation arose a plan. A plan that she, and she alone, had devised. All the hours of conversation with Arthur, all the strategy meetings, all the years of shadowing him had paid off.

The torch was about to be passed.

The police questioned her about MacMillan's "unfortunate accident." She, of course, knew nothing. The bankers, who had known Magnolia for years as Kincaid's smart and trusted assistant, didn't question the power of attorney giving her access to Kincaid's accounts. She was, after all, the logical person to take control. Likewise, the CEOs of the companies that Kincaid controlled agreed to call meetings of their respective board of directors when they learned of Kincaid's stroke. By the time the shareholder meetings were held she would have absolute power to vote the stock of each of the companies.

It would take a trip back to the States for her to fully assert control over the business operations, but that could wait. For the moment, being in command of Kincaid's personal accounts was enough.

After confirming that MacMillan had not acted on Kincaid's order to transfer the million dollars, Magnolia moved the funds into Hawke's trust account, with instructions that it be distributed only upon her authorization. She also paid Hawke an additional one hundred thousand dollars, with the promise that the remainder of his fee would be paid when the final arrangements for painting *The Reaper* were complete.

Now, sipping a glass of Albarino at Drolma, waiting for Juan Carlos to serve her a salad of artichokes, guinea hen and *foie gras,* Magnolia had time to reflect. Soon she would be one of the richest, most powerful women in the world. Arthur had groomed her well—taught her what it took to get there and how to stay there.

"There's bound to be collateral damage," he had once said as they celebrated the completion of a business transaction of dubious legality. She remembered those words now. That's what MacMillan had been, collateral damage. There would likely be more. It was the price to be paid by the losers.

She liked how she felt: strong, powerful, unconquerable.

Funny, she thought. *There was a time when I was so weak I wouldn't have dared to do this, or even to take a sip of wine.*

Arthur loved wine. One evening at dinner, several years after she had gone to work for him, Arthur ordered wine, as usual. She indicated she would like a glass, too, but couldn't. He encouraged her to have a glass, telling her he would be her coach and her conscience.

She drank one glass. She wanted a second but forced herself to refrain. *I can do this,* she had thought. That night she called Arthur at three in the morning. She needed help. He came and sat with her, and the next night as well. By the third night she got through it on her own.

Over the course of several years they had gone through the same sequence on multiple occasions. Each time her overwhelming desire, her addiction, had less grip on her. Now she could have a glass of wine or two without fear that it would spiral out of control. Arthur had said it was because of her strong character and willpower. Magnolia had always thought that she was just lucky—lucky to have Arthur and lucky that her body had somehow shrugged off the addiction after twenty years.

Now she thought that maybe Arthur was right.

A second glass of Albarino brought on a little buzz, and with it a wave of melancholy that eroded her confidence. Could she now find the courage to talk to him—to Hamilton, her son? Would being rich and powerful change how he would feel about her? Would he forgive her? She tried to imagine what he would look like. *Will he be tall? Handsome? Or small like me*? Her one memory was of a little boy standing next to his Grandma, confused, sad, afraid, but she could not bring his face into focus.

How could I have left him?

The question had haunted her for thirty-four years. It was her lone unresolved regret from her early life and she had felt powerless to deal with it. No amount of psychiatric treatment had been able to answer her question. "You were under the influence of a foreign substance." "You knew you weren't able to care for a young child." "You were planning on coming back for him." The shrinks and psychologists had been well-intentioned, but none of their justifications had made her pain go away.

On rare occasions she telephoned her mother to ask about him. The calls always sharply renewed the pain. After each call, she had to fight the hardest to stay straight. The last call had been seven years ago. By then, she knew that Ham had become an artist. Her mother berated her for failing to talk to him. She promised she would. She hadn't. She was afraid.

In her moments of depression, she longed for a way to show her love for him, to relieve her guilt, but she felt like that door had been locked long ago. Then a chance conversation revealed the key.

She and Kincaid were having a late dinner at Drolma during one of their frequent trips to Barcelona. The evening crowd had departed and they were the only customers left in the place, watched over carefully by a patient, professional staff that gave no sign that they wanted these last diners to finish so that they, too, could go home. Chef Agusti Puig came out of the kitchen and joined them, genuinely happy to see two of his regulars. They shared a glass of wine and the conversation turned to art. It was during that conversation that Puig shared the story of *The Reaper*.

"A distant cousin of mine was director of Spain's exhibit at the 1937 Paris World Exposition," Agusti said, explaining that the appointment had come primarily because his cousin was influential in convincing famous artists to do works for the exhibit despite the besieged Spanish government's bankrupt state. Among the artists was Joan Miro.

"Miro painted a mural he called *El Segador*," Agusti explained. "It was supposedly a tribute to a revolt of the Catalonian farmers in the 1600s, but it was done to inspire Catalonia to take advantage of the civil war and secede from Spain, or so the story goes."

Puig told of the riot that resulted in his cousin's death—about the heroic, but failed, effort to bring the painting back to Barcelona, and the disappearance of the painting after the exposition closed.

"The painting has never been found," he concluded. "I suspect it was destroyed by the Nazis, or by Franco's regime after the government fell."

"If that painting was found, what do you suppose it would be worth today?" Magnolia had asked.

Agusti and Arthur answered in unison: "Millions." And with that single word the seed of a plan began to sprout in her brain.

Over the following week she researched Miro, *The Reaper*, and the 1937 Paris World Exposition. She contacted an art curator she knew in Washington, D.C., and asked her to check out an artist named Hamilton Blethen. She believed he lived in Minnesota, or perhaps Chicago. The report came back. Blethen specialized in copying other artists' work. He was pretty good at that, but he hadn't produced anything original in years. He wasn't considered a serious artist by the art community.

The report fit her plan perfectly.

She had been lobbying Arthur for months to leave his fortune for charitable purposes and not to her. He had always been generous to her, compensating her well and including her with small interests in some of his business dealings. She had become comfortably wealthy in the thirty years she had worked for him and felt guilty about the prospect of inheriting his billion-dollar estate. That, she felt, was too much, and it would only confirm MacMillan's opinion of her. *The Reaper*, she hoped, would convince Kincaid to do as she asked.

As she and Arthur relaxed in the comfortable first-class seats on a trip back to Boston, she presented her scheme. They would hire an artist to paint *The Reaper*, pay him a large sum of money for the painting *and* to keep his mouth shut. Arthur could give her the painting as the sole gift to her from his estate. This could be done quietly without arousing any suspicion or publicity. The actual name of the painting wouldn't even have to be disclosed in the court papers.

If she ever needed money she could sell the painting. It would be years before that would happen, if ever, and the skeptics could trace the painting back to Arthur's estate as the source of her ownership. Arthur's reputation for nefarious business dealings, and a carefully contrived paper trail showing a million-dollar payment to an unknown recipient, would stymie investigators and give *The Reaper* sufficient provenance.

The plan had just enough larceny in it to intrigue Kincaid. The idea of turning a multi-million-dollar profit at the expense of snobby art-scene dilettantes appealed to him, as did the thought of giving Maggie a financial cushion. But what fascinated him the most was the prospect of creating controversy and intrigue long after he was gone, adding to his legend.

"Find someone to paint it," he said.

She already had.

Since Arthur had made the call to Blethen three weeks earlier Magnolia had dialed Blethen's phone number several times. Most of the time he didn't answer. When he did, she hung up, but she had heard the voice of her son. Instinctively she knew he hated her. He had to. Who wouldn't hate a mother who abandoned her child for a life of alcohol and drugs and crime? Would giving him financial security make him love her? Surely, her new stature would at least give her the strength to talk to him.

If he didn't forgive her, at least she would have his *Reaper.*

SAINT PAUL

The issue of whether Blethen was going to Europe was answered at precisely 6:30 a.m. Wrapped in a towel, with his hair still dripping from a morning shower, he picked up the receiver on the phone's fifth ring. "Ham Blethen," he answered.

"Mr. Blethen, my name is Henri Hawke. I am an attorney representing Arthur Kincaid. Mr. Kincaid has been indisposed and has directed me to assume all matters related to your services."

"I haven't agreed to provide any services to Mr. Kincaid," Blethen said, his tone a bit testy.

"I propose we discuss this matter in person." Hawke said, not acknowledging Blethen's response. "You will receive a ticket to Barcelona. Delivered tomorrow."

"Really. When am I supposedly going to Barcelona?"

"Tuesday," Hawke said without apparent concern for either Blethen's schedule or his piqued tone of voice. "The return flight will be open."

"I have business to attend to next week," Blethen replied, even though his schedule was open. "I couldn't possibly come until the following week."

There was a pause, and then: "I will tell Mr. Kincaid that you are not interested."

Blethen felt a million dollars slipping away. "What's so important about this painting that it can't wait another week," he said. "Your Mr. Kincaid is already a week late getting back to me."

"Mr. Kincaid is not a patient man," Hawke responded. "I will see if he will wait until next week."

"I thought he was indisposed and you're in charge. If you have to run to Kincaid every time there's an issue, then you're wasting my time. Let me talk to the man, himself. Or is this some sort of practical joke?"

"Very well," Hawke said after a lengthy pause, his voice showing no emotion. "I will send a ticket for the following week, Monday departure."

"Make it for Sunday, June 10, and send two tickets." Blethen pressed his advantage, surprised at his own aggressiveness. "I'm bringing an interpreter."

"I assure you I speak perfect English," Hawke responded flatly, still not betraying any emotion in response to the earlier insult.

"I don't need an interpreter for our discussions, but as long as I'm coming to Barcelona there is a significant amount of research that can be done on *The Reaper*, and I speak neither Spanish nor Catalan."

"Very well." The response was quick, matter-of-fact. "Give me the name of your interpreter."

"Antoinette Chapereaux."

"You will receive the tickets and other arrangements tomorrow," he said in monotone.

"I'll look forward to it."

This time Blethen was the first to hang up.

He took a deep breath and stood for a moment, naked, absent-mindedly drying his still-wet hair with the towel that had been wrapped around his waist. Smugly he replayed the conversation in his head. *I showed that legal prick he isn't dealing with some rube. Wait 'til I tell him the price for The Reaper just went up.*

Blethen was debating whether to call Toni when his phone rang.

"Want to go to a movie this afternoon?" she asked. He suggested *Inglorious Basterds*. She countered with *The Blindside*. They agreed on *The Lovely Bones* with Mark Wahlberg and Rachel Weisz. After the movie they stopped for burgers at the 5-8 Club on Cedar Avenue.

Over cold beer and onion rings ("terrible for you, but I can't resist them," she said), Toni was back to her usual self, rattling off a play-by-play of the events of her day, updating him on the progress of her dissertation, telling a funny anecdote about some absent-minded professor. Her green eyes danced. Her freckled smile lit up the room.

When their food arrived, Blethen could wait no longer.

"Well," he said. "I have good news, more good news and even *gooder* news."

She shifted in her seat to get comfortable, popped the last onion ring into her mouth, and focused the full measure of her green-eyed gaze on him.

"*Gooder*?" she asked. Blethen ignored her questioning his intentional syntax error.

"First, I'm coming to Europe..."

"Oh, Ham. That's awesome." She started to rise to hug him.

"Wait. Wait," he said, raising his hand to stop her before she could stand. "Second, *The Reaper* deal may be back on," he said. She sank back in her chair, the elation suddenly tempered.

"Third, I am going to Barcelona to work out the details, and I have a fully paid ticket for you to go with me."

"Wow!" was her tempered response. "When are you going to Barcelona?" Blethen had expected a more enthusiastic response.

"*We* are going on Sunday, June 10, a week from tomorrow. I have to be in Barcelona on Monday to finish the terms of *The Reaper* deal. We can drive to Albi either Monday night or Tuesday and spend the rest of the week with your family. After the reunion, I thought we'd go back to Barcelona and do some research on Miro and *The Reaper*."

"But I already have a round-trip ticket to Paris, leaving the ninth and coming back Sunday, the seventeenth."

"You can cancel your ticket and get your money back?" he said.

"I'd have to miss two days of the reunion."

"Hmm." There was a disappointed look in his eyes.

"I'm sorry," Toni said. "It's just that I've been looking forward to this for so long. I haven't seen my family in years."

"Sure. I understand."

"You could come to Albi after you're done in Barcelona," she pleaded. "You could take the train and I'd pick you up and take you out to the farm. I know you'd love my family."

"Would you come back to Barcelona with me after the reunion is over?"

"I can see if I can delay my return date. How long would we stay in Barcelona?"

"Probably three or four days," he said. "Just long enough to do some serious research on *The Reaper*."

They got a box for the uneaten half of Toni's burger and drove back to Toni's house, each lost in their own thoughts.

"Want to come in?" she asked as he pulled up in front of her house.

"Not tonight."

"I'm sorry," she said again. "I know you were excited about your good news and I kind of pooped all over it. Sometimes it's hard to balance two lives when you've been on your own for so long."

"Yeah. That goes for both of us. Sorry I'm being a prick about it. I'll get over it."

"I'll delay my return date if you'll promise to come to Albi," she said.

"Okay. See if you can do that."

FRIDAY, JUNE 5, 2009

The phone rang, waking him. With the eye not buried in his pillow Blethen read the red digits on his clock: 1:34 a.m. With a groan he rolled over and picked up the receiver. "Hullo." There was no answer. He could hear faint breathing. Then the connection was broken.

What the hell? Maybe it was a wrong number. Then he thought of Toni. He dialed her number. After several rings he got a sleepy: "H'lo".

"Toni. It's Ham. Did I wake you up?"

"Uh-huh."

"So, you didn't just call me."

"No."

"I'm sorry. I just got a phone call from a caller who hung up when I answered. I just wanted to make sure you were okay."

"I'm fine. Mus' have been a wrong number."

"You're probably right. Sorry I woke you up."

"Thas okay," she blurred her words sleepily. "Thanks for thinking of me."

"No problem," was his perfunctory answer. "Goodnight."

"Goo'night," she said in a warm, fuzzy voice.

Blethen had to stop himself from saying I love you.

He hung up and rolled on his side, now wide awake. *This is the third or fourth hang-up call since Kincaid's call about The Reaper. Who would be doing this? Is it some kind of psychological ploy?* He was certain it was connected to *The Reaper*, but then the name Todd D'Anselmo crept into his thoughts.

As the sky showed its first streaks of daylight, Blethen gave up trying to get back to sleep. He spent the day completing the sketch of *Elaine, Duchess of Saint Paul.* By late afternoon he was satisfied that he had successfully put Elaine's oval face into the Gainsborough portrait.

He and Barca went to Como Park, and he let the big dog run free. Blethen found him with a friendly young woman who was petting and talking to the adoring golden retriever.

"Sorry. Hope he hasn't been a nuisance," Blethen said.

"Not at all. What's his name?"

"Barca."

"Cute," she said. "My name's Cynthia."

"Nice to meet you Cynthia." Blethen hooked Barca to his leash and walked away.

When they got home he checked messages. Toni had not left one, so he called her.

"Hey, sorry for waking you up last night."

"Hey, yourself. It was nice to hear your voice and know you were thinking about me."

"I think about you all the time," he said. "Even in my dreams."

"Thank you, I think," she said, with a lilt in her voice. "Are they dirty dreams?"

"Uh, no. Ah, well, maybe a little."

She laughed. He changed the subject.

"Do you ever see that guy, Todd D'Anselmo? The one that I met at the Artist's Quarter."

"He seems to show up some place every day," she said. "I suppose that's normal since we're in the same grad school program. Why do you ask?"

"I think I saw him coming out of my apartment building the other day. He drove away before I could confirm it was him, but the car was just like the car that we saw outside Mickey's Diner. You know. The Smokey and the Bandit Firebird."

"I can't imagine why he'd be in your building, unless he knows someone there and was visiting," Toni said.

"That was probably it, but he sure left in a hurry."

"Are you sure it was him?"

"Guess I can't say for sure. It may not have been him. Maybe I was just jumping to conclusions because of the car."

This time Toni changed the subject.

"I looked into extending my departure date from Paris. I can do it for fifty dollars."

"Great," he said. "I'll pay for it."

"Does that mean you're coming to my family reunion?" Her always happy voice kicked up a notch.

"I guess it does."

"I wish I was there to kiss you," she said.

SATURDAY, JUNE 6, 2009

Blethen couldn't shake the thought that this was all an elaborate hoax. It didn't make sense that he would be asked—no, ordered—to go to Barcelona. Plus, there were the bizarre phone calls with Henri Hawke. And Kincaid's exaggerated New England accent now, in retrospect, seemed phony. *Maybe the tickets won't show up at all, or maybe they'll be delivered by the practical joker. The whole thing will probably be on camera. Maybe this is one of those reality television shows where they make people look stupid so everyone else can laugh. Million-dollar commissions and free tickets to Europe don't happen to guys like me. I am really going to look like a fool when someone finally says "gotcha."*

Despite his suspicion, two tickets to Barcelona arrived as promised. The envelope also contained typed instructions: "Take a taxi to Hotel Colon, Avenue Catedral 7. There will be an envelope at the concierge's desk with further instructions." That was it. No meeting time or place. No signature. Not even an indication of whether they had reserved a room for him at the hotel.

Even if they have, I think I'll stay at a different hotel. This is just too bizarre to be legitimate.

BARCELONA

"As you directed, I have arranged for your painter to come. He'll be here on the sixteenth."

Hawke and Magnolia were seated in the plush lobby of the Hotel Majestic. They had agreed that all conversations between them would be face-to-face in public places to avoid any chance of wire taps or of tracing call history. She used an alias when setting an appointment so neither his secretary nor calendar would hear or bear her real name. She also didn't want her conversations recorded, and she didn't trust Hawke.

"Where do you want to meet him?" Hawke continued, anxious to make this meeting short.

"First, I want to observe him, and then I'll decide whether to actually meet with him," she said.

"He is quite petulant," Hawke responded. "I think you might want to consider another painter. He was very obstinate in our telephone call. I'm not certain he will even do the painting."

"Oh, he *will* do the painting," Magnolia said, arching her back. "*You* will see to that. He's the only person who *can* do the painting."

"I must insist on the rest of my fee. I have arranged for his presence, but I cannot guarantee that he will do the painting." Hawke looked at her skeptically. *There's something I'm missing*, he thought.

"You get the rest of your fee when the arrangements are complete. I didn't hire you to be a travel agent." She leaned forward and whispered the words.

The usually stoic Hawke glowered at her.

"Everyone has a price," she continued, sitting back in her chair.

"So, you would be willing to pay more than a million dollars for this painting?"

"A million dollars should be enough. Surely you can convince a destitute artist from the United States to paint a picture for a million dollars."

Hawke didn't take the bait. "And if I can't?" he countered, fixing her with his best patrician stare.

"For every dollar that it costs me over a million, I will reduce your fee a dollar."

"Perhaps the *Policia* will find a clue of how MacMillan happened to be in the wrong place at the wrong time," he countered.

Magnolia regarded Hawke over the rim of her teacup. He was probably bluffing since any clue would eventually lead the police to him as well as to her, but it was not worth the risk at the moment. It was only an issue of money and she had no shortage of that.

"Very well," she finally said, lowering her cup. "I will go up to $1.5 million for the painting—if necessary."

Without knowing it, Hawke had just become number one on her collateral damage list.

SUNDAY, JUNE 7, 2009

SAINT PAUL

Blethen finished drying himself, put on a sweat suit and dialed his Grandma. Somehow it didn't seem right, or comfortable, calling her without clothes on. Grandmas had vision that didn't have anything to do with being able to see. At least his did. *If I was naked, she'd know it. I just know she would.*

"Hello."

"Hi, Grandma. It's Ham." He had to stop himself from saying "I've got clothes on."

"I recognize your voice, dear," she said. "It's nice of you to call again, and so early in the morning. There must be something very important." Even when she was being a little sarcastic her voice was kind.

"I was wondering if I could move my visit from Saturday to Friday?" he asked. "I have to fly to Europe on business this weekend."

"Of course, dear. Friday would be fine. Will your lady friend be coming with you?"

"I'm not sure."

Obviously, Grandma had been thinking about his new *lady friend*, either hoping that he had finally found someone or maybe wondering if she should hide her snow globe.

"I also have a favor to ask. Could you take care of Barca for me while I'm gone?"

"Of course, dear. You know I love to have him here. How long will you be gone?"

"A week. Maybe ten days. Is that okay?"

"Make sure you bring enough food. That dog loves to eat."

Toni and Blethen had made a date to eat dinner together and watch a *Seinfeld* rerun, so he and Barca made a trip to the grocery store and neighborhood wine shop to pick up the fare for the evening meal. Fresh sea scallops the size of hockey pucks seared in chili oil and served on a bed of shredded jicama became the entrée. A root vegetable gratin with yams, onions, and Yukon gold potatoes would be the side dish. Frozen green grapes sprinkled with powdered sugar would become a simple dessert that would complement the meal. A bottle of Rosenblum Viognier and prosecco to go with dessert finished off their shopping trip.

Happily, they trudged home as a light rain began to fall. Every few yards Barca would stop to shake, starting at his head and working his way through the length of his tail. Then, for a few feet, his nose would be in the air and he would have an extra prance in his step.

A guttural growl interrupted the happy trek home. Blethen looked up. Through the mist he saw a Firebird at the end of the block. It pulled away from the curb and drove off as he and Barca, still growling, walked toward it. It appeared the back window was tinted, Blethen couldn't tell if it was the same car that he and Toni had seen outside Mickey's Diner. *Did that one have tinted windows?* He wasn't sure, but it was the third time he'd seen a dark-colored Firebird in just a few days. Coincidence, or had someone with a Firebird just moved into the neighborhood? Or was it something more sinister? Whatever the explanation, it unnerved him, and Barca wasn't happy about it either.

Blethen set the food and wine on the floor in the hallway and fetched a towel to wipe off Barca so he wouldn't leave puddles all over the apartment. Then he took everything into the kitchen and began cutting the vegetables into thin slices.

Toni arrived just as *Seinfeld* was starting. They agreed to defer dinner until it was over. Luckily, it would not suffer from the delay. The gratin, which had been done for several hours, was in the oven warming. The longer it sat, the better it would be. The grapes were frozen, and the jicama shredded and in the refrigerator. The scallops would be seared while they enjoyed a glass of wine.

Over a leisurely dinner they laughed at the antics of Kramer and George in the Seinfeld episode, they had just watched. Toni talked of her upcoming family reunion and of the events since they had seen each other on Sunday, including the fact that Todd D'Anselmo had left the program. There were rumors he had been asked to leave, but she didn't know the reason why. Blethen told Toni that his visit with Grandma had been changed to Friday.

"Did you do that so that I could go?" Toni asked.

"I was hoping you might," he said, fiddling with his fork. "And that way I can give you a ride to the airport Saturday."

"That's sweet. If I get everything done that I need to do before then there's no reason I can't go with you. It probably means I'll have to go home tonight, though."

Blethen put down the fork and stuck out his lower lip in a fake pout, doing his best imitation of Barca's sad eyes.

"Well, maybe I could get up early and go home." Her eyes twinkled.

Blethen didn't mention the black Firebird during the rest of the dinner conversation. He didn't want that twinkle to fade.

After dinner they piled the dirty dishes in the sink and, with the remainder of the chilled Viognier in hand, moved to the couch. Toni sat, snuggled next to Blethen, his arm around her shoulders.

"You've been kind of quiet," she said.

"I've been thinking about 'I love you.' You gave me a lot to think about the other night."

"I meant to. But I didn't mean to upset you. I just needed you to know how I feel about love." She took a sip of wine. "Love isn't something that can be rushed."

"I feel like you give me mixed signals," he said. He had the feeling he had just jumped off a cliff without knowing the distance of the fall. "We'd been together all of what, eight or ten hours before we had sex. I didn't think of that as 'rushing it' but it wasn't exactly a long-term relationship at that point."

He half-expected Toni to get up and leave as many of his previous girlfriends would have. She didn't move.

"Sex isn't the same as love," she responded, looking up at him without indicating any offense at his statement. "Sex is wonderful. It's a necessary part of a relationship but it's not love. I think that real love doesn't happen until the urgency of sex is over."

He leaned away from Toni and gave her a quizzical look.

"Sex, I think, is the main way we are initially attracted to each other," she continued. "A way to get to know each other. If it wasn't for the desire to have sex, I think there would be few relationships between men and women. But once sex is no longer the most important part of the relationship, when it isn't the first thing we think of when we see each other or at the end of a day, I believe that's when real love happens."

"Wow!" he said. "We may never get to be in love with each other."

"If we're together long enough, we will," she said, not buying in to his attempt to lighten the discussion. "The passion and the lust will wear off. If we're still together—if we're still happy and content and considerate and can trust each other—then we can talk about being in love."

"How did you become so wise?"

"I'm not smart. I've just seen my friends rush into marriage and relationships while at the height of passion and it almost always ends in divorce and unhappiness. I've had a relationship based only on passion and it ended up in hurt. On the other hand, I've watched my parents grow over time. I'm sure they had the same lust and passion that we do when they first met, but they endured after the lust was gone and found that the other things they liked about each other lasted. It changed and became real love over time. They're my role models."

"Wow," he said again, seriously this time. "You're giving me some big shoes to fill."

"The shoes aren't big. Don't think of it that way," she said as she snuggled back under his arm. "Don't try to make it more than it is. Let's just enjoy the passion that we have. If it burns out, and doesn't evolve into something more, then we go our separate ways without guilt or pain, knowing that we enjoyed each other for a while but it wasn't meant to be. If it does turn into something more than just passion, then we can talk to each other about love and really mean it."

Their conversation lasted until after midnight. They went to bed sleepy with a little wine buzz and full stomachs. Toni rolled on her side and nestled her back against him and Blethen fell asleep with his nose in her hair—like two spoons in a silverware drawer. Barca volunteered to sleep on the floor.

WEDNESDAY, JUNE 10, 2009

BARCELONA

Kincaid's condition had deteriorated.

Magnolia sat by his bedside and waited without emotion, listening to his ragged breathing. It would not be long.

People do not understand, she thought. Her feelings for Kincaid were like new fallen snow—pure, pristine, uncluttered by the burden and expectancy of sex. She knew him like no one else. He was rich, powerful, cunning and ruthless, qualities to be admired and emulated, but he could also be kind, thoughtful, compassionate. And he had saved her. She would not shed any tears when he passed, but she would miss his wisdom, their conversations, his strength. She hoped she was ready.

As her vigil stretched through the day her thoughts drifted to the son she had not seen in thirty-four years. She hoped she would have the courage to talk to him. The anticipation filled her with emotion. Those tears she fought to keep in check.

There were aspects of her plan she had kept secret. Only she knew that the painter he had hired was her son. Only she knew that she had no intention of ever selling the painting. The plan had always been about her finding peace for the wrong she had so awfully committed so long ago, of finally giving something to her son—financial security—while she, in return, would have something of his to cherish for the rest of her life, his painting of *The Reaper*.

FRIDAY, JUNE 12, 2009

ZUMBROTA, MINNESOTA

"You can call me Lorraine, dear. At least until we get to know each other better."

Grandma Blethen studied Toni. *She looks like Little Orphan Annie,* she thought as Toni went into the explanation about her hair. Reflexively she touched her own thinning white tresses. *I need a permanent.*

Toni nervously rattled on in her usual rapid-fire fashion, verbally hopping from hair to how she met Blethen, to art, to France, and back to Blethen and Barca.

My grandson has hooked up with another oddball. Damn his mother. She ruined him. It's her fault he can't find a normal girl.

Introductions and explanations behind them, they spent the morning planting flowers, sipping lemonade, shooing Barca out of the flower beds and chatting. Toni's nervousness subsided as Lorraine's snide humor kept them laughing. Lorraine's first opinion of Toni mellowed some, too, as they planted daisies and poked fun at Blethen's dislike for worms and similar crawly creatures they found in the soil.

As they sat down to lunch, he presented Lorraine with a birdbath for one of her flower gardens, his birthday gift to her. Toni had taken the time to buy her a birthday card and packet of sachet.

"Why thank you, dear," she said to Blethen, and then to Toni, in her best saccharine voice while thinking, *why does everyone think old people like to put these stinky things in their drawers?*

After lunch of bologna sandwiches and chardonnay, served without apology, Grandma Lorraine hugged them both and sent them on their way back to Saint Paul.

"That one's doomed from the start," she said out loud to Barca, who lay in a patch of sunlight in the living room. His tail thumped against the wooden floor, raising dust visible in the sunlight. "You agree with me, don't you, old boy?"

"Don't take it personally," Blethen said, responding to Toni's observation that his Grandma was very nice, but a little "in-your-face" (*Were your parents carrots, dear?*). "The last woman I brought with me a couple years ago stole something. There were also a couple others who were a little out of my Grandma's comfort zone—tattoos, smoked cigars."

"Great. And this time you bring a frizzy carrot-top with a motor mouth. I'm sure she was impressed."

"She'll be impressed when I bring you back a second time. I've never brought anyone to her place twice. I think she was really warming up to you."

"Well, I like her. She speaks her mind and makes a mean baloney sandwich. And she loves you. You're lucky to have someone like her so close. All my relatives are thousands of miles away."

She noticed Blethen glance in the rearview mirror, and then do a double-take. "Something wrong?" she asked, turning to look.

Behind them, about a quarter-mile back, was a black, low-slung car.

Blethen took his foot off the gas. As their car began to lose speed, the black car came closer then slowed, keeping distance between the two vehicles. Blethen sped up. After falling back further, the black car accelerated to reestablish the quarter mile between them.

"I'm going to turn off at the next intersection," Blethen said. As he turned, they slowed to a crawl and stopped. He got out just as the black car went past the intersection at a high rate of speed. It was definitely a black Firebird with tinted windows.

"What was that all about?" Toni asked as he got back in the car.

"I haven't wanted to say anything," Blethen explained, "but there's been some really weird shit going on since I got the call about painting *The Reaper*. That's the fourth or fifth time I've seen that car. I'm pretty sure it's the one that I saw Todd D'Anselmo get into outside my building. At least I think it was him. The last two times I've seen it, it's like it's watching me. When I try to get close it runs away. And I've been getting hang-up calls."

"You think it's all tied to *The Reaper*?" she asked.

"I don't know, but I'm sure as hell going to find out in Barcelona."

SATURDAY, JUNE 13, 2009

Blethen picked up Toni at her house while it was still dark. She gave him the phone number for her uncle's farm in Albi and promised to call him when she got there. They kissed, lingering until a car, waiting to disgorge its passengers, honked. With a sheepish grin, Blethen waved at the driver.

"I'll see you in Albi in a few days," he said to Toni with a final squeeze.

"Good luck in Barcelona," she replied. "And be careful."

He wanted badly to say, "I love you" but swallowed the words instead.

PARIS

Sitting in a cramped seat of a DC-9 as it rolled toward Terminal 2E of DeGaulle Airport, Toni's thoughts drifted to her Grandpapa and memories of herself as a tiny girl in his lap: of stories and fairy tales told in a lilting voice, of a wrinkled face with a winsome smile, of a pleasant smell that was peculiar to him. She was excited to see him.

She took a paper copy of a photo from her purse and studied it. Her Uncle Jean had emailed it to her, a picture of himself holding a sign that said "Antoinette." He said that he would be waiting for her, holding the sign. She stepped off Delta Flight 1432 into the unfamiliar surroundings of Charles De Gaulle Airport and her native France. An involuntary shudder coursed through her body. She was going to see her family face-to-face for the first time in nearly twenty years and she realized she was scared. *What are they going to think of me? No one knows me, and I know no one looks like me.* She wished Ham was with her. For an instant her confidence waned, and, if she could have gotten back on the plane, she might have.

With a deep breath to calm herself, Toni plucked her luggage from the carousel. She hesitated, not sure which way to turn until she heard her name. Spinning, she saw the sign, the broad smile of Uncle Jean, and a large group of people, many of whom looked familiar. Spontaneously, tears began to stream down her cheeks. Without knowing how, she was suddenly in a throng of hugging, weeping, happy Frenchmen. Her fear was gone, and supportive hands and arms literally carried her to the waiting car. Toni felt them gather her, support her and love her. No questions. No conditions. She was home.

The caravan of tiny cars, each jammed to capacity, made its way south on E05 through Orleans. They stopped at a small café in Olivet where they rearranged tables so everyone sat in a circle, equidistant from their American guest of honor. There were thirteen in all, about a quarter of the number expected for the reunion. An equal number awaited at the family farm tucked against the Tarn River just north of Albi, another five hundred kilometers to the south. The rest would arrive over the next few days, including Toni's parents.

Toni found herself struggling to be understood in her native tongue as volleys of questions were launched. She had always considered herself "French," but twenty years without regularly speaking the language left her a bit rusty and her responses, labeled "Frenglish" by one of her cousins, brought guffaws from around the table. By the end of lunch, helped by numerous bottles of wine, the gathering had become uproarious.

She remembered little of the remainder of the trip, falling asleep in the back of the car shortly after it left Olivet, afloat in a golden sea of family warmth and humor. It was past midnight when the caravan pulled into the cul-de-sac around which the large farmhouse, barn and out-buildings were arranged. More relatives—Chapereauxs, Flouriens, Pinets—poured from the house, anxious to take up the baton as Toni's next welcoming party. The first light of morning was showing in the east by the time she crawled into bed.

SUNDAY, JUNE 14, 2009

The blaring of car horns and the clanging of cowbells jolted Toni out of her sleep. More family was arriving. She scrambled out of bed and slid into a soft robe hanging on the clothes tree in her bedroom. The rest of the Pinet clan had arrived from Narbonne, bringing with them the best wine the family vineyards had to offer. Hugging and good-natured cajoling was the order of the morning, and Toni was quickly drawn into the middle of it. Opening several bottles of the family Chablis on the front lawn brought a torrent of toasts to *famille, fraternite* and *patrie*.

As the frivolity subsided, the newcomers disappeared into the farmhouse with their valises, getting settled to await the arrival of Grandpapa Emile, whose ninetieth birthday party on Friday was to be the highlight of the reunion.

Toni stood on the expansive veranda of the farmhouse, savoring a glass of *Pinet Chablis 1997* and soaking in the beauty of the French countryside.

"So, tell me more about this man."

Coming from her Aunt Marion, it was not so much a request as a demand. Marion, a sturdy French farmwife with a don't-mess-with-me demeanor, tended to tackle things directly, not mincing words nor accepting generic explanations.

"He's tall, dark and handsome." The levity of the morning and wine on an empty stomach rendered Toni a little silly, prompting the flippant answer.

"Enough with the clichés," her aunt scolded, crossing her arms across her ample bosom. "Why do you like him enough to drag him all the way here to meet your crazy family?"

Toni considered the question.

"Because he's a unique blend of most of the things I admire in a man," she finally answered. "He's talented and smart and tender and thoughtful. He has a wonderful sense of humor and isn't afraid to make himself the butt of his own jokes, but he also has a serious side. He's not tied to material things. He's a good cook and an awesome lover. He likes animals. And he *is* tall, dark and handsome."

"What are the things you admire in a man that he doesn't have?" Aunt Marion went straight for the jugular.

"Like most men, he confuses lust with love, but we're working on that. He's thirty-eight years old and never been married, so sometimes he has difficulty remembering that there are now two sets of wishes and desires that need to be considered…"

"Thirty-eight, handsome and never been married," Aunt Marion interrupted. "Is he gay? Or one of those switchers?"

"No, I'm pretty sure he isn't either. He was abandoned by his mother when he was four, and it's taken him a long time to get over that. I think he's still bitter, but he's coming to terms with it."

"Oh lordy, child," Marion burst out. "You are taking on a project. My advice is screw him 'til you're through with him and then move on. Enjoy the moment, but don't make it a life sentence."

Toni was shocked at her aunt's bluntness.

"I…I think you should meet him before you pass judgment," she murmured, wishing this conversation would end.

"Oh, I will, and I'll give you my honest opinion. Don't worry, I won't embarrass you in front of him, although I may ask him an uncomfortable question or two." The smile on Aunt Marion's face turned serious. "I'm just saying that getting involved with someone with his kind of baggage is asking for trouble more times than not."

Toni found herself nodding. *Maybe it wasn't such a good idea to bring Ham to meet her family.*

It was late afternoon when Grandpapa Emile arrived from Toulouse, chauffeured by one of Toni's many cousins. With them was a surprise guest, a distant relative with a colorful past. "Tsk, tsk" could be heard rippling through the farmhouse as family members learned of her presence, exacerbated by the commotion caused by finding a suitable place to sleep for the unexpected visitor.

They were sitting on the veranda in wicker rocking chairs—light coverlets on their laps to fend off the cool of the evening—as Toni approached, her first chance to reintroduce herself to Grandpapa Emile. His voice still had the same lilt, and his smile, now full of wrinkles, was just as mischievous. He remembered her and her bright orange curls.

"I wondered how long it would take for you to come and talk to me," he said. "You have grown up beautifully."

"Oh, Grandpapa," she said. "I have been looking forward to seeing you for such a long time. You have aged magnificently. I think we should go dancing."

"How could I turn down such an invitation, but perhaps it could be later. My old bones are very comfortable right here in this rocker at the moment."

Then, looking at the woman to his left: "Allow me to introduce you to my rocking partner. Antoinette, please meet your Aunt Monique. She really isn't your Aunt, more like a fifth cousin, but everyone considers her their aunt."

She greeted Aunt Monique, a small woman with an aristocratic air, dressed in elegant but outdated clothes.

"Pleasure to meet you, Antoinette," said the elderly woman, offering her hand. "I understand you are studying art. I was in art once."

"Monique and I were both born in 1919," interrupted Grandpapa. "Grew up together. Still argue about who's oldest," he chuckled. Aunt Monique gave him a patronizing smile.

The next person in line to greet Grandpapa moved in, and Toni moved on. She would spend more time with Grandpapa during the week. She also felt a curious need to learn more about her fifth cousin/aunt.

MONDAY, JUNE 15, 2009

BARCELONA

Blethen arrived at Hotel Colon travel weary and ready for a drink. He was too tired to hunt for another hotel, so he checked in and tipped the bellman five dollars to take his bag to his room. He picked up the promised envelope from a chatty concierge who informed him, among other things, that Joan Miro was once a regular patron of the hotel. At the moment, Blethen didn't care.

Seated in the hotel bar, he downed a third of his gin and tonic in one swallow and studied the unopened envelope. There had been no "surprise" or "gotcha." He realized this was no practical joke. He was being asked to forge a painting, and he knew it. If he opened the envelope he was headed down that treacherous path. He could say he changed his mind, didn't want to do the painting, turn around and go home on the next flight. Then he remembered the newspaper story of the mutilated, dead forger. He knew the clipping had been a message.

Kincaid is powerful, has a lot of money and is ruthless. On the other hand, all he did was ask me to copy a painting, just like any other client. He never said the word forgery, or asked me not to sign it, or asked me to paint "in the style of" Miro.

Long ago Blethen had learned the words "in the style of" were an automatic signal that a forgery was being painted. A forger painted "in the style of" some great painter, then passed the work off as the real thing—a long-lost painting worth millions. If the forger was good, the experts were fooled and the forger got rich. If not, he was disgraced, or went to jail, or, worst of all, ended up like the guy in the newspaper. It seemed to Blethen that all forgers, even the very best, ended up that way.

Maybe those are just the ones they write about. He reconsidered. *Maybe there's a bunch of forgers out there that are living long happy lives and we never hear about them.*

He argued with himself as he finished his drink and ordered another. Mentally, he made a list of all the things that made him believe

The Reaper was intended to be a forgery: Kincaid's reputation and lack of any apparent interest in art, the emphasis on discretion and silence, the huge fee, the fact that the painting had disappeared over seventy years ago so it couldn't be compared to the copy he was to paint, the strange phone calls with Hawke, and even this trip.

Meanwhile the envelope lay on the table, staring at him.

As the second drink arrived his doubt took a new tack. *What would Toni think? I'm pretty sure she'd walk away if she knew I was painting a forgery. But she wouldn't have to know. Shit, I don't even know. And there's no guarantee that we'd stick together anyway.* His past relationships hadn't lasted, although, he had to admit, this one felt different. There was something innocent and honest about her that set her apart. And she was smart in ways that he hadn't even considered. Did he want to risk this relationship over a painting?

He wanted to call her, but decided it was too late. He ordered a third gin and tonic instead.

A million dollars. That's really the issue. Is a relationship with Toni worth a million dollars? He pondered the question for a moment. *How the hell would I know. I've never had a million dollars and our relationship might not last regardless of what I do. And there are other considerations besides Toni and the money.* He knew his rationalization was a cop out.

Blethen sat, chin in his hands, staring at the envelope. His drink arrived and he asked for the check. *What do I know for sure? Someone is willing to pay me a million dollars to copy a painting. That's all I know. What don't I know? Why the client wants the painting. Whether my relationship with Toni will last. What the future holds.*

Blethen finished the drink in one swallow and slammed the glass loudly on the table. "Here's to the future," he said aloud. "Whatever it may hold."

He ripped open the envelope.

TUESDAY, JUNE 16, 2009

Magnolia sat alone at a table in the corner of Casa Calvet with an open line of site to the table where Hawke waited. They had chosen this particular restaurant, not a regular locale for either of them, to assure that Hawke and Blethen would not be interrupted, and so that Magnolia could watch anonymously. A busy lunch hour crowd would provide the necessary camouflage for her to observe the meeting without detection, although it would prevent her from hearing any of the conversation. That would come later, when she listened to the recording of the meeting Hawke would discreetly make.

She watched as the hostess escorted a tall, dark-skinned man to Hawke's table. A puzzled look etched her face. *Wait! This must be a mistake.* But the hostess seated the man, who shook hands with Hawke.

Confusion crept into Magnolia's mind. Her recollection was of a tousle-haired little boy, standing on the front porch as she drove away. She didn't remember him having brown skin. She tried to bring the memory into focus but couldn't. She struggled to recall other memories of her son. *I had him for three years! I should remember something, for Christ's sake!*

In truth, Ham was with her for only a few scattered weeks during those years as Magnolia ricocheted between jail or rehab or month-long drug binges. He had been taken in by her friends, or lived in foster homes, or, when he was with his mother, in drug houses where people came and crashed and went in a constant carousel. She'd been in a constant chemical haze and Ham was seldom her priority. By two-and-a-half he had learned to subsist on his own.

During one of the rare times he was with her she made a spur-of-the-moment decision to go to the West Coast with a couple of drifters who had passed through the house. Having to drag a kid with her had been too big a burden. She dropped Ham with her mother on the way west, with a promise she'd be back in a couple of weeks.

She'd never gone back.

But this can't be my son. He looks like he's from the Middle East. Or

India. For the very first time Magnolia wished she had known, or at least could remember, the father.

"Four million dollars, a million up front, the rest when I deliver the painting," Blethen said. His words sounded more confident than he felt, but if he was going to paint a forgery he was going to make sure it was the only one he'd ever have to do.

"Mr. Kincaid has agreed to pay a million dollars, which is more than generous for a copy of this painting," Hawke countered. "I have no authority to pay you more than the agreed amount."

"I told you, I didn't agree on that or any other amount." Blethen's voice rose. "If you only have authority for the million, why did you drag me to Barcelona?"

"Because, Mr. Kincaid wanted me to meet with you so that I could give him my impression of you. Are you trustworthy? Do you have the stability to take on a task such as this? Do I think you'll actually deliver the painting?" Hawke said quietly.

The squat little man in the rumpled suit and 1930s barbershop hairstyle sat back in his chair and stared at Blethen.

"Truthfully," he continued. "I'm not impressed. You appear to be perpetually angry, and your estimation of your own worth is outlandish. Four million dollars is ridiculous. There isn't a copy of a painting in the world worth four million dollars. Unless, of course, it was to be passed off as the real thing, and Mr. Kincaid has no intention of doing that. That would be illegal."

It caught Blethen by surprise. He thought he'd come to negotiate a deal for the painting. Instead he was there for an interview.

"Well that makes everything different," he said, shifting in his seat as his face flushed. "From the way this unfolded I thought I was being asked to paint a forgery. That's why I asked for four million. I figured *The Reaper*, on the open market, would be worth sixteen mil. I thought a quarter for me, a quarter for you as the broker, and half for Kincaid as the investor. It sounded fair to me."

Words wouldn't stop running out of his mouth, and he felt a dampness on his skin as he tried to salvage the deal. "As long as it's not a forgery, I have no trouble with the million. I think a million's fine, as you say. I can deliver it. I could have it to you in three months if you're in a hurry."

"We may want to interview other painters," Hawke said.

May want to interview others. Blethen weighed the words. He didn't believe Hawke was going to interview anyone else.

"You'd be wasting your time. No one's as good as me. I'm the only copier who can make a copy look the same age as the original." Blethen regained his swagger.

"*The Reaper* is seventy years old," Hawke replied. "It doesn't have to be aged as if it were an old master."

"But it still has to be made to look authentic," Blethen argued. "*The Reaper* wasn't painted on canvas. It was painted on industrial wallboard. It will be as difficult to make it look authentic as it would be if I was copying a Rembrandt."

Blethen noted a slight tic in Hawke's right eye when he mentioned the wallboard. He knew he had hit on something and decided to press the advantage.

"I'll do the painting for a million, but there'll be some significant expenses involved. I'll need an additional hundred thousand to cover them. I'll need it up front."

"I can agree to fifty thousand up front but it comes out of the million," Hawke said. "You get the remaining nine-fifty when the painting is delivered."

Relieved and excited, Blethen walked out of Casa Calvet and placed a call to Albi, to the farmstead of Jean Chapereaux. After fumbling through what little French he knew, he finally got someone on the line who spoke English. They summoned Toni to the phone.

"I've closed *The Reaper* deal," he said, excitement in his voice. "I have to wait around until tomorrow to pick up a check, but I might be able to catch a late train that would get me into Albi tomorrow night. Does that work for you?"

"Absolutely. I'll pick you up. Probably have a bunch of cousins with me, all of whom can't wait to meet you. Tell me about today."

"I'll tell you when I see you. Just know that we have reason to celebrate, and a lot of research to do."

"He asked for four million but settled for the million. I agreed to give him fifty thousand in advance to cover expenses." Hawke handed Magnolia a cassette tape and a small recorder. "The whole conversation is on there."

"*That* was Hamilton Blethen?"

"Of course. Who else did you think it was?"

"I just pictured him differently," she said. "I didn't know he was middle eastern."

Hawke shrugged. "Listen to the tape," he said. "I'll expect the balance of my fee tomorrow."

She returned to the penthouse at The Majestic and ran the tape through her portable player. There was no discernible accent in the voice of the man speaking to Hawke. He was clearly American. He identified himself as Hamilton Blethen.

She picked up the phone and got the hotel operator. "Please place a call to the United States," she said, giving the operator the number.

She waited as the call was put through. As expected it rang several times and then clicked over to voice mail. "This is Ham Blethen. Not available now. Please leave a message." It sounded like the voice on the tape. She thought for several minutes, then, preceded by a sigh of capitulation, called the operator again to place another U.S. call. This one was to her mother.

"Hi, Mom. It's Mary." Magnolia still used her given name when talking to her mother.

The only response was the television Magnolia could hear in the background.

Finally, Lorraine spoke: "I haven't heard from you in a long time."

"Three, four years I think."

"More like seven," was Lorraine's terse answer.

"How are you, Mom?"

"Fine. Why are you calling?"

The abruptness stung, but Magnolia had expected it.

"Have you seen Hamilton recently?" she asked.

"Just two days ago. Why?"

"Can you describe him for me?"

"What? Why?"

"Because I think I may have just seen him."

"I doubt that," Lorraine said. "He's in Europe."

"That's where I am," Magnolia answered. "In Barcelona. I think I just saw him at a restaurant here."

"Well, wouldn't that be a small world. But I don't know how you'd know him if you did see him. He doesn't look anything like you, and you haven't seen him in over thirty years."

"But, can you *please* tell me what he looks like?"

Lorraine fumbled with describing her grandson, saying he had black hair and was quite tall. "Oh, and he has a sharp nose and really dark brown eyes."

"What color is his skin, Mom?"

There was a long pause.

"Brown. He has brown skin," she finally said.

Maggie hung up from the unsettling phone call. She didn't remember him as brown. *Could they have switched kids? Maybe in foster care?*

She placed one more call to Boston Children's Hospital, to a doctor who was a friend of Kincaid's and whom she had met multiple times over the years.

"James Vasavada," was the answer when the connection was made.

"Dr. Vasavada, this is Magnolia Kanaranzi, Arthur Kincaid's assistant."

"Hi, Maggie. To what do I owe the pleasure?"

She bristled at the familiarity of his greeting. Only Arthur called her Maggie. But she set aside her pique. "I have a question that I thought you might be able to answer."

"I'll try."

"When babies are born, babies of color, does their skin get darker as they get older?"

"Everybody gets darker to some extent through exposure to the sun. Over the years it can accumulate somewhat. It really depends upon the parents and the level of melatonin in the skin," he answered.

"I'm talking about a child of mixed-race parentage. Say, the mother is white and the father is Egyptian. Could their child be born with fair skin and then turn brown as years passed."

"That would be an extreme case, but it would not be unusual for a baby's skin to darken as he or she got older," Dr. Vasavada said. "How dark the child's skin becomes would depend partially on the skin pigmentation of the parents, but it's not uncommon."

"Thanks, Jim," she said. "That helps clear up some things. I really appreciate your help."

"My pleasure, Maggie. Any time. Say hello to Arthur for me."

"I will," she promised, seeing no reason to extend the conversation by mentioning Arthur's deteriorating health.

She sat, staring out the penthouse window into the Barcelona night.

This changed everything. She was about to take her place in the highest levels of society, to be accepted in the inner circles of power, a status few women ever reach. It would not do have it all derailed because she had an illegitimate child of color.

THURSDAY, JUNE 17, 2009

Before boarding the train, Blethen confirmed that fifty thousand dollars had arrived by wire and was safely nestled in his bank account. Now, he was ready for the scenic five-and-a-half-hour journey through the beautiful Pyrenees Mountains, content and happy. He had more money in the bank than he'd ever had in his life. He had a million-dollar commission. And he was going to see the woman whom he was pretty sure he loved, even by Toni's standards. Blethen settled into his first-class coach and watched passengers milling about the station platform. *Life can't get any better,* he thought.

He was wrong. The greeting at the Albi train station took it up a notch.

Blethen stepped off the train literally into the arms of Toni and a long, steamy kiss that took his breath away and made the small hairs on the back of his neck stand up.

"Whoa!" he gulped, trying to regain his composure. "I missed you too."

Toni's smile lit up the terminal as she spun him around. "I'd like you to meet my cousins Paulette and Elise. Ladies, Hamilton Blethen, famous artist and my new beau."

Blethen didn't have time to dispute the veracity of the introduction. The cousins, both younger than Toni, greeted him as if he was a rock star, hugging and fawning and chattering in a combination of French and English of which he caught only a word or two. Elise, a diminutive brunette who spoke little English, held tightly to his left arm, an elated look on her face, opposite Toni who was comfortably holding onto his right arm and enjoying every minute of the attention he was getting. Paulette, compact and athletic, picked up his bag and slung it over her shoulder. They walked four-abreast, down the concourse, out of the airport and to the parking garage, with Paulette peppering him with questions all the way. Neither the questions nor the adoration abated during the hour-long trip to the farm.

Thanks to Aunt Marion, information about Blethen had spread quickly throughout the farmhouse. He became more handsome and more talented as each person retold what they had heard. Anxiously they awaited his arrival, even holding the evening meal for all but the small children and the elderly.

Seated at a huge table filled with platters of fragrant meat, vegetables and bread, he was introduced to the rest of the family as Toni's *petit ami,* and a painter of immense talent. Toni's introduction was punctuated with comments from Paulette and Elise, usually resulting in abundant laughter and multiple toasts. He blushed at the flattery but, even as the potent wine made his head fuzzy, Blethen thought it best to leave Toni's introduction unchallenged. There would be time enough to explain the sometimes-blurred line between art copying and forgery.

It was after midnight by the time the festivities wound down and Blethen and Toni were finally alone. He had felt a genuine acceptance from her family. There were no furtive glances, curious stares, or uncomfortable comments; nothing, in fact, to indicate that anyone perceived his skin color or ethnicity as different from their own. Indeed, they were not a homogenous group. There was a Nigerian woman, Patience, who was married to one of the Pinet cousins, and an older, dark-skinned woman, who appeared to be the companion of one of Toni's aunts. And now him.

"Your aunt, with the female friend, are they a couple?" Blethen asked.

"Aunt Mamie? Her friend's name is Lakshmi," Toni answered. "They've been together about twenty years. Both of them were married and their husbands died. I don't know the story of how they got together, and I don't know if they're a couple in the sense of being romantically attached, but you never see one without the other."

"And what about the older woman with Grandpapa Emile? I got the sense she wasn't really part of the family."

"That's Aunt Monique. She's like a fifth cousin," Toni said. "Most of the women of my mom's generation don't like her, and most of the men find her fascinating. Rumor is she was a Nazi sympathizer during World War II. She moved to the United States for a while and then came back to France and led quite the sensational life as a writer and a socialite in the sixties and seventies. Said to have been the courtesan of at least one prime minister and a couple movie stars. She lives in Paris now. A little dotty I think."

"Why do you call her Aunt Monique if she's a cousin?"

"All the cousins call her 'aunt.' It's how Grandpapa introduced her. They grew up together. She's a surprise guest."

They chatted about other family members, until Toni asked, "So, what happened yesterday? You said we were going to celebrate. What are we celebrating?"

Blethen purposely drew out the suspense, taking his time pouring them each a fresh glass of bubbly.

"I negotiated a deal on *The Reaper.* When this is over we're going back to Barcelona to do some hands-on research on Mr. Miro and his lost painting, and we're going back in style."

"Congratulations." Toni's smile reflected her happiness for Blethen. She was curious about the size of the commission but reticent to ask. *When he wants me to know, he'll tell me,* she thought.

BARCELONA

Arthur Kincaid died at 8:45 p.m. Magnolia got the call at 9:10 p.m. It was 3:10 p.m. in New York.

From her room at The Majestic she quickly placed calls to confirm that the stock in Kincaid's companies had been transferred into her new trust. All but one transfer had been made, and that would be completed by the end of the day.

She would wait until the next day to notify the companies of Arthur's passing.

As soon as she completed arrangements to have Kincaid's body returned to the States, she would head back to Boston on the next available flight. First, however, she needed to deal with Henri Hawke.

FRIDAY, JUNE 18, 2009

Magnolia met Hawke at Drolma for an early lunch.

"Mr. Kincaid passed away yesterday," she said. "Your services are no longer needed. Please take the balance of your fee from the money in your trust account. I want the remaining eight hundred thousand dollars wired today to the following account." She handed him a folded piece of paper.

Hawke opened the paper, looked at it, then refolded it and put it in his vest pocket. “Very well,” he said. “Our business is then concluded. There is no need for us to exchange false pleasantries over lunch. I shall arrange to wire the funds immediately.”

“Before you go, I have something for you.” Her words stopped Hawke’s exit. She reached into her purse and handed him the same recorder that he had given her two days earlier.

“This is yours,” she said. “You may want to listen to the tape that’s in it. It’s a recording of every conversation we have had.”

Hawke started to say something, but she interrupted him. “You were not the only one recording conversations, Mr. Hawke. I have several copies of this tape. Some of them are in the hands of my associates, with instructions on what to do with the tape if something ever happens to me, and that includes if I were to be implicated in certain activities, if you get my meaning. I hope you understand that this is entirely defensive on my part. I bear you no ill will, but I do expect your absolute discretion and silence. I also understand that you could also use the tape in the same way if I were to implicate you. As is often the case in chess, let’s just call this a stalemate.”

Hawke took the cassette recorder and left, looking like he had just eaten something sour.

Her last call of the day was to the Boston law firm of Horst, MacMillan and Roper. She spoke with Tyron Roper, expressing her horror and regret over MacMillan’s tragic death in Barcelona, and making an appointment to discuss Kincaid’s estate. Magnolia hung up the phone, a slight smile on her face. She checked her airplane ticket to confirm her departure time the next day, and took a final, leisurely stroll down La Rambla, enjoying the sights and sounds of Barcelona. She doubted that she would ever return to the city.

ALBI, FRANCE

The novelty of his arrival had worn off by the next day, and Blethen eased into the bustle of the family reunion. Toni tried to teach him piquet, a centuries-old two-handed card game, with little success.

"I'm a terrible card player," he apologized. "I lost a lot of money in the minor leagues playing gin rummy. Well, a lot back then was like two bucks. Realized then I was just bad at cards."

"You can redeem yourself tomorrow," Toni said. "They've organized a petanque tournament. That would be more up your alley. It's the French version of bocce ball or boules. You can join our team, be the clean-up hitter."

"Who's on your team?" he asked.

"Paulette. I left the third spot on the team open when I signed up, hoping you'd join us."

Blethen agreed.

Later in the afternoon, with Toni busy helping prepare the evening meal, Blethen strolled into the backyard and watched a petanque game in progress.

"Can you explain this to me?" he asked a cousin named Philip who was also an observer.

"You stand in that circle," Philip said, pointing to a small plastic ring, barely large enough to get both feet inside. "You toss or roll the balls, the bigger steel ones, and try to get them as close to that little wooden ball as possible. A team scores if their ball is closer to the little ball—it's called a *cochonnet*—than the other teams. There's more to it than that, but that's the essential part of the game. Whichever team is the first to score thirteen points wins."

He thanked Philip and watched the various pitching styles of the players. He noted one consistency: the steel balls were thrown with backspin. The better players would lob the ball most of the distance to the cochonnet. The backspin allowed them to stop the ball quickly once it hit the ground.

After the game was over, Blethen picked up one of the steel balls. It was about the size of a softball, although significantly heavier, with a pattern of grooves cut into the ball's surface. He made an underhand toss, trying to mimic style of the better players. The ball landed about half way to the cochonnet. *This,* he thought, *is going to be a challenge.*

Blethen had his first opportunity to have a conversation with Toni's parents after dinner. Her mother, Francine, a woman of about fifty with long blonde hair and a ready smile, was as loquacious as Toni. She carried the conversation with questions about how he and Toni met, about his art and about his younger years. She expected detailed answers and prodded until she got them. Her father, Maxim, dark haired with olive skin, spoke less but listened closely and watched Blethen with a penetrating gaze, like a father trying to see what was inside the man who was sleeping with his daughter. Both parents were dressed expensively.

Blethen told them of college, playing baseball, his stint in Desert Storm, studying art and how he and Toni met. He talked about his plan to paint her portrait, about her unique "look" and her "glass is always full" personality. Thinking it best to make full disclosure to her parents, he explained how he made his living and how an art copier was different from an art forger. When asked by Toni's mother where they might see some of his work, he told them of several public locations where his copies were displayed. He didn't mention the two paintings hanging in well-known galleries presumed, by the curators, to be originals.

A question about his childhood brought a terse response. "I never knew my parents. I was raised in foster care, never adopted." That ended the inquiries into his early years.

"What are you currently painting?" Francine asked, anxious to restart the conversation.

"I just finished a Vermeer, *Girl with a Pearl Earring,* for a jewelry store in Cleveland, and am now working on a Gainsborough for a private client," Blethen said. "and I've just been hired to do a Miro. That's how I happen to be here. I just closed the deal a couple of days ago in Barcelona."

"It's nice to have an artist in the family," Francine said.

"Francine!" scolded her husband. Then to Blethen: "She's anxious to marry off our daughter. I apologize."

"I wasn't even thinking of that," she replied defensively. "I just meant it was nice to have someone here who is knowledgeable about art. Someone who can call Aunt Monique's bluff." Her disdain for the elderly, distant relative was apparent.

"But now that you've met us," she continued, "you're part of our family, even if you don't marry Toni."

Maxim sighed, shaking his head in mock resignation. "You're incorrigible," he said.

"That might be a little premature," Blethen interjected, feeling obliged to say something. "We've only known each other a few weeks, but I will tell you that I am very smitten by your daughter."

Francine beamed. Maxim, not so much.

The conversation turned to less delicate matters, like how Francine and Maxim met, got married, lived their lives—she, an advertising agency customer representative, and he a trader for a large New York investment house. His occupation led to a discussion about the collapse of the junk bond market and the demise of Wall Street giant Drexel Burnham Lambert.

"Stupid choices caused by greed and lack of ethics," was Maxim's diagnosis. "When personal greed overrides your clients' well-being, the system fails. You lose their trust and, *poof*, you're out of business."

"Not much different for me," Blethen responded without thinking.

"I would think artistic talent was the only criteria for success in your business," Maxim shot back.

"Um, no, ah. Certainly, you can't succeed without it, but, ah, you need ethics and trust, too. Like any business." Blethen's fumbling response, in an effort to avoid explaining why discretion was a required trait of an art copier, seemed to confirm Maxim's thoughts.

He leaned toward Blethen, his hands on his knees.

"I initially judge a man by who his family is, what he does for a living, and the firmness of his handshake," he said. "If any of those things are missing, it takes a long time for me to trust someone. If two of those things are missing, that's also a lot of assumptions to overcome, particularly if I'm being asked to entrust that person with the most important thing in my life, my daughter."

With that he stood and offered his hand to Blethen. As they shook hands, Maxim looked him directly in the eyes. "So far, I've only seen one of three."

He walked away, Francine following quietly behind. Blethen now knew where Toni inherited her damn-the-torpedoes-full-speed-ahead style.

Later, still shaken by Maxim's pronouncement, he and Toni sat on the veranda.

"I had a chance to talk to your parents," he said. "Your Dad doesn't like me."

"I do," she said, "and I'll bet my Mom loved you. Don't worry about Dad. He was in papa bear protective mode. He's always like that at first, but he'll come around."

"I'm not so sure. My lack of a family really seemed to bother him."

"Oh. You got his family, work, handshake speech. I've heard it a dozen times. Give him a day and then go have a glass of wine with him. Showing him that he didn't intimidate you will go a long way toward overcoming his reservations."

Blethen nodded. "Maybe I'll do that tomorrow," he said.

"No. Give him a day. If you do it tomorrow he'll think you're too anxious. Maybe after his money. If you want to do something tomorrow, spend a few minutes with my Mom. She'll be thrilled, and the word will get back to Dad. Then talk to him on Friday."

As they got ready to go to bed, Blethen recalled something else from his conversation.

"Your Mom indicated that Aunt Monique was somehow involved in the art world. What's that about?"

"Oh, it's just one of the many things my Mom and the other women find distasteful about her," Toni replied. "Aunt Monique claims to have been involved in some art scandal when she was young. It supposedly involved the German high command, Hitler and Goering, whom she claims to have met. They think it's just a story she made up to make her sound important."

"What do you think?"

"I have no idea. I hear stories about her flamboyant life back in the day, but I don't know how much is true, and how much is family fiction. She does have this imperial air. If you're already inclined to dislike her, she could certainly rub you the wrong way."

"I'd like a chance to talk to her," Blethen said.

"That's not a problem. If she's not with Grandpapa, she spends most of her time by herself. She'd probably welcome the company, but you may want to be a little discreet. Giving her attention won't ingratiate you with the women of the family."

"If you and I talked to her together, would that be less distasteful?"

"Probably. If someone questions it, I'll tell them you wanted to talk to her to see if there was any truth to her story."

"Good."

"I don't think you'll know if what she says is true, though, if she talks about it at all," Toni said. "She may not remember anything because of her dementia."

They lost, 13-11, in the first round of the petanque tournament. They trailed 11-5, saved only by Paulette's skill, until Blethen started to get the hang of it. He was much better at knocking the other team's balls out of scoring range than he was at stopping his own close to the cochonnet, but with Paulette's finesse and his aggression they rallied to tie the score at eleven before a superb final shot by Uncle Jean scored two for his team and ended the game.

"I think you'd be pretty good with a little practice," Paulette told him after the game.

"You, on the other hand," she said turning to Toni. "There's no hope." The cousins laughed and hugged and promised to practice for the next reunion.

"What does Paulette do?" Blethen asked as he and Toni walked away.

"She's a student, and a part time physical education teacher. She was a boy once, you know."

"What?"

"She was born a boy. A girl in a boy's body. Had a bunch of operations to change her physical body to match her psychological gender."

"Wow." Blethen said, shaking his head. "Your family's amazing. No wonder no one thought I was peculiar. You're like the world melting pot all in one family. She's quite attractive."

"She has a boyfriend. They're thinking about getting married," Toni said.

Blethen gave his head a shake, as if trying to assimilate the surprising information into his thought patterns.

"Americans are really hung up about stuff like that," Toni went on. "I think Europeans are more open to things like gender and racial stuff. Maybe it's because we've been seeing it for centuries and realize that it's just normal. Some people are gay. Some people are dark-skinned. Some people are born in the wrong bodies. Ho hum. Just another day in the life of Europe."

Blethen put his arm around her. "Maybe we should stay in Europe," he said.

They found Aunt Monique sitting by herself in the back yard, the fragrance of lavender saturating the air, carried by zephyrs from an adjacent field.

"May we?" Blethen asked, motioning to a wicker loveseat opposite the plush chaise on which she was reclining.

"As you wish," she said, flipping her hand in patrician permission.

"I understand you spent some time in the States," Blethen said as they sat down.

She nodded.

"How long did you live there?"

"Several years. It was dreadful, so I left."

Blethen waited for an explanation, but only the sound of crickets filled the void.

"I live in the United States," Toni said, breaking the silence. "What didn't you like about it when you lived there?"

"Do I know you?"

"I'm Antoinette. Maxim and Francine Chapereaux are my parents. You and I are cousins."

"I don't know any Chapereauxs with red hair," Monique said. Another silence followed.

"My name is Hamilton Blethen. We met last night at dinner. I'm the reason dinner was so late. Because I came in on a late train." He sat back down.

Monique nodded again, a vacant look in her eyes.

"Why are you in my home?" she asked.

"This isn't your....." Blethen stopped, realizing that trying to correct her would be fruitless. "I'm here to celebrate Grandpapa Emile's ninetieth birthday."

With the mention of Emile, her eyes lit up. "Are you his son?" she asked.

"No, I'm a friend of his granddaughter, Toni...Antoinette." Blethen put his arm around Toni to make his point.

"Thought you might be his son. Emile always loved the women. All sizes and colors." It was said without malice. "What's your name?"

"Uh, Hamilton...Hamilton Blethen."

"You remind me of a man I once knew. I think he was a Basque gypsy. Anton. Played the guitar. Great lover."

This time Blethen didn't let her surprising response derail him.

"I hear that you met both Adolph Hitler and Hermann Goering," he said. "How did that happen?"

"They were at the exposition in Paris. I met them there. Reichsmarschall Goering was a very nice man. Very polite. Hitler was...how do you say it...*un con*...a prick. Threw a tantrum and broke the door." She said it like it happened yesterday.

"When was the exposition?"

"1937."

"Are you sure?"

"Young man…do you mind if I call you Anton?"

"Hamilton, please. I hope you remember me some day as fondly as you do Anton."

"Hamilton," she repeated. "Good name." Her concentration drifted off.

"Aunt Monique?" Toni interjected, trying to bring her back. Monique jerked, as though startled.

"Who are you?" she asked, looking at Toni.

"Remembering the Paris Exposition," Blethen jumped in, not wanting her to wander off in another direction. "How did you happen to be there?"

"I worked there," Monique said, still looking at Toni. "I met my husband there. He's why I didn't like living in the United States."

"What did you do at the Exposition?" Blethen pressed on, trying to keep her on track.

"I was a tour guide."

"Did you lead a tour for Hitler and Goering? Is that how you met them?"

"How did you know that? Were you there?"

"I was just guessing," Blethen said. "Where was the tour? Were you the guide for Hitler and Goering?"

"In Paris," she said. "I already told you that."

"I mean where in Paris? Where at the Exposition? Why were Hitler and Goering touring the Exposition?" He realized he had asked too many questions at one time. He tried a simpler approach.

"Why did Hitler throw a tantrum?" he asked.

"Because he didn't like the painting."

"What painting."

The lines in Monique's forehead furrowed as she concentrated. "It had cows in it. And a horse. And people screaming. I can't think of the name."

"Was it *Guernica*?" Blethen asked.

"Yes. That was it. *Guernica*. It was bloody and awful."

"Were you a guide at the Spanish pavilion at the exposition?"

"Yes...I think that's where I worked."

"Do you remember a painting called *The Reaper*? By Joan Miro?" Blethen's voice rose in anticipation.

Aunt Monique yawned. "Would you help me to my room dear," she said, turning to Toni. "It's time for my nap."

Toni rose and gently took the old woman's elbow. "Be careful of the sticks," she said, nodding toward the twigs and leaves scattered on the patio.

"What's your name?" Monique asked her.

Blethen repeated his question.

Monique looked at him as if seeing him for the first time.

"*The Reaper*?" Blethen asked again.

"Oh, it's in the attic," she said. "Why are you in my house?"

"What do you think?" Toni asked after she returned from taking Aunt Monique to her room.

"That was crazy," Blethen said. "I can't tell if she's concocted the whole thing, or if there are threads of truth in it. I'd start to believe her, and then she's say something that was just factually wrong."

"Like what?"

"Well, she said she met Goering in 1937 but then called him 'Reichsmarschall.' Goering wasn't the Reischsmarschall until 1940, after the fall of France. And she called *Guernica* bloody, but *Guernica* is in black and white. Bloody suggests something red. I don't think there's even anything in the painting that would suggest blood. And then there's the attic comment."

"I think she's more to be pitied than ridiculed," Toni said. "She's obviously losing her mental faculties. That's got to be an awful thing, especially if you remember bits and pieces and are still aware enough to know you're losing it."

Blethen nodded. "You can tell your Mom, and Aunt Marion, that there's no way to tell if her story is made up or real. She's mentally too far gone to tell fact from fantasy."

MONDAY, JUNE 21, 2009

BOSTON

"There is one more thing I need you to do," Magnolia said, sitting on the visitor's side of a huge mahogany desk occupied by Tyron Roper, attorney at law. "After he was diagnosed with cancer, Arthur became interested in art collecting. I didn't pay much attention until he became obsessed with recreating a painting that disappeared nearly a century ago. It's named *The Reaper* and Arthur agreed to pay a million dollars to have it done. He paid the painter a retainer of fifty thousand dollars. I don't know if the painter has started yet, but I want the agreement terminated and the fifty thousand dollars returned. Arthur is gone, and I see no need to spend a million dollars on this."

"You are the executor of his estate," Roper said. "You have the authority to make that decision. If the painter has started the work we may have to pay him something, but we'll get right on it. Is the agreement in writing?"

"Not that I know of," she replied. "I wasn't involved in the negotiating, and I don't believe there is anything in writing." She gave Roper the details and Blethen's contact information, and then left the offices of Horst, MacMillan and Roper.

She would attend MacMillans's memorial service the next day, putting on her best stoic face, offering to help in any way she could, agreeing to put up a reward for finding his killer. The following week would be filled with board meetings—the first step in consolidating her power over the Kincaid media empire. Everything was proceeding smoothly except for one thing: what was she going to do about Hamilton Blethen.

She wished she didn't need to do anything. He had no idea who she was or what she looked like. Perhaps she could go on ignoring him. He did not know of her involvement in *The Reaper* deal, and no one knew that the would-be painter of *The Reaper* was her son.

She could just stay away from him, except for one thing. At some point, if she hadn't already, her mother would tell Hamilton about the phone call, about them both being in Barcelona at the same time. What if he went back to Hawke? Her "arrangement" probably wouldn't prevent Hawke from divulging her involvement in *The Reaper*. Blethen would put two and two together, and he would find her.

A man wouldn't have to worry about this, she fumed. *But a woman with a colored child who is an art forger?* First it would only be whispers and rumors. Then it would become media fodder. She knew it would bring her down. Suddenly, she was no longer a mother who felt the remorse of abandoning her child. She was a woman on the verge of immense power, of being an inspiration for other women, of shattering glass ceilings and allowing other women to rise up. Hamilton Blethen could not be allowed to derail that. He was not her son. He couldn't be. He was only an obstacle to be overcome, to be dealt with.

That afternoon a message was left on Hamilton Blethen's voice mail: "Mr. Blethen. My name is Tyrone Roper. I am an attorney in Boston. I'm calling to inform you that Arthur Kincaid has passed away, thereby effectively terminating the agreement between you and Mr. Kincaid. Please call me as soon as possible."

ALBI AND BARCELONA

Blethen and Toni had spent the final two days of the family reunion enjoying her family and the French countryside.

"I told you my Dad would warm up to you," Toni said as she sat, snuggled next to him on a train bound for Barcelona. "And my Mom loves you, all the women in my family do."

"Even Aunt Monique, once she remembered my name," Blethen

chuckled. "I think parts of her story are true. The problem is trying to figure out which parts."

"Regardless, she seemed to enjoy her conversations with you. She perked up quite a bit the last couple of days."

"So, what did your Aunt Marion have to say?" he asked. "I saw the two of you in deep conversation this morning."

"She had warned me, before you came, about loving an artist. Her exact quote was 'Screw him until you're through with him, and then move on.' This morning she told me she really likes you, but she hasn't changed her mind. She said that artists are creative, and they're always looking for someone new to be creative with."

Blethen scratched the tip of his nose, looking thoughtful.

"So," he said with a grin, "when you say all the women in your family love me, they really just want my body."

"They can't have that," Toni said with that familiar twinkle in her green eyes. "At least not 'til I'm done with it."

Their verbal foreplay eventually evolved into more serious conversation about researching Miro and the lost *Reaper*. They decided the first stop would be a visit to the Miro Museum, Fundació Joan Miró, where a great deal of Miro's art and personal history was on display.

"I think what we do after that will depend upon what we find there," Blethen said. "It might be valuable to look into the archives of local newspapers or art periodicals from 1937, but I don't think either of us has adequate Spanish skills to do that. We might have to contact a local college to see if we could hire someone to do the research. Maybe we'll go to Majorca. He spent many years there and there's a museum that used to be his studio."

Well after midnight they checked into Hotel Rialto as Mr. and Mrs. Hamilton Blethen. It seemed like a natural thing to do. They spent the weekend touring the city and taking pleasure in each other.

TUESDAY, JUNE 22, 2009

After breakfast, before heading for the Miro Museum, Blethen checked his voice mail.

"Probably full," he said. "It's been almost a week since I checked." It was, but there were only two messages of consequence. The first was from Elaine Ravalo.

"I've got to see you right away!" There was urgency in Elaine's voice. "Call me as soon as you get this." The message had been left on Friday, the day Blethen and Toni had left the family reunion.

The second message was from Tyrone Roper informing him of the death of Arthur Kincaid. Blethen sank into the chair as if he'd taken a punch to the gut.

"What's wrong?" Toni asked.

"Arthur Kincaid is dead."

Toni stared at him with a confused look on her face.

"Kincaid is...was...the guy who hired me to paint *The Reaper*. The message was from a lawyer. He says the *Reaper* deal is off."

"Oh, Ham. I'm so sorry."

He sat in the chair with a stunned look in his eyes.

After several minutes of silence, Toni asked, "Should I start packing up?" That snapped Blethen out of his trance.

"I suppose I better call...oh, shit, it's only three in the morning in Boston. Yeah, I suppose we better pack up and see about getting an earlier flight."

The hotel concierge rebooked them on a flight to New York that afternoon. Thanks to the time zone changes, and a quick connection in New York, they would be back in Saint Paul that evening.

Blethen called Roper during the layover in New York.

"He wants me to give back the fifty thousand," he told Toni after the call.

"What fifty thousand?"

"Oh, I thought I told you," Blethen answered. "I got a fifty-thousand-dollar advance against my commission to paint *The Reaper*. To cover expenses."

"A fifty-thousand-dollar advance!" Toni blurted. "How much was the commission?"

"A million dollars."

They sat in silence for several minutes. Finally, Toni spoke: "That doesn't make any sense unless…."

"Unless, what?"

"Unless he intended to resell it as the real thing," she said.

"That's what I thought, too, but I was told point-blank that was not the case. Kincaid wanted it for himself. Why, I don't know."

The pall of the lost commission, the prospect of having to disgorge the advance, and brain-sapping fatigue hung over them the rest of the trip. Blethen slept fitfully on the flight to Minneapolis/Saint Paul.

WEDNESDAY, JUNE 23, 2009

He slept no better in his own bed that night, a nightmare of flaming paintings and violence waking him at 4 a.m. in a pool of sweat. He didn't go back to sleep.

Realizing delivery of the morning newspaper wouldn't resume until Monday, Blethen put on a pot of coffee, got dressed and walked six blocks to a twenty-four-hour gas station to get the paper. The fresh air helped clear his head but walking without Barca seemed strange. He would have to go get him today. He bought two apple fritters at the gas station. At least he would be able to eat them in peace without a long nose on his leg and big brown eyes staring at him.

At eight o'clock, with the pot of coffee, both apple fritters and the newspaper consumed, Blethen called Roper. He asked to keep half of the advance to cover his expenses and time spent, ultimately settling for $15,000. He promised to mail the balance of the advance immediately. He wrote the check to Roper's trust account, as directed, and felt better, realizing the balance in his account was still healthy thanks to the recent payment from the jewelry store in Ohio and Elaine's advance payment.

Elaine. Oh, shit. I forgot about her call. He dialed her number.

"Elaine, this is Ham. I'm sorry it took so long to get back to you. What's up?"

There was a long pause on the other end.

"Yes, that would be fine. Where can we meet?"

"What?" Blethen responded. It was definitely Elaine's voice, but the words made no sense.

Another long pause. "How about Dunn Brothers Coffee on Third Avenue in an hour."

"Okay." She barely waited for his answer before hanging up.

What the hell is this all about? Some new ploy to get me into bed, again? But her answers were bizarre, and she had sounded upset in the earlier message she'd left. Blethen searched his voice mail and found the message. The tone of her recorded voice was agitated, maybe even scared. *She's such a diva. It could be all an act,* he thought.

Blethen called Toni and told her of the strange call with Elaine. Without being asked, she volunteered to meet Blethen at Dunn Brothers.

It was a quarter to ten when he walked in the front door of the coffee shop. Neither Elaine nor Toni were there yet. He ordered a small cup of the dark roast of the day for himself and a caramel macchiato for Toni, then grabbed a table in the far corner of the second level, hoping for a bit of privacy. Toni found him a few minutes later. They sat and waited.

Elaine, nearly a half hour past the appointed time, made her usual flamboyant entry. They could hear her place her order, ending with: "Oh, dahling, would you please bring it to my table." There was a clumping sound as she ascended the wooden staircase to the second level, and a wave of acknowledgment when she saw them, but the look on her face didn't match the flamboyance of her entry. She looked tired and worried.

"Thank God you're here," she said in an uncharacteristic half-whisper as she pulled out a chair.

"What's going on?" Blethen asked.

"Sorry I couldn't talk on the phone. George was there. He and

I had a blowup last week. He's been having me followed. He said he knows I'm having an affair."

The words reeled through Blethen's mind.

"You mean he thinks you and I are having an affair?"

"Yes," she said. "He says he has pictures."

"Pictures? What the hell kind of pictures could he have of us?"

"I don't know," she said. "Maybe pictures of us having lunch together at the club, or of me going into your studio. I don't know. Oh, shit. You don't suppose he has copies of the photos you took a couple weeks ago."

"How could he have those?"

"What kind of photos were they?" Toni asked, a chilly tone in her voice.

"Innocent enough, but considering what I was wearing there may have been some that didn't leave a lot to the imagination," Elaine responded.

Toni shot Blethen a dark, questioning look.

"I took pictures of your face," he said. "I don't think there was anything suggestive or revealing. Maybe some cleavage in a couple of them."

"I don't know," she said, traces of despair in her voice. "He says he has pictures."

Blethen cocked his head, thinking.

"Just before I left for Europe there was this suspicious car, a black Firebird, that I'd seen several times before, parked outside my building," he said. "I saw a man come out of the building like he was in a hurry. I was suspicious, so I checked to see if anything was missing from my place. There didn't seem to be, but I didn't think to look for the photos I took of you. I'll check when I get back to my apartment."

"Are you having an affair with anyone?" Toni asked Elaine, matter-of-factly.

"Or a flirtation?"

"I have flirtations with every man I meet," Elaine said, truthfully, "but there isn't any affair. At least not now. God, I never thought it would come to this!"

"How long ago was your last affair?" Toni continued. There was no accusation in her voice, just a search for information, as uncomfortable as it might be.

"I haven't seen him in months." Then, referring to her husband: "I don't know what's gotten into George. He's never been concerned about my dalliances before. He's never cared what I do as long as I'm there when he wants me to be."

"Has anything changed?" Blethen asked. "Between the two of you?"

"Not that I know of."

Does he have a new girlfriend? Does he want a divorce? Has he had enough of being a public cuckold? The thoughts crossed Blethen's mind, but he didn't say them out loud. Elaine had enough to deal with right now and so, apparently, did he.

"Meet the lion in his lair." It was Toni's suggestion.

"Since you have nothing to be guilty about, meet the issue head-on," she repeated. "Tell Elaine's husband about the portrait, and let him know that there is no affair. Defuse all the innuendo and false assumptions and suspicion."

"He already knows about the painting," Elaine interjected. "I even showed him the check I paid for it. He said it looked to him like I was paying to get laid and the painting was just a cover."

"But if the person he suspects is your lover meets him, face-to-face, and denies the affair, it will be different than you denying it," Toni persisted. "Most men screwing somebody's wife wouldn't have the balls to confront the angry husband. By Ham doing it, you overcome that assumption and the claim of innocence has credibility."

The suggestion might have made sense if not for the affair two years ago. *Maybe the pictures are from back then, and he was just waiting for the right time to use them,* Blethen thought. *Maybe doing another painting for Elaine was what triggered this.*

"I'll have to think about that," he said. "Sounds logical, but I'm not sure an angry husband is going to think logically."

Toni turned to Elaine. "Has he asked you for a divorce?"

"Not yet. He's just threatened to cut me off. I may need the money back from the Gainsborough." Elaine said.

"If you don't go through with having the painting done," Toni said, "won't it just confirm his suspicion that you two are having an affair? Apparently he has pictures of the two of you together. If there is no painting to show for it, what logical reason is there for the two of you to be together?"

"Thanks for saving my commission," Blethen said to Toni as they stood on the sidewalk outside Dunn Brothers. Elaine had left, placated, seeing the wisdom in Toni's reasoning. She had agreed Blethen should finish the painting. Blethen had agreed to look for the photos. She would continue to deny the affair, and they would wait and see what George Ravalo did next.

"I wasn't saving your commission," Toni said. "I was trying to keep you from getting offed by some hot-headed Italian lawyer who probably has connections to the mob, and, having said that, I still think you should meet with him. Open communication is still the best way to head off a crisis. And I was just kidding about the mob connection."

"Not something to kid about," Blethen said. "Remember that Elaine and I did have an affair. What if he's got pictures from back then?"

Toni thought for a moment.

"Make an appointment to see him in his office. That's the safest place to meet him. Take someone with you so you have a witness. Tell him you are not having an affair with his wife, and about painting the Gainsborough. Take your sketches with you. If he has photos from before, then you'll need to admit it. Tell him you knew it was a mistake then, and that you've taken precautions to make sure it won't happen again. Offer to not finish the painting, to give the money back."

"And if he doesn't have pictures from before?" Blethen asked.

"Then deny you're having an affair with her, show him what you're doing, and convince him there is nothing to his suspicions. You could still offer to give the money back and not finish the painting."

"Whhhhhhh." Blethen exhaled, sounding like the rush of wind.

"Coughing up two commissions in twenty-four hours? That really sounds great."

"It's the honorable thing to do," Toni said. "It could save Elaine's marriage. And it will definitely keep you from being offed by the mob."

"Don't joke about that," he said. He was serious.

The photos of Elaine were missing from the desk in his studio.

At first Blethen was furious. His space had been violated. Things that belonged to him had been taken. Who is the sonofabitch in the black Firebird? But as he calmed down, he realized that this was probably good news. If Elaine's husband hired someone to burglarize his apartment, and all they took was a bunch of photographs, it probably meant that he didn't have earlier pictures. Plus, it gave Blethen leverage. If George Ravalo showed him the photos of Elaine taken just two weeks earlier, then he was guilty of burglary, or breaking and entering at the very least. Blethen guessed that would be enough to get Ravalo before the ethics board; maybe get his license revoked. Maybe send him to jail.

His confidence grew. At least he wasn't going naked into a meeting with an irate husband. He had a bargaining chip.

He called Jim Benson. They agreed to meet over wine.

"I have this little problem and I need your help," Blethen said after they'd sniffed, swirled and sipped a new Napa Valley cabernet.

Blethen explained his predicament. "Would you come with me when I meet with this guy?" he asked.

"I took a course in grad school on dealing with difficult people, but it didn't include irate husbands." Benson shook his head, a sardonic smile on his face. "You lead the most interesting life. Did you ever think of getting a legitimate job?" The moment he said it, he regretted it. "Of course, I'll come," he said, quickly. "Just try to set the appointment after two thirty so I don't have to cancel any classes."

"I'll let you know when," Blethen said, setting his partially full wine glass on the bar and rising to leave.

"I didn't mean it. About the legitimate job," Benson blurted.

"Yeah. Sure. I'll let you know."

Blethen had forgotten about Barca until he walked through the door that evening and missed the usual exuberant greeting from his four-legged roommate. He called Toni and asked if she wanted to ride with him to Grandma's to pick up Barca the next day.

"I'm glad you called," she said, a noticeable quiver in her voice. "I'm feeling a little creeped out right now. Todd D'Anselmo was waiting for me when I got home this afternoon, sitting on my front step."

"What the hell did he want?" Blethen interrupted.

"Said he just stopped to say 'Hi.' He asked what was going on in the program. He asked about you, and whether we were still seeing each other. I couldn't get rid of him, and I sure didn't want to ask him in. I finally made up an excuse and he left. Now I have the feeling I'm being watched."

"I'll be right over," he said. Twenty minutes later he rang her doorbell. An ashen Toni opened the door a crack, pulling him inside as she wrapped her arms around him,

"You okay?" he asked. He could feel her shudder. He squeezed her tighter, then stroked the back of her head, buried in his shoulder. After a minute Toni's rigid body began to relax.

"I think I just had a panic attack," her words muffled, spoken into his shirt.

"What do you want to do?"

"I'd like to go to your place," she said. "Let me get my computer and throw a couple of things in a bag."

"I'll take a look outside while you're getting your stuff together. Did you see what kind of car he was driving?"

"I didn't even think to look. He was just so creepy, all gaunt with his eyes sunken in. I think maybe he was on drugs."

Blethen went out to the sidewalk and looked up and down the street. There was no black Firebird and no sign of Todd D'Anselmo.

"Has he ever shown up at your house before?" Blethen asked as they drove to Saint Paul.

"No, and I hope he never does again."

FRIDAY, JUNE 25, 2009

ZUMBROTA

The white cargo van slowed. The driver leaned forward, peering to read the name on the mail box. His destination confirmed, he turned off the highway into the gravel driveway that led to the white farmhouse with green shutters.

Lorraine could see the words "Bert's Appliances" on the van doors as she watched it come up the driveway. It crunched to a halt next to the wooden stoop, less than a dozen feet from her front door. A young man dressed in dungarees, work boots, a uniform jacket and work gloves got out of the passenger side.

Lorraine opened the front door a crack, not waiting for the man to knock. "Barca, get back," she said, pushing the big dog away from the door with her leg. "Can I help you?"

"We're here to deliver your new appliances," he said.

"You must have the wrong place. I didn't order appliances."

The man looked at his clip board. "Are you Lorraine Blethen?"

"Yes."

"Says here that we are to deliver these to you and take away your old appliances. Says they're a gift from Mary Blethen."

"What? Let me see that." Lorraine opened the door wider and the man handed her his clipboard. "Well, I'll be," she said.

"Can I come in and see what we have to remove?" the man asked.

"Of course, come in." Lorraine stepped aside and swung the door fully open. "Don't worry about Barca," she said, referring to the golden retriever wagging his tail. "He wouldn't hurt a fly."

The man signaled the driver who got out of the van. He was dressed the same, but shorter with a barrel chest and massive arms. His left eye squinted in the direction of a small, half-moon scar a half-inch from his eye socket, pulling up the left corner of his mouth and giving him a whimsical look. He tousled Barca's ears as he entered the house. "Okay if I give him a treat?" he asked.

Less than ten minutes later the two men left the house, climbed in the van, and left.

Blethen had been checking his rearview mirror as he and Toni rode south on Highway 52.

"Black Firebird?" Toni asked.

"No, but since he followed us last time we were on this road, I'm checking."

"Do you really think it's Todd D'Anselmo?"

"With him showing up at your place the other night, I'd almost bet on it," Blethen responded.

"Maybe, but you said you started seeing the car right after you got the call about *The Reaper,* and now we know that Elaine's husband has been having you followed."

Blethen nodded, perplexed. "I know. There are all sorts of possibilities. I guess we won't know until I catch him."

"And then what will you do?"

"I'll…uh…I'll at least know who is following us. I guess I hadn't thought about what I'd do."

"Well, maybe when you talk to George Ravalo next week you can ask him if he knows anyone with a black Firebird, and if he's having them follow you."

"Yeah, I'll make sure I do that," Blethen said sarcastically. It would be difficult enough to face Ravalo without accusing him.

As they exited off Highway 52 they could see red emergency lights flashing in Grandma's driveway a half mile away. Blethen hit the gas, accelerating the half mile, then braked hard and careened into the gravel driveway, narrowly missing the two police cars and an ambulance parked in her yard. He pulled around the cars and parked on the lawn, next to an old Chevy Neon. He jumped out of the car and could hear Barca barking. Toni was right behind him.

A local policeman was standing in the open door to the farmhouse, blocking their way.

"What happened?" shouted Blethen. "What's going on?"

"Who are you?" the policeman asked over the barking, growling and shouting coming from inside the farmhouse.

"My Grandma lives here. This is my girlfriend, and that's my dog inside!" Blethen shouted.

There was more shouting from inside and a county sheriff deputy came out. "We're going to have to tranquilize that dog," he said as he passed the policeman and headed for one of the squads.

"Wait! Wait! That's my dog," Blethen shouted.

The policeman stopped. "Then get control of him. Call him off."

They followed the deputy into the house. A snarling Barca was straddling Lorraine, who lay crumpled on the living room floor. Foam and drool dripped from the dog's jowls, forming a puddle on Lorraine's dress. A half dozen uniformed personnel circled the dog and fallen woman, making sure to keep a safe distance from the crazed animal. An older woman in a house dress cowered in the corner.

"Barca! Barca! Sit!"

The familiar voice transformed the dog. He carefully stepped over Lorraine's body and sat beside it, a low growl still emanating from deep within him.

"Come, Barca. Come." Blethen's voice was firm but with less volume. Barca bounded across the room, his tail wagging, as EMTs and law enforcement officers backed against the walls of the living room. Blethen hooked a finger under Barca's collar and led him into the kitchen.

EMTs immediately rushed to the fallen woman and checked vital signs. It took only a minute. "No pulse, and she's not breathing," one of them said. Blethen felt a leaden weight in his chest.

"Is she?" He managed to say as he stood in the kitchen door, still holding Barca's collar. The EMT nodded. "I'm sorry." He mouthed the words, not wanting to say them aloud.

For the next hour Blethen and Toni sat, or wandered through the house, numbed by the suddenness of Lorraine's death, listening and asking questions, trying to piece together what had happened.

The old woman from a neighboring farm had been hanging laundry on her clothesline when she saw a white van pull out of Lorraine's driveway. As it drove past she saw the signage on the van door: *somebody's appliances*. She couldn't remember the name, but she was sure it was a man's name. She wondered if Lorraine had gotten that new stove she'd been talking about for so long. When she finished hanging clothes, she poured a cup of coffee and walked to Lorraine's to see. She knocked but there was no answer, so she stuck her head in the door and shouted for Lorraine. There was a muffled bark from the bathroom. She shouted for Lorraine again. When no answer came, she decided to peek in the kitchen to see if there was a new stove. As she walked past the living room she saw Lorraine on the floor. When she couldn't wake her, she called 9-1-1.

The police arrived just minutes before Blethen and Toni. The neighbor had let Barca out of the bathroom as the police were coming through the front door. Barca was astraddle Lorraine's fallen body, not about to let anyone come near his fallen grandmother.

"There's bruising on her arms, and one big bruise on her left thigh," Blethen overheard one of the EMTs tell the Goodhue County sheriff's deputy who seemed to be in charge of the scene.

"Tripped over something? Fell?" the deputy asked.

"Maybe, but it's both arms. Could be signs of a struggle."

"We'll have Jake take a look."

Blethen had been eavesdropping. "Who's Jake?" he asked.

"Jake Long. He's the county coroner. Who are you, again?"

Blethen and Toni were questioned by the deputy and a Zumbrota city policeman, Blethen receiving extra scrutiny until he showed the officers a framed picture of him and Grandma Lorraine on an end table.

"Did she have any enemies? Anyone who might want to do her harm?" the deputy asked.

"Not that I know of," Blethen said.

"Relatives?"

"Besides me? I know she has a sister and a brother. They both live on the West Coast. Oregon, I think, but I don't know how to get in touch with them."

"Any others?"

"My mother, I suppose, but I have no idea where you could find her. Grandma hasn't mentioned hearing from her in a long time, probably in five, six years. I haven't heard from her in twenty."

"Name?"

"Mary. Mary Blethen. Or maybe she changed her name. The last thing I heard from her was a card that was signed Magnolia."

Heading north on highway 52, back toward Saint Paul, Blethen drove in silence. Toni sat, watching the fields pass by the passenger's window, leaving Blethen to his thoughts. Barca curled up in the back seat. Tires rolling on concrete at seventy miles per hour provided a white noise backdrop to the anesthetized mood in the car.

As the fields evolved into the shopping malls and housing tracts of the suburbs, Toni broke the silence. "Who's going to plan the funeral?"

Blethen shrugged. "The police will try to get hold of her brother and sister," he said, a ragged edge to his voice. "We can't get into her house because they're treating it like a crime scene, at least until they do an autopsy. They said they'd let me know when they got the results, but that probably won't be for a week, so I guess everything will have to wait."

"We at least ought to call a funeral home," Toni said.

He nodded and lapsed back into the void, the EMT's words "signs of a struggle" kept coming back. *Now I know what I'll do*, he thought, harking back to his earlier conversation with Toni. *I'll kill the sonofabitch when I catch him!*

MONDAY, JUNE 28, 2009

MINNEAPOLIS

Benson had made the appointment with George Ravalo for four o'clock. Blethen wished it had been earlier. He had spent the entire day, and most of a sleepless night, oscillating between the why of Grandma Lorraine's death and the meeting with his accuser. By the time he and Benson were sitting in Ravalo's plush reception area, Blethen was flushed, sweaty and on the verge of a panic attack. To keep a lid on his emotions he focused on the artwork that tastefully adorned the waiting room. It was apparent that Ravalo had good, and expensive, tastes.

A secretary ushered them into a large conference room with one windowed wall looking out on the Minneapolis skyline, and offered them water or coffee. Blethen and Benson both declined. They sat at an expansive conference table polished to a sheen that brought out the depth of the wood grain. A moment later Ravalo, short and bald with the nose of a pugilist, entered the room, dressed in a suit Blethen was sure neither he nor Benson could afford. A younger man followed. Ravalo stuck out his hand as he made his way down the conference table. "Mr. Benson?" he inquired.

Both Benson and Blethen rose, Benson taking Ravalo's hand, acknowledging his greeting.

"This is my associate, Anthony Vincent," Ravalo said, nodding at the younger man. "And you are?" he said, turning to Blethen.

"Mr. Ravalo. My name is Hamilton Blethen." His voice sounded strong, which surprised him. At the mention of Blethen's name Ravalo bristled.

"I believe there is a misunderstanding that needs to be cleared up," Blethen pushed on.

"I know who you are." Ravalo snarled.

"Perhaps it would be better if we talked in private," Blethen offered.

"No!"

Ravalo's voice turned immediately calm, calculating, the inflection venomous. "I want witnesses for anything you have to say. Perhaps we should record this conversation." Blethen felt like a rat in a box with a cobra, but he forced his rehearsed speech out of his mouth.

"Mr. Ravalo, you are a formidable person, and it took a great deal of courage for me to come here today. More courage than I thought I had, but I have come to tell you that I am not having an affair with your wife." He exhaled. *There. I said it.* "I am an artist, painting a portrait of your wife in the style of the English artist, Thomas Gainsborough, nothing more. We are not having an affair."

"I have people who say you're a liar, and I have pictures that prove it."

"You mean the pictures stolen from my apartment?"

Ravalo's young associate flinched, but the accusation didn't faze the older lawyer.

"Those and several others," he said. "I believe you've been having an affair with my wife from the first time you did a painting for her."

"I can assure you that I have never had an affair with your wife," Blethen said, hoping there was nothing in the pictures to prove his lie. "I have painted two pictures for your wife. I am currently painting a third. Our relationship has been purely professional."

"Explain these!" Ravalo said pulling a stack of photographs out of the pocket of his suitcoat and slamming them down on the table. They scattered on impact.

Blethen recognized most of them as photos he had taken. There were two showing him and Elaine having lunch. There were also photos of Elaine entering his building. There were none from their earlier liaisons. He internally exhaled. His lie was safe.

"Mrs. Ravalo and I had lunch to discuss the painting I'm currently working on," Blethen said, pointing at the two luncheon photos. "These were taken at your club. Do you think we'd have lunch at your club if we were having an affair?

"She asked me to paint Gainsborough's *Georgiana, Duchess of Devonshire*," Blethen went on, not waiting for an answer, "but she wanted me to substitute her face for that of the Duchess. For me to do that she had to sit for me so I could draw her face into the portrait."

Blethen pulled four sketches from a portfolio and spread them on the table. "These photos," he said, pointing to the ones showing Elaine entering the door to his building, "must have been taken as she came for one of the two sittings."

"I took these other photos," Blethen continued, referring to the remaining pictures, "in the event I needed to refine some detail during the actual process of painting her face into the portrait, so she wouldn't have to come back for additional sittings, and for reference regarding skin tone, hairlines and things of that nature."

"If you are only interested in her face, then why did you take these?" Ravalo snarled, not buying into the explanation. He pointed at two photos showing extensive cleavage, her blouse struggling to cover her double Ds.

"Mr. Ravalo," Blethen sighed in apparent resignation. "Your wife is a very flamboyant woman. What she wears seems to reflect her personality. I am not responsible for that, although sometimes it makes me uncomfortable." He had practiced the answer several times on the way to the meeting, anticipating the question.

Blethen bent down from his chair and withdrew a carefully folded copy of *Georgiana, Duchess of Devonshire* from the portfolio. He laid it next to the offending photos. "As you can see, Gainsborough's work is a full upper torso portrait. Please note that in these photos Mrs. Ravalo is seated in exactly the same position as the *Duchess* in Gainsborough's painting. And now look at my sketches."

He positioned them next to the two photos and the copy of the original painting. "Note that the woman in my sketches is also seated in exactly the same position. They have, to the best of my artistic ability, your wife's face in them. And they show no cleavage."

Both men looked back and forth between the painting, the two photos of Elaine and the four sketches.

"I took these photos to duplicate the lighting Gainsborough used in his portrait. See these shadows?" Blethen continued, pointing first at the portrait and then at the same shadows in the photos. "The two photos are the same except they were taken with two different backgrounds. I was trying to soften the shadows in the second photo to more closely match those in the portrait."

Vincent and Benson simultaneously sat back in their chairs, nodding.

Ravalo fought against seeing the logic in Blethen's explanation, but his face lost its hardness. "Hmmmph," was all he could muster.

"Look at each of the photos your man took from my studio," Blethen went on, now careful to avoid any inflammatory words like *burglary* or *thief.* "All but these two," referring to the two cleavage shots, "are of your wife's head and face. If we were memorializing an affair in photos, do you think these two would be the raciest photos we'd take?"

Vincent was still nodding his head. Ravalo looked like a bulldog with his teeth pulled.

Blethen reached for the picture of *The Duchess*, folded it and put it back in the portfolio. He did the same with his sketches. "If you don't mind," he said. "I'd like my photos back so I can finish the painting." He squared them up on the tabletop, careful to leave out the ones he didn't take, and put them in his portfolio without objection from Ravalo.

"I don't know who's been telling you that I'm having an affair with your wife," he finished, "but they're the ones who are lying. Not me." He looked squarely at Ravalo.

"I want you to stay away from my wife," Ravalo's demanded, the edge in his voice returning.

"I can't control your wife, but I will not initiate any contact with her, and if she contacts me I will discourage any meeting. If she insists, I will let you know the time and place of the meeting in advance."

That seemed to satisfy Ravalo.

"I will need to deliver the painting when it is completed," Blethen said, trying to make sure all loose ends were accounted for. "Do you want me to deliver it to you here at your office?"

"No. Just have it delivered to my home by courier.

"It will be delivered COD," Blethen said.

Ravalo abruptly concluded the meeting. "You can show yourselves out," he said as he walked out the conference room door.

"You were great," Benson said as he and Blethen descended in the elevator. "Man, you should have gone to law school."

"Dodged a bullet," was all Blethen said. He felt drained, dirty. He wanted a shower and a nap but agreed with Benson to stop for a beer to avoid the rush hour traffic—and to thank Benson for sticking his neck out for him. During his second beer he called Toni to tell her how the meeting had gone.

"Congratulations," she said, "but you don't sound very happy."

"Exhausted," Blethen replied. "When the meeting ended all my adrenaline went with it. Just the after-effect of the last three days."

"Why don't you come to my place so you don't have to drive all the way home."

"Barca..."

"I'll go get him. You can both stay over."

Blethen was too tired to argue. "Thanks," he said. "I'll see you in an hour or two."

By the time he was headed south on I-35W the sun had set. He'd stayed longer and drunk more than he planned, and Benson had buoyed his spirits. He was in a good mood, with just a few cobwebs in his head, and he stopped to buy a bottle of wine to give Toni a chance to catch up to him.

After browsing for a few minutes, he selected a Bordeaux from the Pomerol region.

The price approached a hundred dollars, but he was feeling giddy.

Maybe I'll even ask Toni to marry me tonight. He looked at the wine. Had he really just thought that? *She'd say 'too soon.' Shit, I don't even have a ring.*

The hundred-dollar bottle of wine was gently put back on the shelf. His thoughts muddled, Blethen selected a nice Pinot Noir from Oregon instead and saved sixty dollars.

He drove the last few blocks lost in his conflicted thoughts. The black Firebird materialized out of the night, sitting in front of Toni's house.

Sonofabitch! Rage engulfed him. *This has got to end! What the fuck are you doing in front of her house?*

Focused only on the object of his fury, Blethen slammed his car into the curb at a forty-five-degree angle in front of the Firebird. *You're not getting away this time, you sonofabitch!*

He bolted out of his car and dashed to the driver's door of the Firebird. He yanked on the handle hard. It was locked. He tried to peer through the tinted window to see if anyone was inside.

He heard the crack of his backbone before he felt the pain. He spun from the impact of the blow and saw a tall, hooded figure with a baseball bat as he went down. There was another impact on the side of his head, and his body changed directions as it hurtled toward the ground.

The side of his face was against the pavement. The eye that could see watched a black puddle slowly get bigger. He could hear his phone ringing in the distance, fading…fading…

Nancy Crawford was on her way home from work after pulling a double shift at Abbott Northwestern Hospital. Fatigue wracked every fiber of her being. All her concentration was on getting home to the bed beckoning her weary body. Suddenly the tail of a car sticking out in the traffic lane jumped out at her.

She swerved to miss it, fought for control of the car, then slammed on the brakes.

There, lying in the street beside the oddly-parked car, was a body. There was blood. Lots of it. Her nursing instincts kicked in. Dialing 9-1-1, she grabbed a first aid kit from her backseat and sprinted toward the inert form on the concrete, all fatigue forgotten.

Within minutes, the police were on the scene, followed by an ambulance and paramedics. The flashing lights brought out the neighbors to gawk and brought out Toni who had been waiting.

"Oh my God!" Her shriek drew the attention of the police. One grabbed her by the shoulders to stop her as she rushed toward the bloody scene.

"Do you know him?" he asked when he had succeeded. Toni sank to the pavement, her legs giving way.

"Do you know him?" the officer repeated, louder. Toni's eyes rolled back in her head. "Medic!" the policeman shouted.

An EMT revived Toni with smelling salts and left her with the policeman, returning to help Blethen.

"Is...it...bad?" she asked, fearful of the answer. She had seen the blood and his crumpled body.

"He'll get the best medical care in the world," the policeman said. "I'm sure he'll be all right." In these circumstances, it was his job to give comfort, not to be accurate. Tears rolled down her cheeks. *It's my fault. He would never have gone if I hadn't pushed him.* Her shoulders convulsed and the tears became a flood.

The ambulance screamed through the night, carrying Blethen to emergency surgery.

"Thank God a nurse found him or he'd already be dead," one of the paramedics said.

"Not likely he'll make it anyway," said another. "He's lost a lot of blood. Plus, he has at least three broken ribs on his right side. Maybe a punctured lung. Back might be broken too."

The two grimly continued to work over the body of Hamilton Blethen, trying to keep life's thin thread from breaking before the surgeons could try their luck.

After the ambulance left Toni had been escorted back inside her house by the uniformed policeman, and he stayed with her until the sobbing ceased and she regained control. Minutes later, the officer in charge, notepad in hand, had taken a seat across from her on the couch and had asked preliminary questions about Blethen, about Toni and about their relationship.

"Do you know what happened?" Toni asked the officer.

"We were hoping you could tell us," he said. "It appears Mr. Blethen was struck with a blunt instrument. Do you know anyone who would want to harm him?"

Toni thought for a moment.

"Yes."

"Who?"

"A man named George Ravalo."

"Why would he want to harm him?"

"Because he thought Ham was having an affair with his wife."

"Do you…" the officer started, but Toni interrupted him.

"Ham met with Ravalo today to tell him there was no truth to the rumors." She put her head in her hands and wept without making a sound. "It was my idea," she gulped.

The officer called in George Ravalo's name. After a moment he touched Toni on the shoulder. "Are you able to answer a couple more questions?"

"Yes," she said, gathering herself.

"Mr. Blethen's car is parked at an odd angle. It appears that the right front tire hit the curb with some force. Do you have any idea why he would park that way?"

"Well, if he was hurt…"

"We thought of that, but there is no trace of blood in the car, and he was lying in front of the car.

"I don't know." Toni's voice was barely a whisper.

The officer nodded. "I may have more questions later." Toni walked him to the front door.

"Where did they take him?" she asked as he was leaving.

"Abbott Northwestern. Great hospital."

She nodded.

George Ravalo opened the front door of the magnificent colonial mansion, annoyed that someone would be ringing his doorbell at such a late hour.

His attitude adjusted as he stared at the badge held out at arms-length by a man in a dark suit.

"Mr. Ravalo? I'm Detective Schwartz. This is Lieutenant Sylvester. We're with the Minneapolis Police Department. We'd like to ask you some questions."

"What's this about?"

"Can we come in?"

"Oh, of course." Ravalo stepped aside, and the two officers stepped into the vestibule. "Come into my office." He led them, in his stocking feet, past a wide, curved white marble stairway that disappeared into the second floor. A massive crystal chandelier hung over the stairway, scattering light throughout the foyer. Ravalo opened a heavy wood door just off the corner of the foyer. "C'mon in. Take a chair," he said, motioning toward two over-stuffed leather chairs. Ravalo sat behind a large writer's desk that dominated the middle of the room. Walls of books flanked both sides of the room. Behind Ravalo a large window looked out into the blackness of the night.

Schwartz tried to adjust himself so he didn't sink completely into the soft leather, noting that the chairs were positioned so that the occupants of the chairs had to look up at Ravalo. "Do you know a Hamilton Blethen?" he asked.

Sweat beads popped on Ravalo's forehead. "I've met him."

"Did you have a meeting with him today?"

"Yes," he said, steadying himself. "I and another lawyer from my office met with him."

"What was the meeting about?"

"That is confidential."

"Is Mr. Blethen your client?"

Ravalo paused, twisting in his seat. "No."

"So, then, what was the meeting about?"

"It was a personal matter. I'd rather not say."

Detective Schwartz already knew, from his questioning of Toni, what the meeting was about. He decided to take another tack. "Was it a friendly meeting?"

Ravalo shifted uncomfortably. "Not exactly."

"What time did the meeting end?" Schwartz continued.

"About five o'clock, I think."

"Did you and Mr. Blethen leave together?"

"No. I left before he did. He was with another man named Benson. I assume they left together. I went to my club to play tennis. I left there about seven and came home."

"Were you with anyone?"

"Yes. I was playing tennis with another member of my club. Why are you asking me all these questions?"

"Because Hamilton Blethen was assaulted tonight. He's in the hospital undergoing emergency surgery as we speak."

"WHAT?" Elaine had been standing in the foyer, listening to the conversation. She charged into the room, yelling, "WHAT DID YOU SAY?"

"Are you Mrs. Ravalo?" Schwartz asked.

"Yes. What happened to Hamilton?"

"He was assaulted. He's in critical condition."

"You bastard," Elaine turned on her husband. Lieutenant Sylvester stepped between Ravalo and his onrushing wife.

"I had nothing to do with it!" he screamed back at her. "I was with Vincent. You can ask him."

"Then you had someone do it!"

Sylvester stopped her charge toward her husband, but she tried to twist around him. Schwartz's voice of authority brought order to the chaos.

"Mrs. Ravalo, please go with Lieutenant Sylvester into another room! Stay with her," Schwartz directed Sylvester. "After I've finished questioning your husband, I'll want to ask you some questions."

A half hour later, Sylvester and Schwartz walked down the long sidewalk toward their unmarked car.

"You think they were having an affair?" Schwartz asked his partner.

"She's pretty emotional about it. Maybe he was painting more than her portrait."

Schwartz snorted, suppressing a laugh.

"We'll check out Ravalo's alibi and then track down his nephew," he said. "See why he thought Blethen was having an affair with Mrs. Ravalo."

Sylvester took his note pad out his pocket and flipped it open. "Todd D'Anselmo, 1646 Fourth Street Southeast, Apartment 201. Think we should talk to him tonight?"

"Right now, I'm more interested in checking out Ravalo's alibi," Schwartz said. "Let's stop in at his club and see what we can find out. Then we'll talk to Mr. Anthony Vincent, counselor at law. He probably won't talk to us, attorney-client privilege, but it's worth a try."

She had talked her way in, begging the nurses, telling them that he had no family, that she was the closest thing to family that he had. The severity of the situation and earnest pleading had gained her admittance to the surgical wing. Toni sat in the surgical waiting room. It was 1 a.m. and Ham was still in surgery.

When she had arrived about ten thirty, Ham had already been in surgery for an hour. It had now been three and a half hours. No one had come out to say anything to her. She went to the nurses' station for the sixth time. "Any word on Hamilton Blethen?"

"Nothing yet," the burly nurse replied. "I'll see if I can get someone to come out and give you a status report."

"Thanks."

No one came. She fell asleep, emotionally spent.

She woke with a start. Something had touched her! *Where am I?* Then she remembered, looking up at a woman dressed in scrubs.

"Mr. Blethen is out of surgery," she said. "He's being moved to recovery."

"Can I see him?" Toni asked. "Is he all right?"

"He has not regained consciousness," she replied. "They should have him in recovery in about fifteen minutes. You can ask the nurse, and she'll tell you when you can see him."

"Was…was the surgery… a success?" She was afraid to hear the answer.

"Mr. Blethen's skull is fractured and there are several brain contusions. His back is also broken. He lost a lot of blood. The surgery went as successfully as possible under the circumstances, but we cannot tell at this time the extent of any brain damage or the prognosis for recovery."

At least he was alive. That meant there was a chance he would recover. Toni thanked the surgeon, then stood with her hands clasped over her mouth, watching the surgeon walk out of the waiting room. *What will happen now?* She remembered the words of the surgeon and hurried to the nurses' station. "When can I see Hamilton Blethen?"

"I'll let you know as soon as he's settled. Will you be in the waiting room?" Toni nodded.

Toni paced the waiting room. *The mad dash to the Barcelona airport when The Reaper deal fell through. Grandma Lorraine's death. The confrontation between Ham and Ravalo, and now this.* Her mind was a blaze of pain, sliced like a knife each time she remembered it was she who had urged Blethen to meet with Ravalo.

More than an hour later, the nurse said she could see Blethen. He was swathed in bandages with only one eye, one cheek and half his lip showing. Tubes and wires disappeared into a cast that encased his body. Monitors kept track of his heartbeat and breathing.

Toni pulled a chair next to the bed and sat, holding Blethen's hand and talking softly to him assuring him he was going to be fine, that he would recover, that she loved him. And then she began to cry softly. *He may never get to hear me say I love him.*

It was starting to get light in the east when she got home. She took Barca out. Her street seemed foreign, dangerous in the early-morning light. She knew she would never again see it as a friendly, welcoming place.

Exhausted, with no more tears to shed, she crawled into bed. Barca jumped up and snuggled next to her. She wrapped her arms around the big dog and held him tight until sleep overtook her.

2012

MONDAY, OCTOBER 1, 2012

SAINT PAUL

"What's this word?"

Blethen was sitting in his wheelchair, the remnants of an oatmeal, stewed prunes and toast breakfast on the table beside him. The morning *Pioneer Press*, affixed to a metal frame attached by a cantilevered arm to the back of the wheelchair, was suspended in front of him. A laser pointer in his mouth pin-pointed the word.

"That's *accolade,*" Toni answered, looking over Blethen's right shoulder. "It means an award or statement to acknowledge some accomplishment."

"They're giving Mauer an accolade even though the Twins have lost ninety-three games," Blethen said. "I'm not big on individual *accolades* when your team stinks."

"I know, honey, but you can only do the best you can do. If he's done well, and some of the other players haven't done so well and the team is losing, he can't control that. He still had a great season. That's why he's being praised, being given an accolade."

Between rehab stints, one of Toni's tasks was to keep Blethen's attitude positive. Although his mental capabilities were being gradually restored, he was, for all practical purposes, a quadriplegic, and it was easy for him to slip into depression. Baseball kept him entertained despite the Twins' dismal record, but the season was winding down and Toni worried.

"Are you done with the sports page?" she asked. "Should we turn to something else, like the variety section or business? Or would you rather watch TV?"

"Just want to sit and think for a while," he said.

Through physical rehabilitation Blethen had regained enough movement in his left thumb and index finger to move the joy stick that controlled his electric wheelchair. He maneuvered through the door into his old studio so he could sit by the window. Barca followed and laid down beside the wheelchair.

"What are we going to do, old fella," he said to his dog. "Need to figure out something to do to keep me from going stir crazy. Need to figure out who killed Grandma."

A month after the incident Toni had learned that Blethen was Grandma Lorraine's sole heir, but what seemed to be good news turned out to have a dark side. The Goodhue County coroner concluded that Grandma Lorraine had been suffocated with a pillow from her couch. That confirmed that the farm was a crime scene, the site of the first homicide in Goodhue County in five years. It had taken the Goodhue County sheriff, the Zumbrota city police and the state Bureau of Criminal Apprehension nearly a month to complete their examination of the farm and let Lorraine's siblings in the house to inventory its contents.

They found her will and, much to their dismay, learned Hamilton was to get everything. It also made him the prime suspect in the murder of his grandmother.

For nearly a year Blethen's injuries and slow recovery prevented the authorities from interviewing him. When they finally did, the investigation dragged on for another year before the Goodhue County Attorney concluded that there was insufficient evidence to charge him.

By that time the trail had grown cold and no one was ever charged with the murder of Lorraine Blethen. The case was closed. The lack of resolution weighed heavily on her grandson.

While they were coping with the stress of the criminal investigation and his recovery from his injuries, Toni and Blethen were forced to confront dwindling finances. They had sold a few of his works, including the impressionist painting *Woman with Greyhound in a French Garden.* The sale of the paintings, and the refusal by Elaine Ravalo to take back the money she had paid Blethen even though he never completed the Gainsbrough, had enabled them to stretch his savings until he qualified for Social Security disability. Hundreds of thousands of dollars of medical costs were paid through veterans' benefits, including extensive rehabilitation and equipment such as his wheelchair.

Toni had moved in with Blethen when he was released from the hospital, and became his full-time caregiver, sporadically working on her doctoral thesis when she could. The money from the sale of her house was deposited in an account which Toni called their "emergency fund," but Blethen adamantly refused to use it.

"I created this situation," he yelled during an argument. "I'm sure as hell not going to let you spend your money to bail me out."

"Us," Toni responded. "Bail *us* out."

"There is no *us*," he said, immediately regretting it. "You aren't going to spend the rest of your life with a cripple."

His words ripped at her, brought tears, but she refused to participate in his pity party. She hugged him until she felt the tension leave his body.

Besides the criminal investigation and the issue of Toni's nest egg, it was the sale of *Woman with Greyhound* that seemed to bother Blethen the most. "It's the one thing I painted that was any good," he had lamented on many occasions. "Now it's gone, and I'll never paint anything again!" It frequently came up in their arguments over money.

Time and again Toni tried to walk him away from the edge of depression. "You still have your knowledge and love of art. You could become an art critic, or a teacher, or an art historian like me," she would reason.

His answer was always the same: "There would be no chance to create. I'd have to answer to someone. A boss. I haven't done that since college, and I didn't do it very well then."

"You'll find something," she would say, wrapping her arms around him. "And you still have me…and Barca." It always calmed him for the moment.

It was after yet another money argument a year earlier (one in which Blethen shouted: "*Was.* I *was* a talented painter. Now I'm just a vegetable!") that Toni verbalized something she had been thinking about for nearly three years.

"Let's get married," she said.

Blethen did a double-take. "You're joking, right?"

"I couldn't be more serious."

"You don't want to be stuck with a cripple...."

"Shut up and say yes," she said.

He did.

They were married by a judge in the Fort Snelling Chapel on May 26, 2012, with Toni's parents and few close friends in attendance. They took a ten-day honeymoon to Hawaii, using part of Toni's nest egg to pay for it. Each night, and every night since, Blethen would end the day with these words: "Thank you, Mrs. Blethen. I don't know what I've done to deserve you."

Despite the joy of the marriage and toasts to a bright future, Toni had yet to find a job, and their financial reserves were rapidly eroding. "Maybe I should get a job waiting tables or in retail so we have some money coming in besides your disability," Toni offered, but the prospect of leaving Blethen alone for hours at a time caused her to procrastinate, and within a month after returning from their honeymoon the sale of the farm brought them financial relief.

TUESDAY, OCTOBER 2, 2012

BOSTON

"Obama is going to win in a landslide. Won't be close. Question is, how do we cover it to make the inevitable seem exciting?"

The strategy session in the newsroom of a local television station was boring Magnolia.

"Why don't we just declare a win for Obama now, and quit covering the election?"

The heads in the newsroom pivoted, jaws agape, eyes incredulous.

"I'm just kidding," she said. "If you want to make this interesting for our viewers, find something seamy. You, know. Romney has six secret wives. Obama's ancestors were slave owners. Stuff like that. You boys figure it out. I've got other things to do. But I don't want to see a carbon copy of *The Globe's* news coverage."

She left the newsroom and checked her schedule: lunch at Meritage with the administrator of Mass General where she was being recruited to serve on the board; 2 p.m. board meeting of her investment company; 7 p.m. speech at Wellesley. That left dinner open. She dialed her administrative assistant.

"See if you can line up an early dinner for me, about five thirty, with Annie Sullivan from the Celtic Center. Call Romine at No. 9 Park to get a table. If Annie's not available, try Meredith Glenn from the Museum of Fine Arts. Call me back as soon as you have something set."

It had been this way since Magnolia had ascended to the pinnacle of Kincaid Enterprises. "Make every minute count" was her motto. From the time she left her brownstone at seven in the morning until she returned between ten and midnight, her days were purposefully filled. It kept her in the forefront of people's thoughts, constantly in the media she controlled, and fueled her rise in Boston's social circles. It also didn't give her time to think about how she'd gotten there.

With deft maneuvering and swift decision-making, she had taken control of Kincaid Enterprises within a month of Arthur's death. She spent the first year gaining the confidence of management, terminating those who opposed her and replacing them with people loyal to her.

Disturbed by how few qualified women she found in her search for replacements, she established the Arthur Kincaid Foundation to fund scholarships and endowments for women in business. Using the vast fortune she controlled, Magnolia established a political action committee to champion women's issues, particularly equal pay legislation and defense of abortion rights. Her name was now being frequently mentioned as a potential candidate for public office.

As she waited for her lunch companion to arrive, she scrolled the newsfeed on her phone. A headline far down the list caught her attention: "Painting Missing 75 Years Found." It was the sub-headline that made her go to the full story. "Miro's *El Segador* found in Paris attic."

A MONTH EARLIER

PARIS

"What a pile of junk," the *Commissaire-preseur* observed to his wife, who was sorting her own equally large pile of junk on the other side of the attic. "It's amazing how much people, even poor people, accumulate."

"Well, she lived here for fifty years, so it's not too surprising," his wife responded, "but I'm not seeing much here that will bring anything worthwhile at the auction." The couple had been hired to conduct an auction of the contents of the small, shabby house at 4327 Avenue Villemain by the niece of the old lady who had lived there.

"I think the niece probably took anything of value," the auctioneer responded, "but there is some glass that will bring a few euros, and she missed the marbles, or didn't know what they were worth."

"She missed these, too," the woman said. A roar of a passing train shook the house. She waited for it to pass, then walked across the attic with a small wooden box in her hand. Inside was a bundle of letters, daintily tied together with a piece of lace ribbon. "What should we do with these?"

He studied the top letter. It looked too fragile to take out of the box. "Take the box back to the office," he said. "They're probably nothing, but we can be more careful with them there. If they have sentimental value we can send them to the niece. If the stamps have any value, we can auction those."

They completed their exploration of the attic and carried a few items to the edge of the opening in the attic floor. He climbed halfway down the spring-loaded ladder, took the largest box from the edge of the opening, and completed his descent. She followed with a smaller box and an old lamp, handing them to her husband. They transported the rest of the items they had selected in similar fashion. Finally, she took the wooden box from the edge of the opening and stepped down carefully until she was off the last rung of the ladder.

The auction was two weeks away, giving them ample time to tidy up the few things they'd salvaged and segregate them into lots. Their commission wouldn't be large on this one, but they had learned to take what came their way. As a mom and pop auction house, they were never considered for the large, wealthy estates, but occasionally they would get lucky. This time their luck was in the marbles. The marbles would bring several thousand euros with the right collectors present.

They lugged four large tins of marbles to their van and locked the house as another train rumbled past. The marbles and the box of letters were the only things they would take with them for now. They would catalog the glassware and a few other potential collectibles in the next day or two.

Back at the auction house he searched through the rows of dog-eared catalogs until he found the one he was looking for. He sat down on the bench, opened the first tin of marbles and began flipping through the catalog. "Get me a bunch of those little plastic bins, please," he called to his wife. In a few moments she came in from an adjoining room with a stack of bins and sat them beside him.

"I'm going to look at those letters while I'm thinking of it," she said. "Otherwise I'll forget and they'll end up getting tossed." Sitting at an old roll-top desk, she opened the wooden box and carefully lifted out the stack of letters. Gently she pulled on the lace ribbon, increasing the force until the fifty-year-old ribbon began to slide through the bow.

She sorted the envelopes by date. There were nine in all, addressed to Monique Picard, the woman whose life they had been sorting through that day. All were from Francois Picard, *probably her husband* the woman thought, sent from Chicago, Illinois, United States. The most recent letters had been sent by airmail.

The airmail stamps might be worth something, she thought.

She held the edges of the top envelope between her thumb and index finger and pushed slightly, then blew just hard enough to force apart the thin paper. With two fingers she removed the fragile letter written on onion-skin. It was dated May 30, 1960.

"Dearest Monique," it read. "I miss you already."

The letter had been written the day Monique Picard had left the United States, returning to France.

The woman read the letter, and the next two. Monique had fled to the United States just as World War II started in Europe. It appeared she had left not because of the fear of the war, but because of persecution from her own countrymen. The reasons for the persecution were not made clear by the letters. She had found her way to Chicago and married a French expatriate, Francois Picard. From Francois Picard's words, the woman could tell that he was desperately in love with his wife, a love that was apparently not reciprocated. She gleaned from his words that the marriage had been short on intimacy and long on silence, until finally she had had enough and returned to France, despite his protestations.

The letters from Francois followed, the first three each a month apart, filled with longing and melancholy and declarations of love.

In the fourth letter, postmarked October 11, 1960, there was a marked change in the tenor of the language.

"I have lost my job," it read. "I have looked for weeks and have found nothing. I do not know what to do. The money I had been saving to come home to you is almost gone."

The desperate words continued, creating a heaviness in the room.

The click of the auctioneer sorting marbles was barely audible as she read on, fully absorbed in the lives of the star-crossed couple.

The fifth letter was postmarked December 22, 1960. Anguish poured from the thin scrawl of his pen. He wanted to send her a gift, to see her, to hold her, but he was destitute. The letter was short, tragic. He swore his undying love for "as long as I shall live." The ending had an ominous feel.

More than a year passed before the sixth letter was posted.

She must have died a thousand deaths, not knowing how he was, if he was alive or dead. Or did she even care?

The letter was filled with apologies and self-loathing. He had suffered through severe depression but had never stopped loving her. In fact, his love for her was all that kept him alive. Now there was hope. He was a handyman and gardener for a rich family. He lived on their estate. The pay was not a lot, but it cost him almost nothing to live. He would save his money so some day he could return to France and they would be together.

There was another gap of three months before the seventh letter was posted. He had saved a little money and was optimistic. It would take time, but they would be together once again. He alluded to something surprising that he had discovered about his employer—they had met years ago at the World Exposition. He didn't give any details.

The eighth letter came a month later, full of guarded optimism. What he had discovered about his employer could result in great profit for them. He told her to be patient a little longer. Her faithfulness would soon be rewarded. As always, his love for her was undying.

It was only two more weeks until the final letter was posted. With anticipation, the woman blew open the envelope.

> *"My Dearest Monique,*
>
> *"By the time you get this letter I may already be in your arms. I can't wait to see you, to hold you, to kiss you, to love you.*
>
> *"I always knew that I would return to France and that we would be together, but I feared that I would come home in disgrace, a pauper, and that you would not want me anymore. I would have died, broken and depressed.*

"But for once luck has shined upon us. Two months ago, I learned that my employer was a man I had met briefly a long time ago at the World Exposition. Back then he purchased a painting that was at the pavilion. You may remember it. It was by Joan Miro and it was titled El Segador. The purchase was under unusual and somewhat dishonest circumstances. I had known about it at the time but was not in a position to do anything about it.

"In April of this year I was asked to go to his summer home and ready it for the family. I had never been there before. I was shocked when I entered the home. Covering one of the walls was the painting. I could not be mistaken. It is very large. I had looked at that painting for six months and disliked it very much. But it was by a famous artist. It was then that I realized that my employer was the man I had met back then.

"For weeks I kept the information to myself, not knowing what I should do. Then, in the newspaper one day, there was a big headline that my employer had decided to run for governor of Illinois. He's very wealthy and influential. The newspaper talked about his great honesty and what great things he would do as governor. I realized why I had discovered the painting.

"I will tell you all the details when I see you, but I must say this: your husband is a brilliant negotiator. My airline ticket is paid for and I am coming to you with enough money to buy a house for us, and an auto, and enough left for us to live for several years.

"I love you, my dearest Monique.

"Francois."

Scrawled below the signature was a postscript:

"I almost forgot, he also gave me the painting and offered to pay for its shipment back to France. He said it needed to go back to where it came from. I think he wanted to be rid of it so that no one would ever find out how he got it. I don't know what we'll do with it. I think it's ugly."

The woman sat back. She looked again at the last letter. It was postmarked: Chicago, Illinois, U.S.A., June 2, 1962.

"Louis," she turned to her husband. "Do you remember the

book—about two years ago we read it—about the painting that disappeared from the Spanish pavilion at the 1937 World's Fair?"

"*The Reaper*," her husband responded. "The book was called *The Reaper*. It was about a painting by Joan Miro.

"I think we need to go back to the house on Avenue Villemain."

"Why."

"Remember the stack of wallboard in the attic?"

"Yeah. I tripped over it more than once"

"We should go back and see what's on the other side, the side facing down. It might be *The Reaper*."

TUESDAY, OCTOBER 2, 2012

SAINT PAUL

"I found a job opening today," Toni said. "A museum is looking for an assistant curator. How would you feel about moving to Boston?"

"Okay with me, as long as there's room for Barca." Blethen replied. "It would give us new places to explore. I could become a Red Sox fan."

Toni snorted. "You'd never give up on the Twins. You aren't that fickle."

"Well, the Red Sox could be my second favorite."

She smiled. "Oh, and I got a letter from cousin, Paulette," Toni said, holding up the envelope for Blethen to see. "Do you remember her?"

"Remind me," he said. It was a frequent line for him. He found it got a better response from Toni than just saying "no."

"You met her at my family reunion. We played petanque together. Short and kind of stocky. Good athlete."

Blethen thought for a moment. "Was she the one that had a sex change?"

"Yes."

"I liked her. What does the letter say?"

Toni opened the envelope and began to read, relating the highlights to Blethen.

"She's gotten married...they're thinking of adopting...might be coming to the States next year...mmmm...mmmm...oh, Aunt Monique died...Paulette's taking care of her estate...hah!"

"What's 'hah?'" he asked.

"You were named in Aunt Monique's will. She gave you a painting."

"Who's Aunt Monique?"

"She was the really old woman at the reunion. Kind of aristocratic. You talked to her quite a bit. She had dementia."

Blethen looked puzzled. "Why would I talk to an old woman with dementia?"

"She supposedly worked at the Paris Exposition in 1937, where *The Reaper* disappeared."

Blethen nodded and Toni went back to the letter. "Mmmmm... too bad Paulette didn't find the painting when she went through Aunt Monique's house."

"Did they look in the attic?" Blethen said.

"What?"

"Did they look in the attic?" he repeated with a grin.

"You *do* remember!" Toni shrieked, rushing to wrap her arms around the man she loved.

BOSTON

Her assistant had successfully scheduled dinner with Meredith Glenn, curator of the Museum of Fine Arts. As they shared an escargot appetizer and sipped sauvignon blanc, Magnolia quizzed her about an upcoming exhibit of Degas's paintings. Meredith, in turn, kept gently pressing Magnolia for a financial commitment to the museum.

"Say, did you see the news article about the Miro painting that was just found?" Magnolia said, changing the subject.

"I did," Meredith responded. "It's caused quite a stir because everyone thought it had been destroyed."

"I have a little history with that painting."

"How so?"

"Oh, that's a long story for another day, but I might consider making a contribution if you bought that painting and put it in your permanent collection."

Meredith's eyes opened wider. "You mean you'd donate enough money to buy the painting for the museum?"

"Maybe," Magnolia replied, suddenly wishing she hadn't gone down this path.

"That would take something between ten and twenty million, I'm guessing," Meredith responded.

"Oh! No. I had no idea it was that expensive. I had something more like a million in mind."

Meredith shook her head. "Not even close," she said.

"Tell you what," Magnolia continued, trying to save face. "I'll donate a million if you can raise the rest of the money needed to buy *The Reaper*." She was confident that her million dollars was safe.

THURSDAY, OCTOBER 4, 2012

SAINT PAUL

The call from Paulette came two days later.

"You've got to hear this," an excited Toni said as she put the headphones on Blethen.

"Hi, Ham, this is Paulette," she said in her beautifully accented English. "Do you remember me?"

"How could I forget? I think you scored all our points playing pentanque."

"I have some good news for you. We found the painting that Aunt Monique left you. It's apparently quite famous, by a painter named Joan Miro."

"Is it *The Reaper*?" Blethen interrupted.

"How did you know?"

"And I'll bet you found it in the attic."

There was silence on the other end. "How did you know that?" Paulette finally said.

"Because I have a long memory," he replied.

THURSDAY, NOVEMBER 15, 2012

BOSTON

Magnolia had underestimated Meredith Glenn.

"We agreed on thirteen million," Meredith said as she watched Magnolia write out a million-dollar check to the museum. "Thank you for your contribution." She took the check from Magnolia's hand. "Yours was the first commitment, and your check is the last one needed to complete the purchase."

"Who's the seller?" Magnolia asked.

"They prefer to remain anonymous," Meredith replied.

That afternoon Meredith wired the funds and notified the media of the museum's newest acquisition. *The Reaper* would arrive in Boston by the end of the month. The first public display of the painting, lost for seventy-five years, would take place immediately after the first of the year. It promised to be a prodigious year for the Boston Museum of Fine Arts.

Magnolia got home after midnight. She checked her phone messages just before going to bed. There was a message from Henri Hawke. She hadn't spoken to him since he'd walked out of the restaurant in Barcelona three years ago. *What the hell would he want,* she thought. *This can't be good news.* It was 6:30 a.m. in Barcelona. She dialed Hawke's number. *Maybe I'll wake up the greasy little sonofabitch.*

FRIDAY, NOVEMBER 16, 2012

SAINT PAUL

"I got the job! We're moving to Boston." Toni was to be the new assistant curator of the Boston Museum of Fine Arts. "I just got a call from the curator, Meredith Glenn."

Toni danced around the room, stopping to give Blethen a hug. Not only had she gotten the job, she had done it on her own merits. She had persuaded Blethen to keep their identity confidential as the sellers of *The Reaper* so it wouldn't influence her job application, and she had been rewarded.

"When do you start?"

"As soon as we can get things wrapped up here. They'd like me there by December first if possible."

"I'll have to give notice to the landlord. The earliest we could get out of the lease is December 31, but you could go to Boston by the first," Blethen said. "You can find us a place to live, and I can stick around here until everything is taken care of. We can celebrate the new year in Boston."

"But, how..."

"We have money now, honey. More than we'll ever need. I'll hire a live-in nurse until I come to Boston."

Toni acquiesced, but not without reservations, which were soon lost in the excitement of new beginnings and bustle of planning the move, a project which seemed to energize Blethen.

BOSTON

"It is my business to know such things." Hawke's voice came over the telephone with a smugness that made Magnolia clench her teeth.

"And why would I be interested in this information?"

"Because there will surely be lawsuits and investigations. I thought you might want to retain my services to make sure those investigations and lawsuits did not include you."

Magnolia thought for a moment. Hawke was right. There could be a legal battle over who was the rightful owner of *The Reaper,* but why would that lead back to her? Hawke, himself, was the only link between her and the painting, and they already had a mutual agreement that would be asinine for either of them to break.

"I don't see how any of this pertains to me," She said.

"Because you don't know who claims to be the rightful owner."

"Who?"

"None other than Hamilton Blethen."

"What? Oh! Shit! That bastard sold us a forgery!"

Now Hawke didn't understand. "Repeat, please," he said.

"Never mind." Magnolia's mind spun in circles. "All right. I'll retain you. But just to keep me informed of what is going on. Five thousand a month, U.S. not euros. If I want your services for more than just information *I'll* let *you* know."

Magnolia told Hawke where to send his first invoice and then hung up.

"That sonofabitch. He painted it after all. And he sold us a forgery." She said it out loud with just a touch of pride. He is, after all, *my* child.

She would have to be very careful with this. Everything she'd accomplished was at stake.

WEDNESDAY, DECEMBER 12, 2012

SAINT PAUL

"The landlord found a renter for the apartment," Blethen told Toni over the phone. "He let us out by the fifteenth so he could paint before the new renters move in. Movers are coming Friday morning, and I'll arrive at Logan Airport at eight-thirty Friday night. Can't wait to see you, babe, and our new home."

"The nurse will be flying out with you, right?" Toni said.

"I have an attendant from the same agency who will take me to the airport and get me on the plane, but I'm flying by myself, so you better be there to pick me up or I'll be a homeless waif in a wheelchair."

"I will be there," she confirmed, "but I wish someone was flying with you."

"There will be. I had Barca designated a service dog, and he has his own ticket. Not to worry, my love. Your hubby has become quite self-sufficient. Barca and I will be just fine."

Blethen left the apartment at noon for his one-thirty appointment. Even though he was only going downtown, less than a mile away, everything took more time now. The medi-cab delivered him to the St. Peter Street entrance to the Hamm Building just after one. It took him fifteen minutes to get to the elevator and to the third floor. He hoped that the information he had been given about how to gain entry to the office was correct.

He sat in his wheelchair for a moment, reading the words on the opaque window in the middle of the antique door: "Monet Detective Agency" read the big letters arcing across the window. Below, in smaller print: "Veronica Brilliant, Holly Bouquet & Carrie Waters, Private Investigators." Next to the door was the promised button. He took the stylus from his pocket with his lips and pushed. There was a buzz inside. A moment later a young woman opened the door.

"You must be Hamilton Blethen," she said. "They're waiting for you." She led him into a small conference room. Seated on one side of the conference table were three women. Behind them was a large picture of *Water Lilies.* Blethen remembered that the original Claude Monet painting had sold at auction earlier in the year for forty-three point seven million dollars.

"If that's the original," Blethen said with a chuckle as he took his place on the opposite side of the table, referring to the painting with a slight nod of his head, "you don't need my business."

"We certainly wish it was," said the woman in the middle. "But it's not, and we'd love to have your business."

"This is Holly Bouquet," she said, referring to an attractive blonde woman on her left, "And this is Carrie Waters." Waters put out her hand to shake Blethen's.

"Nice to meet y…Oh…I'm sorry." She pulled back, blushing at her faux pas.

"No worries," Blethen said with a smile. "I appreciate the thought. 'Wish I could reciprocate."

"I'm Naomi Brilliant." the woman in the middle introduced herself in a melodious baritone. She looked to be six feet tall, with broad shoulders and a narrow waist. Her hair was jet black, cut in a short, tousled style. "How can we help you Mr. Blethen?"

"I'll pay you a million dollars to solve the murder of my grandmother, Lorraine Blethen."

THE END

The saga of *The Reaper* continues in *The Sower*, the second book of the *Chimera Chronicles*, by Rob Jung

"KANARANZI WINS PRIMARY"

The headline shouted the news. Magnolia Kanaranzi, media mogul, darling of the women's movement and owner of one of the greatest rags-to-riches stories in recent history, was now the odds-on favorite to become the next Senator from the State of Massachusetts.

"Early polls have you up by eight points over Metzger," said Jim Bean, Kanaranzi's veteran campaign manager. "Part of that is probably the bounce from the primary. I would guess your lead is closer to five points."

The staccato clicking of her just-manicured fingernails drumming on the conference table punctuated her impatience. She scanned her circle of advisors, seated haphazardly around the cluttered campaign office, most nodding in confirmation of Bean's assessment.

"I don't view five points as a lead," she said. The intensity of her voice, always surprising coming from a person of such diminutive stature, brought them to attention. "Metzger hasn't unleashed his attack dogs yet, and we all know he's capable of making up things if he can't find any actual dirt. We need to hit him first."

Bean ran a hand through his unruly hair, trying, but failing, to make it look more presentable for his boss. "We started doing oppo research last week," he said. "So far we've found nothing that isn't already public knowledge."

"We can attack him on his record. Tie him to the President," offered Aaron Feldman, Kanaranzi's chief policy adviser.

"Thanks for stating the obvious, Aaron," Magnolia answered. Dressed in rumpled pants and a wrinkled shirt, looking like he'd slept in his clothes for the past week, made it easy for Magnolia to dismiss him.

Turning to the others, she said, "We need something sordid, something perverted. Something the voters can hate him for."

"Well, we know he smoked marijuana in college," another staffer interjected. "Flannery uncovered that in the last campaign."

"Yes, and Flannery lost by ten points. I don't think an attack based on marijuana smoking thirty years ago, coming from the campaign of a reformed drug addict, would really be very effective, do you?" The staffer hung his head under Magnolia's glare.

"Get on it. All of you," she barked as she rose from her chair. "This is the number one priority for everyone. Hire outside investigators if you must. See what the national committee suggests, but we need *something* to bring his character into question."

As she passed Bean, she leaned over and whispered in his ear, "Find a replacement for Feldman. We can't have someone looking like *he* does appear in public on behalf of the campaign. Find him a project that will keep him busy for weeks. Have him develop a comprehensive Middle East policy for us. That should keep him busy.

Press secretary Sara Jones, nearly a head taller than Kanaranzi, followed the candidate as she left the room. As they crossed Boylston Street, Kanaranzi began giving orders.

"No news conferences until next week, Sara, unless something comes up that requires an immediate response. Just keep feeding the media our daily press releases with my itinerary, a germane policy blurb, and a quote or two from me. For now, you can get the policy stuff from Bean. Make up the quotes, but pass them by me before they go out."

A uniformed chauffeur, standing next to the open rear door of a white Cadillac limo, offered his gloved hand to Magnolia.

"Ma'am." Jones said.

Kanaranzi stopped, turning her head, her hand extended toward the chauffeur. "What?"

"Someone has been digging around in newspaper archives, asking about you."

"Metzger's wolves already at work?"

"My contact didn't think so," Jones replied. "He didn't recognize the person. It wasn't one of the usual political research hacks. It was a private investigator from Minnesota."

"Minnesota?" Kanaranzi's reaction was too quick, her voice too shrill.

Quickly composing herself, she took the chauffeur's hand and slid into the back seat of the limo. As she settled herself in the lush leather, she looked up at Jones. "Did your contact get his name?"

"It's a her. The detective is a woman. She told my guy her name is Ronni Brilliant."

Kanaranzi nodded, and the chauffeur closed the door. She dug in her purse, looking for her phone. Finding it, she scrolled her contact list until she found Henri Hawke, then tapped his number. She got his voicemail.

"We need to talk. There's someone from Minnesota digging around in my past. How does that happen? You said you took care of everything."

ABOUT THE AUTHOR

Born in the wine country of California, brought up in a beautiful little Mississippi River town in Wisconsin, and educated in the Minnesota State University system and Harvard Law School, Rob Jung now lives the writer's life in suburban St. Paul, Minnesota, with his wife, Kathy.

A newspaper writer for seven years while getting his undergraduate degree, Jung has practiced law for 47 years.

A life-long student of history, geography, and religion, Jung has traveled in every continent except Antarctica, and his stories often find their origins in historical events from countries outside the U.S.

Jung also lists among his "credits": inventor, entrepreneur, gourmet chef, master gardener, fishing guide and storyteller. His best work: three grown children, four grandchildren and one great grandchild.

He has written four novels, the first two of which are safely tucked in the back of a drawer to prevent injury to either reader or the literary world. His first published novel, *Cloud Warriors*, can be purchased online or at select bookstores. The Reaper is his fourth, and second published, novel.

Jung can be contacted through his website: www.robjungwriter.com, or on Facebook at Rob Jung Author.

Follow Jung through his weekly blog, "The View from Middle Spunk Creek," which can be found on his website.

*Rob Jung is the pen name of Robert W. Junghans. He also writes limericks and tells stories under the name "C.J. Rackham."

CPSIA information can be obtained
at www.ICGtesting.com
Printed in the USA
BVHW030755110819
555603BV00002B/294/P

9 781950 685028